DAKOTA FLAME
SONYA T. PELTON

ZEBRA BOOKS
KENSINGTON PUBLISHING CORP.

ZEBRA BOOKS

are published by

Kensington Publishing Corp.
475 Park Avenue South
New York, NY 10016

First printing: July, 1989

Printed in the United States of America

For My Beloved Family

How strong, how free the spirit of the wind
   rippling through fields of wildflowers
   across this glorious land.
'Tis the spirit of independence,
   the spirit of belief in a sweet dream.
'Tis freedom—
   only if it could burn in every heart,
   what a place this world would be.
                              —Johanna Salmi

Part One

Savage Journey

Came the spring with all its splendor,
All its birds and all its blossoms,
All its flowers, and leaves, and grasses.
　　　　—Longfellow, *Hiawatha*

Prologue

THE SIOUX, (or in their language, THE
DAKOTA) hungry and knowing they had been
tricked at the Treaty Table, went on the warpath
in 1862 when they attacked the Redwood Indian
Agency. They then carried their bloody campaign
down the Minnesota River to New Ulm, where
they took scalps and prisoners in what the
Dakotas called Hot Moon.

After the outbreak had been crushed by forces
commanded by General Sibley and the regular
army of officers, President Lincoln ordered the
mass execution of thirty-nine leaders of the
Dakota Nation. Of these, thirty-eight were to be
hanged at Mankato in December, 1862.

MANKATO, December, 1862

The Indians had painted their faces. They shook
hands with the friendlier officers with sorrowful good-
byes, as if merely going on a journey. Then the Dakotas

11

chanted their monotonous but very moving death song. Hoods were placed on their heads, leaving only a small area of their painted faces still visible.

The Indians' shame was evident. They were humiliated. All singing had ceased. At the scaffold they were delivered to an officer and then proceeded to make their ascent to the gallows. One Indian raised his eyes to the huge hawk perched on the gallows' tree. Then Red Hawk lowered his eyes, scanning the crowd for his son; he felt Wild Hawk was out there but could not see him. The pouch should go to him, for Wild Hawk would take it to Red Hawk's Spirit Lodge.

Breaths in the crowd were held, and the scene was cold and gray. Thirty-eight Dakota Indians awaited the moment when the platform would fall and they would be finally still. They heard the three slow measured beats on the drum, and then a man standing by cut the rope. A prolonged cheer went up. Bodies dangled and twitched. In twenty minutes the Indians were declared dead.

And now a hawk lifted and soared on widespread wings into the wintry sky. . . .

Chapter One

Minnesota River Valley, Winter 1862

Across the cold sweep of the Minnesota sky there were clouds; they were a wintry bluish-gray. A low wind caught the breath of their coolness and moved across the hills, down the valleys and frigid rills, creeping across the face of a land that was beautiful and green in summertime. But now it was winter—a cruel winter. The cold wind came swiftly and crossed the land, dipping between the hills and finally into the bustling town of Mankato, where it seemed to sigh forlornly.

The wind swept down the drab, colorless street, past the little house. Audrina Harris looked up from her ironing, feeling a thrill race along her spine as she stopped to stare out the window.

Audrina had been up and working since daybreak. She had awakened and dressed while it was still dark outside, while her Aunt Kate was still abed. Katherine was the town seamstress and her niece often helped

13

iron the pattern pieces and the recently altered clothing.

Now a few leaves left over from autumn skittered across the frozen mud and grass of the yard, past the window to the main street, then tumbled after the curious strangers who thronged the town.

Placing the heavy iron into a pie tin, resting on its side over a folded cloth, Audrina went to stand before the window. It was a long time before she moved a muscle. . . .

The frontier town of Mankato had been bustling since long before daybreak, but now it was a beehive of activity. With curiosity alive in her moss-green eyes, Audrina gazed out the window, watching folks scurrying by until she felt compelled to go outside to mingle with the growing crowd. As she turned from the window, the morning light caught the many fiery shades of red in her long, glossy hair. Audrina shivered, reflecting on what was going to happen out there today.

Her sweet features clouded gloomily.

It was a sad and tragic moment in history. She abhorred killing, and the Indians and whites had been doing so much of it lately. Dakota Indians had ridden through the Minnesota River Valley, through isolated homesteads and over tiny settlements, their war whoops carried in the wind. She and her Aunt Katherine had been spared, only because they lived at the edge of town where there had not been so much killing. But the Sioux had gotten to some of their outlying neighbors. They had driven away stock, burned houses and barns. Hundreds of settlers had gone to their graves and many more had been left

14

without homes or places to go.

Now, today, thirty-eight Sioux warriors were going to be hanged by the neck until dead. Audrina told herself she shouldn't go out there; there wasn't any need. . . .

Still . . . I have to go. . . . Something beckons me.

"Aunt Kate?" Audrina called into the kitchen.

"Yes, dear." Katherine stepped into the larger of the two rooms, wiping flour dust off her fingers and onto her old cotton apron. When she saw her niece taking her burgundy-colored coat down from the peg, she sternly voiced her opinion. "I don't think you should be going out there, Audrey. Not today . . . of all days."

Lifting her long, dark red hair over the collar of her coat, Audrina faced her aunt with a pretty smile. "I won't be long, Aunty. I just want to take a walk and get some air."

Shaking her graying head, Katherine warned, "There's all sorts of riffraff out there, and you don't know when one of those strange men might come along and kidnap you. They see a pretty girl like you all alone and they're going to get ideas." She regarded her sweet-tempered niece with loving concern.

With her shining mane of naturally waving dark red hair, the streaks at her temples of a paler, coppery shade, a small, delicately formed nose, exquisite dusky rose lips, olive-gold skin, and large uptilted green eyes with long, silky eyelashes below slightly arched brows—not to mention the slender shapeliness beneath her coat—Audrina was a tempting target who could easily capture the eyes of a stranger bent on inventing evil schemes. There were hardly any suitable young men in town to tell her that she was breathtakingly

15

beautiful, and only Katherine knew the reason why they kept their distance. Painfully, she wondered how much of the truth her niece had guessed about her Indian heritage.

"I can take care of myself, Aunty. I am twenty years old now, remember?" She smiled sweetly and began to button up her coat while Katherine watched.

Katherine's heart wrenched as she concealed her sadness from her lovely niece. Audrina was lonely, for almost all the young women, married and unmarried, cruelly snubbed her. Even the unattached males pretended she did not exist, and their indifference was even more apparent because of the war that had been going on between the Indians and whites. There was one young soldier by the name of Joe Powell who wanted to court Audrina, but she wouldn't give him the time of day. Katherine was certain that Powell could not be trusted; there was something dark just beneath the surface of Joe's pleasant and easygoing nature. She'd not like to see Joe as Audrina's mate.

Katherine sighed inwardly. The truth of the matter was that Audrina possessed both Cheyenne and Sioux Indian blood, and Katherine had tried to protect her by keeping the fact a secret. Audrina was not aware of the whole truth, and Katherine was ashamed of wrapping lies around her tongue all these years to save her niece shame and humiliation. What good had it done? Though Audrina hadn't been born with the half-breed looks, rumors nevertheless persisted that her mother, known to the whites as Melissa Harris, had really been Gray Dove, daughter of the great Oglala chief Standing Eagle and Tashina, his wife. All were now dead.

16

Audrina had finished buttoning her coat and stood staring at the only guardian she had ever known. "Aunt Kate, what are you thinking about? You seem so far away." Audrina looked at her with a wistful little smile. "Is there something you wish to tell me?"

Katherine shook her head to clear it. "There's a lot of troublemakers out there today, because of the multiple hanging. They came from far and near just to see those savages hang." Katherine moved closer, taking something out of her apron pocket. "Here, take my small handgun with you for protection."

Deep auburn lashes lifted. "I really won't be needing it."

"Take it . . . please."

Audrina tucked the long, luxuriant wave of hair behind her small, shapely ear and planted a kiss on her aunty's cheek. Then she tucked the revolver inside her coat's deep pocket. She looked back into Katherine's worried face. "Wait a minute. . . . Why don't you come with me?"

Katherine seemed to shiver. "You know I don't like big crowds. Besides," she grinned, "I have to make you that cherry pie, remember?"

Audrina licked her lips, saying, "Now I remember. I can almost taste it already."

"Don't be long, dear," Katherine called over her shoulder as she went back to her kitchen and her baking, first stirring the contents of the vegetable-beef soup. Her hand halted in midair then. Still worrying, she listened for the front door to open and close.

Audrina paused only a moment longer, and then she reached down into her coat pocket and withdrew the revolver. Watching to see that Katherine stayed in the kitchen, Audrina bent to lift a cushion off the sofa and placed the gun beneath. Then she patted the cushion and went to the door.

As Audrina walked along the main street, crowds of well-bundled folks jostled her. Shouts and ribald laughter filled her ears. Civilians mingled with squads of blue-coated soldiers . . . and then she saw Joe Powell.

Joe was wearing the dress of the Cavalry Troopers— a short-waisted blue coat trimmed with brass buttons, brass buckles on a black belt, breeches dyed a lighter shade of blue than his coat and tucked into calf-high black boots. He was blond, trim, and good-looking. The only thing that detracted from his handsomeness was the fact that his nose was slightly crooked . . . and he was always drunk while on leave.

Joe was laughing, and Audrina heard him cracking jokes about the Indian prisoners who now sat in a cold stone building behind barricaded windows. He snickered smugly about the fact that the condemned warriors had been chained to spikes driven into the timbered floor. He bent to his soldier friends, showing them something he had in his possession, something Audrina could not see, nor did she really care all that much about it. All she noticed was that the other officers appeared surprised, and some even frowned over what Joe showed them.

Some of the townsfolk, especially the elders, thought Joe Powell was a disgrace to the blue uniform he wore. Audrina herself avoided Joe, for she had never liked him. For one thing, Joe could not keep his eyes or his hands to himself while in her presence. He was totally self-centered, Audrina had often thought, if he could not understand she was not interested. No man was going to frighten her into submission. Even though she was lonely and dreamed of finding the perfect mate who would love her and want to marry her, she was not going to jump into just *any* man's arms.

Audrina turned her attention to the crowd. Thousands of people had crowded into Mankato. Farmers and journalists, businessmen and politicians, and whole families had already started to arrive on Christmas Day. She could not explain her own compassion for the Indians, knowing that several of her neighbors and Aunt Katherine's acquaintances had been killed by them. But those citizens who had lived through the raids had violently attacked the Indian captives while they were being moved through the town from the Lower Agency to Camp Lincoln. An older Indian who had been hit on the head with a brick could not walk and had to ride in the crowded supply wagon. That day General Sibley's men had had a hard time trying to drive the enraged and bloodthirsty citizens back.

As Audrina walked, she was jostled and bumped, stared at by half-breed scouts and white men alike. She began to wonder how so many people could be drawn to the ghastly spectacle of a mass hanging. Some, she knew, were kinfolk of whites killed during the uprising, who had come to watch their fierce and spiteful revenge being played out.

She, herself, should not be here, but Audrina wished there were something she could do to help the poor warriors who were about to hang. But she could accomplish nothing. They were so many—the embittered folks, the soldiers, the white leaders. She was only

19

one woman in a vast sea of people. Besides, she too had come to fear the Indians and their violent attacks.

Early snows had melted during the warmer days, and the streets of Mankato were drab and colorless. She could see the crowd converging on the center of town. She could not turn back and found her feet automatically taking her to the site of the gallows, where thirty-eight nooses dangled twenty feet above the street.

A pair of dark, hostile eyes trailed the redheaded beauty. The watcher wore a heavy coat with furred Eskimo hood. His skin was the deep shade of old copper. He was a lean, buckskin-legged individual with high cheekbones. Gleaming black hair hung past his shoulders but was hidden now in the depths of his hood. He continued to watch, then a sea of laughing faces surrounded her and she suddenly vanished. The primitively handsome, bronze-skinned face drew into a taut frown.

Wild Hawk felt some compelling force draw him like a magnet to the girl with the hauntingly beautiful golden face and long, flowing red hair. He would name her *Petala,* Precious Fire, just to keep her memory alive in his mind but never in his heart. Indians did not fall in love with little *wasichus*. And his heart was full of hatred for the white man this day . . . especially for one white soldier.

Wild Hawk's dark, piercing eyes shifted to the uniformed guard just coming to stand beside her. *Him.* The white soldier whose cruelty had sown this intense hatred in his heart.

Wild Hawk's eyes turned into wrathful pools of darkness as he stared at Powell . . . with the lovely young woman beside him. The white soldier had not

20

allowed him to pick up his father Red Hawk's belongings. He had seen Powell a short time ago, proudly displaying the stolen item to his officer friends. Wild Hawk kept his eyes trained on the couple, aware of nothing but the familiar placement of Powell's hands on the pretty *wasichu*. She is his woman, he told himself with dissatisfaction and loathing.

Audrina's eyes scanned the area. Over a thousand soldiers, including hundreds of mounted troops, had been stationed around the scaffold to keep the crowd back. The merely curious and the coldly bitter spectators mingled. They leaned out of windows. They stood on roofs. They lined the streets and even hung in trees. Audrina had never seen so many people in one place at one time. They even stood on the opposite bank of the Minnesota River, watching.

When Audrina turned at the sound of soft giggling, she was surprised and annoyed to find an old schoolmate there with her grandmother, blood lust shining in their crystal-blue eyes. Audrina looked around; she would find no response of brotherly or sisterly love here. She could not even smile or greet these people; they always snubbed her, making her feel like an outcast.

With a faraway look, Audrina gazed off into the gray, wintry sky. She had never known her parents. Her mother, Melissa, had died giving birth to her, and her father had run off not long after. Aunt Kate had come to fetch Audrey Tina Harris from the kindly preacher when she was only a baby. Aunt Kate had always been vague about Audrina's past. Once, when she was a little girl, she had come home after overhearing town gossipers call her half-breed and had

21

asked Katherine why. Her aunt had laughed nervously, saying, "Don't think anything of it, honey. They're just jealous because you're so pretty."

A voice broke rudely into Audrina's reflections. "Well, well, what brings lovely Miss Harris out into the cold, to a mass hanging, no less?" Joe Powell placed his gloved hand on her shoulder, his fingers moving familiarly over her back and beneath the mass of fiery hair swirling in ringlets chased by the wind. "Cat got your tongue, honey?"

"Mr. Powell," Audrina began, flinching away from his hand, "I wish you wouldn't do that. And my name is not *honey.*"

"And what are you going to do about it, princess, huh? Pull away and make a scene? I know you don't like to have attention drawn your way. If you just relax and lean toward me"—he pulled her unwillingly closer—"it won't look as if you're struggling." He lifted her chin and gazed into her frightened eyes. "Now, you be a good girl, and no one will notice that a thing is out of place."

Placing her hands on his uniformed chest, Audrina pushed away. "Please, Mr. Powell . . ."

"Call me Joe, princess. I told you that many times before. I used to live here when you were just a child, remember that? I used to pull those long red braids and you would run away from me. Now that I'm back in town, you and I are going to get better acquainted." He grinned, showing a row of straight white teeth while he hooked his thumbs in his army issue gunbelt.

"Y—you're always back in town, Mr. Powell." Audrina's lashes lowered embarrassedly over huge liquid eyes. "I'd appreciate you not standing so close."

22

Just then, Joe saw some of his friends waving him over, and he reluctantly excused himself from Audrina's presence. "I'll see you later, Audrey. If not then, I'll be back in three months." He grinned wolfishly. "You'll be waiting for me, won't you?"

Audrina turned and put her back to Joe Powell, hissing under her breath, *"Never."* She was about to make her way back home when she felt a ripple of excitement race through the crowd.

"Look, the savages are coming!" Lianne Nelson loudly exclaimed to the man standing next to her. "I can't wait to see them twitch and breathe their last!"

Audrina pursed her lips. And Lianne Nelson calls *them* savages?

Her head turning slowly, in the same moment that the condemned Indians appeared, Audrina found herself staring into the darkest hawk-brown eyes she had ever seen. For one split second, she had observed the proud and regal bearing of the man; then he vanished like thin smoke. She tried to find him in the crowd, turning away just as the Sioux death song began. *Hi-yi-yi.* Audrina watched as the Indians began to sway to the rhythm of their music. Their breaths fogged the frigid air.

The Indians reached for each other one last time with bound hands. Some of them managed to grasp hands of men beside them, while others grabbed and clutched at each other's blankets. One, still smoking his pipe, stood cool and patient as Job.

The nooses had already been placed about their necks by the time Audrina forced herself to look up again. The Indians began to shout in Dakota and called out their names to their friends. Audrina shivered as

23

the strange litany rang out over the crowd, few understanding the beautiful words and even fewer caring about the impressive and cherished names of the thirty-eight warriors.

Where is the love and compassion? Audrina wondered. She felt part of what they were feeling. Sad, forlorn, lost. Dying for want of land and the friendship they never received from the whites. The Indians have been cheated and abused while being pushed to the edge of starvation, Audrina thought. Dying because they had been tricked and deceived over and over.

Listen to me and my thoughts. . . . I sound like an Indian, Audrina told herself. *I am white and should be feeling sorry for the families of the lost loved ones.*

Now, more than ever, Audrina wondered if the rumors of her Indian blood could possibly be true. At times, of late, when she walked through town, she could hear the sibilant whispers: *half-breed.*

Audrina could not watch anymore. She tore herself away and pushed through the crowd. Angry looks and voiced taunts fell upon her, but she did not care. And she did not see the silent hawk swoop down and lift something in its powerful talons. From the fringe of the crowd, another did not see this either. His bronze hands clenched in frustration and helplessness as his dark eyes turned away and the hawk lifted effortlessly into the hushed air and then wheeled around.

Officer Joe Powell was so engrossed in the hanging that he failed to notice he had the medicine pouch no longer. In all the excitement, he had dropped it on the ground below the gallows.

The hawk soared on widespread wings into the wintry sky. In sharp, powerful talons, the great bird carried the leather bag filled with small objects that would hold special meaning to its next carrier. . . .

When Wild Hawk scanned the crowd with his ebony eyes and found that the young woman with the moss-green eyes had disappeared, he went to find his companions. He had no wish to watch his father perish from this cruel death. But his beloved parent, Red Hawk, had already died, even before his virile, handsome son of thirty summers turned away.

Much later, when the crowds had thinned out and most of the folks had gone home, Wild Hawk lurked in the shadows, waiting for Joe Powell to step out of the house where a raucous, drunken party had been going on from midnight into the wee hours of the morning. As he waited, he had time to ponder and reflect back . . . and to grow more bitter.

The white man's greed and insatiable desire for land had led to the Indians selling Minnesota. Unjust policies and routines had created conditions that presaged a serious conflict. All that had been needed was a tiny spark. It had come, within a small community of settlers in Acton, in August, 1862, when angered and hungry Dakota hunters killed five settlers. One of the settlers had told the Indians to "Eat grass." The white men had gone on to live prosperous and successful lives, but the Dakota faced defeat, starvation, and exile on the Great Plains. Wild Hawk knew his people would eventually end up there. . . . There, or on the reservations where Indians lived with limited horizons, unable to hunt freely as they were accustomed. He was one Indian who would never live on a reservation!

Wild Hawk had not joined his people in warring

against the whites that last tragic and fateful time, but Red Hawk, his father, had changed his mind at the last minute and had joined the others. Wild Hawk had remained behind, heeding the words of their relative Little Crow: "You will die like the rabbits when the hungry wolves hunt them in the Hard Moon." Little Crow had warned the angry and bitter Dakota warriors on the eve of the bloody conflict. At the last minute, even Little Crow had not heeded his own words, but like Red Hawk, he agreed to join the War. He had told the other chiefs he would not die a coward, but would die *with* them.

Little Crow's prophesy had proven accurate for, when the end of The-Moon-when-Plums-are-Scarlet—September—arrived, the Dakota had been defeated and the white leaders of Minnesota were getting ready to inflict harsh punishment on the Indians. The white soldier, Joe Powell, had not allowed Wild Hawk to visit his condemned father, Red Hawk, before the execution, when the braves might hand their most prized possessions to their loved ones . . . in this case the medicine pouch, which he had needed to take from his father and return to Red Hawk's Spirit Lodge. Powell had been cruel to deny him that, but Wild Hawk could not serve his father's people by getting killed himself. He must tread cautiously with the soldier named Powell. But somehow, he must get back the pouch.

It was still dark when, like a silent wraith, Wild Hawk crept closer to the wall of the house. Then he saw Powell, emerging drunkenly with several other men with young, painted women clinging to their arms. Wild Hawk could not attack the man until he was alone, for he would be caught and hanged just like the others.

Wild Hawk watched from the shadows as Powell boisterously called a "Good night" to the others and began to walk down the street alone, singing a bawdy tune of wine, women, and song.

Joe Powell didn't know what had hit him. In his inebriation, he thought it might have been a vicious bear. He struggled futilely, and then all of a sudden he was being dragged into the overhanging shadows of a dark storefront. A long, wickedly gleaming Indian knife was held to his throat. His hand went for the Colt dragoon pistol in his waistband, but it was wrenched from his holster and tossed aside.

All was quiet, but for the deep, masculine hiss of Wild Hawk's voice.

"Tonight you will surely die, white man, if you do not listen to me . . . and listen well."

Joe listened. It was the same dangerous-looking Indian who had come to ask for his father's pouch the night before. Joe had been acting cocky, lording it over the ruggedly handsome savage. Now he was in trouble. For one, he didn't have the pouch any longer; he must have dropped it somewhere. Now he was out here alone with a wild savage, ironically one who could speak perfect English, who was probably going to kill him and take his scalp. Maybe he would do that first, Joe thought as the Indian added pressure at his throat with the sharp edge of his blade.

Wild Hawk stood behind the white man, his voice threateningly low and demanding. "Where is my father's pouch? You would not give it to me when I came for it last night. Now I ask you again, white man.

27

Bring it to me, or you will surely die."

"I lost it," Joe barely got out in a croaking voice. The Indian applied more pressure. "I must have dropped it in the crowd."

"Perhaps you lie. Perhaps you have given it to the beautiful white woman you were speaking to—and fondling—earlier today."

"Audrina?" Joe's head spun in circles.

"Your woman?" Wild Hawk fiercely asked.

"Ah . . . yes," Joe lied, hoping to stall the Indian and give himself more time to think . . . *think,* damnit! It was awfully hard to do that at the moment, with the savage's arms crushing him, his blade ready to slice him from ear to ear. "Audrey and I are going to be married."

"When?"

His voice was harsh, grating on Joe's shaking nerves. Joe tried to clear his head so he could think. . . . Lord, he shouldn't have had so much to drink.

"Next summer," Joe answered, hoping the Indian would feel some compassion and let him live to see his wedding day. Then he jerked with a start as Wild Hawk began to search him. When he was finished, his hands had left no part of Joe's body untouched.

"See," Joe said, "I—I told you I didn't have it."

"I will warn you." Wild Hawk's breath was close to Powell's ear. "If you tell the others of this incident, you will die . . . as will your woman."

"I don't have your father's medicine pouch. I don't want Audrey killed; she's my woman. She's a *good* woman, an angel. Promise, I'm not going to tell the others."

28

"I will take your promise to heart, Powell," Wild Hawk said in a deep, ominous voice. "Remember this: I will be watching you . . . and your beloved woman. I will never be far. You need only turn around and you will find me stalking you."

Joe was vowing at this very moment, even while his life was at stake, to some day get back at this Indian warrior whom he already hated with an insane passion. He didn't care that Wild Hawk was mightiest of all Wahpekute Sioux, a warrior feared and hated by his enemies. He didn't care that his people depended on Wild Hawk's fighting spirit, his courageous heart, and his matchless skill with both the rifle and the bow. Wild Hawk was the last of the proud warriors who could not be cajoled to live on a reservation the rest of his life . . . but if Powell had anything to do with it, he would see him there with the rest of his savage lot.

Joe backed cautiously away after Wild Hawk allowed him to go. The coppery savage melted into the shadows like a vanishing wraith. . . .

In the morning Joe awoke to an invading blast of sun in his eyes, and he sat up in his bunk. He held his aching head in his hands as fragments of the night before swam inside his blurred consciousness. No, it could not be, he told himself. He must have dreamed it all. Wild Hawk had not attacked him in the street; it had to have been a dream . . . a damned *nightmare*.

"Powell," a stern voice called from the doorway. "Up and at 'em. We have to get the regiment back to New Ulm. On the double!"

"Yeah, yeah." Joe hung his aching head between his shoulders. Then he rose unsteadily. "No, it wasn't just a dream. . . ." He looked into the mirror, seeing the livid bruises at his throat and the small slash where Wild Hawk's blade had cut him. Joe's anger grew. No damned filthy redskin was going to treat him like this and make him afraid of every step he took. He wasn't going to alert the others . . . no, he was going to find his own sweet revenge on the one Indian warrior he hated with an insane obsession.

Audrina had quickly returned home after the hanging; she had been unable to watch the Indians draw their final breaths.

As she neared the little house, she could smell the delicious odor of cherry pie wafting in the crisp breeze. But she had lost her appetite suddenly.

Just then, something in the sky caused her to look up.

A big red hawk was circling above her, its cry ringing out over the rooftops. Audrina turned about as the hawk wheeled and soared; there was something strange about the wild, winged creature. Then she realized what it was. The hawk was carrying something in its powerful, lethal talons.

Her eyes were full of awe and wonder as the hawk circled and came back, then dropped a six-inch object right at her feet. She stared in astonishment and disbelief, then bent to pick up the soft leather pouch. She turned it over in her hands, caressing the soft deerhide.

Audrina looked up into the blanket of gray, but the beautiful, mysterious hawk was only a vanishing speck in the gloomy western sky.

"Aud—rina Har—ris?"

The Indian woman stood framed in the doorway as Audrina held the door open for her. Before leaving in her wagon, Katherine had told Audrina that the Indian woman's name was Minowa, which meant Moving Voice, and Audrina had been expecting her. Minowa had never before been to her aunt's house. Katherine spoke to Indians once in a while, but only to gain information about their movements so she could travel about freely in her wagon to visit neighbors and customers and to do good deeds, far and near.

"Your Aunt Kather—ine sent for me," Minowa said, pausing in a shaft of pale sunlight in the doorway.

"Yes, I know. . . ." Audrina paused to release the breath she had been holding. "Please, do come in. You are welcome here."

"Thank you." Minowa walked slowly toward the young woman, thinking what a very pretty female she was. The small face possessed a childlike innocence. There was fire in her long red hair, and the eyes were an unusual shade of green that reminded Minowa of deep summer, and of the Dakota/Lakota word *gnugnuska,* grasshopper.

Minowa smiled as the young woman led her to a chair. "No." She shook her head, her graying black braids asway. "I will sit on the floor . . . here."

The Indian woman sat in a feminine fashion on the old carpet on the wood floor. She looked up to find Audrina Harris perched on the edge of the chair. Minowa giggled, then just as quickly grew serious once more.

31

"Huka, I am not afraid," the Indian woman stated. "Why are you afraid like the *mastincala?"*

"What is a *mastin . . . cala?"* Audrina asked, feeling strange trying to say the word just right.

"Little rabbit," answered Minowa. A gentle spring wind breathed against the house, and just then Minowa's eyes fell upon the soft hide pouch. "That is it."

Audrina followed Minowa's gaze. "Yes. It—it sings to me and Aunt Kate says the songs are Dakota." She would not add that her aunt had told her many times to get rid of the thing or else she was going to be under a curse. Audrina had not listened; she had a great desire to know more about it, somehow feeling it held her destiny. "It does not make sounds *all* the time," she added.

"There are voices, talking Dakota, and drums and songs?" Minowa asked.

"Yes." Her eyes twinkled at the Indian woman. "You may think this strange, but sometimes the pouch makes me feel . . . as if it holds *me* captive." Audrina's smile faded. "That *is* strange, is it not?"

"Perhaps . . ." Minowa's eyes traveled the room and the curtained doorway leading into another room. "Where is your aunt now?" She gave a sideways glance at the pouch and began to frown as she leaned forward; she wanted to touch it but was afraid of the power it held.

"Katherine has taken her wagon to a farm in Milford Township. She is going to pick up a girl by the name of Sadie Peterson. Her parents perished in the battle of New Ulm, and Sadie has been staying on with neighbors there until Katherine can come to get her."

32

Minowa frowned. "Your kind aunt should not go so far in order to help others at this time. It is most dangerous to travel far from one's home."

Audrina studied the woman's heavy features, then said, "But I thought the wars were over?"

"There are many Indians who have been greatly angered by this conflict. Just as with the whites, there are the good and the bad Indians. The white man must learn to distinguish between them. He is safe with the farmer-Indians. The white traders began many of the problems that have led to war. I have seen a Dakota man swallow the gold coins given him during the annual treaty payment. He swallowed them in order to keep the traders from cheating him out of his money. Any bonds that existed between the two peoples have been severed by the war. The white people of Minnesota are in danger when they travel alone."

"It is a very confusing war, Minowa. I just wish everyone could get along. There is room enough for all here on God's beautiful and spacious earth." Tears sparkled in Audrina's gentle green eyes.

The Indian woman nodded. "You speak wisely for one so young, Aud—rina."

"How is it that you speak English so well?" Audrina asked, eager to get on with the real purpose of this visit: to discover why the pouch was in her possession and what it meant for her to have it, and if she truly was in danger as her Aunt Kate believed.

Minowa stared at the bold streaks of sunset that danced on the windowpane, then she leaned forward and back again. She looked very wise and very old when she finally spoke once more.

"My father Tasa, who has gone to the Great Father,

was a farmer-Indian, and like Mazakutemani, who is known to the whites as Little Paul, Tasa cut off his hair and put on white man's clothes. He became a Christian. Tasa learned to speak English very well. His grandfather had gone to the white man's school for many years. And I am medicine woman, just like my sister, Rain Lily, who has left this earth."

Minowa's eyes widened and something within her spirit began to throb. A soft cry broke from her lips. She leaned forward this time and, in a high singsong voice, began to speak. "It is inhabited by a spirit, in the form of a man." As Minowa said these things, Audrina stared at the medicine pouch as if another Indian would suddenly appear in the room, and as she touched her throat, her slender fingers shook. "He is a very powerful man." Minowa reached for the pouch and merely touched it. "There are secrets here that are only to be known by a few."

Audrina bit her lip as she puzzled over Minowa's strange words. Softly, she asked, "What *are* they?"

Minowa turned to Audrina. "One day you will learn them. For now, guard it with your life. You will go on a mission with this powerful totem; you will go far, and you will find a trying time with many perils ahead. There might be many who will try to snatch the pouch from you. Do not give it up to anyone. You must fight like the she-cat who defends her young. You must hold it until your destination is reached. From there you will go even further. This is your destiny... *White Feather.*"

"What did you say?" Audrina leaned closer, her face full of confusion and concern. "You called me a name.... What was it?"

Minowa rose from the floor, looking as if she were in a trance. Then, without a word, she went out, closing the door softly behind her.

"Wait!" Audrina rushed to the door, but when she opened it there was no one there. Not in the drive leading to the main road. Not in the spacious yard.

Audrina stepped outside, her eyes darting to the dark green line of pines off to her right. . . . Minowa could not have gotten there already. Then . . . *where was she?* Audrina went back inside, shaking her head at the wonder of it all as she closed the door.

Audrina approached the table where the pouch still lay. *This is your destiny . . . your destiny. You must fight like the she-cat who defends her young.*

Sighing heavily, Audrina turned to the window to gaze out at the deep blues and lavenders heralding the coming night. A warm shiver ran up and down her limbs as she recalled the hawk-brown eyes with ebony flecks, swimming, boldly swimming toward her as they had the morning of the execution. The strong virile face loomed before her. The room seemed to be filled with a strange new fragrance, something sweeter than spring flowers and scented grass. She expanded her lungs and breathed deeply. . . . It was as if he were close again. Out there . . . somewhere in the misty lavender twilight.

Audrina closed her eyes, unaware that someone *was* outside, watching through the window as she lifted her hand to her throat and swayed and let her head fall back. She felt so warm and so sensuous. The face of the dark stranger was not as clear as it used to be; it was fading.

She tried to hold the vision a little while longer. Her

35

breaths were becoming shallower and the tips of her breasts were growing taut and hard. She felt strange and tingly all over, even in her most secret places. . . . She was warmth and awakening passion.

Her arms crossed over her breasts and Audrina hugged herself, wishing . . . oh how she wished . . . Her eyes flew open and she gasped for breath. She caught hold of the table, leaned over it dizzily, and then shoved away.

What had come over her? she wondered. Never in her wildest reveries had she experienced or visualized anything quite like this . . . so alive . . . as if the dark stranger in the Eskimo coat stood right here in her aunt's house!

With sublime effort, Audrina shook herself from her erotic daydreams. *Enough* of this, she told herself. She headed toward the tiny kitchen and stood in front of the wood stove. Lighting a match, she just stood there and stood there until the tiny orange and blue flame burned her fingers.

"Ouch!" Audrina shook her hand. She heaved a deep sigh and peered around the darkening room, wishing that Aunt Kate would come home.

Audrina stared at her slender arms as she rolled her sleeves up, getting ready to prepare some biscuits and leftover vegetable soup. Running a hand over her forearm, she felt the fine, soft reddish-brown hairs rise at her touch and her flesh turn goosebumpy. With quick, efficient movements, she lit a kitchen lamp and tried to forget about the effect a pair of black-brown eyes was having on her body.

Her *body*. That was it. Every time she envisioned those disturbing eyes and dark, compelling visage, she began to feel hot and strangely tingling all over. Ever since that day, she would lie awake sometimes at night and her heart would drum in her blood, for she would envision the dark stranger towering above her bed.

"Oh, come now, Audrina," she said, disgusted with herself. "You really cannot be in love with a total stranger!" She stared at her blurred reflection in a pan suspended from the blackened oak beam. "You are more intelligent than *that,*" she told herself, stirring the thick stew of meat and vegetables.

Pushing the spoon into the soup and then ladling a portion, Audrina shook her head as she smelled its rottenness; the meat had gone bad. She carried the spoiled food with her to the weather-beaten door, unlocked it, then leaned out to dump the smelly contents into the garbage barrel. So she thought, but her aim was less than accurate.

A dark figure stepped out from the shadows and Audrina clamped a hand over her mouth. She stared at the spoiled stew sliding off the man's coatsleeve and exhaled slowly.

"Good evenin', Miss Harris," a slurred voice drawled.

Audrina pursed her moist pink lips and one slim hand went to her hip. "Mr. Powell, what are you doing standing right beside the kitchen door?" A shiver crept along her spine as she wondered if Joe had seen her through the living room window as she stood there in a dreamlike state.

Joe shook out a handkerchief and wiped the mess off his arm. "Thanks for all your assistance in helping me clean up, Audrey."

"I'm sorry. Aunt Kate made the stew last Friday and

37

our ice melted two days ago. I just forgot when I warmed it up tonight." What was he doing here? This was the first time Joe Powell had ever stopped by when Aunt Kate wasn't home.

"You must have been in a daze if you didn't smell *that!*" His grin turned roguish. "The night is unseasonably warm. Look"—he pointed to the sky and wavered a bit—"there's a big romantic moon to spoon under."

"You've been drinking, Mr. Powell. A little too much, I would say. I do believe you should go home and sleep it off."

"I don't have a home, Audrey love. Not tonight, anyway." He laughed. "Mama would kick me out if I came home smelling *so* sweet."

Joe was built solidly. She knew he was hard-muscled because he used to push her on the swing in the Powell's backyard after church on Sunday afternoons, and he had always brushed an arm or a leg against her, pretending it was accidental. For years he had done that and she had never thought much of it; then she grew older and realized he was being overly familiar. She shivered to think what he would have done if she had been alone with him at that time . . . alone, like she was now.

She didn't want Joe Powell courting her: He was the right age for her, but there was something dark lurking just beneath the surface. . . . And he was always inebriated when in town, strolling the streets with ladies of questionable virtue hanging on his arm.

Leaning against the side of the house, Joe said, "What were you doing a while ago in front of the window? You looked like you were waiting for your

38

lover to come along. Who were you burning for, princess?"

Joe reached for a loose curl of her hair and Audrina jumped back, banging the pan against the house. "Keep your hands to yourself, sir!"

Joe's blond hair hung over his lazy, drooping eyes. He slid a shoulder against the wall a little closer to Audrina. "Do you realize just how pretty you are? I love it when your green eyes flash and throw sparks at me. You've got the shiniest auburn hair, too, and when you wear it in that fat braid down your back, you make my heart go crazy. When you walk down the road in the sunshine, you're like a slender golden flame . . . your perfect hands . . . your perfect *everything.*"

Audrina was so nervous she blurted the first thing that came into her mind. "I don't think I like you very much lately, Joe. I heard you making fun of the Indians who were imprisoned in that cold room. You laughed at their discomfort and misery."

For a moment, Joe's mouth hung agape. "Those savages? Hell, Audrina, they weren't even humans; they were *animals.*"

She glared at him. "I always thought there was something about you, Joe. Now I know what it is. You are cold and unfeeling. You are the kind of person Minowa was telling me about." Audrina thought for a moment, then asked him, "If you could change the course of history and go back to the treaty table, would you have deceived the Dakota Indians out of land that belonged to them? If it was in your power?"

"Hell yes!!" Joe snorted. "Have you gotten a little loco, Audrina? You're a white person just like I am."

39

His blue eyes squinted and he asked, "Or are the rumors true? That you got some Injun blood, that your mother Melissa was one-half Oglala Sioux?"

"I don't know what she was." Audrina shook her head sadly. "She died when I was born." She glanced down at her warm golden skin, even more tawny and lustrous under the moon. Who am I, really? Where do I belong? I feel so out of place here, with this man, this town and its people. The only one I really love and care for is Aunt Kate.

Audrina shook her head. When her eyes lifted, she found herself staring at the most romantic moon she had ever seen. A thrilling sense of anticipation shot through her and she felt as if she stood on the very edge of the world, waiting to fall off or be caught.

The face of her dream-lover was growing dimmer, but she would never forget those compelling eyes. It had been like gazing into another world, wild and invitingly warm, and she had lost herself in the thrilling pools of deep, dark brown. If only she could remember what his face looked like, but his features had been hidden by so much fur circling his face. . . .

"Come on, Audrina, quit pretending you don't like me." Audrina gasped when Joe grabbed her arm, and when she looked up into his eyes, she realized he was very serious. The pan was still in one of her hands, and she clutched it tighter, meaning to use it as a weapon if she had to.

"Stay away from me, Joe. I'm warning you." She backed into the kitchen, holding onto the door with one hand, the pan with the other.

Joe leaned forward and shocked Audrina with a warm, wet kiss. He grinned devilishly, and when he went for her lips again, she saw her chance to let him know just how serious she was, too. Before his lips touched hers, Audrina quickly stepped back and, in the same motion, brought the pan up and swung the door.

Joe stepped back just in time, as the pan fell and clattered to the floor. Audrina tried shutting the door, but Joe stuck his foot between and snarled into her face, "Wait just a damn minute! I'm not leaving until we have a nice long talk."

He was back in the room in a flash, slamming the door behind him and driving the bolt home. Audrina stared at the vicious snarl on his face. He was very close. Joe's nose had never looked more crooked than at this moment, and she noticed that his blond hair was already thinning a little in the front.

"What do you want, Joe?" Audrina's heart quickened and then sank as Joe looked up and down her body.

Joe chuckled nastily, "What I'm gonna *get,* princess." He leaned closer. "You're going to be just like clay in my hands, honey. Just like clay."

Dear God, Audrina thought frantically, I'm all alone with a drunken madman!

Chapter Two

Audrina's eyes widened as Joe pulled her toward her bunk in a curtained corner of the kitchen. Frantically, she thought of the handgun she had hidden under the cushion months before. If only she could get to it quickly enough, she told herself, then thought miserably that maybe it was not even there anymore; maybe Aunt Kate had taken it with her. Whatever the case, Audrina wished to God she had the weapon in her hands this very minute!

"Enough, Joe!" Audrina shouted at him as he pinned her between his eager body and the bunk. "You have gone far enough!"

"Oh no, princess, not far enough yet. We've still got a long way to go."

His eyes blazing with lust, Joe gazed into her dark-lashed green eyes, then on down to her perfectly formed breasts straining against the bodice of her dress. "We are going to go all the way. Wait until you get your first taste of me, Audrina, you'll want more and more. Then you'll be so greedy you'll never want to quit. You'll see."

"Joe, you *are* drunk." Audrina felt a sickening lurch in her stomach as he found a tender spot on her neck and began nibbling. "You . . . are . . . frightening me." She shoved at his chest, angered and resentful that this man could come along and paw her body as he saw fit. "How could you even *think,* after all these years being acquainted with me, that—that I would so easily perform the act you have in mind?"

"Come on, lovely Audrina. Answer my body with your sweet and passionate one. You're mine; I always knew it."

Bringing her knee up, Audrina shoved with all her might. She gasped as she felt his manly parts shift as bone contacted flesh. She stepped aside as he collapsed from the waist down and pressed his forearms between his legs. She heard the breath suck through his lips. Then she moved quickly, leaving him while he was not looking, making a beeline for the sofa in the living room. If only she could get to it in time . . .

Joe was in such pain that he was doubled over and surprised to find he could not unbend. Taking a few deep breaths, he slowly straightened and searched around the kitchen, but Audrina was nowhere to be found. "Where'd you go, Audrey? Come on back. I promise not to force you anymore." He neared the door frame in the kitchen wall.

Her voice came from somewhere close by, "We'll *talk,* Mr. Powell . . . on my terms."

All of a sudden the nose of a pistol was shoved into his line of vision. He looked up into a pair of shining green eyes. "Right," he said, "we'll talk."

"I said as much," she responded crisply, and waved

the gun back and forth. *"Now,* Mr. Powell, I want you to leave my aunt's house." She indicated the door with a jerk of the gun. "I have grown tired of your company."

"There's no need for such haste, princess." He was so close he could see the hint of freckles spread across her nose and fine high cheekbones. Her bright auburn hair had come loose in her struggles and it floated about her like prairie fire.

"And *please* do not call me *princess.* Just leave this house as quickly as you can move in your inebriated state."

With the swift reflex action of a trained and well-tried soldier, he reached out and latched onto Audrina's swinging hair. With his other hand, he quickly and expertly relieved her of the dangerous and threatening gun.

Now *he* had it in his hand. Audrina stared down at the gun pointed at her, mentally kicking herself for being so easily caught off guard. What had she been thinking of in that moment to have allowed him such easy access to her one and only means of saving herself from being ravished?

Just as quickly as he had snatched it from her, Joe unloaded the gun and tossed it aside, then reached out and gripped her hard and painfully by the shoulders. His arm hauled her against him and his lips crashed down on hers, slanting bruisingly, nipping the corners of her delicate lips, biting her chin. A long graceful leg was caught between his and he felt like a crazy man in his deranged lust.

Audrina felt nothing but repulsion and outrage. The grinding of his teeth against her soft lips was unpleasant, and the bold thrust of his tongue shocked and shamed her. His foul breath was in her mouth, and she promised herself never to drink liquor, for it would always remind her of Joe Powell and his offensive kisses. Now he was lifting his hand to touch a breast; she could feel it creeping alongside her ribs.

"No!!" she cried in his ear. "Damn you, *no!*"

She reached out a hand to claw his face, but Joe caught at her wrist. "That's the last trick in your bag, Audrina. There's none left." He caught her around the waist in a bear hug and began to carry her to the bed in the corner of the room.

She struggled and fought him hard, but he was now more determined than ever.

He picked her up and tossed her onto the bunk, then followed her down with his lean and muscled frame, pinning her there like a poor butterfly.

"I'm in a hurry," he said, panting. "So excuse me if I fail to be the gentleman, Miss Harris."

"You're mean and—and terrible!" Audrina shouted at his face. "I hate you! I mean, I *really* hate you. Do you understand? God, how can you take a woman who despises you so thoroughly? Have you no respect? Are you a man or what?"

Pinning her down with a large, strong hand, Joe fumbled with the front of his trousers, got them open, then began to tear and yank at her skirts. Audrina scissored her legs and bit and scratched and kicked, but to no avail. His foul kisses made her feel as though she might retch.

"Keep still, you little tigress, or I'll be forced to tie you up." Joe spent his energy furiously, removing every stitch of Audrina's clothes until she lay writhing on the

45

bed, a scattered pile of white underslips beneath her and her pink and green striped calico dress tossed carelessly onto the floor along with her camisole and bloomers.

"Why don't you find a woman who is willing? I'm sure there are plenty who would—" Her pleading words stuck in her throat as his eyes widened over the delicious perfection of her golden silky body, with its tiny waist, perfect breasts, gently flaring hips.

Dear God, Audrina prayed fervently, Help me escape this lecherous man before the worst is accomplished. "Mr. Powell . . . *please* . . . I have never lain with a man before!"

With those words ringing in Joe's ears, Audrina slithered between his arms like a slippery fish, hopping off the bed and grabbing for a piece of clothing as she sped across the kitchen and fled from the house. All she could manage to snatch in her flight was her bloomers.

The sudden coldness struck Audrina like a slap in the face. The springlike day had vanished with the sunset, the night bringing back a hint of frosty air and nipping north wind. There was nothing but thin, cloudy moonlight and shadows.

Audrina sped along like a graceful doe, but her shapely bottom felt like two cubes of ice; it was shocking and queerly embarrassing to be outside without a stitch on. She couldn't slow down to tug the bloomers on, so she just carried them and kept running, hugging her shoulders as she fled, her long limbs a flash of white as she ran.

The streets were deserted; there wasn't a soul about. She could see the black and simple geometric figures of houses, but they seemed so far away. She would wait

46

outside until Joe left. Audrina ran up to a tree and hid behind it, stepping into her bloomers and pulling the drawstring at the waist, trying to catch her breath as she peeked around the trunk to see if Joe had come out. But the door was as she had left it, slightly ajar. She breathed a small sigh of relief. . . . At least he wasn't giving chase. Not *yet*.

She failed to see him coming toward her while she hugged her shivering form and peered over her shoulder. . . .

Wild Hawk had returned to the Minnesota River Valley. He rode slowly now, cautiously, along the moonlit stretch of lonely road. His long black hair floated down his back; his single braid had two golden eagle feathers woven into it. He did not feel the March winds; to him they were mild and invigorating.

The season of the Hard Moon—cold weather—was over. It was now early in the Moon-of-the-Red-Grass-Appearing. Wild Hawk was glad. He could move about now, silent as a nighthawk, and not wear as much clothing.

The Bear, Wild Hawk's black-as-midnight horse, moved on great, muffled hooves, almost unseen in the land they had traveled by night. Wild Hawk had persuaded two of his most trusty warriors to accompany him, but the other superstitious four would not come into town—not since the public execution of their Dakota brothers and fathers. They would ride around the town instead. His two braves were not far behind, traveling in the dark of the moon, swiftly flitting from shadow to shadow in the patches of light.

Wild Hawk made a strikingly handsome figure as he drew his horse to the top of the hill and came to a halt. With the barrel of the Indian rifle resting in the crook of his arm, he stared down into the moonlit valley, seeing nothing but silvered light and shifting shadows, and a few rooftops with spiraling gray smoke lifting into the star-studded heavens.

Wild Hawk's gaze shifted to the right. There was the house of the lovely *wasichu* Audrina—Powell's woman. He guessed her to be of nineteen summers, though he had only looked upon her twice and those times had been disappointingly brief. Her lovely face was fading from memory. He would like to see her again, to look into her moss-green eyes, maybe even touch her to see if she were real. She had lived in his mind and in his dreams all these three Hard Moons since he had gazed upon her in that crowd of *wasicuns,* white men, and then once again when he had seen her enter the house below the hill, her hair a bright beacon in the early morning light.

Wild Hawk had been drawn to this hill overlooking her dwelling twice before and had looked down as he was doing now, a puzzled expression on his face, strange emotions tugging at his heart. He had heard eerie sounds, too, like voices singing in Dakota . . . soft drums, and he had felt the movement of a wandering spirit. Where were they coming from? He could not pinpoint the exact spot, but he came closer each time he visited this hill.

As Wild Hawk asked himself these questions, he found his eyes gazing down at the little house with the big smoke curling from the roof. Her house, Audrina's house. He had seen the compassion in her face and eyes

48

that day for the doomed warriors. He had wondered at her sadness. Then she had flown from the crowd as if her heart had been breaking. For his people? She was a *wasichu*. How could she feel these things?

Wild Hawk's father, Red Hawk, had been leader of the Cetan/Wahpekute tribe, the Indian word *Cetan* meaning Hawk or Small Falcon. His mother, Rain Lily, had been Oglalahca, or true Oglala. His father had followed Rain Lily into the Spirit World. One other immediate family member remained, Rainbow, his sweet and lovely sister. And he had a plentitude of distant relatives, cousins mostly, like Fox Dreamer.

His dark eyes shifted as he stared again at the back door of the pretty woman's house. He wondered if she were German, that strange word for settlers who had never wanted to learn the Indian's way or make friends with his people. The Sioux resented those Germans and other white-skinned men because they had refused to share food with hungry Indians; his own culture had always been based on sharing.

Wild Hawk had learned the white man's tongue and spoke English fluently now. His grandfather, Standing Hawk, had worn white man's clothes and had attended school for several years. Red Hawk had followed Standing Hawk in this, as had he, Wild Hawk. Now he could almost spit on their English words, for he could not help but feel bitter and angry toward the whites. They had cheated and stolen the Indians' land. They had deceived again and yet again. . . . And they had cruelly taken his father captive and executed him.

"I should take a captive. I have never taken a white woman and kept her," Wild Hawk said in his beautiful and flowing English voice. It was deeply resonant and masculine. There was one especially he would like for his captive. The green-eyed woman with the flaming hair, *Petala,* Precious Fire. She would be his *Winu,* his captive woman, forever, and he would never lose her. . . .

Wild Hawk sighed. Alas, this was not to be. More trouble with the whites he did not want, nor did he wish to hang, nor did he really wish to clip Petala's wings. It was a mystery to him and his warriors why he even visited Mankato and sat here gazing down on the pretty female's house. No one could unveil the overpowering mystery of what drew him to this spot. He surmised the only reason he came here was to listen. If he sat as if carved from stone, he could hear something . . . like soft drums and urgent whispers on the wind.

"Why do you not just search the house?" *Miyaca,* Prairie Wolf, had asked of him on more than one occasion. "If what you want is there in the pretty *wasichu's* house, then you must take it. If it is the woman herself you want, then take her for your captive woman. If you must take her and all she owns, then do so. You have never shown fear before, Great Warrior. You keep us in mystery, Mighty Chief. Our people cannot wait for you to join them in the prairie woods in the Dakota lands."

"It is my wish to remain near the woods and rivers of Minnesota." He looked sad, adding, "Some day our People will return to the upper River Valley."

"But we are hunted in Minnesota. We should not come back here anymore. The white man will catch us and put us on the reservations. Do you not wish to be free, Wild Hawk?"

50

"I am free; I want to remain free," Wild Hawk had spoken sternly, "—as much as any other Dakota chief."

"The great chiefs have been cheated. Many have perished within the hangman's noose. We should go far from here. We distrust the white traders and settlers. They have broken the land with their white man's plows. They have cut down the forest and scared off the game. They have never attempted to build kinship ties with our People."

Left Hand stepped in and concluded, "We are not worthy of being called human beings by the *wasicuns*. They have driven us from our own lands with their big guns!" He spat on the ground.

This was true. Wild Hawk had often felt bitter frustration sear his soul. In the battle of Wood Lake, Little Crow's warriors had been defeated by the superior weapons of white soldiers, and Little Crow had been forced to lead away several hundred mounted Dakota warriors. They had gone toward the western prairies, and Little Crow had stated, as he rode from the Minnesota River Valley, "We shall never go back there."

Red Hawk and his men had been caught; some had been let go. Little Crow and his band were still wandering through Dakota Territory. Wild Hawk had seen him only once since he had left Minnesota. Dakota Territory was still beyond reach of white civilization, and it was there to the Suland that Wild Hawk would return, to battle to preserve his people's heritage and identity, but not to the Black Hills, not into hiding, not unless a reason arose to force him.

Something fierce was brewing in the wind, and Wild Hawk was unaware that the reason for flight was not far off.

The new chief of the Cetan/Wahpekute tribe rode down the hill and was about to join the others in the shadows when a stirring to the left caught his eye. The wind had picked up, and when Wild Hawk turned his head, the eagle feathers in his long lock of ebony hair stirred against his bronze cheeks.

"Hai!" came the startled sound from one of his warriors as he rode out of the deep shadows of evening. "Wild Hawk, do you see what we see? There, a woman . . . She runs from behind a tree where she was hiding."

Wild Hawk's eyes narrowed into obsidian slits. "The white female runs like a deer." *Could it be? . . .*

"She wears nothing but a long breechclout!" exclaimed Prairie Wolf. "And look! A man pursues her."

"We must leave here," Left Hand said as he rode up. His black eyes shifted from the half-naked woman and rested on Wild Hawk's face. *"Hiya,* you do not hear?"

"Never tell me I must do something, Left Hand, for *I* give the orders and you, my brave, obey!" Wild Hawk ordered the argumentative brave who could never hold his tongue, not even when they had played together as young lads. "Leave if you wish; I remain."

"I stay also," Left Hand said.

Wild Hawk was fascinated by the long hair flowing over the slender, naked torso touched by the moon— hair like red flames. . . . There was something familiar about this woman. A secret smile lurked on his well-defined lips. Then he frowned as the man closed in on the swiftly fleeing wraith and, with a sudden forward lurch, tackled her about her slim waist, bringing the captivating creature to the ground. "This is none of our affair," Left Hand said, looking on the couple with disgust. "They ravish their women without reason. They beat their children without reason. White people are crazy. Let us leave this place, Wild Hawk," Left Hand snorted. "I feel an evil spell being woven around us. There is something foreboding which comes closer and closer. . . . Can you not feel this?"

"I feel nothing but anger," Wild Hawk hissed. The nostrils of his wide, straight nose flared and the muscles of his strong body flexed in readiness for action.

"They only play a white man's game," Left Hand said, flinging out a hand. "See how she relaxes her struggles. Her body is ready for his taking now. Do you not wish to turn your eyes from this ugly ritual of the white man's?"

Wild Hawk felt the gentle touch of Prairie Wolf's hand on his arm as he said, "He speaks true words, I think."

The Bear shifted under Wild Hawk as if he, too, were willing him to go from this place. "Perhaps you are right. We will go now."

They were just nearing the lone stand of pines when the scream rent the stillness. To Wild Hawk, it was as if the cry had pierced his heart. He looked up at the cold moon, then wheeled the Bear about and sent him off at a gallop. Prairie Wolf and Left Hand stayed where they were, watching their leader go to the woman's rescue, neither of them believing she was really in need of rescuing. Besides, they had never seen Wild Hawk react so strongly to a white woman's distress.

By the time Wild Hawk reached the two, the man was dragging her, screaming and kicking, back into the house. There was a moment when the moon was shrouded by dense gray clouds and Wild Hawk could not see what was happening. Then, when the gray clouds were erased, the Indian looked upon an empty yard.

Wild Hawk was suddenly alerted when he realized that the house he had come to was Audrina's dwelling. He had never been this close to her home.

"Hai." What is this? Startling sounds were coming from within. It was as if he were being drawn inside by a powerful and magnetic force. The sounds of the drums and chanting *hiye-hey-i-i* were louder now, louder than he had ever heard these mysterious sounds to be.

With a blanket wrapped around her, Audrina shivered even harder as she crouched in a corner of her aunt's bed and heard the Dakota words and drums again. A look of hatred crossed her weary features as she stared across the room at Joe; he was standing in the living room with a frown on his face.

"I don't hear anything." He shook his blond head, sweat glistening on his high forehead. "You must be hearing things." Rushing over to her, he knelt on the floor with one knee. "I must have hurt you, princess, for you to hear such things as drums and such."

Her pulse raced, not from fear of Joe, but from the strange foreboding she felt. "Please, stay away from me."

With a shaking hand, he pushed the blond wave from his eyes. "Lord, I need a drink." He frowned. "What the hell is wrong with you? You look as if you've seen a ghost, princess."

54

Audrina rose from her aunt's mussed bed, where Joe had almost had his way with her. But he had sobered up in time, when she had begun hearing the ominous and exciting sounds from the pouch again.

"I asked you never to call me that again." Audrina shook out her long mane of silken red hair, and the ends swirled about her tiny waist. "Now, please . . . *please,* leave this house."

"You're too high and mighty, girl." He puffed up his chest and sighed impatiently. "I guess I'll have to teach you some lessons if you're going to be my woman!"

With that, Joe stepped on a corner of the blanket, and Audrina walked out from the safety of its folds and into the arms of an Indian who had only seconds before burst into the room like a pouncing cat!

"Indian!" Joe yelled, dancing backward from the bed. At first he did not recognize the Sioux as Wild Hawk; he shook his head violently to clear it.

Audrina covered her cheeks with her trembling hands, her green eyes large and full of terror.

For a pulsating space in time, the three of them looked at one another. Only their eyes moved, nothing else. For one crazy moment, Audrina found herself comparing the two men. Joe Powell paled beside the copper-skinned Indian with the shining blue-black hair.

Then everything happened lightning fast. Joe went diving for a gun he couldn't find at the most crucial moment, not realizing that he had emptied it, and the Indian, who Audrina could see was in superb physical condition, shot forward and knocked Joe out stone-cold on the floor. Joe's leg twisted as he was propelled backward. Audrina stared down at Powell in horrible

55

fascination, and then at the tall Indian. She was about to let loose a scream when he lunged forward and covered the lower half of her wildly shocked and terrified face with a big bronze hand.

He muttered a strange guttural word as Audrina stared into the eyes of this handsome savage who was holding her, naked and half swooning, in his arms. His eyes were the eyes of a dark hawk's feathers, eyes she had gazed into once before. This was the last thing a weakened and disoriented Audrina saw before her head spun wildly and she thought: her lost man with the fathomless and soul-penetrating eyes. *He's an Indian*. Then her mind was floundering in a whirling dark mist and she sunk into a faint.

Audrina opened her eyes. She was lying on the bed and someone had covered her nakedness with the red and blue blanket. She was shivering and wished fervently she could go get her clothes, but the Indian was searching the house—for what she could not say. Maybe food, or valuables, or both. From her vantage point, she could see him poking in the kitchen cupboards.

Then the questions hit Audrina like a tumultuous spring flood. What was he doing here? Who was he? She had seen moving shadows lurking in the periphery of her vision when she had been outside, struggling with Joe Powell. Had it been the Indian in the shadows? More frightening, were there more of them?

Audrina lifted her head, tried to rise, and swayed in dizziness. What had happened to Joe's body? He had been lying unconscious on the floor when she fainted, but he was nowhere to be seen now. Had the Indian already disposed of Joe for good? Was he going to get rid of her in the same way?

By the time Audrina finally managed to sit on the edge of Aunt Kate's fluffy feather bed, with the blanket worn Indian-fashion around her body, the tall coppery-visaged Indian returned. He halted at the foot of the bed and Audrina stared in awestruck wonder at his magnificence. He was a superb male, matchless, Audrina thought as a shiver raced up and down her spine.

Pin-drop silence reigned.

She had never seen such a beautiful male animal. He was tall, bronze, graceful, and she was struck by the profound mysteries she saw in his eyes; also, she could detect some sadness within the liquid ebony depths. He seemed to see and know her true heart. She felt as if she had always known this handsome and virile man who at once terrified and fascinated her.

As Audrina studied the Indian, Wild Hawk's gaze read her thoughts and realized proudly what she was seeing. He glorified in his virility and savage prowess, and was unashamed of the way he dressed.

His headband had been fashioned of buckskin and colored cloth; floating down the back were feathers that had been taken from the living golden eagle *wiyaka,* and one from a wild hawk, too. Each feather represented a deed of valor he had performed. On his large and strong body, he carried only the barest essentials for surviving. There was his hunting and skinning knife, and around his neck was a strike-a-light pouch of dyed buckskin decorated with black-and-white beads and quills. He wore a buckskin shirt and

57

leggings; when the weather warmed even more, he would wear nothing but fringed leggings of shorter length. When necessity called for it, Wild Hawk wore the white man's clothes, as he had to his father's execution.

The revelation had already dawned on Audrina that this man's dark eyes were the same ones she had encountered that tragic day, those penetrating eyes that had left a definite and lasting impression on her young heart and mind.

Wild Hawk stared back at her. Her brilliant and lustrous hair was the color of the wild Dakota sunset. Her clean-cut chin had a willful thrust, even while there was a childlike innocence about her oval-shaped face. The sparkling light in her deep green eyes revealed a flashing spirit and a restless heart.

Wild Hawk's shoulders squared as he thought: Here is a woman destined to walk beside a great warrior. One named Wild Hawk, leader of the Cetan/ Wahpekute tribe. Yes, she would be his . . . and very soon.

Wild Hawk thought of the beauty and softness beneath the blanket she wore. In her struggles with the white man Powell, he had noticed her breasts were high, firm, and full, her waist so small his own warrior's hands could easily span it. Her hips were sweepingly curved, with exquisite roundness in her buttocks. He glowed inside at the tempting thought of touching her and had to force himself to still his irregular breathing.

The dark eyes roved over her, resting upon her mouth. At the moment, there was the suggestion of a pout in her lower pink lip. He could well imagine her as a lonely young woman, pining, awaiting her first love.

Here was the same young, brave beauty Wild Hawk had seen at the execution. He had been witness to her forlorn expression, looking lost in the crowd and saddened by the Indians' fate. His face hardened. But he knew his thoughts were incorrect. She was not a lonely young woman, nor did she care for his people even a little!

"Huka," Audrina said, clutching the blanket modestly to her breast. *"Huka,"* she repeated when he did not respond to one of the only Dakota/Lakota words she knew . . . thanks to Minowa, the mysteriously disappearing Indian woman. "I said *Huka!* Do you not understand?"

Audrina caught hold of her lower lip with her teeth. My God, what if he's not a Sioux? She might have just offended him with her hasty words. Audrina swallowed the fear lumped up in her throat and squared her chin as she stared up at him.

He remained very still. "I understand that your vocabulary of our language is very limited." Wild Hawk employed his best English and wondered why he should wish to impress a mere white female. He shrugged and said, "You are not afraid."

Audrina blinked wide. "N—no." She felt something under her thigh, beneath the blanket, and slid her hand down inside to come in contact with the medicine pouch! She clutched it tight against her naked thigh and watched the Indian approach her.

"You will give me what I have come for"—his eyes glittered strangely as he stood before her, his toes almost touching hers—"and if you do not, I will be forced to take you with me."

"Wh—what you have come for?" Audrina experi-

59

enced a new kind of fear.

"Indeed, I desire that which the white man has given you." Wild Hawk glanced around the room. "He has gone. My braves have not been able to find him. Someday I will see that Powell dies. . . . For now, you will give me what I ask for."

His tall frame filled the boundaries of her vision; nothing else could she see. "G—give you what Powell . . . has given . . . *me?*" Audrina repeated and gasped with delayed surprise. He speaks English. . . . She was standing here talking to an *Indian.*

"You will give the pouch to me now, Audrina."

Blushing hotly, Audrina lifted her eyes quickly from the spread-eagle legs and strong, sinewy thighs . . . from the prominence there at the junction of his thighs.

Wild Hawk's eyes narrowed suspiciously. "You will answer me!" he suddenly lashed out.

"P—pouch?" Then it hit her and she all but swooned. *Pouch.* No . . . no . . . she couldn't allow him to take it from her! *You must fight like the she-cat who defends her young,* Minowa had warned her.

Clutching the pouch beneath the folds of the blanket, Audrina stammered, "I—I have no pouch." Her eyes widened as, for the first time, she noticed that his forehead bore a thin white zigzagged scar running into his black hairline.

"You, then, will be mine"—he peered down at her from his towering height—"in exchange for the pouch. I shall not ask you for it again. . . . For now, you must pay the price of its loss."

"Please . . ." she begged, her eyes full of apprehension.

"Please? What do you beg me for?"

60

"Don't take me . . . *please.*" She held onto the pouch for dear life . . . even while her freedom was at stake.

Menacingly, he shook his raven-dark head. "You will be mine, Audrina, in every way."

She stared down at the floor, frozen, expressionless. It seemed he knew everything about her . . . even her name. But he did not yet have knowledge of *one* thing:

Her secret.

Chapter Three

"You will go and get dressed now," Wild Hawk ordered sternly, the urgency in his tone unavoidable.

Quickly, Audrina stood and walked away from the rumpled bed and the Indian who watched her. He has knowledge of my fear, she thought with a new sense of dread, and he will use it to his advantage. Whatever was going to happen from here on out, it was going to be up to her to make certain he did not realize her fear. But what was going to happen now? Would he take her captive? Audrina shivered fiercely at the thought. There was a chill in the house, because she had forgotten to replenish the wood in the stove . . . as if there had been time to do that this night!

She felt the cold floor beneath her bare feet and quickly moved across it to the curtained-off area in the kitchen that served as her bedroom. She stared at her small bed, her drawings of wild animals on the walls, the washstand with its pretty speckled porcelain basin, her clothes hung neatly on the wood rack—but for the ones Joe had strewn on the floor. This was the only home she'd ever known. Loving parents had never existed for her, but Aunt Kate had been a wonderful guardian, and Audrina had never wanted more. She loved Katherine; her aunt had never spoken an unkind word, and Audrina had never given the older woman trouble when she was growing from toddler to teen to young woman. Her life had been uneventful and she had never wanted for anything, but now everything had been turned upside down. She could truthfully say that the excitement had commenced when she had first stared into the eyes of the compelling savage who had this night come back into her life; she'd never thought to see him again. What was to happen now? Was she going to be taken captive? Would she ever see her beloved Aunt Kate again?

Retrieving the clothes from the floor, she dressed as fast as she could manage with shaking hands and fumbling fingers. She hurried, afraid the Indian would come looking for her. Or would he just leave? Dear Lord, that was not possible, not the way her luck was holding out. No doubt she would be carried away to become his captive. Neighbor women had talked about what happened to white women while in captivity—a fate worse than death itself! She shouldn't worry, Audrina told herself, swiftly donning the calico dress. Joe had probably revived and gone for help. She smiled wryly. Rescued by the man who had almost ravished her? She doubted rescue was imminent; he would leave her to her cruel fate, for she had withheld her favors. Never, but never, would she give herself to a man she did not love and cherish.

When Audrina began to button the calico dress in front, she discovered the sleeves were torn and the skirt

63

was split up the middle. She groaned and quickly tore it off, reaching instead for a full green wool skirt that had been folded neatly atop her dresser. It was warmer than the calico, anyway, she thought, unaware that she was dressing as if she planned a long journey.

"Dear Lord, help me through this night," she prayed as her fingers shook. She stared around the small area that was her bedroom. . . . If only there were a window she could escape from!

She was just buttoning up a snowy white blouse of heavy linen when a fierce-looking savage flung back the sliding curtains. He stared with narrow, menacing black eyes, which had an evil look about them; she stared back, and her thoughts turned wildly frantic. He was frowning darkly at her.

"Who . . . are . . . you?" she asked, not expecting an answer.

All he did was grunt, deep in his throat. Audrina wished she could sprout wings and fly. Then the Indian with the hawk-dark eyes returned. He looked restless and impatient as he watched her fumble, trying to fasten the last button. He stepped up to her, reaching out to complete the task.

With a weak smile, Audrina looked from one to the other, and then did a double take as a third Indian appeared in the flimsy doorway of her bedroom. This man was younger and appeared kinder than the fierce-eyed one. She was surprised at the gentle look on his smooth face.

It dawned on Audrina just how much her life was in peril. She backed to the edge of the bunk. "No!" she cried, clutching her wool skirt, wanting to discredit what she was seeing.

64

Not one, but three Indians!

"Catka, take her to the horses," Wild Hawk ordered Left Hand, placing a fringed buckskin jacket over the frightened young woman's shoulders. She trembled very hard now. He halted the Indian who was about to take her, then motioned for a stunned Audrina to sit down and put on a pair of high leather boots he thrust into her hands.

"Th—these are my b—boots," Audrina said dazedly and without thinking; she was so nervous.

The tallest and most powerful looking of the three, the one with the hawk-brown eyes, nodded that he realized they were her boots, and he turned from her. Wild Hawk understood that she was terrified and nervous, but this could not be helped. She was coming with them.

Audrina dawdled, unconsciously stalling for time as she moved to toss some things into a bag. She was so frightened that she didn't realize what she was doing. But the Indian understood and he pulled her around to face him. Audrina stared downward, at the strong fingers clamped like a vise over her suddenly trembling arm. Gazing up into his dark face, she began to struggle and try to wrench away from his powerful hold.

"It is ridiculous for you to struggle, woman, for my strength is far greater than yours, and you will be swiftly caught if you try to run. Don't even think of it. You will come with us now." He took her by the arm and propelled her from the kitchen.

In an agony of fear and disbelief, wondering what shock she would receive next, Audrina moved stiffly and warily as the second frowning Indian ushered her ungently out the door. In the deep pocket of the full green wool skirt was the pouch; Audrina felt it bump against her thigh. Now, at the last minute, she wished she had left it behind. There just might be some serious repercussions for bringing it with her. But what did she care? She was going to perish of fright soon enough, anyway. Either that, or they would kill her.

A quick, painless death would have been preferable, for when Audrina stepped outside into the brisk night air, her captors surrounding her like bodyguards, she received that next jolt she had been fearfully anticipating.

There, in the wagon just pulling into the backyard, sat her Aunt Kate, the ridiculous old battered hat pulled low over her forehead, with the sloping rim almost touching her cheek at one side. Though Audrina could not read Katherine's expression, she knew the woman must surely be horrified coming home to a yard full of Indians.

Audrina prayed her aunt's rifle was loaded. She wanted to yell "Run!" but could tell, just by looking at the Indian leader's long limbs in taut buckskin leggings, that he could no doubt run like a deer! Then her eyes fell on the girl beside Katherine—Sadie Peterson. She was all alone in the world now but for Katherine, who had taken her under her wing.

Only seconds had passed since Audrina caught sight of the wagon. She stopped so abruptly that the grim-faced Indian walked right into her tensely rigid back. Then the Indians moved as quick as lightning on a stormy night. The one with the ugly frown and black glaring eyes grasped her arm painfully from behind while the other two went to meet Aunt Kate's wagon. Katherine leaned down, brought her rifle up, and was surprised when a strong bronze hand lifted it from her grasp. Audrina's mouth fell. The one she thought of as Hawk-eyes had taken the weapon away.

Joe, nursing a swollen jaw and sprained ankle, watched the curious scene from behind a large live oak. Swift and silent as ghosts, the Indians snatched up their victims, unhitched the horses, and departed, Katherine Harris riding one, Audrina the other, and Sadie mounted in front of a mean-looking Indian. Joe watched them go, thinking they were almost invisible as they moved like foxfire in the night.

With a balled fist, Joe struck the tree and grimaced in pain. He could have done something; he should have gone for help, he supposed. Or he could have rescued the ladies like a gallant knight. But he had no shining armor, nor did he even have a horse. Three ruthless savages were too many to battle, he had warned himself.

Joe had recognized Wild Hawk. Since that night the Indian leader had viciously attacked him in town, Joe had asked around in the regiment and of others what they knew about Wild Hawk. He was rumored to be very fierce in battle, though he had not fought and killed many whites. His ferocity was in fighting renegade bands, like the Rebel Indians Joe had heard so much about.

Joe grimaced at the pain in his leg; he couldn't go after help now even if he wanted to. He mused on the Indians for a moment longer. Some of the Sioux warriors had been beaten and defeated; many were devoid of hope. But Wild Hawk was not beaten; he was still a brave warrior who would lead his people with pride. Too damn much pride, Joe thought now. Wild Hawk should know when his people were licked. He was a smart Indian, Joe could give him that. He recalled when he had turned the son of Red Hawk away when Wild Hawk might have visited his father before execution. Joe knew he had been downright mean to turn Wild Hawk away when all he had come for was his father's possessions. "The Devil made me do it," Joe had laughed to his fellow officers just before the execution. The best Joe could explain his dislike of Wild Hawk was that the Indian was just too damn handsome, clever, and arrogant for a savage.

As Joe limped away from his hiding place, plans ticked fiercely in his mind. He liked the way this had turned out; it suited what he had in mind for Audrina. First, he wouldn't tell their neighbors what had happened. Several days would pass before the townsfolk would miss Audrina or her aunt, and they'd be long gone by then. And Sadie Peterson, the orphaned girl who'd lost her parents in a raid, wouldn't be missed at all. Yeah, Sadie was sure pretty, with her long blond hair and big brown eyes. Sadie probably wouldn't mind a savage or two fighting over her. But not Audrina . . . *She* would fight the savages tooth and nail.

Joe had to take time to ponder this matter carefully. He was crazy with the need to possess Audrina. He had lusted after her ever since she had shown signs of becoming a shapely, pretty woman. She was no heiress; she had no money. He only desired her ravishing young body, and of course he wanted to control her mind, too, and tame her wild spirit. One thing was certain: Audrina had some Indian blood. Joe planned to make her his Indian mistress, and now the prospect seemed more exciting and challenging than ever.

Joe decided to go home, get a few hours' shut-eye, and then go after Audrina—alone. Those three would be headed toward Dakota Territory, Suland, with their captives, and they were known to move *fast*. Joe, being an officer, knew the paths well. While the Indians slept, one moonless night, he would rescue Audrina. She would be forever grateful to him!

Audrina felt the leader's night-ebony eyes burn into her back as they rode wildly away from town. When civilization was left behind, with only a few distant twinkling lights from farms off to the right or left, her breath quickened and her heart surged with the dangerous excitement of their flight. She could almost enjoy this night flight, if only she were not so filled with trepidation! She also felt that at any moment they would be pursued by soldiers on horses, firing warning shots into the air for the Indians to halt with their captives.

As they continued to ride, Audrina's anticipation of rescue lessened. In her mind she had named the leader Hawk, because of his dark eyes with their unusual shadings and ebony depths. He was just like that bird of prey, too, swooping down on her and carrying her off in his powerful talons. Audrina shivered and her heart thumped heavily in her chest.

She felt the Hawk's presence as he rode like a silent apparition at her back. Her auburn locks were loose and Audrina thought she must look wild with her hair streaming down to her waist . . . almost like an Indian squaw.

She glanced over her shoulder and found him watching her, his keen eyes mysterious and glittering. Audrina felt her heart pound, but not from fear this time. It was something else, a certain magical yearning and curious wonder. The one arm about her waist tightened, and Audrina could feel the steely cords and the pressure of his mighty strength. She chided herself for her tumultuous feelings that were becoming too dangerously daring.

Wild Hawk felt his heart pound in measure with the thunderous beat of the Bear's hooves. He peered down at the girl who rode so silently in front of him. Her eyes had glowed like green fire when she glanced at him. Her beautiful hair was tangled by the cool brisk wind, flowing wild and free, occasionally whipping against his brown skin. His eyes brightened, and his blood pulsed wildly through his body

There was so much he would know about her thoughts and her past, and from her own lovely lips he would hear it. She held something of import from him, a deep secret; he could tell. He would force it from her if need be. He knew of very pleasant ways to make her talk, or perhaps he would employ sterner methods. He could satisfy her fully and give her time to speak her heart and mind. Would she fight him? Maybe so.

Wild Hawk could not wait to be alone with his captive, to show her he could awaken in her a desire she had never known. Perhaps it would be an easy task to tame her heart and learn her wild secrets. Perhaps not.

Wild Hawk would give her time . . . yes. She was his captive now, and one way or another he would find what she held from him.

They rested on a curve of the Watonwan River. Audrina rubbed her aching backsides as she came down off the old gray wagon horse and gave the faithful beast a pat. She had served them well the last seven years. It was too bad that the leader was forcing her to ride the poor mare to death. For the last several hours, her captor had allowed her to ride the old mare, but he had fastened a rope leading from his wrist to hers. Before stopping, he had untied the rope before walking a short distance away. Now she rubbed her wrists where they were red and chafed.

Audrina was just walking over to join her aunt when the Hawk gripped her shoulder and spun her about to face him. Suddenly, he appeared angry. With a deep shudder, she wondered what she could have possibly done to upset him.

Looking up at him in surprise, she gazed into those dark, fathomless eyes that bore straight into her soul.

Abruptly, he spoke. "I did not say you could visit your friends. You must learn to ask when you want to do something, and you must heed my commands if you would wish to remain healthy." He was aware that some of his braves listened closely, curiously.

With a look of bold defiance, she faced him squarely. "Would I have to ask your permission to ease my hunger?"

Sternly, he said, "You will do what you are told, or

71

you will *not* fill your belly."

Quickly, she returned, "Then I will not eat your food."

Audrina tried not to panic as he stepped closer. Staring down from his towering height at her lifted face, he noticed that her defiantly thrusting chin quivered. Coils of shiny flaming hair curled over the mound of one breast as if placed there purposely, temptingly. Reaching out, Wild Hawk lifted an irresistibly lovely curl and rolled it back and forth in his fingers. The slight brushing motion of his fingers was feather-light against her breast. She looked up into his eyes, and what she saw in them made her feel weak all over and shaky at the knees.

With a deep, commanding growl, he caught her wrist. "We will see." Bringing his compelling face nearer, he folded her arm behind her back.

Audrina struggled against his hold, then ceased her movements suddenly, peering up at him and becoming aware of the dangerousness of his expression. "What are you going to do?"

Leading her over to his mount, he removed a buckskin pouch and a length of rope. She stared up at him as he brought her arms in front and tied them at the wrists. He then pushed her down next to a tree and hunkered before her, holding out a strip of dried meat. "Eat," he commanded. When she shook her head, defiantly refusing the food, he went on, "You will eat now, or I will be forced to punish you." Again she shook her head in denial of nourishment. He leaned into her, his lips grazing her cheek, his tongue probing her ear. She gasped softly and he breathed the erotic words into her ear. "Every time you disobey, I will

72

touch you, a little more each time." Seeing her eyes widen with alarm, he continued. "Little by little, Petala, until you are fully mine."

Drawn by the fierce light in his eyes, Audrina slowly opened her mouth and took a bite of the proffered food. She took several more bites while he grinned triumphantly, his stern demeanor diminishing, his straight teeth glowing whitely in the rough satin of his compelling face. Mesmerized, Audrina watched as he slowly took a bite himself, and then, bringing her shakingly to her feet, he released her hands from the bindings. Relaxing his grasp slightly, he murmured, "Petala"—he felt his braves watching closely—"you *must* obey."

Audrina did not realize that her small hand was wrapped around his wrist until she felt her nails pressing hard flesh. She gazed upward again, to black hair with the sheen of a raven wing; to intimately smiling eyes dark as obsidian, reflecting her own wide green gaze. "Why do you want to take me captive?" She indicated her aunt and the other young woman with a slow jerk of her head. "Why take them, too? If you really have to take me, couldn't you at least allow Sadie and my aunt to return home?"

"That is impossible. They would warn the others that we had taken you." With his back to his braves, he gazed upon her with warm sensuality.

"But . . . why do you want me?" she repeated her first query.

"Petala will walk beside Wild Hawk. If it is meant to be forever or for a short time, I cannot say."

"Who is Wild Hawk?" she asked. "And who is Petala?"

He answered only her last question. "You are Petala, as I have named you."

"My name is Audrina." Then, realizing her outburst of defiance, she said in a calmer tone, "My name is *not* Petala."

"This I know." He released her arm and was shocked to see that he had bruised her. . . . Or had the white man done this to her? "You may join your people. You will eat the dried meat and berries. Your strength will be gone and your hunger great if you do not. The trail is long from here and we will not stop frequently, Petala."

"I am not—" Audrina's mouth hung in mid sentence. He had turned away, and already his steps had eaten up the distance between her and the resting horses.

As soon as Audrina joined Katherine and Sadie, the older woman took her niece by the arm and whispered a question in her ear. "Oh, my darling, has he hurt you?"

"No. I'm all right." She hugged her aunt around the waist. "But how about you? You were not hurt, were you? My God, I don't know what I'd do if they harmed you in any way, Aunt Kate."

Katherine peered into her niece's tear-filled eyes. "I'm all right, love, it's you I'm worried about. I don't know Indians too well, but I believe that the leader is a dangerous man. I—I only wish there were some way to escape them."

Sadie was snuggled close to Katherine, holding her hand for dear life. "Ever since the Indians killed my parents, I've been terrified that they'll return and kill me, too." She hung her blond head. "I should have died with them in that raid." She grimaced as she accidentally touched a tender bruise, one that the

74

crueler of the Indians had inflicted on her tender flesh.

Katherine turned to face Sadie Peterson. "Don't you be thinking that way, honey. You survived. It's as it should be; God willed it so."

Sadie shivered. "I'm so cold, I wish I could warm up." Katherine leaned over the girl and buttoned up her coat.

"This will help, dear. You forgot to button up."

"Thank you, Katherine," Sadie said in a choked-up voice. "You're so kind to me." She looked over at Audrina just then, greeting her. "I know it seems kind of silly of me to mention it now, but I didn't have a chance to say hello, Audrey."

"I understand, Sadie. It is strange, to say the least, us getting acquainted now after we only said hello in passing on the street in Mankato when you and your family came to visit the neighbors."

"I knew who you were," Sadie said with some shyness now. "The Nelsons used to talk . . . about you. . . ." Sadie looked away quickly and bit her lip.

"It's all right, Sadie." Audrina smiled warmly. "And I know what they were saying, too." She shrugged. "It doesn't matter anymore, does it?"

"But it does, Audrey. I've always liked you, even though I heard you were a half-breed." She did not ask if it were true, and Audrina did not reply to the statement.

Katherine daintily bit off a chunk of dried meat. "We should eat now to conserve our strength, girls. We will no doubt be moving on soon again." Katherine looked away, unable to meet the young, vulnerable eyes of Audrina and Sadie. She had knowledge of what the Indians would do to them if they managed to get them to their village. She had heard that redskins raped all white women they took and held captive. Men, women, and children were murdered and tortured to death. . . . Dear God in heaven, that this should happen to her girls!

Sadie hunkered down, remembering but trying not to. It had all started with hatred and bitterness in the white folks' hearts. She considered how the white man first treated the Indian by taking his lands away. Wicked and brutal acts were committed on both sides. People gossipped continually about Indians shedding white man's blood, but little was ever said about the crimes against Indians. Still, she could never, ever forget the savage bloodshed the day the Sioux had killed her parents. She had remained hidden in a flour barrel until they had gone. She might not have harbored any hatred for them and had even felt a little compassion before that raid, but she certainly did hate and fear them now!

"Audrey. Sadie." Aunt Kate peered through the darkness to her niece's moonlit face, then at Sadie's. "You are both so quiet and you are not eating. Please, try to eat something, if only to keep up your strength."

The girls nodded and sat quietly chewing while the Indians moved like wraiths in and out of the shadows and patches of moonlight.

Katherine kept her great fears to herself, but the terrible words Lianne Nelson had spoken not two weeks ago haunted her now and rang ominously in her head: "The Sioux commit the most hellish sins imaginable against the white man. They tear unborn babies from their bleeding mothers. They violently rape young girls until they're dead. The soldiers should have killed them all when they had the chance or President Lincoln should have had them *all* hanged by the neck until dead!"

Sadie's head nodded against Katherine's shoulder and she began to doze, picturing the awful scene of her parents trying to flee from the Indians while she hid in an empty flour barrel. After the screams had died down, she had gone to look. Both her parents lay dead in their own bloody pools. It was strange, but her mother's body had not been sexually violated. Her father's rifle lay empty beside his bloody form, and an Indian lad of no more than fifteen summers lay dead not one hundred feet away.

The words of Mankato's town gossip came to haunt Sadie, as they had Katherine, as Lianne had said to her last time she visited: "They ain't normal, those savage Sioux, and you are lucky, Sadie, that you didn't get ravished, with one of them after the other on top of you!" Lianne had snickered under her hand, "Otherwise, you'd have had a savage brat to raise in nine months, and you wouldn't have known whether to call him Hawk or Eagle, or Bat or Rat!" In her dozing mind, Sadie told herself she could not have remained alive after such an experience, and if she had, she would have taken her own life instead of suffer the cruel taunts of such a one as Lianne Nelson!

With a cry and a jerking of her body, Sadie came fully awake, her soft brown eyes round as saucers. "Oh, Katherine, I—I'm so *afraid!*"

"Hush now," Audrina whispered. "They are coming back with the horses. The tall leader speaks and knows all English."

"I'm cold," Sadie whined as the Indians approached.

She peered up at the nearest man, who happened to be Left Hand, and shuddered. She looked longingly at the two thin blankets he had folded across the back of his horse, but she said nothing. Left Hand reached out and yanked at her long, silky hair. His English was very poor; he could only say a few words. "What white hair want? Say!" he demanded.

Katherine shot forward and grabbed his arm. Their eyes locked in combat for several moments, Left Hand's fierce and threatening. "Leave her be," she warned.

Left Hand was surprised at the white woman's defiance and peeled her soft fingers from him as if she had a disease he didn't want to get. *"Tankala!"* he hissed.

Prairie Wolf could not help but chuckle, for Left Hand had called the *wasichu* woman by a derogatory term meaning "too big for one's boots." But Prairie Wolf knew that the woman had overstepped her bounds; Left Hand would not forget this. The older woman's days were numbered now, and it did not matter to Left Hand what their leader thought. Even in childhood, the two had clashed, and as they grew to men, Left Hand and Wild Hawk competed over everything from the number of arrows they shot straight to the number of coups called. Left Hand would surely find a devious way to harm the white woman.

Sadie swooned and Audrina reached for the girl to steady her. "Sadie," Audrina whispered urgently, "do not show them how weak you are. Here now, stand straight. You can have my blanket if you are that cold."

"Oh, Audrey, why don't we run the first chance we

78

get? It would be better than being rav—"

"Be still!" Wild Hawk ordered the blonde. "We will mount up and ride for the hills now." He nudged his horse over to Audrina's old mare, fastened her wrist to his, and ordered Sadie to ride with Left Hand again, Aunt Kate with Prairie Wolf. Then they were off. Audrina took a moment to wonder why she was allowed her own horse, then thought it was perhaps for the sole reason that the chief wanted to ride alone to look more important . . . with the rope strung between them like a leash. It made her appear all the more like a captive.

They rode on into the night. Audrina was lulled into drowsiness by the constant movement of her horse, and at one point, when she allowed her eyes to close, she almost fell off. She awoke to strong hands lifting her before she could slip all the way to the ground. Sleepily, she gazed up into the Hawk's face, then felt a delicious tingle in her spine when his muscles slowly flexed against her arm. He was so close to her his body emitted a strange animal heat. His deeply wondrous eyes sparkled in the moonlight.

Audrina's heart pounded hard as she wondered what he would now do. They rode side by side, so close it was as if the horses were Siamese twins. The Indian's leg and thigh were pressed into Audrina's. Even their hips brushed now and then with the rhythm of the horses. Audrina felt the soft eagle feathers blow against her cheek and tickle her. Shouldn't she be afraid? she asked herself. Most women in this situation would be. And then, before she could think about it more, he said something into her ear.

"My *petala*," he murmured. Then there was a

commotion up front, where Left Hand rode guard.

"Please." Audrina placed a hand on his arm before he rode away. "What is your name? I want to know it."

He gazed deeply into her eyes. "In your language, I am known as Wild Hawk," he said, and then he went to greet the other six warriors who had ridden up to join them.

Wild Hawk, Audrina silently thought. She had known it was something like that. It suited him. His name thrilled her but did not make her like him any better; he was still the cruel savage who had captured them.

She rode up to where Wild Hawk sat as the central figure in a circle of eight other Indians. "My God, where did they come from?" she asked under her breath. How many more were going to join them? Audrina stared at a strong-looking Indian with delicate features. . . . Why, it's a *woman!* she realized.

Audrina flushed crimson. Dear Lord, she had to find some bushes, otherwise she was going to burst! Her uncomfortable circumstance was made almost unbearable as the handsome warrior woman continued to glare at her, the black eyes obsidian beneath the shining moon and twinkling stars.

Wild Hawk was watching his warriors ride off in different directions, while the same two Indians remained with him and the captives. Something in the blurred darkness caught his side vision. He spurred his mount with soft high-topped moccasins and came face to face with Audrina. "You are troubled? Speak! What is it?"

"I—I—" She swallowed hard, then her shoulders straightened tall. "I have a need . . . a *natural* need."

She blushed furiously. "It is . . . very private."

"You must not be offended by something indeed so natural, Audrina." He loosened the rope between them. "Go. I will not be far away. And I warn you, do not try to escape or you will indeed suffer punishment at my hands."

Audrina rode down a small hill in search of a private spot, while Wild Hawk turned and rode several yards away to afford the young woman her privacy.

As the virile chief waited, he tried to think of anything other than the recurring vision of Petala—Audrina—without her clothes on in the little house in Mankato. Wild Hawk knew he would never reach their destination swiftly and safely if he could not put his mind to other more important ponderings.

For a few crazy moments, Audrina thought seriously of escaping. It would be a dangerous and stupid thing to do, really, and they'd be sure to catch me, she warned herself. She would either be beaten or ravished by the handsome savage—or both. Besides, she could not leave Sadie and Aunt Kate.

When she returned, Audrina stared up at Wild Hawk as she was mounting her horse. The moon silhouetted his lean and powerful physique, and Audrina found herself wondering what it would be like if he were kissing her, caressing her. Would she find him gentle? Or would he become brutal and indifferent to any pain she might experience? There wasn't going to be any physical pain, she told herself firmly, because she would never let him get that far.

Early in the morning, when the sun peeped lazily over a hill, Wild Hawk finally came to a halt in some woods running along the crest of a bluff. There were

81

myriad trees all over and below was sluggishly running water. The spring thaw had come early in this sheltered spot, which had already been discovered by the warming rays of the sun.

Wild Hawk filled his water skins and returned to the camp. He stiffened as he noticed that Audrina was nowhere in sight. He frowned as he caught Left Hand snoozing beneath a tree, and a distance away, gentle-hearted Prairie Wolf was entertaining the ladies in his broken English with amazing tales of courage and daring. *Istahota,* Gray Eyes—Audrina's relative—was just falling asleep against a tree. The other warriors he had scattered and sent out to scout the area were nowhere in sight. Staring down, seeing where dainty tracks led, he tossed aside the water skins and set off at a run into the dense foliage and trees.

Audrina had not gone far when she spied the wild crocuses in the woods. The sun slanted in and found her. The warming rays felt deliciously vibrant on her back. She was tired and every bone in her body ached; when she tried sitting on a rock it felt like she was covered with bruises. She rose again, then found a comfortable spot beside a tree, too weary to think of escaping.

She only meant to rest there for a few minutes, but her eyes kept closing. She tried to keep them open, but after several tries, her lashes fluttered and her eyes drifted shut. A lustrous curl of her auburn hair was caught between her fingers, for she had been brushing it out of her eyes before she fell asleep.

A shadow fell over Audrina as she slept. It remained

and did not move for several minutes, closing out the rays of the warm and radiant sun. Several more moments passed before the shadow moved and shrunk as the Indian hunkered down in front of her.

Wild Hawk was caught in a magical web of enchantment and could not move away from her or awaken her. He experienced immeasurable delight of the senses just gazing down upon his lovely sleeping captive. A purple and white crocus flower bloomed beside her face in all its natural loveliness. In all his thirty summers he had never known such intense and powerful emotion. He was a full-blooded, lusty male who had known much vigorous loving upon his mats with very willing females of his tribe and others. He had even been with mixed bloods. He studied his surroundings now and nodded. There had even been a time or two in the woods, if he remembered correctly. In all those times he had never known such pleasure as he was now receiving just from gazing down at this gentle sleeping maiden. Soon, he knew, looking would not be enough for him.

A warm feeling was spreading through Wild Hawk and soon, if he did not do something, it would be like wildfire. He had never been in a battle as fierce as this one. All his defenses were up. His blood churned and leaped as it did when he was going in for a kill. Wild Hawk swayed dizzily, then let himself down all the way. He had gone for three days without sleep.

Wild Hawk closed his eyes, meaning to rest for only a short time. He felt safe and secure, for they were far from any towns or farms or white people, and his men were out scouting below the bluff.

Long black lashes fluttered. He slept.

83

Chapter Four

Audrina stirred in her warm bed and snuggled to get closer to her fluffy pillow. She could hear the birds chirping vibrant springtime songs outside the house, could feel the sun warm on her face; she was so cozy and comfortable in her delicious bed. . . . But there *was* no window in her bedroom, no sun streaming through.

It was a dream, but everything in it was very real and beautiful. A wonderful sense of well-being prevailed. Now she walked in the fragrant, pine-smelling woods, overgrown with thick green foliage and tall bushy trees. The smell of rich brown earth and growing things rose up to titillate her nostrils and Audrina inhaled deeply, feeling a gentle stirring in a soft, sweet breeze laced with wildflower blossoms. Tilting her head, she could see the noble, princelike figure of a man up ahead, black silken strands lifting from bronze muscled shoulders. Beckoning brown hands drew her along the trackless path and she followed, curious and unafraid, moving now in a force so powerful, so beautiful, that she was awestruck.

"Come with me," the beautiful male voice urged and tantalized in deep soothing tones; and then in Dakota, "Come, Pay-TAH-lah."

Audrina began to hurry, going faster and faster to keep up with him, while branches reached out to slap her in the face and tug at her long hair. The figure became a quick moving blur. She began to run, too. With powerful strides, he went even faster. Her heart thudded wildly in her breast and she was afraid she could not reach him before he disappeared altogether. The forest sped by and became a blur of greens and browns and wildflower colors. . . . He was going . . . going. . . . Audrina cried out, willing the savage prince back to her.

"Wild Hawk!"

The cry reached into Wild Hawk's dreamless slumber and pulled him up to wakefulness. With a sudden jerk, he opened his eyes and found himself staring into Audrina's stricken face. Her green eyes were wild and reminded him of the frightened doe he had come upon nursing her fawn in a shadowed patch of tall buffalo grass. *"Ah-ah,"* he used a child's Dakota term to calm her. "I am not here to hurt Petala." He stared at her for long, tender moments. She had moved with unconscious seductiveness against him, and when he felt the brush of her bare limb, he shuddered with an ecstasy he had never experienced before.

Audrina found herself staring boldly back. "I—I am not Petala," she whispered. "My name is Audrina. Audrey Tina Harris."

"Audrina," he began in a beautiful flow of English. "It is a nice name, but to me you are Petala, my Precious Fire. If this name displeases you so much, I

85

will think of another name for you."

A deep blush crept over her fine cheekbones as his forefinger caressed the line of her chin lightly with a sensuous, slow touch. Audrina tried to move but found her arm pinned beneath him. She stared into dark eyes of deep mystery and profound intelligence, fear of him suddenly making her heart hammer.

Audrina dropped her eyes as she felt her face grow hot. "Let me up, Wild Hawk. My arm has gone to sleep."

He shifted in order that Audrina might pull her arm out, and when she lay rubbing the tingling member, it came to her suddenly how close in proximity their bodies were. Wild Hawk lay on his side, she on her back now, and he was staring down into her face. He was so lean, dark, and handsome he made her almost hold her breath. "You have disobeyed me again," he murmured deeply.

Audrina stopped rubbing her arm the moment she felt and saw Wild Hawk's head lowering. It came to Audrina in a flash of wonder: Did Indians know how to kiss a woman? She had only been kissed by Joe Powell, and that was like being thrust against a wet rock. What did a wonderful kiss consist of? Maybe she was about to find out, she told herself, her blood pounding fiercely within her body. "I needed some time alone, Wild Hawk."

Audrina stiffened as Wild Hawk's dark, lean face hovered merely inches above her own. They were suspended in time and space it seemed, floating sensuously about in each other's curious and wondering eyes.

86

Wild Hawk's arm went around her shoulders and he drew her to him for better access to her mouth. His fingers moving in her glorious sunlit hair, he bent all the way and then his lips touched hers. The shock of his gentle, undemanding kiss reached way down inside her. Something opened from within the core of Audrina and spread like wildfire throughout her body. The feeling was so new and frightening, growing more intense with each moment his mouth lingered on hers. She had to break free, otherwise she was going to burn alive or suffocate.

But Wild Hawk cupped Audrina's face so she could not break the thrilling kiss. She was so sweet and warm beneath his lips. He lifted her with him to slide an arm beneath her back and his lips did not depart from hers for a moment. Audrina was in the circle of his hard embrace, feeling the powerful cords of steely muscle and drowning in the eternal kiss. When one of his muscled legs went between hers, Audrina cried out against his lips, and when he eased up a little, she broke away. Her mouth felt sore, swollen, and her breasts felt strangely the same way.

"No more, Wild Hawk," she cried softly. She glanced up at him, noticing with a shiver that his dark eyes were filled with a strange light and his lips with a new sensitivity.

"You've a cold heart, Audrina," he murmured softly.

"I'm afraid I do not understand," she answered, puzzled.

"You must have a lover. . . ." *He was thinking of Powell.* "One you must look upon with favor?"

"No," her voice shivered. "And you are the first to

have kissed me like this."

"You have not received passionate kisses from any other?"

"Not of that sort . . . no." She would not mention Joe's foul kisses, for she did not wish to discuss her near ravishment. "Why do you say I have a cold heart?"

"You did not wish for me to kiss you and hold you any longer. Do you not think me desirable, Audrina?"

Wild Hawk's breath had burned her ear. "I think you are very handsome—and fierce."

"Do I frighten you so much then?"

"Yes, Wild Hawk, a little . . . at times."

"I would ask you a question, Audrina, and would like for you to be truthful with me."

"I cannot promise to answer it, Wild Hawk."

"Well, then, I will ask it anyway. How is it that a lovely girl such as yourself is not already asked for—or married?" *Would she tell him she was affianced to Powell, or would she lie outright?* Wild Hawk wondered.

"No one has asked me."

"This is true?" When she nodded, he asked, "Why have they not asked? Is there some problem?"

"There were . . . rumors about me."

"What did these rumors consist of? Did they hear of some flaw in your person, some affliction, an ugly marking upon your body?" He looked her over with a sweeping scour, then into her eyes once again.

"Yes, some flaw in my person—no, in my parentage."

"What could that be, lovely Audrina?"

"They cruelly taunted and—" she looked quickly

88

aside, "and they named me *half-breed.*"

He lifted her chin a notch. "You look so downcast, Audrina, my Petala. Did you fear these taunts, these lies? For surely they must have been just that and nothing more. You are not to be married come summer? No? And you are not a half-breed girl?"

"Again . . . no," she answered the second question.

"You are very certain."

Audrina hung her head dejectedly. "I've told you the honest-to-God truth, Wild Hawk. I know nothing of my parents except that my mother, Melissa, died shortly after giving birth to me. And my father ran way when I was a newly born babe. Aunt Katherine told me all this long ago."

"What other secrets are there about you, Audrina?"

Audrina jerked her face to look up into Wild Hawk's, noting the scar that stood out like a livid ridge on his moist forehead. Why had he asked the question in that hard fashion? His voice had deepened; it was as if he was accusing *her* of telling untruths. Or had she only imagined this? she wondered. All of a sudden, he was warm and sensitive once again.

He pulled her into his embrace, tenderly cradling her now. With her face against his chest, her fingers biting unconsciously into his upper arms, she was kept hidden so that she would not have to look at him. He was so near that she could feel his warm breath upon her flushed and heated cheek, and she could hear the thunderous beats of his heart. He smelled so good, his breath fresh and sweet as mint, and even the musky odor delighted her tantalized senses.

"Petala," he said between quick breaths, kissing the

89

top of her head.

Audrina stared down into Wild Hawk's lap, at his fully enlarged manhood. Her heart began to beat with an erratic tempo. Then she stiffened and pushed away from him, rising to her elbows, unable to look him in the face. She heard his deep chuckle and her face flamed even hotter, her eyes flying up to meet his. What she saw there again astonished her—the soft lines of his mouth when he detected her fear, the tenderness that had come into his black and brown flecked eyes.

Fluidly and gently, Wild Hawk lowered Audrina back to the ground. He smiled, and dark jet eyes danced above Audrina, the taut, bronze flesh of his cheekbones and strong jaw lifting upward. He smiled even wider, staring down at her impudently thrusting breasts. Unconsciously, her fingers had lifted to clutch his powerfully muscled shoulders. She found herself studying his masculine nose, which was wide, long, and flared at the nostrils, then his lips, which were full, sensuous, and shapely. Even the thin scar on his forehead did not detract from his savage masculinity. If only we weren't enemies, she thought unhappily.

For many more painful moments, Wild Hawk had to control his strongest sexual urgings, but the lingering sweet heat from her lips and body flashed over him, leaving him weak and shaken. Just the smallest touch of her hands sent him into shivers of wracking desire. He could not take much more, but the terror to mate with him that he read in her eyes made him sick inside.

Wild Hawk groaned and drew her close to him. Her breasts were crushed against his wide chest. He pulled away for a second to shift and to adjust himself. This time he gently flattened her on the cool earth, autumn leaves, and warm grasses the sun had kissed. He covered her feminine curves in a way that did not allow all his weight to crush her, but his body still touched hers in all the favorable places to evoke trembling desire. Until this moment, the only real lover Audrina had consorted with had been loneliness. Now she felt surrounded by warmth.

His body seemed like living flame. Wild Hawk shifted and moved over her, letting her learn the shape and contours of his hard male body. As he moved deftly against her, he stared into eyes the dark green of wild prairie grass and on down to perfect bowed lips the dusky rose of a winter sunset. Audrina met his eyes without flinching this time.

The clean buckskin smell of him tantalized her senses even further, leaving her almost dizzy with sensation. She felt Wild Hawk's body press into forbidden places, skim over mountain peaks and nestle into warm secret valleys, going where no man had ventured before. Warm, delicious feelings were spreading through her whole body, and unwittingly, she lifted her hips to meet him just when he lowered to her in the erotic rhythm. When he pressed her into the warming earth and became still, she cried out and welcomed him in her embrace. Her fingers plunged and entwined in his black, silky hair, and she was unaware of how bold she was being with her untaught body.

Though her mind fought her, Audrina's silken form desired more than a kiss. Her maiden's body had been awakened finally. There was the sparkling of her wild heated eyes, her rapid breaths, the urgent lifting of her

91

body, the frantic writing and twisting. She would blush if she realized how wanton her behavior was, but Wild Hawk was now convinced that she had had a lover before—Powell. She would be easy to make love to, but he did not desire the mating to take place here, where they might be discovered at any moment. They still had far to go before reaching the Dakotas. He wanted to take all the time in the world with Petala.

Wild Hawk gazed into her upraised eyes and knew regret that he must cease this lovemaking. His desire was deepening with every passing moment they were together. They were still too close to the white man's world. If he took her now and one of his braves came upon them, it might forever ruin the precious passion she was already beginning to know and feel for him.

When Wild Hawk moved away from Audrina and stood to his feet, leaving her to go into the bushes, she waited breathlessly for him to return, desiring and yet afraid to again feel the touch of his strong male body against hers. When, after several minutes, he did not appear again, she began to wonder if he would come back.

It was almost more than Wild Hawk could bear, that he should have to restrain himself from loving Audrina totally. He emerged from the cover of verdant spring foliage and saw her wondering eyes. Suddenly, he was alerted by a small sound he had heard in the trees; his eyes lifted, his body moving with Indian caution.

Audrina, embarrassed and ashamed of her behavior, busied herself straightening her skirts and hair. She wished desperately that Wild Hawk had not started the lovemaking. She was more lonely and depressed than

92

she had ever been. Why wouldn't he look at her? He stood stiffly, as if repulsed by her wanton behavior. Well, it was her fault for allowing him to kiss her in the first place. What had gotten into her? She had never acted the hussy around men before.

She was just coming to her feet when all of a sudden Wild Hawk stepped behind her and clamped a hand over her mouth. She should not have trusted him! Now he would rape her! Audrina struggled, wondering why he had not finished the act when it would have been so easy, when she had been a stupid fool to let him get so far. He is a savage; he must like his captives to struggle so he can overcome them, she thought. She should have listened to her Aunt Kate.

"If you resort to force, Wild Hawk, I will fight you tooth and nail!" she cried, her words muffled in his hand. "You will never have me without a fight!" She bucked against him, but he only held her all the tighter.

Wild Hawk had not understood a word Audrina had been forced to mumble against his hand. But she was afraid, that much was certain. Until he knew who or what it was in the woods, he would have to keep her quiet and restrain her wild movements.

But Audrina would not keep still and would not cease her struggles. "Be still!" he ordered sternly. "You will only make it worse." Off in the woods Wild Hawk could see an unfamiliar figure walking about stealthily. She kept on struggling, and he hissed into her ear, "I will be forced to knock you cold!"

"Oh no!" she cried out loud. He would not take a woman while she was knocked out, would he? Had he turned into a bloody savage?

Wild Hawk regretted what he must do, but he was horribly afraid that they were being stalked by white men. He would never allow Audrina to be taken from him now that he had captured her . . . and soon would make her his, heart and soul.

Audrina felt herself being spun about, and the next thing she knew, there was a jarring pain in her jaw. Stars twinkled in her head, and then the lights went out.

Wild Hawk, carrying Audrina, sped through the woods on winged feet. He came to a sudden halt when a figure emerged stealthily from behind a tree. It was his cousin, Fox Dreamer, and he had painted his face in the bold colors of war.

"Fox Dreamer, what are you doing? Why are you painted?" Wild Hawk shook his head and his feathers tickled Audrina's sleeping face. "Where is the battle? I gave no orders to attack anyone."

"Wasichu!" Fox Dreamer then explained in Dakota that he had seen white men along the bluff. "They look for her." He nodded, staring at the sleeping beauty in his cousin's arms. "I did not realize that she was so pretty, for I could not see her in the dark the other night when we joined you and the others."

"How do you know it is Audrina Harris they search for?" he asked his cousin, who only understood a few English words. "Did you hear any words from the white men?"

Fox Dreamer shook his head. "They were too far away to hear every word. I heard only this, "Let'sget'em!"

Wild Hawk repeated the words slower. "Let's get

'em!" He inhaled deeply. "They might be after us, Fox Dreamer," he went on in Dakota. "Take your water skin and some leaves over there and remove the paint." As Fox Dreamer did as ordered, Wild Hawk asked, "Have any of my other braves painted their faces?"

"Only I have," Fox Dreamer answered with a sheepish look.

Before Fox Dreamer could remove all the greasy paint, Wild Hawk reached out to still his cousin's movements. "Someone comes—or many." He held the girl out to Fox Dreamer, saying, "Here, you must hold her."

Fox Dreamer peered down at Audrina's lovely face and shook his head. "I never touched a white woman before. Must I do this, my great cousin?"

"You must."

"*Hu!* I will just put her down by this tree. . . ."

"No! You must hold her!" With a serious expression, Wild Hawk looked into the younger man's grimacing face. "I do not wish to kill any white man. Our people have gone through too many battles with the *wasicuns*. We wish for peace between our people and the white man." Wild Hawk stared into Audrina's sweet, innocent face. "But I will have to slay the white man if they try to take this woman from me. She is my captive and I want never to lose her." He felt the knife at his hip to make sure it was strapped tight and, as he began to move away, said, in a deep, commanding tone, "Keep her safe for me, Fox."

When Wild Hawk had crept off into the woods to warn the others and scout the area, Fox Dreamer began to pace and blow air through his lips, making no

95

sound. Suddenly, he stopped pacing. With a frown, he peered down into the face of the captive woman. A look of concern grew on his boyishly handsome face. She looks too still, he thought. What if she is not breathing? What will I do? My great cousin will kill me. He will think it my fault if the pretty *Winu* perishes in my arms.

Taking her to a tree with thousands of new spring buds weighing down its branches, Fox Dreamer placed only her buttocks on the ground, never taking his arms from around her. He was leaning down to listen for a heartbeat when Audrina's eyes slowly opened. First she felt the pain in her jaw, then she became alarmed when she found herself staring into a head of thick, shiny hair, black and perfectly straight.

The Indian turned and stared into eyes of startling green. *"Hai!"*

A most frightening face with zigzags of blue, white, and red paint greeted Audrina's curious regard. She stared. Her scream was only a huge lump in her throat that would not emerge. As she continued to stare, she repeated, *"Huka,* I am not afraid," over and over, trying to convince herself, too, of this.

"Huka," Fox Dreamer echoed. He nodded that he understood, and then he smiled.

It was like the sun breaking from gray stormy clouds when this young Indian smiled. The lifting of his lips transformed his face, and suddenly Audrina was truly no longer afraid. She smiled back and he nodded vigorously. Then he placed a finger over his well-defined lips, and Audrina was aware that he wanted her to be silent.

Audrina blinked and nodded, her hair swinging and catching the sun in scintillating sparks of many shades of red. No wonder his older cousin found this young woman to be such a precious treasure, Fox Dreamer thought. She was almost as lovely as the blonde he had seen back at the camp, and he had been sorely disappointed to see that Left Hand seemed to have claimed that one as his own. He would like to have been the one to have taken such a luscious prize captive, and he would not have treated her with such unneeded force as Left Hand was doing. The young beauty with the snowy hair had not seen him yet, for he had watched from the edge of the trees as Left Hand handled her roughly. He was also disappointed with his cousin for hitting this redheaded beauty on the jaw, but Wild Hawk was chief now, and he must show force; otherwise, he would lose face with his braves. Still, he should not have hit her; he must really treasure this young woman if he was so afraid to lose Petala.

Again Fox Dreamer grinned and Audrina smiled back at him, feeling as if she had found at least one lasting friend among Wild Hawk's people. Sadly, she wondered if she could ever truly be Wild Hawk's friend; it *would* be nice if that were possible between enemies. She had never made any friends, for no one in her town had liked her very much.

"I would like to be brought to my Aunt Kate now," Audrina told him, then realized that he could not understand her every word.

"Ka-AYYte?" Fox Dreamer said with a grin.

"Yes!" Audrina giggled, smiling into the boyishly handsome face.

This was how Wild Hawk found them, gazing into each other's curious faces and smiling like two children who had just discovered a delicious secret no one else should learn.

"Sunihanble, hakamya upo." Wild Hawk ordered Fox Dreamer to come and follow closely, then gestured for him to bring the girl.

Audrina frowned at Wild Hawk's back as Fox Dreamer took her up into his strong arms again and ran with her behind Wild Hawk. She was thinking how angry he had looked when he stepped out from the trees. Then it all came to her as she watched Wild Hawk's darting figure and noticed his wary and watchful movements. There was a hostile force he was trying to avoid, be it man or beast. She had a feeling it was a man—her *own kind.*

In a flash of realization, the truth of it came to her as she looked up at the young Indian who carried her so gently and carefully. With upraised eyes, she studied him. There was a look about him that told her he could possibly be a relative of Wild Hawk's.

The sun was higher in the sky now. Audrina reflected back to earlier events of that morning and realized she had been mistaken about something. Wild Hawk had *not* been trying to harm her, she understood now. No! He had only been alarmed by something in the woods and had been trying desperately to keep her quiet. That something—or *someone*—must have been very close, and she must have placed Wild Hawk in grave danger by not keeping silent and holding still. He and his many braves would be killed if they were caught holding captives. Why didn't he just let her go? They could arrive at their destination so much more quickly and safely if he just left her and the other captives behind!

Wild Hawk held up his hand for them to halt, and he hunkered down in the brush behind several tall elms. "They are white men," he said to Fox Dreamer close to his shoulder. "I have sent the other braves ahead with the fair-haired girl and the *istahota,*" he said, calling her aunt gray eyes.

Audrina stared at Wild Hawk's arrogant profile, watching the vocal cords vibrate in his throat as he spoke the beautiful Dakota language, listening to the guttural and explosive sounds, some words followed by a sudden expulsion of the breath. He was so noble and powerful that just looking at him took her breath away. Audrina knew she was in danger of falling in love with the vibrant and alluring Indian.

"Wild Hawk," she murmured sweetly as she went to him. With a hand on his buckskin sleeve, she went on, "Please, leave me here. Go on without me, Wild Hawk. You and your braves will be safe. Go quickly. *Please.* I am begging you. . . ."

After he had silenced her with a dark gaze, Wild Hawk turned his face away to stare straight ahead. His voice was at a low pitch, his face wooden. "What about your relative and the other white woman? They have gone ahead with my braves. I will leave you here and take them captive to my village?"

"No." She shivered as if very cold of a sudden. "Catch up with them and then release the women. Whoever these men are, I will hold them back until you are safely gone. When I think you have had enough time to get far away, I will tell them I *think* I know

99

where the other women are. They will go off to 'find' the women and we will return home"—she looked aside—"where we belong."

Audrina was not prepared for Wild Hawk's reaction. She met his gaze levelly and his eyes penetrated to the core of her being. There was soft menace in his look, but Audrina did not see his envious wrath coming until too late. He pushed her away and stood to his feet. He said a few terse words to Fox Dreamer, then he was gone.

Audrina closed her eyes and sat, stunned and dejected. She would never forget the cold rage she had seen in Wild Hawk's beautiful eyes. Miserable tears burned her lids, and Fox Dreamer saw them as he came and bent down beside her.

She looked up and into the young Indian's gentle eyes. He seemed so kind, not fierce and angry like his leader. As he watched the tears slide down her cheeks, he shook his head, his eyes telling her that tears were only for the weak. He lifted her chin in one hand and struck his chest with the other, kindly ordering her to be strong and of big courage.

"My cousin does not mean to hurt you," he said in Dakota. "He is confused that he cares for you so much and does not want to let you return to your people. He is our chief now, and he must be brave and not allow a white woman to break down his power, especially in front of his warriors. I have never seen Wild Hawk so worried over losing a woman that he resorts to anger. In fact, he doesn't even *have* a woman of his own yet. No wife, no mistress."

Audrina stared into the kindly black eyes. "I wish to

100

God I could understand you. I realize you were speaking to me of Wild Hawk."

Out of the corner of her eye, Audrina saw the young brave stand. She turned and watched him give a sign to someone in the woods a distance away, someone she could not see but knew was there. She read it as the sign for "all clear."

Audrina was about to step from the trees when a strong hand clamped on her shoulder. She had been about to make her way down the hill to find the white men. After all, Wild Hawk had let her go, hadn't he? He would certainly be a fool not to. He was only endangering his men by keeping her and the others with him.

The white woman was like a small lost kitten as she stood there, watching Fox Dreamer beckon for her to follow him. Audrina shook her head no, she was not going with them, then when he frowned at her gesture, she firmly nodded her head. Turning away from Fox Dreamer, who was by now several yards away, Audrina smoothed back her tangled hair, pressed her skirts with an unsteady hand, then began to walk away from him.

She was in the open now, where anyone could see her if they were walking along the bluff. She didn't look back; she just kept on walking away. Wild Hawk had pushed her away; that was answer enough for any woman.

"Hiya!"

Audrina heard the deep angry command ring out, but she kept right on, her chin squared resolutely and her head held high. The white men were nowhere to be seen. It was so quiet. The world seemed to stand still and the earth seemed to wait. The sun was warm on Audrina's face. She had the pouch fastened securely at her thigh, under her skirts, and she knew she walked south. If she kept right on walking . . .

When a sound like thunder rose up behind her, Audrina turned and saw Wild Hawk break from the edge of the woods, his huge mount pounding the turf and coming straight for her.

Audrina's feet barely touched the ground as she ran faster than she had ever run before. The trees and dense bushes up ahead were her destination, and if she could get to them in time, maybe she could hide from Wild Hawk. She dashed frantically in the direction of the copse of trees.

When she glimpsed the big horse looming behind her, Audrina changed her course of destination and veered to the left. She became truly frightened, for Wild Hawk was an awesome sight on his big charging war horse. She was trying to watch from the side of her shoulder to see where Wild Hawk was, when the edge of the bluff came up suddenly. There was no time to stop. . . . The thundering was louder.

Wild Hawk saw what was happening before Audrina did. He brought the Bear to a skidding halt and leaped from the horse's back.

The bone-crushing jar knocked Audrina to the ground just before she went over the grass-grown bluff. She rolled with the hard body, and eventually she landed flat on her back, with Wild Hawk on top, one muscled arm beneath her head, the other at her lower back to break and cushion her fall.

She was stunned, out of breath, and suddenly afraid of the dark look in Wild Hawk's eyes. He was not even breathing hard but his nostrils were flared, as if he were very angry. He was straddling her hips, and when he let himself down a little, Audrina could feel the hot shape of him pressing into her. For a few moments they stared into each other's eyes. Her lashes did not flutter, nor did his. A tingling warmth rose from within her and extended clear to the tips of her toes.

"You as much as *said* I could go," she said in a deep-breathing voice. "At any rate, I was not *trying* to escape."

He growled softly, menacingly. "Do not test me further with your paleface lies."

Audrina squealed when Wild Hawk tangled his fingers in her disheveled red hair and hauled her against him as he forced her to stand up. He wrapped his arm about her waist and carried her to his horse, placing her on the Bear's back as he leapt up behind her.

They rode well into the afternoon, stopping once to rest the horses and let them drink while Fox Dreamer, still grinning slyly over the unusual and romantic situation, gave Audrina something to eat. She was growing tired of scout-meat and pemmican, but there was nothing else. Soon there would be roots they could dig to eat, Fox Dreamer showed her in sign language, and Audrina grimaced. She was so bruised and weary that she fell asleep before it was time to break camp again.

Fox Dreamer woke Audrina and signed to her that they had to catch up with the others. Wild Hawk stood silently beside the Bear, waiting for Audrina to come to him. She went, asking him where her own horse was, but he remained silent and indifferent to her. It was as if he had forgotten the English language.

Wild Hawk wondered what had possessed him to act so rashly as to have given Audrina that stunning blow on the chin. Then he had pushed her away, seeing the hurt look that had come into her lovely green eyes. She was special, and he took delight in her tough and tender spirit. What he really wanted was to crush her in his arms, soothe away all her fears, and make love to her until she cried for him to cease. He had not known desire for a woman in a long spell, not until this delicate female had entered his life. He felt as if he had been going through a purifying ritual, for the mere thought of making love had not entered his mind for almost a year. But now his lust was so intense it overwhelmed him with its mercilessly driving ache. He had never throbbed so hard before in his yearning to make love to a woman.

As the horse plodded along, tears sprang to Audrina's eyes. Her body was feeling bruised, sore all over, and it was entirely Wild Hawk's fault! She had only been trying to help, to send him far from Minnesota before the soldiers lit out after them.

As she gazed into the ink-blue of the night sky, the heavens, and the huge stars that glittered, Audrina suddenly surprised herself with the confession that she really cared for Wild Hawk. The moon floated in banks of deep silver clouds as she thought of his touch earlier that same day. She knew there was much more to making love than what he had already shown her. It would not do to tell Wild Hawk of her affection for him, even though she was beginning to care for him deeply. So much, in fact, that it would be hard to go from him when the time finally arrived. . . . But arrive it would.

Before they came to a place where they would make camp for the remainder of the dark hours, Audrina vowed she would never allow Wild Hawk to make love to her. She would fight him at every turn, if need be. She could not let him do that to her, for it would bind them as surely as if a preacher had said the words over them.

In the days that followed, Wild Hawk drove them mercilessly. Audrina learned a few things about the Sioux Indians they were traveling with, for she had no trouble interpreting most of their actions. There was a warrior woman by the name of Tawena. She was the sister of Catka, Left Hand. She was very tall and very beautiful.

Tawena shot Audrina haughty and sneering looks that said, without words, how much she hated her and how displeased she was to see her riding with Wild Hawk. Audrina read in Tawena's black eyes that she would slit her throat if she had the chance.

Audrina spoke only to Sadie and Aunt Kate—both holding up well enough—for Wild Hawk did not converse with her much The Indian leader tersely answered Audrina's questions, giving her the names of his braves and a few other things she wanted to know. Other than that, he remained silent, speaking only to his warriors. He seemed driven by demons to get to their destination. He only spoke to her in the evenings, when they ate the same hard-to-chew scout-meat and mixed some grains with water to make a paste that almost made Audrina choke. At these times, he seemed compelled to teach her his language. So far, she had learned that he was the leader of a tribe called Cetan/Wahpekutes. That was not too difficult to say, but some of the Indian words gave her trouble. He told her they were going to a village in the Dakota Territory, but he would not say where, only that it was still far away.

"Please do not fight the passion within you, Petala," he whispered to her one night as they were falling asleep side by side on the coarse Indian blankets. Then, without another word, he surprised her by closing his eyes. Audrina lay awake for several hours, confused by his strange request.

Early one morning, when Audrina began stirring in her blankets, the sun deliciously warming her face, she peeked out to see Wild Hawk just returning from the stream they had camped by. His back was turned to her, and she noticed the play of muscle and sinew in his long, lean back. Her gaze fell to his slim hips and firm buttocks in taut buckskins. How virile he was. How handsome. She thought she had never looked upon such a superb male. . . .

Oh God, no. Audrina rolled over, telling herself she must stop this foolishness. It would get her nowhere except in the last place she ought to be. If he made real love to her, she would die or be paralyzed from fright. She would then truly be his captive.

"It is time for you to get up, Audrina," he said. When Wild Hawk became aware of the crimson in her cheeks and the wild look in her eyes, he went on to give a more thorough visual search. His gaze caressed her from head to toe, every single inch, until she felt warm and aglow.

A flash of deeply tanned doeskin caught her eye just then, and as Wild Hawk turned to see to his horse, Audrina found herself staring across the way into a hostile and jealous face.

It was Tawena. She narrowed her black eyes to glare at Audrina as she rose from the Indian blankets. The look told Audrina that the Indian woman would like to carve out her heart and serve it to the hungry wolves that howled in shivering intervals during the night.

Sadie and Aunt Kate came to stand by Audrina. She was grateful to God that they were holding up well so far, considering the grueling circumstances of their captivity. For a moment, Audrina was tempted to give the medicine pouch to Wild Hawk. He wanted it more than he wanted her. Many would desire to possess it, Minowa had said. But guard it, *guard* it. If she gave it up, Audrina told herself, then Wild Hawk might allow her, Aunt Kate, and Sadie their freedom. No, she told herself, it was too late for that now; they had traveled too far.

The three captives spoke softly amongst themselves until they were forced to mount up as the sun lifted higher and the spring day warmed delightfully.

The hills and valleys wore a cloak of bright green as new blades of grass began to push up through the earth. The mornings were warm and pleasant, the nights cool, and the earth smelled of black loam and growing things. There was a timelessness about their passage, Audrina often thought, and it was as if the beautiful land stood still to feel their mounts' muffled hooves, which were like soft drumbeats on the sweet-smelling earth. Wild Hawk had finally allowed Audrina to ride the gray horse without the leash between them, and she was grateful for that.

At first, Sadie had been unable to understand the looks that Audrina gave Wild Hawk. When Audrina was not staring at Wild Hawk, he was staring at her. And so it went all day long, seven days a week.

Now Sadie was doing some staring of her own. Fox Dreamer, Wild Hawk's cousin, had caught her eye, and she could not control the growing attraction she felt for him. When he caught her staring at him across the other mounts and riders, she saw the stern young visage soften into boyish handsomeness. He rode straight and proud, his long Indian rifle with feathered thongs riding near a lean hip.

"But he is an Indian," Sadie said under her breath. "And I hate all Indians."

Left Hand, riding in front of her, grunted what sounded like a question. It angered him to no end that he could not understand what the white women were saying, and he mentally kicked himself for never having learned the white man's tongue.

The day came when something changed Sadie's situation for the better. They had been riding for hours, when Left Hand's horse stepped into a gopher hole and twisted his leg. Left Hand leapt from the horse, dragging Sadie to the ground with him as the horse

108

went down. They got out of the way just in time.

Sadie stood with Audrina, who had dismounted to see if the girl was all right. Left Hand was arguing with Fox Dreamer about something the women could not understand. The language was hot and explosive, and Wild Hawk sat his horse, letting the younger men argue out their differences. It seemed to Audrina that Left Hand did not wish to put his horse out of its misery and kept trying to haul the suffering animal to its feet. And every time Fox Dreamer put his rifle to his shoulder, the other one would yank it down.

In Dakota, the two young men argued, while the other Indians seemed not to notice the heated dispute. Except for Tawena, who was obviously interested in the final outcome. Wild Hawk was frowning at Left Hand as he continued to argue and thrust his arms into the air.

"You are very stupid," Fox Dreamer was telling Left Hand. "You must shoot the horse. Can you not see that he suffers? Put him out of his misery, Catka. He cannot even stand, though you try to help him with all your might."

"Be still, I will do this my way. Step aside!" Left Hand ordered Wild Hawk's cousin.

Fox Dreamer snorted. "I know why you would force the poor horse to his feet. You know if your mount perished, then the white hair would ride with me."

"She will not!" Left Hand turned viciously to glare at Fox Dreamer. "White hair will ride with me. Get up, Cecila," he ordered; the horse looked up at his master with huge liquid eyes full of pain.

When Left Hand began to shove at the neck and tug

at the mane of coarse black, Audrina could stand it no longer. She stepped closer. She was enraged at the inhumane treatment of the horse and she meant to say so.

"Put him out of his misery!" she shouted. Left Hand turned and narrowed his black eyes at her. Tawena looked at her with murder in her own black eyes. While the warrior woman was exchanging a look with her brother, Audrina again demanded, "Put that horse out of his misery, or I will!"

"What is the angry white woman saying?" Left Hand turned to his leader, careful to hide his terrible hatred and desire to kill Audrina.

Wild Hawk said nothing. Very calm, he lifted his rifle out of its leather scabbard and, sighting down the bore, squeezed off a single bullet. It entered the animal's throat, killing it instantly.

Left Hand looked aside, squeezing his hands into tight balls of frustration. His eyes darkened like the pits of hell. He wanted to whirl about and spit into Wild Hawk's handsome face. He had always been jealous of Wild Hawk's superior position in all the Sioux villages of the Dakotas and Minnesota. Wild Hawk had always shown more ability and prowess even in the games they had played as lads. Wild Hawk was braver and mightier than any other warrior of the Wahpetons or Wahpekutes. Wild Hawk . . . Wild Hawk . . . Wild Hawk . . . He was sick and tired of hearing that name.

Wild Hawk rode up to where Left Hand stood staring off into the distance. "Catka, it was never in my mind to humiliate you. This was not my intention. The horse was suffering badly. You should have put the poor beast out of its misery before I took the matter into my own hands."

Left Hand glared sideways at his leader, not really looking Wild Hawk in the eyes. "You shot my horse because of the white woman's hasty words. It was her demand you harkened to. You should make her suffer for her defiance!"

"I will hear no more from you, Catka. I will punish Petala my own way. The white hair, Sadie, will ride with Fox Dreamer now. You may ride with whom you wish."

With that, Wild Hawk rode to Audrina and halted before her mount. His eyes were darker than ever as he growled, "Never give orders again! This is not for you to do!" While his mount pranced, he reached out and shook Audrina by the shoulders. Left Hand looked on with stern visage as Wild Hawk continued to berate the white woman. "Hear me well. . . . I give the orders to my men. Do you understand?"

Audrina's chin came up. "I hear," she said. When he was out of earshot, she snapped, "I hear and I obey, my savage master."

Riding behind Tawena on her sturdy mount, Left Hand glared at Fox Dreamer and the white hair as often as he could, his eyes telling of his plans to get even someday.

Left Hand's anger and bitterness increased over the days. He tasted jealousy like bile in his throat, almost choking on its acridity. His nasty disposition grew worse over the days, because of the affection Wild Hawk lavished on the woman he called Precious Fire and because of Fox Dreamer's apparent interest in the

111

white hair Sadie.

Tawena warned her brother, "You must practice more caution in concealing your growing resentment, Catka. I know this is very hard to do. It is hard for me, too." She looked over at Wild Hawk, who was occupied with watching his auburn-haired captive. "Look, he is always afraid she will disappear. The sight sickens me!" Tawena hissed jealously.

"Be careful of your own growing resentment," Left Hand taunted his sister.

Tawena and Left Hand talked softly, making their evil plans. In the past, Left Hand had always thought his sister and Wild Hawk would someday wed. He had thought perhaps he could come to like the powerful man a little. But Wild Hawk had never shown the least bit of interest in Tawena, had not even acknowledged her beauty and the magic of her swaying hips.

Staring at the white hair riding silently behind Fox Dreamer, Left Hand began to feel an ache of lust. He swore under his breath when he saw the white woman's breast unconsciously rubbing against Fox Dreamer's back as she bounced gently up and down. The white hair had never known a man. Left Hand knew this instinctively. Visions of being her first man filled his head. He would ravish the blonde, and she would like it.

Or he would see her perish by his own hand.

Part Two

Precious Fire

The skyline melts from russet into blue,
Unbroken the horizon, saving where
A wreath of smoke curls up the far, thin air,
And points the distant lodges of the Sioux.
                              — *Tekahionwake*

Chapter Five

A playful spring breeze lifted Sadie's white-blond hair as she paused like a slim statue near the water's edge, her rapt gaze following the flight of a powder-winged butterfly. Her soft brown eyes with gold silken lashes lowered to the right, and she found Tawena staring at her with malevolence.

"Stay where you are, or you and the older woman will be tied to that tree!" Tawena ordered when Fox Dreamer was out of earshot.

"I am sorry," Sadie said, exchanging a look with Katherine, who stood beside her, "but I don't understand a word of Sioux." She shrugged, feeling a chill run along her spine.

Tawena nodded her head toward a nearby elm tree. Sadie stayed near the edge of the stream, lest the Indian woman vent more hostility on her.

Though Sadie rode by day with Fox Dreamer, who was not unkind, when dawn awakened or when evening settled and the young Indian male was seeing to the horses, the Indian woman took it upon herself to stand guard over Sadie and Katherine.

Sadie swore under her breath, but Katherine, standing beside her in the first rays of morning sun, had heard the soft curse. Sadie touched the older woman's arm, saying, "I'm sorry, Katherine, but Papa was a cusser and I guess it sort of rubbed off on me. I—I just felt like swearing, and I pray God forgives me."

"It's all right, honey," Katherine said. "I guess we have to try and be a little tougher now—you, Audrey, and myself. I'd like to cuss, too," she laughed lightly, hiding her own apprehension, "but I've never been a *cusser*. Come on, dear, we have a little time to wash our faces and freshen up a bit. . . ." She gazed at the loppy-winged butterflies. "We will be moving on again pretty soon."

Sadie looked along the stream to where Audrina stood silently with the leader of the savage party. "He follows her everywhere; hardly ever lets her out of his sight."

"What, dear?" Katherine looked up, following Sadie's line of vision. "Oh, yes. Audrey says his name is Wild Hawk." Katherine shivered slightly. "He frightens me. He's so powerful and . . . so much the noble Indian. I've never seen his kind before."

"Noble?" Sadie scoffed. "Maybe noble-*minded,* you mean." She bent to scoop water onto her face, shivering from the ice-cold sensation, then lifting the hem of her skirt to pat her face dry.

"He's one of a kind. A high-ranking Sioux," Katherine explained. "I believe he's very proud—and strong. You can tell that."

"Why, Katherine, you almost speak as if you *like* Wild Hawk." Sadie wrinkled her pert nose in disgust.

116

"I hate all Indians, noble or otherwise."

"There *are* kind Indians, Sadie, like the ones that are Christians. I've met some."

Sadie stared away from the water and into Katherine's face. "Is—is Audrey really part Indian? I've heard rumors. . . ."

Katherine looked away, and then back at Sadie. "I might as well tell you. Yes, *she is.*"

Katherine didn't know if they would survive this savage ordeal. Why not tell it like it really was? "Her mother, Melissa, was one-half Oglala Sioux. I have kept it from dear Audrey to protect her, because I love her. But . . . I don't think it did much good, Sadie. Everyone in Mankato seemed to have knowledge of her Indian heritage. Maybe it was cruel of me. . . ." She sighed. "I don't know."

"You did what you thought best, Katherine. You didn't actually lie. What Audrey doesn't know couldn't hurt her . . . I guess."

"But . . . it did, somehow," Katherine said, biting her lip. "It did. I would like to tell her about *both* of her parents. . . ."

"Maybe you should tell her now," Sadie advised.

"Lord, I just don't know if this would be a good time, considering the circumstances." She stared at the fresh-eyed girl who had seen so much bloodshed in her lifetime, as she had herself as a young girl. "We don't know what's going to happen to us, Sadie."

"You're so wonderfully strong and kindly, Katherine. I see why Audrey turned out the way she did. I've come to know her better, and I can truly say she is my friend. You were a good parent for Audrey . . . you *still* are."

117

"Oh . . ." Katherine's eyes misted. "I don't know if I'll be looking after her much anymore. I cannot seem to get close to her now—now that Wild Hawk has taken over her life."

"Jesus, Katherine, I hate Indians," Sadie said with fervor. "I'll *always* hate them—the full-blooded ones."

"Even the young brave who seems to have taken you under his wing?" Katherine asked, her gaze wise and discerning.

Just then, Fox Dreamer walked to the dawn-lit stream, leading a pair of spotted pinto horses to the water. For a moment the rising sun was obscured by a bank of snow-white clouds, then it cleared and the sun shone brightly again. Birds called from the trees, making a sweet and melodious sound.

Sadie's blood began to tingle wildly as she watched the slim bronze Indian walking straight as an arrow and proud in manly bearing, his feather-thonged Indian rifle always with him.

"What is his name?" Katherine asked, knowing that if they were to survive this trek, it would only be because of Wild Hawk and the younger, boyishly handsome Indian. Katherine did not like the one with the slaty eyes, the one who'd been rough and mean with Sadie before his horse went down. Neither did she care for the Indian woman who watched them with hatred in her eagle-eyed glance. Katherine detected jealousy in the Indian woman, who obviously did not like Audrey.

"Audrey says his name is Fox Dreamer. He's not mean, like the first one I had to ride with," she confirmed Katherine's thoughts. "He only knows a few English words . . . simple words. He's still an Indian— a Sioux—and my parents were killed by their kind!"

118

But Katherine couldn't help noticing that Sadie's eyes never left the young Indian.

Halting beside the water's sky-hued edge, Fox Dreamer paused to let the horses drink their fill. The new morning wind murmured through the trees like a thousand primitive voices and lifted the ebony strands of his thick hair. Fox Dreamer did not look in the white hair's direction, but he felt her spirit-thrilling eyes studying him. Fox Dreamer knew the moment she looked away; her hostility and her fear wounded him deeply.

"He's just like all the rest," Sadie told Katherine. "He hides his savageness better, that's all."

"I suppose you are right. . . . I just don't know what is going to happen, Sadie."

The young blonde returned, *"All* we can do is continue to pray, for God is our strength in time of need."

An involuntary sigh escaped the older woman as she said, "True, Sadie . . ."

The sun was just lighting the valley floor with the colors of dawn when Audrina walked with Wild Hawk to the stream. Her spine tingling, she turned to face him. She found herself staring directly into the hawklike face, the dark bronze of high, sculpted planes and the deeper copper of shadows. Her eyes lifted slowly and she saw the frown draw his coal-black brows together. His hawk-dark eyes never left her face, even for an instant. As she watched him, she noticed that he seemed to be listening. She was apprehensive of his stern expression, and she clutched her skirts with

119

one hand, her fingers brushing the bulge of the medicine pouch fastened about her slender thigh.

Audrina blanched as her stomach growled noisily. Looking downward, she noticed that he was wearing a different pair of buckskin breeches. These were tighter and molded the contours of his manly shape like a second skin. Once again she felt a longing for something alien in the core of her being, something she had only had an intoxicating taste of so far.

Automatically, her hand pressed down over the flat planes of her stomach as she said, "I washed a few things when I came down here earlier with the Indian woman. It was still dark outside, but there was enough moonlight left to see by." She blushed and indicated the tiny items of clothing she'd hung on a nearby branch. "I wanted to wash my hair, too," she went on, "but the water was *much* too cold."

He merely looked at her with that strange expression as if, again, he was listening. Then she realized what was bothering him: He had lost faith in her. She had tried to escape and he did not trust her not to try again. But why, she wondered, had he misunderstood her motives when all she had wanted was to keep him safe? Maybe he did like her just a little and was angry when she had tried to leave him. She should try to be stronger. After all, she was a captive white woman and could not expect to be treated fairly. Neither should she fancy herself falling for an Indian.

Audrina started to back away from him, mindless of the deeper water behind her. He reached for her arms and caught her just as she slipped on the bank and would have fallen in. She had never seen anybody move so fast! It was like lightning striking.

"You should be more careful, Audrina." He held her arms, reluctant to let her go, his eyes searching her face and reaching into her thoughts.

While Wild Hawk held her from him, she glimpsed the water over her shoulder, saying, "It's not very deep here, is it?"

"It is very deep indeed," he said, "and cold—for a white woman."

"What does that mean?" Audrina snapped. She shrugged out of his hold, then saw her mistake as she caught the dangerous glitter in his narrowed eyes. Why can't I hold my tongue? she asked herself. All of a sudden she felt tense—and frustrated. Was it because of his nearness? Did he feel it, too? Whatever it was, when they faced each other and stood close, she felt a tremendous tension.

"A moment ago you said you could not wash your hair because of the cold water. Indian women wash their hair in cold water and never shiver like the *wasichu* woman." His eyes were caught and held by the dainty underthings hanging over the branches.

Slowly, Audrina remarked, "Surely they cannot be *that* immune to the cold; they must shiver a little."

Wild Hawk said nothing, and Audrina wondered how many admiring squaws with thumping hearts must be waiting for him at his village. They must be very pretty, she thought, with long shiny black hair, dusky skin, and the wistful eyes of a doe. No doubt the Indian maidens had figures that would put hers and Sadie's to shame.

"What are you looking at?" Audrina slowly asked, cocking her head. A gentle smile lifted a corner of her dusky pink mouth. Her long-lashed gaze followed his

121

line of vision, and she blushed furiously as he dragged his eyes from her dainty unmentionables. Now she could think of nothing to say. But her face was red; she could feel its heat.

Wild Hawk watched her unbelievably long lashes rest shyly against her smooth, high cheekbones. "We will be leaving soon." He jerked his head in the direction of her wash hanging over the branch. "You must take them down now, Audrina, dry or not."

Audrina watched him walk slowly away from her, still wearing the same bemused frown he had greeted her with minutes before. "Strange . . . I wonder why is he being so kind all of a sudden?" she murmured in a moonstruck daze.

Audrina could not even glance at Wild Hawk without a delicious warmth stealing over her. Today, she was allowed to ride with Sadie for a while. Audrina liked it this way, for she could watch Wild Hawk. When she rode with him, she could not even think straight, much less catch her breath. He rode with such command in his noble bearing. Even Aunt Kate cast him admiring glances every now and then, and Tawena watched him like a hawk. She noticed that even Left Hand gave Wild Hawk grudging respect. Everyone did, except Sadie, who shot him looks of pure hatred from beneath the floppy brim of her hat. If looks could kill, Sadie's would do the job.

Katherine recognized the land they were riding through, the places they had passed, and the country they were entering. She whispered to Audrina as much as she knew of each area, just in case her niece should need that information someday. Sadie knew this one area, too, for she had lived in the township of Milford. If they ever escaped from the Indians and something happened to her, Katherine wanted the younger women to know the area as well as possible in order to survive. What Katherine did not know was that Audrina had already learned more about surviving from Wild Hawk than she would ever learn from Aunt Kate in a lifetime.

New Ulm was far off to the right and behind them now. The town was situated near the junction of the Cottonwood and Minnesota Rivers. It had presented an attractive target to the Indians during the Sioux uprising. The Indians had known that some of the town's young men had gone south to serve in the Union Army. The people of the town possessed few guns and ammunition, and it was evident to the Sioux that the terrain would make defense difficult, for the land rose some two hundred feet in two giant steps from the Minnesota River to the top of a high bluff behind the town proper. Most of the houses were spread out along the lower terrace, with an occasional one situated up on the second terrace. The wide "steps" provided the Sioux with sloping springboards for invasion. To make matters worse for the townsfolk, there were woods along the crest of the bluff behind the town, and a slough extending the length of the settlement between the second terrace and the bluff, offering attackers ample cover.

There had been a festive air that morning in New Ulm, Sadie was telling them one evening while they ate the usual dry fare the Indians doled out. The low campfire made Sadie's face glow enchantingly as she gave the account. The people of New Ulm were preparing to give a rousing send-off to a recruiting party, heading west over the prairie to enlist Civil War volunteers among the farmers working in the August sunshine. "This group," Sadie went on, nervously chattering because Left Hand was watching her, "was ambushed in Milford Township. The survivors went racing back to New Ulm, telling the terrifying news that there had been an Indian breakout nearby."

"Were you there . . . in New Ulm?" Audrina asked in a low voice, keeping her head down as she ate, for the Indian woman was narrowing her eyes their way again.

Sadie's gaze shifted when she saw the Indian with the slaty eyes, Left Hand, frowning darkly at her as he walked to the water to care for the horses. "First off, the whole town was in panic. Sheriff Roos and Jacob Nix organized the men into militia units. Some of our neighbors had pitchforks and other crude weapons to fight the Indians off with, because there were only about forty guns available. We left before that and—" Sadie sighed forlornly, "and I wish we had stayed in town. At least we could have hidden in the Dacotah House with the others. But it got so crowded upstairs at the hotel that the women had to go downstairs, take their hoop skirts off, and pile them in the backyard. There was no way to talk Papa into staying. He said we'd all just be sitting ducks for the savages."

"What happened then?" Audrina asked, munching the scout-meat that she was beginning to dislike very much. But it was food, nourishment, so she choked it down with water as best she could.

"Sheriff Roos tried to get Ma and Pa to go back into town, but Pa wouldn't do it. So Ma and I went with him. The Indians hit the town first. About a hundred warriors dismounted on the bluff behind town and began firing. Lots of the townsfolk fired back. Some of the houses were burned at the upriver end of town."

"I heard the first person killed was a thirteen-year-old girl named Emilie Pauli."

"Yes. I knew her," Sadie said, looking sad. "She had been trying to cross the street to get to her parents while the fighting was in progress. Five others lost their lives, and at least five persons were wounded. The Indians kept coming back and the siege lasted for many days. At the end of the fighting, the defenders of New Ulm lost thirty-four dead, and sixty were wounded."

From the deep shadows of the pines, Fox Dreamer watched the girl with hair like liquid sunshine. She grew more beautiful to him each day. Her eyes held him enchanted, having deeper serenity than the forest itself. He felt a hunger for a woman, which he had never known before. When she had ridden before him on his horse, he had felt the urge to reach for her thin shoulders and bring her soft peach-hued lips to his. He was torn between the desire to seize her in his embrace and the need to shield her purity. The confusion of Fox Dreamer's bold emotions left him shaken and dizzy. He dragged his heated gaze from the blonde to the older woman who was speaking now, then he stepped out into the clearing, heading for the water, moving with a lean, muscular grace.

Across the clearing, Sadie watched him breathlessly for several moments, then turned to Katherine to say something.

"Shh," Katherine warned. "The leader is coming back. We'll talk more later; it's good medicine for you."

"You're right, Katherine, it does help to talk about it—even at a time like this."

And the war is not over yet, Audrina was thinking, and how strange that they were sitting here discussing the Sioux uprising when they were captives of Indians themselves. But Sadie was right to get it off her mind. Oddly, it helped to relieve the tension—and Sadie's hatred.

As Wild Hawk came to stand over them, Audrina was just reaching out to rub Sadie consolingly on the back. He looked down into Audrina's flushed face for a moment, at Sadie, at Katherine, then walked away, his long strides pantherlike and powerful.

The Indians were constantly on guard, for Wild Hawk knew that twenty or thirty miles to the north one of the headquarters for several Minnesota regiments was situated at Fort Ridgely. The white warriors patrolled designated areas daily to guard against Indian raids and prevent whites from plundering deserted settlements.

It seemed to Audrina that they must have been riding for weeks. She saw, in the distance, wisps of smoke hovering above the trees, and then, as they drew closer, she could make out the points of several tepees crisscrossed against a blue sky, with fleecy clouds scudding northward. Audrina's heart picked up its beat. Here was food and shelter, even though it was an Indian encampment.

She had been allowed to ride with Sadie again, and now she could hear the loud gasp behind her, feel the violent hammering of Sadie's heart. "What is wrong, Sadie? Are you afraid?" The flawless hands came around Audrina's waist and held tight.

"I'm terrified! Haven't you heard what happens to captive white women in Indian villages?" Sadie shuddered against Audrina's back.

Audrina thought about that for a moment. Wild Hawk, or the others, could have forced them a hundred times already, but the Indian leader hadn't even attempted to kiss her again after his first embraces. "Hold on, Sadie." Audrina patted the hand gripping her waist. "If they have not ravished us by this time, I don't see why they would do so all of a sudden when we enter their camp."

"They just might," Sadie returned. The young blonde sunburned easily, and the tip of her nose under the floppy brim of her hat was like a ripe tomato. "They didn't do anything before because they were afraid of being caught by white soldiers. But now we are farther from civilization. Why," she swallowed hard, "anything could happen in Wild Hawk's camp."

Katherine, riding one of the old plodding wagon horses, had been about to say something, but just then Wild Hawk rode up beside Audrina. "This is not our camp," he explained, watching Audrina closely. "My village is much farther. Wambliitanka is chief here. He has not come to greet us, so he is not in the village now."

"Where is your village, Wild Hawk?" Audrina gazed up at him as he rode beside her—a dangerous and proud Sioux Indian, who strangely made her heart beat so hard and fast it was like a hundred galloping horses in her veins.

"Much farther, Petala. We will cross many rivers and climb many hills before my village is reached."

Audrina felt a wild thrill, for she had detected a

127

warm, sensitive spot in Wild Hawk's nature before he kneed his mount and rode ahead, a feathered hank of braided hair slapping at his back as it rode up and down with a gleam of pure jet. She felt the flaming heat spread across her face. Then, as quickly as the stunning emotion had claimed her, it disappeared and in its place was a feeling of bewilderment. She had been so caught up in her tangled emotions after captivity that she hadn't given much thought to the medicine pouch. Why was it in her possession? Why had the hawk dropped it at *her* feet. Why had Wild Hawk been asking about it before taking her captive? *He had taken her in its place.* What did this mean? When would the secret be revealed? Would it be up to her to decide, when they finally reached their destination? All she knew was that she would guard the pouch until the time arrived to divulge its golden secret.

Audrina wondered if it was drums beating or only her helpless heart. Up ahead lay two circles of tepees, a smaller circle inside the larger one. From one of them came the sharp cry of a baby, and farther on was heard the faint musical tinkling of bells.

Sadie's eyes followed the long, lean back of Fox Dreamer as he rode to catch up with his cousin. She was not aware that she was staring until she was brought rudely awake when three Indians neared them. They formed a flanking guard around the three captives and proudly rode into the encampment. Left Hand looked none too happy about what he had been ordered to do. He would rather the white women be forced to trot behind their horses, as captives had been forced to do in the old days.

128

The horses trotted between the hide-covered conical structures and Audrina saw the hostile looks on the women's faces, while the wrinkled old men just looked on with disinterest. Just that many more mouths to feed, their bored and disgusted looks said. But the children were wide-eyed with excitement, their reddish-brown hands holding sticks as they tried to get a poke at the white captives. Audrina glared a warning at one lad who lifted his stick in a threat to her.

They came to a halt in the center of the camp. An elderly Indian was walking toward Wild Hawk with a smile of greeting on his toothless face. Audrina and her companions could not understand the words exchanged between the old man and Wild Hawk, nor could they imagine the thoughts of the Dakota Indians who stared in awe at Wild Hawk: Here was the leader of the Cetan/Wahpekutes, Hawk People who Shoot in the Leaves.

However, the looks on the red-brown faces told Audrina that Wild Hawk was a man of tremendous importance in this tribe. Their dark eyes admired and respected the man. The young maidens could not stop staring, and their soft little giggles floated in the air.

Audrina's nose twitched at the aroma wafting about. Was that food she smelled? Like a stew? Of course it was.

"Ouch!"

Sadie's cry was loud in Audrina's ear, and full of distress and fear. Audrina looked down in time to see a stick being jabbed at Sadie's thin white legs. No one else seemed to notice or care that Sadie was being tormented; they were all watching the medicine man and Wild Hawk conversing, and the young maidens

129

were in rapture, ogling the taut stretch in the backsides of Wild Hawk's leggings. Only Katherine and Audrina noticed what the nasty Indian boy was doing to Sadie.

Audrina reached down to try and make a grab for the large, sharp stick when the boy lifted his hand, but she missed. For her efforts, all she received was a stinging blow across her own bare knuckles.

Audrina winced in pain but she would not cry out, nor would she allow them to make a coward out of her. They could beat her until she was bloody, and still she would not let them see that they won, for they would not intimidate and reduce *her* to cowardice.

"*Huka*," Audrina said, loud enough for those Dakota near her to hear. "I am not afraid. *Huka*." She nudged Sadie. "Say it, say *huka*, Sadie. It means you are not afraid."

"Say it?" Sadie swallowed hard. "How can I say something I don't mean?"

"Say it anyway!" Audrina pleaded with the blonde. "They might leave you alone."

"*Huka. Huka. Huka*," Katherine began to chant, her gray eyes blinking wide. "Oh, *dear*," she cried, pausing to take a breath.

Wild Hawk turned just then, hearing the captive women as they repeated the Indian word simultaneously and endlessly. It was clever of Audrina, he thought, and watched the Dakota grin and nod their heads in her direction. She was nodding, too, and waving her arms, and soon they had several Indians joining in to repeat the word like a tribal chant.

From the fringe of the crowd, Fox Dreamer took up the weird, guttural chant. He smiled across to Sadie and she shyly returned the gesture of genuine friendliness, hoping it arose from Fox Dreamer's heart. Tawena and her brother Left Hand stood staring around at the Dakota, their lips curled into sneers of haughty disapproval. They stared at the beautiful redheaded Audrina in withering contempt, and Tawena knew great jealousy.

With his bronze hands on his lean hips, Wild Hawk stood with a curious smile, watching his precious captive. Not only was she very beautiful, but she was, at the moment, also recklessly brave.

She was brave now, Wild Hawk thought to himself, but how long would she remain like this? There would be many tests and trials for her in the days and weeks and months ahead. And how brave would she be when he finally took her in his arms and pressed her body into the lush new grass or his soft robes to fully possess her? Would she become like a weak white woman and cry out? Would she whimper and beg for him to stop? Could she take all he was hungry and aching to give her? He knew a great *cin* for her, and he hoped that one day she would feel this same desire for him. He longed to plunge into the moist, warm secrets of her alluringly vibrant body and make her rise and soar like a shooting star. He would have her, he vowed, and before the fat summer moonrise, perhaps in the Moon when the Ponies Shed, the month the *wasichus* call May.

When the bold red splash of sunset heralded the night, Katherine and Sadie were brought to a tepee, and Audrina was taken to the huge lodge in the center of the encampment. With supreme effort, she emboldened herself to suppress fear. Why was she not allowed to join Sadie and Katherine? And whose dwelling was this she had been taken to? Perhaps she would soon

131

have answers to all her complex worries.

Forgotten were all her exhaustive questions as she looked around the spacious interior. It was not as large as a house, but it looked comfortable and liveable. And there was something cooking in a huge pot over a fire in the center of the dwelling. Her mouth watered. She only hoped it was more palatable than what they had been consuming the last several weeks. Or had it only been days? It seemed that they had traveled forever, into another time and place.

The lodge had many comforts of home, crude though they might be. Everything was neatly in order—cooking utensils, baskets of corn and grains, baskets of berries and nuts, robes covering mats for beds. There were several other items she could not begin to name. Some must be weapons, she deduced.

Walking about the lodge, she noticed a medicine bundle much like the one under her green wool skirt. This could be her chance to be rid of it. All she had to do was leave the pouch here, with the other Indian possessions, and no one would notice. She had been tempted many times to drop it in the woods, but she always found it difficult to part with the pouch.

Maybe she should not have brought the medicine pouch with her. Even though Minowa had foretold a secret mission, Audrina had a feeling of great danger just having it in her possession around other Indians. She would have to take care that Wild Hawk did not discover it. He would take it from her. She would feel a great sense of loss then. . . . Perhaps, she thought with a smile, perhaps Wild Hawk was the one who was fated to deliver her to her destination. Still, she couldn't be certain. . . . She wasn't going to take the chance of losing it now. Maybe there was some special magic in the pouch that protected her. Yes, she decided, that was it. In fact, Minowa *had* said a powerful spirit dwelt in the pouch.

Audrina worried then about Sadie. Two braves were watching and ogling her closely, and Audrina wondered which Indian would try ravishing her first. At least Katherine could take care of herself in that area. Katherine, she smiled poignantly, beloved Katherine, if anything happened to her aunt, she would be utterly devastated. Her smile deepened as she remembered the Christmases they'd shared together, presents under the tree purchased with earnings from Katherine's job as town seamstress. She, herself, knew how to properly wield a needle and thread, but not as expertly as her aunt. Perhaps someday . . .

"You find something amusing?" Wild Hawk asked from the entrance to the large tepee. Moving into the spacious area, he regarded her closely when her answer was not forthcoming. "I thought you would have attacked the food by now."

Facing him squarely, Audrina answered his first question. "I was just remembering old times with my Aunt Kate . . . special times." Her heart fluttered oddly when his look softened almost to tenderness. "I am very hungry, yes, but I would not eat"—her eyes twinkled merrily—"without seeking permission first."

He nodded toward the cooking area in the center of the tepee. "The utensils for eating are there. You may make use of them, Petala, and there is food aplenty here in Wambliitanka's village. This is his lodge and we may use it in his absence."

Going over to seat himself on a mat near the

cookfire, he waited for her to serve him. Suddenly, he announced, "We are not the savages you think us to be, Petala."

"I did not mention a word about you being a savage, Wild Hawk." She almost giggled aloud then, thinking of his name, which was anything but civilized. She walked to the cookfire. "Could I wash up first, my face and hands, please?" *Sir Savage*. Audrina hid an impish grin behind her hand.

"Over there." Wild Hawk indicated the pail of water just inside the entrance. "Tatewin has put it there as I ordered. You may wash." He folded his arms across his chest, Indian-chief fashion, his eyes concealing his intense pleasure at having her perform wifely duties for him. *Wife*, Wild Hawk thought. Suddenly, the word sounded appealing to him—for the first time ever.

Audrina glanced over her shoulder as she went to pick up the pail. His dark eyes never left her and she felt a shiver along her spine. "Are you going to watch me?" she asked over her shoulder, flinging back the long, thick braid of reddish-brown hair.

"I have seen you without your wrappings, Petala, and"—his eyes warmed mischievously—"you will not be showing Wild Hawk anything new. I have seen many women without their clothes."

Undoubtedly, he has seen hundreds of maidens undress while he watched and waited for them to join him in his soft bed, Audrina thought. As she washed only her face and arms, she began to wonder about other things. Wild Hawk might have several wives waiting for him to return. Squaws, they were called. They were probably very lovely. That thought depressed her.

Deep in thought himself, Wild Hawk recalled all the many women he had made love to, but Petala's beauty and charm far surpassed all of them. He interrupted his warm thoughts to say, "This is the first decent meal I am to eat in a long time, and I insist you share it with me now, Petala. You may wash your whole body later in the stream."

Audrina turned to face her captor, her eyes like huge glittering emeralds. "The water is cold this late at night," she softly murmured. Was he planning something for her later? Her body warmed thrillingly as she imagined what he had in mind.

"Let there be no argument over this matter, Petala. You will wash after our meal, and you will find the water as pleasant by night as by day—despite the late hour."

Hesitating only a moment more, Audrina went to fix two bowls of the stew for them. He spoke hardly at all, only indicating with a wave of his deeply bronzed hand that he wanted some more pones with his stew. All of a sudden, he stopped eating.

"You are not hungry?" he asked when she kept staring into her untouched bowl.

Dark fluttery lashes lifted. . . . The images that had filled her mind for an instant had been sweetly erotic. "I am," she nodded vigorously, picking up a cornpone. "Yes, I am very hungry."

"Good," he said. "You will need your strength later, Petala."

The pone she had been carrying to her mouth halted midway, and she stared with wide, astonished eyes until he had finished. He set down his clean bowl and unceremoniously stood, walked to the entrance, picked

135

up a huge bow and a quiver of arrows, and exited without another word. What she had failed to catch was the deep amusement in his hawk-brown eyes, his white teeth bared, his lips curved sensuously in a smile.

Setting down her food, Audrina quickly rose from the mat and hurried to the entrance. She only meant to peek outside, knowing it would be foolish even to think about escape while the Indians still moved about. She was not prepared for the pair of deep-socketed eyes that greeted her nor the huge arm that crossed her chest, barring her from stepping out. "Oh!" Audrina exclaimed, greatly alarmed.

The strange Indian grunted a word into Audrina's startled face and she needed no further coaxing, swiftly pulling her head back inside. She screwed up her winsome mouth. So much for making plans to find Sadie and Aunt Kate, much less trying to escape later. That ugly Indian would no doubt be camped outside the entrance the remainder of the night.

Returning to her food, Audrina sat down and began to eat slowly. Then, when she found that the stew was not all that bad, she ate hungrily and even put away another pone before she was finally finished.

Patting her yawning mouth, Audrina looked around the spacious area and spied a comfortable bed in the corner. If she could just rest for a time . . .

Audrina was sound asleep on a fluffy fur robe when Wild Hawk returned to the tepee. He had succeeded in killing two rabbits, which he had brought to Tatewin for her stew pots. The heavyset woman was a good friend, but Tatewin despised the *wasichus* with a passion. Wild Hawk had almost been afraid to go hunting and leave Petala by herself. He was not positive that a member of Wambliitanka's tribe would not wish to take his lovely captive for his own, so he had posted Wolf Spider outside for extra protection. Too, there had been the need to get away from her to indulge in vigorous exercise. It was going to be an agonizing labor of mind and body to wait until he reached his own village to possess her. But this was his aim and his desire. He would endeavor to stick to it—if possible.

Most of the people of the camp were abed by now. Wild Hawk bent to shake Audrina gently awake.

"Come with me now, Petala, it is time to bathe in the stream."

Sleepy eyes peered up at Wild Hawk. "Now?" she asked, wishing she could return to slumbering so peacefully.

Determinedly, Wild Hawk said, "Now."

Despite her weariness, Audrina followed him outside into the moonlit night. Tossing her braid over her shoulder, she drew a deep breath of the invigorating night air into her lungs. The soft call of night birds enchanted her with romantic visions of love and passionate desire.

Directly up ahead, the stream looked like rippling diamonds under the spellbinding moon. Wild Hawk watched from the bank as she stripped and walked like a glorious wood-nymph into the water. All shyness and modesty had deserted her, and all she felt was a need to get clean, to rinse the day's soil from her long hair.

She was grateful for shadows that the moon did not find, but when she stepped into the invigoratingly cold water, she looked down and saw that the moon played mischievous tricks, highlighting her slender form upon her own mountainous peaks and delicately shaded tender valleys.

Beneath a widespread oak, Wild Hawk watched Petala, pleasuring his senses with the lovely sight, the moon beaming down all around this beauteous creature. Wet, she was like a silvery moon-goddess. Her hair was dark, scintillating fire and her lips were mauve like the taut nubs of her breasts. Her legs were long and perfectly slender, and the dark blurred patch between her thighs caused his manhood to harden almost painfully. As she walked into the deeper water, he could see that she fought not to shiver. He knew a great desire to join her, to warm her, to remove his garments. . . . Not yet, he warned himself. But soon . . . when he knew they would be safe. Perhaps . . . in the lodge . . . tonight.

Audrina knew Wild Hawk was watching her. It made her feel tingly and warm. Her nipples hardened into vibrant buds, her breasts blossomed larger, and the secret place between her legs fluttered as if warm rays of sun had discovered its secret valley. She washed her body and her hair quickly, for it was cold in the stream, but her blood was nigh onto boiling.

Walking fluidly from the water, Audrina saw he was waiting silently, like a magnificent statue carved from bronze. The handsome statue moved and came to life, handing her a soft blanket to dry off with. Wondrously, he stepped closer and began to pat her here and there with a corner of the blanket. Audrina shivered now, not from cold but from passion's kindled flame.

His dark head bent, and long, thick ebony strands of hair brushed her throbbing throat. His kiss was like the wind's softest midnight whisper, melting her lips like

138

wax beneath the fiery sun. She sighed when his hands ran up and down her arms in a sweet, savage caress.

When his lips left hers, Audrina looked up yearningly at the hungry, lustful glint in his night-black eyes. Two moons shone in them, pinpoints of silver light in each orb. She was filled with a strange buoyancy as he continued to stare at her unblinkingly.

"Wild Hawk? Why are you looking at me like that? I would not wish to displease you."

"You do not displease me. I have grown fond of you, Petala Audrina. It will be good with us when finally we mate." His breath was warm against her cheek. "For now I wish only to touch you—like this . . ."

When his hand slid beneath the blanket to cup one of her breasts, Audrina thought she might swoon. His fingers brushed the taut mound and red-hot shivers centered in the nipple.

". . . and like this. . . ."

As Wild Hawk's fingers learned the rounded shape of her breasts, the taut rosebud nipples, he fought the urge to snatch her in his arms and carry her to his love-nest. In the woods, upon a carpet of old autumn leaves, or in the tepee; it did not matter where he made love to her. He wanted this woman more than ever, and his desire blossomed to a burning ache in his loins.

Gazing into the liquid jet eyes, Audrina shivered rapturously. He had one hand on her shoulder, the other on her breast. He leaned down to the creamy mound, flicking his warm tongue over the nipple. There was reckless want in her eyes. Her mauve-pink lips parted, youthfully, moistly, invitingly. With tender savagery, Wild Hawk moved to capture her lips and kissed her until silvery bells rang in her head. And he

139

heard some sounds of his own, too, deeper, more like the beating . . . beating of a primitive drum.

Audrina was faint with expectation, wondering what Wild Hawk would do next. His ever-growing desire was between them, and she gasped softly when he moved even closer, cupping her hips, pulling her slightly against him in a loving caress, then tighter, tighter. Pressing his lips to her forehead, he moved back a little so that he could reach down and slip his fingers between her thighs.

The pale gold column of her inviting throat arched and he bent to fervently kiss her there, a few strands of her hair caught like stinging silk in the tender kiss. Rapturously, languorously, her head fell back even further when he pressed his palm between her thighs. The moon began to spin with the stars as she gazed into the heavens.

Audrina lost all sense of time and place. There was only the liquid fire pulsing through her blood and the delicious fluttering of unfamiliar sensations between her legs. She began to ache for something more than mere touching; kissing didn't satisfy her any longer. She was swimming in a sea of burning, aching desire. She couldn't tell where she was any longer, for she was merely sensation, her head spinning dizzily.

There was a smile of triumph on the Indian's face, and when he moved to caress her more deeply, she cried out a name. Audrina had felt the hard, probing finger and her virginal body had sent out rapid signals of alarm.

"Mr. Powell!" she cried, unaware that she had experienced a frightful flashback of Joe's near ravishment. Unaware, until it was too late.

Suddenly, Wild Hawk became very still, his expression cold and harsh. His eyes were transformed into hard black glass. Powell. White warrior Joe Powell. The cruel man who had not allowed him in to see Red Hawk before his execution. The same man who had planned to make Audrina Harris his bride in the summer.

Pushing Audrina away from him, Wild Hawk stood glaring into her suddenly confused and frightened eyes. "Powell. The white man is your lover?" When she shook her head in denial, he went on with a livid snarl. "I believe it is so. You and Powell were playing a white man's game." His face turned hard as stone. "You had just finished making love with the soft white man who would have become your husband." Wild Hawk nodded, turning his face aside so he didn't have to look at her bewildered expression.

With a gasp, Audrina murmured, "My *husband?*" She shook her head to clear it, her wet lashes spiky and long as she stared up at him with incredulous wide eyes.

"Put your clothes on!" he ordered with a pointing finger. "Make haste, and then follow me." He caught the fear in her eyes as she backed away. "You have nothing to fear, Audrina Harris. I have no desire to touch you now, nor do I believe I shall ever again."

"What did I say?" Audrina asked under her breath as she dressed quickly, making sure she had the pouch in her skirt pocket. She was always careful that Wild Hawk did not touch the medicine pouch. She would exercise even more care now that his anger had been sparked. But how?

Audrina searched her mind frantically as she followed Wild Hawk back to the large tepee in the

141

center of the encampment. Oh no! Now she knew. She had cried out Joe's name when Wild Hawk had grown too intimate with her. She had been frightened, that's all. Lord, what a mistake that was!

"Wild Hawk, there is something I must tell you. It is about Joe Powell. He is not my lover. We have never been close at all." She splayed her hands outward beseechingly. "Joe means nothing to me, nothing at all. Can't you understand this?"

"I only understand that you are my captive, Audrina, and I plan to take you with me wherever I go—even into the spirit world."

Controlling her temper by a single thread, Audrina said, "You mean to keep me with you until—until you die?" Incredulously, she stared up at him . . . To go with him—she gulped—into his spirit world? She would be no more welcome in his heaven than in his village, she realized with dread.

"Wild Hawk," she began shakily, "I do not wish to live with you forever . . . and I do not wish to wed Joe Powell. I have a life of my own with my—"

"Be still! I have not complained of your willfulness for many moons, but you have taxed my temper to the limits of endurance, and now you dare speak that one's name to me!"

Dumbfounded by his brilliant command of English, Audrina could only gape at him. "He . . . P—Powell," she stuttered, "he is not to be my husband. I do not know where you have heard this."

Silence . . . silence . . . nothing but the haunting refrain of night birds and insects.

Pushing the damp hair out of her eyes, Audrina shook the heavy tresses back over her shoulder. I will

142

get away from this savage, she told herself, if it is the last thing I do. And it might be, too, for if he catches me, I'm dead. Indeed, he would not treat her leniently the next time.

Falling asleep did not come easily for Audrina that night. The same question repeatedly rang in her head, and she blinked sleepily at last: Was he her enemy, or her love? . . .

Chapter Six

Rays of morning sun poked golden fingers through branches lighting the eastern face of the land and the tepee walls. The captive women were forced to do their share of work in the village, toiling away with the industrious squaws. The Indians had an abundant supply of provisions such as flour, tea, sugar, tobacco, and barrels of salt pork. They also had Indian blankets that had been taken from the government warehouses.

Unfortunately Tatewin, the rotund Indian woman, was in charge. Audrina wore her washed-out white blouse of heavy linen and her green wool skirt. One of the younger Indian maidens had spied her high leather boots, and Tatewin had given them to the young Indian girl. Tatewin was not unkind enough to let Audrina go barefoot, however. In exchange for her boots, she received a pair of pretty beaded moccasins. Audrina did not argue. If the Indian maid desired them so badly, she thought, then let her have them.

Audrina had not seen Wild Hawk all morning. Last night she had watched him slumbering deeply beside

144

her fluffy robes, then she had fallen asleep herself; when she had awoken in the morning he was gone.

All day long, the women worked. In preparing a meal they took flour and made a course dough, then rolled a chunk of it on a flat stone and made a flat cake that they put in boiling tallow and fried until it was brown. They called it fry bread. For lunch, Tatewin gave them each a mug of tea with two tablespoons of brown sugar in it, and a piece of the fry bread. Audrina thought this fare tasted very good after subsisting on scout-meat and raw flour paste for so many weeks. There were also plenty of crushed berries and dried winter apples.

By the end of the day Audrina was exhausted. She had prepared food, hauled water from the stream, and tanned hides until her fingers were raw. When she asked why she could not join Katherine and Sadie, there was no one who could understand her. She did not get an answer until Wild Hawk joined her in the big tepee when the stars were just beginning to make an appearance in the darkening purple sky. He entered the tepee looking fresh and clean, as if he had just washed in the stream. His ebony hair was damp, his wide muscled chest glistened with drops of water, and his breeches were wet at the waistline. Below that, she dared not even glance, because in the past she had always been surprised at the prominence there.

Her breath quickened and her blood surged as she gazed at him. He was bigger than life. So handsome, she thought, his mere presence making her head swim and her heart pound rapidly. The deep black-brown eyes above her were intoxicating, his body alive with vital force. Looking down at her where she sat on the mats before the low fire, he slid his gaze to the creamy peach outline of taut nipples beneath her blouse. She is captivatingly beautiful, he thought, his gaze drifting back to her face, so soft, so sweet. His loins ached to possess her completely.

Audrina's forehead puckered with a frown as he continued to stare down at her, smoldering eyes penetrating hers. "Why can I not join Sadie and my aunt in their tepee? Why must we be kept apart?" she asked all in one breath.

Staring at the red fire in her braided hair, he decided this style suited her innocent face. "You do not like my company?" he queried. He was angry with her for calling out the white man's name in their time of passion. Rage had boiled his blood. He desired Precious Fire for his own, but he was now convinced she had been Joe Powell's woman. She might even be carrying Powell's seed. He should have slain the man while he had the chance.

Wild Hawk would not admit that jealousy blinded him to the truth of the matter. In fact, all he could fathom was his desire for Precious Fire. Nothing else mattered but that she be his—and his only.

He bent to raise her chin, and Audrina's misty eyes were forced to meet his. "You must remain with me, that is all you need know." For a moment there was a sensitive look about his face, then he moved away from her. "You must sleep now. We leave before first light of morning."

Apprehensive, Audrina dared not question him further. That night she put her head on the soft robes and wept softly so he could not hear. The day's events swam before her tired eyes. She could not speak to

146

Wild Hawk of her fears, for he was indifferent to pleas. So many things were happening so fast. Something else greatly troubled her. She was afraid for Sadie, and did not think it would be long before Left Hand cornered her and raped her. He was an evil man, bent on destruction, and his sister Tawena was no better. Wearily, Audrina shut her eyes. . . .

The Indian children were fascinated with Audrina and watched with sad eyes as she left with Wild Hawk, Chief of the Wahpekutes. As she rode away in the light of morning, her long red braid floating down her straight back, the mischievous boy who had slapped her and Sadie with the stick smiled warmly and waved until they were out of sight.

Audrina's heart was warmed, but not so Wild Hawk's. She rode with him again, feeling the taut rigidity of his arms on the leather reins, sensing the indifference of his mood. All day long he spoke hardly a kind word to her. This new Wild Hawk was a foreboding stranger and she thought it would be better if she tried ignoring him, too. After all, she deduced, they were enemies and she was his captive. She would try to escape at first chance.

The topaz day was warm, and spring was in the air. Bright sunlight spilled all around them during the day and nighttime was splendid with thousands of sparkling stars, which were so close that Audrina thought she could reach out to touch them.

One night, Katherine informed Audrina they were nearing Dakota Territory. Several of the Indians had taken leave of the party, no doubt to scout the area up

147

ahead. Tawena and Left Hand continued to stare malevolently at Audrina. First Left Hand would impudently leer at her and then he would shift his slaty eyes to Sadie, as if to say he could have the blonde if not Audrina herself.

After several hours of wearisome travel, Wild Hawk held up his hand, telling his braves, "We will camp here." After fluidly sliding off the Bear, he turned to Audrina as she stared down at him with sleepy eyes. "It is time to hunt for food, for our supply is low. You will stay here with Left Hand and Tawena. Do not try anything foolish, Petala."

Clenching her teeth, Audrina came down smoothly off the horse without his help. She was grateful, at least, for being allowed to join Sadie and Katherine, but her eyes flashed angrily as he continued to turn his back when she would glance his way.

Wild Hawk looked over at Audrina when she obediently sat beside a guarded Sadie and a weary Katherine. Audrina, however, would not glance his way, hurriedly focusing her attention elsewhere when she knew he was looking. She smiled tenderly at Katherine. Audrina loved her aunt dearly and was unaware that this was the last hour to be shared with her.

Speaking almost in a whisper, Sadie said, "I have a feeling that they're up to something. Wild Hawk has gotten us this far, but I think this is the end; something dreadful is about to happen." Pointedly, she looked to Left Hand as she made the statement.

Audrina was thoughtful for several long moments while she passed out the food Wild Hawk had given her. "I think you are wrong, Sadie; he is only disappointed in me."

"Why, what could you have possibly done?" Sadie wondered out loud, taking a chunk of the usual scout-meat and munching daintily.

Staring vacantly at the piece of stringy, hard meat, Katherine, with wise discernment, asked, "Did you disobey Wild Hawk again?"

Swallowing hard, Audrina stared at her aunt with a high blush riding her cheekbones. "It—it is something like that . . . I think it might have something to do with Joe Powell."

"Joe Powell?" Katherine looked confused. "What does Wild Hawk have to do with him?"

"They have met, accidentally and quite unfortunately. I'm not sure what happened to Mr. Powell. One minute he was at the house in Mankato, then he was gone. . . ." Audrina shrugged wearily, trying not to relive that horrible hour in the little house. "Wild Hawk might have killed him, I really don't know."

"Oh," Katherine began, "I understand. Mr. Powell was visiting when Wild Hawk came along to—to capture you."

"That is not the half of it, Aunty. Wild Hawk believes Powell and I were lovers. When Wild Hawk barged into the house, Joe was . . . ah . . . trying to . . . *had* been trying to"—Audrina cleared her throat embarrassedly—"you know."

Worriedly, Katherine studied her niece for any changes that might have occurred while Mr. Powell had *visited*. "I just knew that there was something about that young fellow I couldn't trust. Did he—?"

Drawing her breath in slowly, Audrina said, "No, Aunt Kate, he did not hurt me, not the way you think.

149

He might have, though, if . . . Wild Hawk had . . . not come along. It is amazing. . . ."

"What is?" Sadie leaned forward, wanting to hear more about what had happened to Audrey before she and Katherine had come along in the wagon.

Audrina chewed her lower lip thoughtfully before she spoke. "Wild Hawk saved me from ravishment at Mr. Powell's lecherous hands." Her misted gaze followed Wild Hawk as he rode out of camp with several warriors. "It's ironic," she murmured. "Out of the frying pan . . . into the fire."

Katherine cleared her throat, moving closer to her dearly loved niece. "I—I have something to confess." Her eyes dampened with misty tears, she bit on her lower lip.

Gazing into Katherine's soft gray eyes, Audrina took her aunt's veiny hand . . . a seamstress's wonderfully dexterous hand that could stitch up a gorgeous dress in one day. To make money, so they would have enough to eat, to buy a few things with. So giving, so loving.

"Aunt Kate, I know what you are going to tell me. I suspected it long ago, but now I am certain of the fact." Tears began to fall between the two, and Sadie felt some mistiness cloud her own eyes. "Shhh," Audrina hushed her quietly sobbing aunt, patting her back gently. "I know who I am, but I don't know my mother's Indian name. Could you—could you . . . tell me?"

Gulping back a deluge of fresh tears, Katherine thought, *I can never tell her about her father, Frank Harris, Tall One, never that.* She said quietly, "Gray Dove." She swallowed. "Melissa was Gray Dove, half Oglala Sioux. Oh, my darling, dearest, can you find it

150

in your heart to forgive *me!*" She burst out into renewed sobs.

"Oh, Aunty!" Audrina hugged the sweet lady close. "Of course . . . I love you, Katherine, I love you with *all* my heart."

While Audrina and Katherine continued to tenderly hold each other, evil forces began to swirl about them. Sadie jerked her head up, shaking inwardly as a great sense of foreboding washed over her.

While Tawena stood guard over the captives, Left Hand rode stealthily out to meet with several of the Rebel Indians among the sheltering woods along the Cottonwood River. Tonight he hoped to succeed with their devious plans. They had tried several times before but failed when Wild Hawk had returned too soon; this night, Left Hand knew, Wild Hawk would hunt much longer for their supply of meat.

Covertly, Tawena had been riding out to meet the Rebel Indians whenever Wild Hawk was occupied with the red-haired *Winu* or when he chose to hunt as he'd done this night. They could not afford to be wantonly careless when they made their plans, for Wild Hawk was alert and wise—when he was not staring at Precious Fire's rosy mouth and slenderly curving backsides. For the last week, however, Tawena had noticed Wild Hawk's dwindling interest in his white captive. Left Hand had informed Tawena that Wild Hawk was peeved with Precious Fire all of a sudden.

"He has let those green eyes twist his heart," Tawena had hissed one night when Wild Hawk was out of earshot.

151

Left Hand had grated out, "Wild Hawk is a besotted fool." He struck his chest with the flat of his dark copper hand. "I will be *Itancan* one day. I will never wear Wild Hawk's eagle feathers and his beaded leather armband."

Tawena's mouth twisted wryly. "You cannot wear Wild Hawk's feathers. You have not earned them. Where is your pride and your honor?"

Angered by Tawena's hasty words, Left Hand's face turned murderous. "It left me when he became chief."

"It was meant for Wild Hawk to be our leader. Red Hawk was chief, so it is Wild Hawk as his son who stands next in line. I am jealous, too, brother. Mine is not as yours, however. You covet all he has earned. You are angry because he was elected the leader of the Cante Tinza warrior society. You are most angry because he will now rule the Hawk-People-Who-Shoot-in-the-Leaves."

"What is your jealousy, sister?" Left Hand asked, but he was already aware of what caused her eyes to turn hard like black jewels when she watched the white woman and Wild Hawk brush each other as if accidentally.

"You play games with me, brother." Tawena curled her lip, looking almost ugly. "You know I have always desired him. He arouses deep passions within me."

"Hau. He arouses them but you cannot do anything about them. You desire the handsome warrior, but it is impossible to consider yourself ever becoming his wife. You are like me, Tawena. We are left with crumbs of pride and honor and love while Wild Hawk possesses the whole chunk."

"I shall get part of it, Left Hand. And when I do, you

152

will share it with me. Wild Hawk will make me his wife . . . you will see."

"How is that, my sister?"

"When I have Wild Hawk in my clutches, I will beg him prettily to make you sub-chief."

And I will kill Wild Hawk after that, Left Hand said to himself.

Left Hand's partners, the savage Rebels, were very careful never to let anyone detect their presence when they crept upon the outskirts of their present camp to meet with Left Hand or Tawena. They truly lived up to the name Sioux, the snake, for the Rebel Indians were indeed like snakes in the grass, some of them half-breeds, a few mixed Indian bloods. They—six of them this night—had left their hidden encampment to meet with Left Hand after Wild Hawk rode out with his braves to hunt.

Whirling, Left Hand now leapt onto his pony's back. The Hoha Sioux had finally made their plans and now it was time to execute them. Left Hand sought revenge, if only a little could be obtained this night. Some was better than none, Left Hand thought. It would be good to feel the blood of the white man slippery in his hands when he took a scalp. While Wild Hawk was gone, he would seek his revenge and see it played out . . . on the precious white captives.

Sadie and Katherine had been asleep for a quarter of an hour. The pale misty moon rode high in the sky as Audrina tossed and turned in her blankets, hearing the cry of the hunting wolf shivering eerily in the distance of night. Her thoughts were of Wild Hawk and his distant moods, totally unaware of the hideous nightmare that crept closer and closer every minute.

When a sudden noise startled her, she rose to her elbow, giving a long, searching look into the purple-gray of night. As one of the shadows began to move, Tawena stepped out from the dark, misty gloom. Instantly, Audrina grew wary.

Slowly, her eyes like obsidian, Tawena removed the Dakota knife from her belt, walking toward Audrina with menacing steps. Fog floated at Tawena's moccasined feet and separated as she neared the one Wild Hawk had named Petala, Precious Fire. She would not be Wild Hawk's Precious Fire much longer, for this night she would become very helpless and pitiful when taken captive by the Rebel Indians. The Rebels would all have their turns on her and the other white women. She didn't know why they just did not kill the white captives. But there was fear in Left Hand, fear that if he killed Precious Fire, Wild Hawk would slay him in turn. Left Hand's plan was to make her disappear instead. But first it was his idea to have some fun tormenting her, and Tawena could not wait to see what nastiness her brother had devised.

"You come," Tawena told Audrina waving the knife threateningly in front of her eyes.

Audrina tried to converse with the warrior woman. "Where do you want me to go? And where is Wild Hawk? Are these his orders?"

Tawena grunted, wishing she could understand the questions being put to her. But she had defiantly refused to learn English when others of their camp had learned from Red Hawk and his son. Wild Hawk's sister, Rainbow, could fluently speak the white man's

154

tongue and now, at times, Tawena knew regrets that she only understood and could speak a few words of this popular language.

Tawena repeated her command. Audrina had a hard time figuring it out, for Tawena mixed the language of the Dakota with English.

"*Hakamya upo!* You come . . . Tawena. You come . . . Tawena."

When Audrina still did not respond, Tawena reached down and yanked her up by her long fat braid. Surprisingly, Tawena found Precious Fire's hair was as thick and abundant as her own. The flame-red braid filled her hand and, driven enviously, Tawena's knife blade pressed against the white woman's face.

"*Hownh!* Come, *hakamya upo!*" She ordered the white woman to follow, and Audrina did not have much choice because Tawena was dragging her by the hair.

Stiffening, catching an ominous aura nearing, Audrina watched as suddenly Left Hand approached. When she could make out threatening shadows behind him, her heart lurched alarmingly into her throat. Reading the menacing faces of Tawena and Left Hand, Audrina perceived something evil was afoot. Had Wild Hawk brought them this far only to perform some sort of evil ceremony closer to his own territory? He had had plently of opportunity, however, without setting up something now, all of a sudden. She thought she had her answer.

Apprehensively, Audrina told herself, "It *must* be a pagan ritual." She yanked her arm from Tawena's cruel grip and stood back, warding the woman off as she held her arms up. "Do not come near me!"

155

Tawena frowned as the smaller woman stood her ground, spitting like a sleek, angry cat. "So," Audrina began stiffly, stilling her fear, "Wild Hawk has left you to accomplish the dirty work. What do you have in mind? If you plan to take scalps, you better move quickly, because I'm not going to give mine up without a ferocious battle!"

Exchanging a look, Tawena and Left Hand stood wondering what defiant words Precious Fire had uttered, for they had not been able to fully understand them. But her look and courageous stance said much, telling them she was going to protect herself and the others any way she could.

Audrina fervently wished she had some kind of weapon. Her fingers found and clutched the medicine bundle inside her skirts and she squeezed hard, feeling remarkably safe and protected somehow. She was afraid, however, because this protection did not extend to Sadie and Katherine. A foreboding chill raced along her nerve ends, along her spine.

An evil laugh erupted from Left Hand as Precious Fire valiantly stood her ground, defiance flashing in her green eyes. Here was a woman to walk beside a great warrior. Then he sneered at the color of her hair. He much preferred the rare shade of Sadie's hair, for it was pure and yellow like the sun. Precious Fire's was like dark fire, and he was superstitious about anyone possessing this color hair. There was something mystical and odd about her. She made him feel inferior and a little afraid of the strange power she held over Wild Hawk.

Tawena wondered what ailed her brother. The Rebels were waiting to take Precious Fire away. They would not show their faces, however, for they feared Chief

156

Wild Hawk and his wrath, even though they were fearless rebels and pledged allegiance to no tribe, raiding by the pale light of the moon, stealing from white and Indian alike. Staring from the shadows, their beady black eyes glowed as they took in the entrancing face and hair as richly glowing as the embers in the campfire. As their mounts began to stamp and shift, the Rebels backed further into the shadows, greatly fearing Wild Hawk would surprise them by returning suddenly.

"Catka," Tawena said to her brother, "the rebel warriors have grown restless. They are afraid Wild Hawk will return. They would take Precious Fire and the white hair and be gone. What are your plans? You must strike now!"

"I have changed my plans. The white hair stays with me."

Tawena shrugged. "As you wish. I will take Precious Fire to them now."

"Yes, you take her. I do not wish to touch the Fire-Hair. I am eager and prepared to feel white blood on my hands." He was staring toward the heavier older woman with the slouched hat over her sleeping face. He would take his revenge against the whites upon that one first. . . .

"Do what you will. If you want to slay the *istahota* and take her scalp, you must do so now," Tawena said of the eldest of the white women.

Audrina met Left Hand's eyes, becoming instantly alerted to the bloodlust shining in their slaty depths. He was . . . oh dear God! He was going to kill them all now. . . . Who would be first?

"No!!" Audrina cried, anticipating Tawena's move

157

as she leapt to cover her face, but the young white woman broke away in order to watch what Left Hand was doing. Tawena hauled back and slapped her, knocking Audrina to the ground. But she got up quickly, adrenaline flowing swiftly in her veins. Fragile though she might be, she meant to stand as barrier, to keep them from reaching Katherine and Sadie.

Audrina was about to shout a warning, when Left Hand moved swiftly, like a striking snake. Adjusting the quiver of arrows over his shoulder and removing a single deadly one, he laid it across his bow and let it fly. Accurately, the silent arrow sped across the clearing and met its mark.

Katherine cried out as a burning heat entered her shoulder. She lurched about, knocked the hat off her face, and it was then, horrifyingly, that she saw the arrow protruding from her shoulder. It had entered her flesh and glanced across her shoulder blade, lodging finally in the fleshier upper part of her arm. A six-inch gash had laid Katherine's shoulder open.

Audrina's eyes had followed the arrow's path, her heart seeming to pound in slow motion with hard dragging beats that taxed her nervous system, the look on her face registering paralyzing shock as the arrow entered Aunt Kate's shoulder.

Horrified, she slowly spun about to run toward her aunt, when another arrow sped overhead and reached Katherine before Audrina could get there. This second deadly arrow pierced the woman's chest and entered her heart. Blood squirted and gushed, and in that moment of horrible fascination, her wild tormented gaze flying to Katherine, Audrina watched helplessly as her aunt lurched backward, gasped, and finally breathed her last.

"Ohhhhh!" Audrina screamed, unaware she did so over and over. "Katherine . . . oh, Aunt Kate . . . *noooo!*" Audrina ran to the dead woman and threw herself upon the lifeless heap of soft womanly flesh. "No—no—no . . . my *God!*"

Tawena was there in a flash, ripping Audrina from the dead woman and then standing back to hold her as Left Hand withdrew a knife, bent on one knee, and cold-bloodedly scalped the dead woman.

Upon hearing Audrina's first bloodcurdling scream, Sadie had come instantly awake. In a daze, torn with grief, she now stared up at the bloody trophy Left Hand held up in the air, and as her eyes began to roll back in her head, she pushed her hand against her forehead and fainted dead away.

"Sadie!" Audrina yelled. "Sadie, wake up!" She struggled against Tawena's greater strength, kicking back at her shins until she was satisfied with a painful grunt from the Indian woman.

Fighting for control of her wild panic, Audrina spied Tawena's horse grazing in a moonlit patch nearby. If only Sadie would awake and they could manage to get to the horse, they might be able to escape from these red demons—and Wild Hawk. No doubt, he was waiting until his bloodthirsty warriors accomplished their evil deeds, staying away until all three of them had perished beneath Left Hand's bloody knife.

She prayed. Please God . . . help me . . . save me . . . save Sadie . . . get away . . . from them . . . The pain was too much to bear. . . .

Audrina's stomach pitched and rolled as she went to

stand before the body of her aunt. Then she leaned to the side and retched violently and with a strangled cry. "Aunt Kate . . ." she sobbed, pressing her forehead into her palm. "My God . . . my dear God! She's gone from this earth. . . ." She prayed and mourned silently for her lost one, believing that nothing mattered any more in this life. Nothing mattered . . . there was nothing left. . . .

It was as if a soft voice arrived on the wind just then, tenderly urging, "There is Sadie. You must live, for yourself and Sadie. Live, Audrina, live and be brave. You will find . . . Good-bye, my darling, *good-bye* . . ." The gentlest of voices melted away on a sudden ghost-like breeze sweeping through the camp.

Steeling her nerves and drying her tears, Audrina peeked from between her fingers. Tawena and Left Hand seemed content for the moment to allow her to mourn the passing of her beloved relative. She had to get Sadie out of here. . . .

While Tawena and Left Hand were arguing heatedly, Audrina saw her chance and snatched it. Stumbling blindly toward Sadie and fighting to keep from becoming sick again, she whispered, in a low hiss, "Wake up, Sadie!" She shook the mumbling girl awake. "Wake up, Sadie, we have to get out of here, now!" The blonde peered up at her dazedly, then shook her head.

Grabbing Sadie by the arm and moving catlike as she'd seen Wild Hawk do many times, Audrina ghosted behind a tree. Chilled for a moment, she stood there hardly breathing at all. They exchanged scared glances, then she whispered urgently to Sadie, *"Let's go,"* pulling the shivering blonde behind her and giving her a grunting, heaving boost up onto Tawena's horse.

160

Tawena and Left Hand were not alerted to their absence until they detected soft muffled beats, a horse's hooves leaving the area. For a startled moment, they were both disconcerted and believed Wild Hawk and his braves were returning. Then Tawena saw that their captives had vanished from the place where the dead woman lay on the bloody blankets.

Dumbstruck, Tawena cried, "My horse is gone!"

Left Hand and Tawena were just about to go after Audrina and Sadie when they heard another sound like many horses approaching. Left Hand went to find the rebel warriors, but they were not in the place he had told them to wait, having wisely moved farther into the shadowy woods. He caught the bridle of the first horse he came to and looked up at Yellow Bear, then he fell to his knees, his head down.

With his ear pressed to the earth, Left Hand announced, "Someone comes . . . many!" He stared around at the rebels. "You must go now!"

Yellow Bear questioned fiercely, "Where is the white woman you promised us?" He looked mightily angered that Left Hand had not brought the Fire-Hair to them yet.

"I will get her for you later, Yellow Bear," Left Hand promised lamely. "Wild Hawk and his braves return from the hunt!"

At the mighty name of Wild Hawk, the Rebel Indians vanished like thin smoke, moving like quick and silent wraiths.

Wild Hawk's keen senses were alerted. One hand lifted in the signal for the small party of braves to halt.

161

He ducked low and caught sight of an animal or bird flitting through the moonlit woods. It was too big to be an owl or a wolf, and in fact, peering closer as he came down off the Bear, he saw that it was a horse. A horse carrying two people . . .

Whirling about, Wild Hawk leapt to his horse and had the Bear moving before he was fully seated. He and the Bear flew through the woods at a good clip, darting trees and bushes and moldered logs. He burst into a clearing that stretched out between him and his swift-fleeing quarry. The Bear stretched out his strong tendons as he struck open ground, leaping into a new surge of power.

Up ahead, Sadie shouted to Audrina that someone was giving chase. Audrina shook the reins out and pushed Tawena's horse to the limit of its endurance, but the smaller mount was no match for the powerful steed that was gaining rapidly.

As the racing horse drew closer, Sadie gripped Audrina about the waist and shouted for her to make the horse go faster, faster, faster!

"We're going as fast as we can!" Audrina shouted back, but the wind snatched away most of the volume of her voice.

"What?" Sadie shouted. "Hurry, Audrey, make the horse go faster!!"

"I can't!" she cried, her heart breaking in two at the thought of leaving Katherine behind.

Audrina had indeed pushed the horse to its limits, and the tiring animal, in trying to make it over a jutting rock, clicked its hooves on the obstruction, faltered, and went down.

After they had both tumbled from the horse's back,

162

Sadie scrambled to her feet but Audrina lay like a broken doll beside the rock. She did not move. Her eyes were closed.

Sadie reached down and gasped when her fingers felt the warm, sticky blood on Audrina's forehead. "Audrey!" she cried. She stood up and screamed. "Don't leave me all alone! Katherine's gone. . . . Don't you leave me, too, *Audrey!*"

Wild Hawk recognized the horse as Tawena's right before it stumbled and fell. He had taken a good look at the long, heavy braid of fiery hair and knew who it was he pursued. In a glance, he read the situation and decided that they had been trying to escape. Gritting his teeth, Wild Hawk told Sadie to shut up and bent down to check Audrina. There was blood on her forehead, and if the white hair would have checked further, she would have found the pulse that still beat strongly in the slender wrist.

His hair blowing back like a bolt of raw silk tossed to the wind, he looked upwards, breathing a silent prayer of thanks to *Wakantanka*.

Dropping her wrist, Wild Hawk bent to lift Audrina in his arms, while Sadie followed close behind, breathlessly asking if her friend was going to be all right.

"Why did you chase us?" Sadie asked in a feminine but fierce voice. "Why were you and your men trying to kill us? Why did Left Hand kill and sc—?"

"Be still!" Wild Hawk ordered the hysterical young woman. He indicated, with a wave of his hand, for her to mount Tawena's horse. She stared up at him dumbly and then at the horse with the drooping stance. "He has nothing broken. You may ride him." He gave his horse

163

a nudge with his knees and brought him around. "Otherwise, you may walk," he said softly, unaware of the desolating shock she'd just received from Katherine's death.

Amazed by the warm, sensitive expression she had seen momentarily in Wild Hawk's moon-silvered eyes, Sadie caught herself up short, gaping, wondering if she'd only imagined he'd looked upon Audrina in a special, loving way.

Just then Fox Dreamer rode up to Wild Hawk, his eyes darting back and forth between his cousin and the two women. Fox Dreamer indicated Wild Hawk's feminine armful with a nod of his head. "She has been hurt; will she be all right?"

Apparently worried, Wild Hawk answered, "She will live. She has only received a blow to her head and her pulse is strong."

"The Hohas have attacked our camp." Fox Dreamer's eyes slid to Sadie, who was looking over at him with an expression he could not read. The moon was beneath some clouds, keeping him from seeing Sadie's face clearly. Then he went on, reluctantly dragging his gaze from the lithe blonde. "Left Hand says they murdered and scalped Precious Fire's *hunkapi.*"

Angry with himself for leaving the camp with only a few to guard them, Wild Hawk clenched his teeth and gazed down at Audrina nestled motionlesss against his arm. Sadly, he shook his head. "That is bad." He indicated his soft bundle with a nod. "Does she know this?" Tenderly, his eyes touched on every high plane and shadowy mauve angle of her lovely face.... No wonder she had fled the camp.

Slowly, Fox Dreamer nodded. "Left Hand tells me

164

she became so frightened when the rebels attacked; she had watched as her aunt was slain and scalped. Then Left Hand finally chased the Rebels off. He did not even notice their absence until they were long gone. He was just going to look for Precious Fire and the white hair when I rode into camp." Fox Dreamer ended on a frown, wondering about some things Left Hand had said that did not ring true. But this was not the time to discuss his suspicions with Wild Hawk, when other matters pressed for attention.

Suddenly, Wild Hawk kneed his horse into action. "Where is the body of the *hunkapi?*" he asked softly, his face drooping wearily, the scar on his forehead standing out whitely.

"It is there beside the tree where she slept."

"Please have her buried at once before Precious Fire revives." Caressingly, Wild Hawk's eyes swept over Audrina and his hand gently smoothed the tangled hair back from her cheeks. He gritted his teeth as his hand came in contact with the blood.

"I will do this myself." Fox Dreamer stared down at the sleeping beauty.

Wild Hawk rode slowly as his cousin continued to speak softly to him, and he asked, "Has Left Hand gone after the Rebels? You did not mention if he finally went."

"The braves are weary from the hunt, and I did not order them to go into the chase. The Rebels are like vanishing smoke, and they are like ghosts when they are pursued."

"As are many braves of the Dakota nations," he said proudly. "But those who raid by night, killing white man and Indian alike, are no better than the ravens and

165

the vultures!!" he spat angrily.

Numbly, Sadie kneed her mount closer, wishing she could understand what they were discussing. One thing was certain: They knew she would not try escaping again this night. At least, not without Audrina. Next time she and Audrina would not fail to be free of them. They were murdering savages, and she had been right to say they should try escaping first chance. Now—her throat choked up painfully—Katherine would not be escaping to go anywhere. Katherine was in her final resting place, God bless her, she had been a wonderful, tender soul.

Fox Dreamer looked over to Sadie, shivering inwardly when she did not smile but only glared at him with hatred in her deep brown eyes. She thought the worst, that they were all savages who killed when the mood struck. He could not blame her, for they had taken her and the others captive. And now one of them was lying dead beneath a tree.

"Tell her we did not do it, Wild Hawk," Fox Dreamer beseeched his cousin. "Tell the white hair the Rebel Indians are responsible."

Wild Hawk suddenly lifted his head. Heavily, he said, "I will tell them nothing. They will believe as they wish no matter what we say. Indians do not think like the whites. They have never been friends with and trusted the Indian. Why should they begin to now?"

Audrina returned to consciousness just as Wild Hawk was staring straight ahead. Her heart beating erratically, she thought, So! He had been the one chasing them. They had never gone hunting at all but had waited in the woods, watching while Left Hand and Tawena performed the dirty work. When will he

166

kill us off as he'd had Left Hand kill Katherine? Were they going to be picked off, one by one, until she and Sadie had perished by the blade, too?

Moaning inwardly, she closed her eyes again. He is a powerful man, a leader, one who takes captives and murders at will. . . . She would never forgive him for having Left Hand slay her aunt . . . her beloved Aunt Kate. Wild Hawk had spared her and Sadie, but that did not make her hate him less. Her turn and Sadie's were coming, that was horribly clear and she could not avoid the fact. She just hoped Wild Hawk would be merciful and her death would be quick.

Was there no mercy in Wild Hawk? In his braves? There was not even a merciful bone in Fox Dreamer's body, quiet, sly Fox Dreamer. Why should he treat them any differently, be any kinder?

In moments, the moon and the dark trees began to swirl, and Audrina lost consciousness again, mourning Katherine . . . sweet Katherine. *I will be brave . . . for you . . . Aunt Kate.*

Wild Hawk gazed down at Precious Fire's moonlit face. His dark-fringed eyes were brooding and his heart was troubled indeed—for more reasons than one. He held Precious Fire as if she were a mere child.

The tall shadow of the Indian stretched across the tepee walls as he moved about. Despising her task, Tawena glanced up at Wild Hawk every so often as she bathed Precious Fire's face. He is as restless as the wildcat, she thought disgustedly. His concern is great for this pretty white woman, and this made Tawena spitting mad. She would have to keep making plans

167

with Left Hand and the Rebels, until they could devise some way to be finally rid of this defiant captive. And they would succeed, she vowed, if she had to kill the white woman herself.

"That is all, Tawena. You have worked on Precious Fire's forehead enough." He glanced right past the warrior woman, who was looking up at him strangely. But he saw none of her lust and admiration; all he could see was his white captive, and to Tawena it seemed Wild Hawk stared right through her as if she were not even present. "Did you put the healing herbs on the cut?" he asked tersely.

Humbly, Tawena nodded, wishing she had crushed poisonous herbs into a paste instead of the healing ones. Picking up her things, she stood but made no move to leave. She set them down again and walked around to stand directly behind Wild Hawk. She reached up to begin massaging the taut muscles of his neck and shoulders, kneading with strong and dexterous fingertips.

"Thank you Tawena," Wild Hawk said, reaching behind to remove her hands from his shoulders. "That will be enough, you may go now."

Bristling from the cold rejection, Tawena moved away when he did not acknowledge her continued presence behind him. Once again, she picked up her things, and then pausing at the entrance to the small, hastily erected tepee, she let her black eyes rest on Wild Hawk's proud, handsome profile for a moment longer. Then she was outside, walking huffily toward the blankets on the ground. It had begun to drizzle. Even though they had struck a new camp not far from the last one of the raid and the overhanging branches gave plenty of shelter, she was envious of the warm tepee the white bitch shared with Wild Hawk. They had discovered the damaged tepee a little way out from their last camp. Tawena wished she had never pointed it out.

She glanced over to where the white hair slept peacefully beside Fox Dreamer. They looked cozy and warm. Her lip curled when she heard Left Hand snoring softly near other noisy braves.

Tawena fell asleep, her dreams filled with visions of hatred and revenge.

Back in the small tepee, Wild Hawk wondered why Precious Fire had not yet regained consciousness. He worked quickly to remove her clothes, right down to the very last stitch. His hawk-brown eyes shone as he studied and charted her shapely body. Never had Wild Hawk known such loveliness, such perfection. Only once before had he looked upon such excellence of the womanly form. His eyes darkened to ebony, envisioning the night he had found her with Powell, the night he made her his captive. Such perfection of the female form could belong to only one woman: Audrina. Precious Fire.

Even though jealousy ran thick in his blood as he thought of this woman together with Powell, mating on the *wasicun's* bed, her legs wrapped about his hips in a hot plunging embrace, Wild Hawk could not help it when his body began to throb with passion. His lust was great for her, with her lying helpless beneath his hungry gaze; he could actually kiss and touch her anywhere he wanted. Heatedly, he looked to the

169

reddish patch between her legs and he hardened achingly, torn by a need to fill her completely with his body.

With a curse, Wild Hawk shook his head. Fool! What enjoyment could a man obtain from making love to an unconscious woman? When he took her—and the day was drawing close—he wanted her to be a willing participant. He wanted her desire. He wanted her throbbing with heat, tossing, aching moistly for him to enter her for the first time ever. And he did not care anymore if Powell had had her first. She was Wild Hawk's woman now.

Completing his gentle examination and finding no other wounds but for bruises here and there, Wild Hawk removed one of the folded blankets from beneath her head and laid her back down. Then he stood looking down at her. "When, my Petala, when will you awaken? Or are you only at rest for the night?" He questioned her softly and, turning his back, did not see the long sweep of her lashes flutter and lift.

Awakened by the deep male voice, Audrina opened her eyes to the sight of Wild Hawk's lean, naked back. Numbly, she noted how his bronze flesh glistened. His muscles rippled with strength undeniable. Midnight-black hair had been loosened from its thick braid and hung arrow-straight to his lean waist. She was surprised to find how much longer it was this way. A turquoise beaded leather band surrounded his dark, proudly sculptured head, with golden eagle feathers floating down in back in graceful, manly allure. Handsome . . . savage . . . a bloodthirsty killer just like his evil brave, Left Hand.

Coldly, Audrina said, *"You*—you had my aunt

170

murdered. When will you slay me, Wild Hawk? When will you slay Sadie? When?" she sobbed. *"When, Wild Hawk?"* She choked on her abject misery, torn apart inside at the loss of her beloved Katherine.

Under his breath, he said, "It was not my order, not my men. ..." He shrugged, his chiseled mouth hardening knowing she would believe what she would and nothing he could say would make her believe otherwise.

As Audrina turned her tear-streaked face into the soft robes, Wild Hawk clenched his fists and his jaw. Then he turned abruptly and strode from the tepee, never noticing the leather object that had fallen from the pocket of the green wool skirt.

Outside, Wild Hawk lifted his face to the heavens. A light rain misted over him, making delicate web patterns in his inky hair. Her haunting sobs filled his heart with sadness. He prayed to *Wakantanka* to give him strength to battle these conflicting emotions raging within.

He wanted Precious Fire for his woman, but he did not want another man's leavings. He had only done that with a few of the half-breed whores he had met. Then he argued with himself that Audrina was different, that she was not like the sluts he had bedded and walked away from. She was different, a special breed of woman. Even though white.

He had never looked at white women and desired them for his own. Not a single one of the captives that had been brought to Red Hawk's village. They had been like frightened rabbits. Audrina. Audrina. Woman with autumn fire in her hair. With summer green in her eyes. Golden flesh. Naked wonder.

He had seen desire for him flare in her eyes; she had wanted him more than once. He had felt her urgent need to mate with him, to become one with him, and he had felt aroused and excited to learn of her desire. Perhaps she was ashamed to want an Indian. Was that the reason she had cried out her lover's name? She had been lonely for the paleface. He could have sworn she had never known a man's deep thrust before. Powell must have been Precious Fire's first lover. What else was there between them? What deep, dark secret did Audrina conceal from him? Perhaps the soldier Powell was tracking them even now with his white Army men.

Wild Hawk realized he might be leading Powell right to him and the People. When he reached Red Hawk's village, he would know if the Wahpekutes had gone on to the Pahasapa Hills into hiding. He prayed it was so, that they were already gone. If Powell and his soldiers got to them, they would force the Hawk People onto the reservations. Fiercely, Wild Hawk sought to avoid that. He wanted to be free, as his people wanted to be free. Government charity was not for him and the Wahpekutes; they would starve there on the little fare they received. Not allowed to hunt, they would hardly ever get the meat they so needed. Squaws would be sickly and overworked, the men fat and lethargic, the children unoccupied and sad.

Wild Hawk's heart gave a painful twist when he thought of the children he had always wanted. His own children, to nurture and love. No other people had deeper love of home and family than the Sioux. They never took the name of the Great Spirit in vain as the

172

white people did, nor did they have curse words to equal the violence and profanity of the *wasicun*.

What to do? He desired the white woman for his own. He could leave her now, take his people, and go far from her and her paleface lover. But the fear of losing Audrina was greater even than the fear of dying. Now he raised strong, muscled arms skyward. . . .

Please give me a sign, Great Spirit, Wakantanka. I am in pain. I wish to keep the white woman for my own. I look into her tender face and I am lost. My world has more sun in it with her by my side. The grass is greener and the air happier. My heart sings when I take Precious Fire into my arms. Tell me what I must do.

The feathers in his raven hair stirred in the rain-washed breeze. Soon the summer moon will arrive. . . . These were the words of mystery that filled his head. There was nothing more, though he stood for a long while in silent meditation. Finally he gave up, knowing he was a fool to have ever taken the white girl captive.

With a deep groan of despair and longing, Wild Hawk ran into the woods, running, running faster, faster, until he had winged feet. Moving like the fleet-footed deer, he did not stop until he found himself miles from the camp, staring up at the clearing sky.

Weary from running but mostly from agony of the heart, Wild Hawk lay where he had stopped . . . and he dreamed. He stood at the edge of a vast prairie and all was dark purple around him. Then the emerald moon filled his vision, that and a pair of deep green eyes, hair with the fire of a prairie sunset during summer. The savage angel came to him so clearly that Wild Hawk knew there was no mistaking who she was. Precious Fire, she was the other part of his incomplete soul. Near him came the sound of a meadowlark, calling out sweetly, a gentle, silvery melody bestowing a benediction upon him. When he awakened, he rose from the ground and ran back to the Indian camp.

Chapter Seven

The small party of Indians and white captives led by Wild Hawk broke camp while the morning was still misty and dark. In the dying light of the campfire, Audrina completed tying her small bundle of possessions. Drawing her dark red hair over her shoulder, she braided it, tying the end of the long, thick braid with a rawhide strip. Sadie watched as her friend completed the task; they had been silent, each thinking their own thoughts until Audrina spoke up.

"Sadie, would you like to braid your hair?" Audrina asked. "It will not tangle as much that way."

Sadie gave Audrina a sad smile. "Will you help me?"

After braiding her friend's long, silky blond hair, Audrina fastened it with a piece of the rawhide Wild Hawk had cut into strips for this purpose. "There, how does that feel?"

"Neater," Sadie shrugged, "but I don't know if I'll ever get used to it."

Breathing deeply, Audrina said, "I guess we will have to try."

"Never," Sadie said forlornly. "I'll never get used to looking like a squaw."

Sighing, Audrina pressed Sadie's hand, saying, "We only have each other now."

Thinking of Katherine, Sadie said, "She would want us to stick together. We'll always be friends, Audrey—forever."

"Forever, Sadie, that's a promise."

"If one of us gets away, we'll promise to get help and come back for the other?"

"Of course. I would always come back for you, Sadie."

Audrina and Sadie watched as the tepee was collapsed, the fires killed and covered with dirt. All the while Audrina would not meet Wild Hawk's eyes—and Sadie knew why.

As the dawn opened its golden eye over the earth, Wild Hawk gave the order and they mounted up, riding away from the camp, the woods, and Katherine. . . . Audrina had not been able to watch as Fox Dreamer buried her, but she had prayed—prayed very hard—for Katherine, Sadie, and herself.

Silence hung like a mantle, and no track or trail was visible in all the expanse of prairie country that stretched out before them. Woods and bushes were few and far between, the only shelter in the occasional creekbeds and ravines.

Wild Hawk's next destination was the lower part of the Yellow Medicine River, where there were many grassy ravines and valleys. This was where the Battle of Wood Lake had taken place, where the Dakota had been defeated and began fleeing Minnesota. It was also where the Warrior Mankato, Dakota hero of the battle

176

of Birch Coulee, had been decapitated by a cannonball.

Wild Hawk's mouth took on an unpleasant twist as they rode near the area where he had watched, seemingly long ago, from the tall prairie grasses after the battle as Sibley's while soldiers had scalped and mutilated the bodies of fourteen Indians left on the battlefield. The white *wasicuns* had taken the Sioux scalps and placed them on exhibition in St. Paul . . . and then had the nerve to call the Sioux Indians red devils.

He looked over to Audrina as she rode double with Sadie, the woman his enamored cousin had lately named Snow Maid. There was a time for war and a time for peace, Wild Hawk thought. There had been too much fighting, too much bloodshed. It was time for peace now. He must put aside his bitterness and hatred for what the *wasicuns* had done. Again he looked over to his sweet and tempting captive. How long, he wondered, could he fight this hunger for her? He wanted his captive beauty willing, but if she continued with her defiance, he knew that force was the only answer. She had already been given the warning: Every time she disobeyed, he would take his lovemaking one step further. She knew what to expect. She had been with a man before. Perhaps she had enjoyed the chase, running naked while soldier-boy Powell pursued, caught, then dragged her back to the place the whites call "house."

Wild Hawk wondered if Powell had come after them, if he was, in fact, at this very moment, tracking them with other white warriors. Or had Powell crawled away with his tail between his legs like a coward? More troubles with whites he did not want. He had witnessed and participated in enough violence and cruelty and senseless killing to harden his heart forever. If only he could rid himself of this last tiny bit of hatred. *If only he could become able to give himself completely to love. Then he would be a new man, reborn in his heart, body, and soul.*

Audrina knew that Wild Hawk had been watching her for a long time now. "What is he thinking?" she whispered to herself. Warm, tingling sensations ran through her when he looked deeply into her face, and she gazed back without tearing her eyes away. She did not realize it at the time, but green fire danced enticingly in her eyes when she looked at Wild Hawk. The warrior's sparkling gaze hungrily devoured her, from head to foot, coming to rest on her rosy, generous mouth.

Then, as quickly as her eyes had lighted up, they darkened into midnight-green. Katherine's words came back to haunt her: *Think of yourself and Sadie ... You will find ... Be brave, my darling ... be brave ... good-bye ...* What had the ghostlike voice been about to whisper? You will find? ... Find what?

Wild Hawk was surprised when Audrina's face suddenly hardened into a mask of mistrust and she turned aside. "What is wrong now?" he asked himself. He knew she must still be thinking of and blaming him for the death of her relative. He would let her believe what she would. In time, she might realize he had had nothing to do with it. He realized his pride stood in the way of explaining to her that he had not been responsible for her aunt's death. He would tell her all, in his own good time. Perhaps she, too, would have something to tell him about that night.

Now Wild Hawk sought out his warriors, one in particular. Left Hand rode off to the side with his sister Tawena, and both of them had their eagle eyes trained on the white captives. Wild Hawk was pleased. When they stepped near a stream and the women went into the bushes, Tawena watched closely and carefully to make sure they did not escape. He had always thought he could trust them. But then there was Fox Dreamer's worry. . . .

Fox Dreamer had come to him just that morning with his suspicions. His younger cousin had informed him that something did not ring true in Left Hand's and Tawena's account of the Rebel Indians' attack. Wild Hawk asked to hear everything they had said.

"I believe you are watching them too hard, my cousin, and seeing things that do not exist," Wild Hawk had said with a deep chuckle, believing that Fox Dreamer was only jealous of Left Hand's admiration and lust for the blonde.

"You are too trusting, my *Itancan*. Look," Fox Dreamer drew his cousin's attention, "Left Hand always has his greedy eyes on Snow Maid."

"Ahh, so that is it. You fear he will take her to his blanket before you can. You feel a great *cin* for her, my young cousin?"

"Yes, it is true. I desire Snow Maid and wish to make her my woman. Never shall I desire another. She is *mitacante,* my heart."

Wild Hawk's black eyebrow rose in the air. "You want only Snow Maid, a white woman, for the rest of your life?"

Fox Dreamer sat his horse straighter. "You question me, my great cousin? Only I see your secret desire for

179

Precious Fire, for I am experiencing these same emotions. Yes, I wish to take Snow Maid as my only woman, as my only wife for the rest of my life."

"Then do it!" Wild Hawk said, his white teeth in sharp contrast to his deeply bronzed skin and black hair. "What keeps you away?"

The head with the gleaming black braid lowered. "She will be frightened if I force her. I do not wish to make her afraid of me; I want Snow Maid to trust me. Only then can she learn to look into my eyes with love in her heart."

"Yes, my young cousin," Wild Hawk said. "But he who hesitates is lost."

Fox Dreamer watched Wild Hawk urge his horse ahead, and he said under his breath, "You would do well to practice what you preach, my great warrior."

The Indians rode slowly across the fiery sunset. Left Hand, riding in front of Tawena for the time being, snorted wryly after Wild Hawk studied him unwaveringly and then stared straight ahead once again.

Over his shoulder, Left Hand said, "I have a new worry."

Tawena sighed. "What is it now?"

"The white bitches saw me do the killing. When do you think one of them will speak of it to Wild Hawk?"

"You should have thought of that before you did the slaying and the scalping!" Tawena shot Audrina a glare from her black eyes. "Precious Fire will not speak of it."

"How do you know?" Left Hand said. "We did not get rid of her. And the white hair, when will she speak of it? She is beginning to look back at me with defiance. I do not like it."

The clean line of Tawena's strong jaw hardened. "I will make sure she does not speak of it. She is easy to threaten, for I have forced her to hold her tongue before when walking her to the stream. I pulled her hair and warned her, with my knife at her throat, to keep quiet."

Left Hand lifted a haughty chin. "We cannot warn them, Tawena; we do not speak their language."

In a near whisper, Tawena said, "You are right. Precious Fire will know Wild Hawk had nothing to do with the killing that night. We want her to believe he had some part in it. Even though Wild Hawk was not present at the killing of the older *wasichu,* she must be made to think he did not care if her relative perished by his warrior's hand or not. She might even be thinking Wild Hawk ordered the killing just to be rid of the troublesome woman."

"As you say, Tawena. We will watch Precious Fire close, and if Wild Hawk becomes friendly with her again, we must end their intimate relationship by any means we can."

"I think that will not work. . . . We could always just kill her one night while she sleeps," Tawena said.

"You do not fear Wild Hawk's wrath?" Left Hand asked.

"No," she said in a shaky voice.

"You do not know how unconvincing you sound, my sister." Left Hand chuckled low. Then he remembered something. "The *wasicun* warrior Wild Hawk knocked aside in the house," he said thoughtfully, his eyes narrowing blackly.

181

"Who do you speak of, my brother?" Tawena asked with excitement in her voice.

"He was chasing Precious Fire in the town of Mankato. This was where she lived with the white relative I have slain. Precious Fire was fleeing from this man; she was naked but for a woman's breechclout. He carried her into the dwelling and that is when Wild Hawk went after them. Wild Hawk knocked the *wasicun* to the floor, but the clever white warrior disappeared as we searched the house."

"What was Wild Hawk searching for?" Tawena inquired.

"I do not know what Wild Hawk wanted. Perhaps only the young white woman. He was acting strange and made haste to take Precious Fire for his captive."

Tawena sneered as she glowered at Audrina riding tall and proud as an Indian, the thick braid hanging down her back straight as a flaming arrow. Tawena recalled the way she had fought, kicked, and scratched like a spitting-mad tigress. Her full, pointed breasts bounced maddeningly under the soiled white blouse she washed every chance she got. Whenever she was waiting for it to dry, she would wear the deerskin shift Wild Hawk carried on his horse. It was too large for her, and she looked very small, very lovely in it . . . like a dangerous little wildcat.

Tawena told her brother, "We have no way of knowing if this *wasicun* will be coming after her." She glanced over her shoulder, scanning the hilly horizon. "I will be looking from now on, and if he is spotted by the Rebels or by one of us, we will make sure the Rebel Indians do not harm him and he gets her back."

Grinning wide, Left Hand muttered, "You are wise,

Tawena. Wild Hawk will never think we were responsible for her loss. You might yet become the bride of Wild Hawk."

After the warm topaz day had ended, they made camp at the base of a low hill covered with short new grass and dotted with scrub pine. Audrina sat her horse long after Sadie had gotten down, staring reflectively off into the moonlit distance, seeing but not really seeing the meandering stream sparkling like sapphires in the night. The sight did not register at the moment. Then she felt the hard fingers clasp her knee and give it a shake.

The voice was so close, so deep and manly. "Audrina, you may eat and go to the stream and wash. Just to rinse off, not to fully bathe. But you must eat now, for I have not seen you nourish yourself the whole day."

"I am not hungry," she lied, feeling Wild Hawk's compelling nearness. Truth was, she could not look another piece of scout-meat in the eye, nor could she choke down any more of the pasty meal.

"You must eat to keep up your strength," he said in a stern voice, his thumb lazily brushing her forearm. "I demand that you eat something."

After a tense moment, she said softly, "I really am not very hungry." All of a sudden food was indeed the farthest thing from her mind; so she did not lie this time.

The chiseled male mouth lifted intimately. "Remember the last time I punished you for disobeying. . . ." He moved closer, as if to kiss her. "Every time you disobey,

183

I will go a little farther."

Not liking the sound of that warning, she said quickly, "I'll eat." She came down off the horse while Wild Hawk stood back. He looked into her upturned face for several more moments, then walked away like a cat on silent, padded paws.

Across the low campfire Audrina caught Tawena staring at Wild Hawk while they were sharing the preserved meat. The warrior woman was always watching Wild Hawk, but he never returned her lusty perusal. Audrina shrugged and stared at the miserable hunk of meat, trying to work up enough saliva to swallow the piece in her mouth.

Audrina looked at Sadie and stopped chewing, wondering how her friend could eat with such relish. When Audrina's jaws took up the chore once again, she found herself meeting Wild Hawk's eyes. He was looking at her, and Tawena was looking at him. Fox Dreamer and Left Hand both stared at Sadie, each vying for a single look from her. But Sadie just kept munching, her young face glowing in the dark fire, happy and content to be filling her stomach with scout-meat and the grains that had been softened with water boiled over hot embers.

Wild Hawk rose to go and speak with the other warriors who kept guard outside the pale circle of light, which was hidden from any possible travelers between the walls of the ravine. Tawena walked Sadie and Audrina to the stream and then the bushes. But as soon as the camp bedded down, Wild Hawk killed the fire and walked to his blanket, which had been spread out not far from Audrina's.

He said nothing to her as he pulled the edge of his

blanket over his shoulder and put his back to her. Soon it was very still, and only the yip or the howl of a distant coyote or wolf sounded forlornly in the velvet night.

Audrina stared up at the white slice of moon with a single twinkling star beneath it. The sky was a deep evening-blue, and traces of the wild sunset still lingered in a shade of lavender-rose in the west after the fiery sun had melted from the earth's rim.

Sighing deeply, Audrina rolled to her side. She could see the dim shape of Wild Hawk and she wondered if he were sound asleep. Audrina's eyes burned with lonely tears, for she would never hear Aunt Kate's soft snore again. Even that exasperating sound would be welcome this night, she told herself.

Suddenly, Audrina felt impulsive and daring. After a tense moment, she moved, ever so carefully.

Getting up, Audrina straightened her skirt and blouse, then bent to adjust the blanket and bunch it so that it would appear that somebody was still in it.

Wild Hawk had not moved a muscle. Audrina stood indecisively and chewed on her lower lip. He had not moved; he was asleep. She looked around the camp. . . . They were all asleep!

Taking a few steps, Audrina then whirled around to make certain that he still had not moved. He was in the same position. Good.

Audrina crept up to Sadie's blanket and was about to give the girl's shoulder a shake when she spied Tawena walking from the narrow stream.

She watched as Tawena tied her horse to a rope that strung the horses together between two scrub pines. Audrina collected her frantic thoughts and sat with her slim haunches resting lightly on the backs of her

185

moccasins. Relax. Take it easy. You can do it. All you have to do is wait for Tawena to go to sleep.

Looking over to where Sadie slept soundly, Audrina pursed her lips in disappointment when she saw that they had fastened the blonde to a scrubby bush by a length of rope. And someone had done a good job of it, too! It would take some doing to untie the thick knots in that rope!

Audrina frowned. Why hasn't Wild Hawk or anyone bothered to tie me up? Don't they think I will try to escape if unbound? Not without Sadie, she answered that question quickly enough.

Kneeling by the length of rope, Audrina decided to give it a try. Once she got Sadie untied, they could lie back down and pretend to be asleep. Then when Tawena finally bedded down, they could make their escape!

Tawena's shifty black eyes caught the movement over by the white hair's blanket. Creeping low to the ground, she unsheathed her knife and headed toward the shadow. As Tawena neared, she saw that the slim shadow belonged to Precious Fire—and she was trying to escape with the white hair.

Tawena asked herself, Why not let them escape? Perhaps she should even help them. She shook her head. No. If Wild Hawk found her out, he would banish her from the tribe and from his life forever. She could just sneak up and kill them, and say there had been a struggle. Again, no. Wild Hawk would discover her deception. He would be roused from sleep as soon as there was one tiny whimper. She had to be careful from now on; she and Left Hand had taken one dangerous chance already.

186

She watched as Precious Fire's fingers tore and bit at the rope to make it come loose, but to no avail. Tawena had tied that special knot herself, knowing that Wild Hawk had been watching. One slip and it could be loosened, but one had to know the secret way.

Tawena stood back then, her mouth gaping wide. Precious Fire had slipped the knot! *But how?* Now Tawena noticed another movement, and quickly she shrank into the shadows and moved away.

Audrina was just about to shake Sadie awake when hard fingers clamped over her shoulder in a viselike grip. She looked back, then up, and shook at the fury in Wild Hawk's eyes. "Sadie was having a nightmare and I had to awaken her," she barely got out.

Wild Hawk appeared calmer now as he said, "Sadie is fast asleep, have you not noticed?" He shook his head, reaching past her to secure the knot, doubly this time. He straightened and stood looking down at her pale moonlit face. "You have forced me to do something I thought there would be no need for." He fought to suppress the hunger flaring in his eyes.

Audrina tried to keep up with his long stride as he pulled her along behind him. "What is that?" When he would not answer, she went on, "What are you going to do, Wild Hawk?" Still he would not answer.

Thinking Audrina had deliberately enraged him, Wild Hawk came to a halt and stared down at the length of rope he had beside his blanket. He stood in thoughtful contemplation for a moment, then turning to her, he said, "I will take you to the stream now. You may wash, and then when we return, I will fasten that rope between us. Your wrist to mine, Audrina, for you have pushed me to the very limits of my endurance."

187

That last part did not register, only the first. "Wash?" Audrina stared up at Wild Hawk uncomprehendingly. "*We* are going to wash?"

Wild Hawk almost smiled as he stared into her wide green eyes. "You are going to wash, Audrina, and I have already washed while you were preparing for bed."

Audrina looked down at her disheveled clothes and then down at the blanket. "It didn't take me long to ready for bed; I still have the same clothes on," she automatically said. Looking up, she felt a thrill of anticipation just staring into the ebony eyes.

"And it did not take me long," he said, drawing her eyes to his still-damp hair that shone jet beneath the silver moon, his buckskin breeches that were still damp around the waistline.

Audrina looked back up at Wild Hawk and gasped. "You were awake all the time! Oh, you saw me creeping to Sadie's blanket and saw me trying to undo that knot!"

"And you did very well—for a white woman."

Audrina squared her shoulders. "You always make that sound like a swearword: white woman."

"The Dakota have no swearwords, Audrina. We never curse and never take the Great Spirit's name in vain as the *wasicun* does."

"Can we forget the bath?" She pretended a yawn. "All of a sudden I am tired. . . . I'd like to go to bed, Wild Hawk."

His eyes glittered strangely. "You will, my Petala."

She stood waiting, looking into his dark, secretive eyes. "I cannot remember if you have already told me what that means . . . Petala."

188

"My little fire," he said, intense feelings of passion running deep within him. She had constantly tested his patience, almost daring him to possess her. As captor, it was his right to possess her body whenever she disobeyed.

Suddenly there was a jerk on her arm and Audrina was pulled unceremoniously down to a deeper ravine, and then to the bank of the meandering stream.

"You may undress and wash now," he said, finally releasing her. He reached out a hand to yank at the soft leather tie holding the hank of hair in a fat braid down her back, then his smile gleamed wickedly as he folded his arms across his chest Dakota fashion.

Audrina felt the silken strands of her hair coming unbound at the tips as she began to undress. She took care not to drop the medicine pouch from her pocket as she gingerly stepped from the circle of her skirt.

When all her garments were off but her bloomers, Audrina crossed her arms over her breasts and ran to the water. She stuck a toe in and yelped over her shoulder, "It is cold, Wild Hawk!"

"Good." He chuckled warmly. "It will wake you up."

After she had bathed—and quickly—he held out the deerskin shift he had brought along for her. While she dressed, quickly again, moving furtively to stuff the leather pouch into the shift's low pocket, he came soft and catlike to her side. "You live inside me now. Let me feel you by my side the rest of my life. You are like the sun, the velvet night, and gentle breeze against my face."

Audrina shivered, this time with emotion. "How beautiful, Wild Hawk. What is that?" Sweetly tilting her face, she watched as he lifted a turquoise beaded leather armband, white and soft, and tied it about her arm. "What is this for?"

He stared into her eyes. "You are my woman, Audrina. My Precious Fire," he repeated possessively. "And this binds us together forever and forever."

A smile trembled at the corners of her lips. "That is a long time," she said on a deep sigh as he moved closer.

"I do not believe you have much say in the matter," he said with a devastating grin, showing a flash of white teeth.

"For *always?*"

"For always," he murmured huskily right before he lowered his head. "You shall always be with me, Precious Fire."

Audrina ducked before his lips could capture hers. She pressed her palms against his rock-hard chest and peered up at him. "Does this mean we are married?"

Smiling mysteriously, he reached out with one bronze hand to capture an auburn lock, which he wrapped around his finger. Audrina shivered, but not from fear of being hurt. It was more a fear of losing herself to him completely, heart and soul, with nothing left over but crumbs of weakness. She had seen this in some women with their brutal, demanding husbands. And she never wanted to be reduced to a cowering slave like that.

With the muscular grace of a sleek cat, Wild Hawk slowly pulled her into his arms. "I demand," he began softly, urgingly, "that you do not turn away from me. Give me your lips, your heart, your soul, Audrina . . . Precious Fire."

Wonderingly, she lifted her face. Her lips were moist, as dew on a wild rose, and his harder, more masculine

190

ones settled into hers, gentle as swan's down. As his kiss went deeper and deeper still, Audrina was unaware that she moved closer and closer, returning the kiss wholeheartedly. She was wrapped in a cocoon of delight until she was brought abruptly to reality as she realized his hand was moving dangerously close to the medicine pouch, which was slung low against her thigh.

"Oh!" she cried, stepping back a little. "Wait . . ." She could see the hurt and anger in his eyes, deciding she would have to exercise more caution. What he would think and do if he were to discover the medicine pouch on her person she didn't want to dwell on. But now she saw that the situation demanded an answer. This was the closest he had ever come to touching and discovering the pouch. She waved a hand in the air. "I am very tired, Wild Hawk, so weary that I feel I will drop at any moment." Audrina lied. She had never been so awake in all her life!

Strong hands gripped her arms in a painful vise. "Do not push away from me again," he ground out. "This night you will feel everything my heart, my soul, my body is saying to you, Audrina."

"I—I just got dressed." Her voice quivered as she stared into his moon-silvered eyes. "I do not wish to be undressed again, Wild—"

"I will not tear your clothes from you, if that is what you are afraid of." His breath fluttered down over her, warm and golden. "I hope this is not what you are thinking, for I have already told you, Audrina, I am not a ruthless savage. It will take much for you to anger me."

Audrina licked her lips that had suddenly become dry. She must not let him discover the pouch, for

Minowa had warned her to guard it with her life. Not until she knew the answer, knew why she had been chosen for a secret mission, would she allow it to be taken from her.

Narrowing heavy eyelids, he softly questioned, "What is it that you hide from me, Audrina? I would like to own the golden key to unlock this secret and unravel the mysteries of your heart. Why do I hear disturbing and lovely sounds at times when you are near? I do not hear them at all times. Lately, again I have heard them and this makes me wonder about you."

"S—sounds?" Audrina asked, her eyes blinking innocently. Did he hear them too? The songs and the drums? Audrina smiled then as an entirely different fantasy came to her. "It could be . . . maybe you are in love with me?" Her voice was soft and her heart stood still.

In answer, Wild Hawk pulled her up against his hard body and kissed her almost savagely. He drove his fingers into her hair, spilling the fiery silken mass all about them. He tangled the strands about his long coppery fingers and gave her head a gentle tug backward, and she cried out as he exerted his authority over her body. "It would be a deep insult to my male pride if you push me away again, Audrina." He kept the harsh sternness from his voice, not wishing to frighten her needlessly.

Audrina placed her trembling hands on his chest as if to protect herself from him as his tongue went deeply into her mouth. He pulled her closer and she inhaled the musky fragrance of his manliness. She was suddenly reminded of the savage tales of Indians who raped and mauled their white captives. She started to panic when she thought of their naked bodies touching, his thrust tearing into her with vicious strokes. Then she reminded herself quickly that he had never hurt her, and she did not believe he would, for he was treating her with loving tenderness, his lips and hands moving over her flesh with graceful rhythm, with fingers that heated every inch of her womanly form.

Audrina had vowed never to let Wild Hawk have his way fully with her, but she could see now that she was going to lose that battle if she did not do something—fast.

"Wild Hawk." She broke away from his deliciously fiery kiss. "Please don't kiss me any more."

"Why not, Audrina? You allowed me to kiss you and caress you many times before. I even touched your body intimately. Now I want to do what I should have done at the start."

"What is that?"

"Made you my woman." He pulled her close again. "I know you want me, Audrina. Your body shivers and betrays your mind when you are in my arms. This time if you call out your lover's name, I shall not stop. Nothing will stop me this time."

"Nothing, Wild Hawk?"

"Nothing on this earth or in heaven above, my Precious," he said thickly.

His eyes burned with a look that made her suddenly afraid. He cupped her face so she could not escape his kiss this time, and he bent his head to brush his lips against her cheek. Then his caress moved lower, and he captured her lips in a more demanding kiss than before.

This time she found that she did not want to struggle

and fight him, for the wildfire ran rapidly through her, so quickly she thought it might consume her. She moved closer and brought her hands to the nape of his neck, his jet hair feeling silken, cool, delightful to her sensitive fingertips.

She wondered with a little shock what it would be like to have him move inside her, thrusting deeply. Audrina was happier than she had been in a long time, and surprisingly she found she was not afraid now. She was only alive with the splendor of his silken, questing kiss, which seemed to go on forever and ever.

Then she almost swooned when she felt the hard fingertips at her bodice, brushing it aside, exposing a tautly aching nipple. The delicious sensation shot through her like a golden arrow as he took the tip, held it, and brought his hot tongue licking across it. Wild Hawk could feel his manhood bulging and rising as he flicked the tiny bud back and forth, then sucked at the nipple until it was as taut and hard as his swelling organ. His lips returned to hers, and kissing her tenderly, he lowered her to the new spring grass and came against her gracefully slim frame with one leg over hers. Her hand brushed against that unmistakable swell between them and Wild Hawk groaned deep in his throat, then captured Audrina's hand and placed it over him. Her eyes widened in shock at how large and hard he was. His desire was obvious, even beneath her wondering gaze that fell between them and then swiftly flew away.

"Oh, Wild Hawk," she breathed and, removing her hand, stared up at him, wanting him, wanting him so dearly, wanting to feel Wild Hawk in the innermost depths of her body.

With the unspeakable agony of wanting her for so long, Wild Hawk moved over her and placed his hands at her waist. Before she could blink twice, he had her bloomers past her hips, then to her knees. Wild Hawk felt her jerk of panic and he left the bloomers bunched right there.

While he busied himself undoing the front of his breeches, Audrina lifted her hand and gasped when she saw the medicine bundle. Dear God, she had it clutched in her hand! She must have automatically taken it from her pocket when he began to tug at her bloomers. She tried hiding it again, then she forgot everything as Wild Hawk pushed the shift higher, the bloomers lower, and nudged her knees apart. Audrina began to breathe harder, to pant as the shaft of his manhood poked along her thigh, rubbing and titillating. Deftly, he took his manhood in his hand then and rested it against her furry mound, dipping just a little bit lower every second.

When he drew back, ready for the thrust home, Audrina tensed up as sheer terror began to plummet through her slender body. "Why do you tense like a virgin? It is not your first time."

"N—not a virgin?" she squeaked out.

Just as Wild Hawk was about to enter her, Audrina whipped the medicine pouch between her legs. She held it there, guarding the precious entrance where Wild Hawk knew paradise finally awaited him.

Bracing his weight on his forearms, Wild Hawk groaned. "Do not close your thighs to me now, sweet Audrina." His fingers contacted a soft leather object and he frowned darkly. "What . . . is . . . this?"

Audrina tried to snatch the bundle away but Wild

195

Hawk already had it clutched in his hand. He shot to his feet, dragging his breeches with him.

Audrina snatched up her clothes and prepared to run, but Wild Hawk stepped abruptly in front of her. His tall, lean frame barred her only escape. On one side was the water, the other side *him.*

His scar was livid, his mouth a thin line as he peered down at her and interrogated, "Where did you get this medicine bundle? Did your lover give it to you? You will tell me!"

"Wait a minute!" Audrina cried. "How can you question me about something that belongs to m—" Then she sealed her lips, reflecting on Minowa's warning: Guard the pouch with your life . . . like the she-cat who guards her young . . . a secret mission.

Wild Hawk watched her with an ominous countenance as he tied the drawstrings of the pouch to his leggings. Audrina stepped back as she took in the menace in his eyes. "No, Wild Hawk. Don't do this," she said, reading the intent in his face to do her bodily harm. "I can explain . . . but I can't explain *right now!*"

All gentleness gone, Wild Hawk forced her back to the blanket he had spread there earlier on the grassy earth. He knew now why he had heard the Dakota spirit songs; they were coming from the medicine bundle. Only he and his closest loved ones could hear the sounds. Only those with the Dakota Indian blood of his ancestors heard the spirit songs. But most of his closest loved ones were gone, but for his sister Rainbow.

Wild Hawk saw red . . . fierce, angry red, as he held Audrina down with one foot while he yanked his leggings off again, now with vicious jerks. Coldly, he stared down at her. "Your paleface lover has stolen this pouch of my father's; or both you and the *wasicun* you were rolling with on your bed."

"What?!" Audrina stared wide-eyed at the enraged Indian. "This is my pouch!" She glared up at him. "Well, not really, but I am supposed to—"

"Be still!" he ordered. "Now I shall treat you as a white captive should be treated. *Wasicun* woman."

Audrina's lips trembled; they were already tender and bruised from the many kisses he had shared with her. But now they were not going to share anymore, she knew. He was going to *take*.

Mystified and frightened, Audrina was drowning in the liquid onyx of Wild Hawk's eyes as he took both her wrists in one of his large hands and pinioned them above her head. Next he pried her legs apart and Audrina could not help but shiver in hot anticipation. She had told herself she would not respond to his lovemaking. But this was not going to be love, it was going to be rape. Now she was going to learn what it was like to be ravished by a real savage . . . all because of a mysterious medicine pouch! How she wished she had gotten rid of the troublesome thing long ago. It was too late now for wishes.

Biting her lip, Audrina anticipated the cruel thrust into her body that would mark the end of her virginity. Her eyes were squeezed tight. Her hands were balled into fists. Her shoulders were rigid. She had imprisoned her breath in her throat.

Slowly, her eyes opened as the delicious waves began to wash over her. Wild Hawk was not ravaging her in a cruel way, but in a most tender and wonderful fashion. His lips were at her throat, nibbling

197

and sucking, and his lower half was pressed into her, rocking with the rhythm she knew must match lovemaking. His hard body was fitted against her naked flesh and then he shifted, his fingers finding and massaging her secret inner core.

Beginning to ache for his possession, Audrina lifted and unconsciously brought his tender caress deeper into her body, then she cried out softly as the hard flesh endeavored to tear into her maidenhead.

Wild Hawk gave the expression of wonder. Delight filled every corner of his mind and body. Precious Fire is a maid untouched! Triumph rang in his ears and made him dizzy with happiness and longing as he gazed down at his beautiful captive, seeing that she awaited his next move. To him, she looked like a frightened rabbit anticipating the kill. "Trust me, Precious, it will hurt only for a few moments. I shall be quick and try not to cause you much suffering."

It was too late to call a halt to their mating. Though afraid, she was as hot and ready as he was. Already he had felt the soft yielding of her thighs, her inner core unfolding and awaiting his eager thrust, the rigidity melting from her slender limbs.

Audrina's whole being was concentrated in Wild Hawk's bold caresses. She ought to fight him and not give in willingly. Resist him, her mind argued, while her body began to flutter and melt like sun-warmed wax.

For a moment Audrina could feel the hot, hard shaft pressing her thigh, and then she felt a full, burning pressure as he thrust forward and entered her. She gave a soft cry of pain, then he remained still for a full minute, kissing the bright spots on her cheeks. She had never known that pain could blend so sweetly

198

with rapture.

"I am sorry if I have hurt you. Ahh, Precious. Precious Fire."

Audrina murmured bravely, "It was not . . . too bad, Wild Hawk."

Hard thighs brushed soft thighs. Long flesh moved slowly to enter her more and more. Then his hands grasped her buttocks firmly, one globe filling each hand. Her own hands sought and found the powerful corded muscles of his back, grasping him tightly, her nails digging into his hard flesh.

A small cry of ecstasy escaped her lips when he rode her with powerful strokes. His joy filled the air with rich laughter when she rose into an arched position, naturally meeting each savage thrust.

Then something wonderful and glorious began to happen. She panted with a wild, almost painful need to burst the bubble that tensed inside of her. Her lover whispered unknown Indian love words into her ear. She did not understand what he was saying, but she knew it had to do with love, sweet, sweet love, their souls entwined in the magnificent splendor of love's fiercest possession.

"Audrina . . . meet me . . . accept my love!"

Fire consumed them both. Every tight nerve and muscle in her body tensed with expectation, and when he shouted *"tecihila"* and stiffened on top of one bold thrust, her heightened climax burst. It expanded and exploded into a bliss that shattered every part of her into quivering ecstasy.

After the mounting of equal fulfillment, Wild Hawk pulled her close and they lay panting, happy and spent. He kept murmuring those strange words as he stroked her long, tangled hair. He looked at her tenderly, brushing her hair from her flushed cheekbones. "My woman . . . Precious Fire," he said lovingly. When he began to breathe slowly and evenly, she pulled the blanket up over her chilled backsides.

Audrina's eyelids fluttered. She knew a wonderful contentment. Profoundly touched, she gazed at the moonlit profile of the sleeping savage, his fine handsome face, the full sensitive mouth. She knew no shame for what they had just shared. There was only a simple joy as she lay in the arms of this handsome savage her young heart would always remember. In time, her eyes closed, and in the deep purple shadows of the moon, surrounded by lush green ferns and growing mosses, they slept together, their love consummated, each softly beating heart tranquil.

Chapter Eight

Recalling the fires of shared passion in the misty moonlit vale, Audrina could not meet Wild Hawk's eyes for days afterward. He had carried out his plans to keep her close to him, her wrist bound to his at night. He rode with her. He took all his meals with her. He took her to the stream to bathe.

"He has not spoken ten words to me in the last three days," Audrina told Sadie when she found a chance to speak with her friend. Actually, Audrina thought to herself, in all the three days since that splendorous night they had made love—the night he had discovered the medicine pouch on her person—he had remained almost totally silent toward her.

"Do you wish he would talk to you?" Sadie asked, her chocolate-brown eyes filled with curiosity.

"Yes, of course," Audrina answered truthfully. "I hate wondering if he is planning murder or something, with those dark looks he sends my way. There is more, Sadie, but I cannot speak of it just now. Maybe in time, when I know more about it myself."

"Well, as for murder, Audrey, I doubt his wrath extends that far. Talk about it when you feel ready." She grinned. "I'll never be far away, you know."

They had moved on again, and Audrina was grateful for the furious pace Wild Hawk put them through. There were no more campfires. The dismantled tepee had not been used again, but it still bounced along in a travois one young brave pulled behind his horse.

Audrina mourned the loss of her aunt, but the pain was beginning to lessen a little; she wore Aunt Katherine's beloved battered hat low over her face, but that did not keep the freckles from spreading enchantingly across her nose when the sun slanted early in the morning and later in the afternoon. And strangely, she missed her most guarded possession, a secret no longer, for Wild Hawk carried the medicine pouch now, concealed on his person somewhere.

"How long will Wild Hawk keep up his indifferent attitude toward me?" she asked herself under her breath. And when would he question her about the medicine pouch again? What had he meant when he had said it was his father's pouch? She had tried to explain to him that the pouch was important, that it was hers to deliver—she was on a noble mission—but he had been too angry to listen to her story. He had even implied that she and Joe had stolen it. What did Joe have to do with this? Could this secret mission have something to do with Wild Hawk's father? Were they journeying to a special place? What would happen there? Audrina shivered to think what it could be.

Wild Hawk rode before her on the black Appaloosa, his black hair and strong wide shoulders filling her vision. His feathers hung, tip down, over his shoulder and tickled her face sometimes in a sudden breeze. His black braid gleamed and his striking profile glowed bronze from the rising or the setting sun. Like a great warrior, he sat proud and erect, and she longed to caress the strong tendons in the back of his neck. Seated against him as she was, the auburn peaks of her breasts grew to pebble hardness, making her skin prickle pleasurably. With the horse's back moving rhythmically against her thighs, she tried to ignore the strange aching in her limbs and secret place, but the motion only heightened the feeling. It was a purely sensual experience, riding on a horse with Wild Hawk.

Audrina could feel Wild Hawk's muscles flex. He was powerfully built and his aristocratic head, gift of Dakota forefathers, poised majestically and proud. He could order people to be killed. He could snatch her from her home and force her to become his unwilling captive. He could make love masterfully, and she could not deny that his lovemaking had given her such intense, forbidden pleasure.

Studying Wild Hawk's profile again, wishing she could shake him and make him understand, she wondered how he could remain so coldly angry. It was his fault she was here; she was his unwilling captive. It was his fault she had enjoyed the act of lovemaking with him. It was his fault her aunt was dead, even though he had not done the actual killing.

She had vowed never to let Wild Hawk have his way with her, but fool that she was, she had let him. She could have fought him like a wildcat, but she had not; she had given in easily after he had awakened her desire. Never, she told herself, would he assert his power over her as easily again.

When the sun was straight up, they halted the horses for water and a little grain. Fluidly, Wild Hawk came down off his horse, stood, and waited for her to dismount by herself. For several moments, he found himself staring at Audrina. She was like the small mountain cat. She had displayed courage and daring beyond any other white woman he had ever known. He watched her come down off his horse, her long coppery braid swinging with the action. She still wore the beaded leather armband he had given her, and he had lately made her don the deerskin shift. Her skin was several shades darker, possessing a warm golden tan. With the battered hat and long fat braid, she could be mistaken for a beautiful half-breed woman.

Wild Hawk shifted his ebony eyes to Sadie, the lovely girl his cousin had named Snow Maid. He perused her fine blond countenance. Her skin was downright red. When they had to pass on the outskirts of a settlement or a fort, Snow Maid was given the battered hat, her long silver-blond hair stuffed up inside. She had lost her own hat.

With Fox Dreamer mounted beside him on his own horse, Wild Hawk gazed at his white captives with narrowed eyes. "From a distance no one can tell if they are Indian or white now. This is good. It will make for a safer journey to the Pahasapa Camp."

"Yes," Fox Dreamer said. "They should make beautiful squaws."

Wild Hawk's gaze shifted to Audrina as she walked to Sadie, stretching and massaging her slim arms. He still believed that Powell was Audrina's secret love, that they had been close to making love the night he had burst upon them in the house. Why Powell had

204

brought the medicine pouch to Audrina's remained a mystery to him. Soon he would have the answer, and from her own mouth would he hear it. He was too angry to question her, unaware just how deeply his jealousy cut into him. Audrina was his own. He would allow no one to take her from him. Never.

Walking his horse to the stream, barely a trickle in the cleft of earth, Wild Hawk began to ponder other matters out loud to Fox Dreamer. "I have seen the riders following from a distance and believe them to be the *Hoha*." The Rebels. Or the Hoha Indians, as the *wasicun* called them.

Fox Dreamer spat on the ground with contempt. "They raid whites and Indians alike, never caring whose land or dwellings they lay waste. They would come and fight their own brothers, much like the whites fight with one another and embrace war. They have as much dignity as the garden snake."

"I have been aware that they fear me greatly," Wild Hawk said.

"They say you have *wakanda,* that you can affect and control others with your inner magical power."

"I do not profess to have any such thing." If he had it or not, he could not say. "This is up to Wakantanka, the Great Spirit, as is everything else in this life."

Fox Dreamer readily agreed. "It is up to the Great Spirit if we are to join with the white women and be their husbands."

"Yes . . . that too," was all Wild Hawk said on the subject. "I pray for a dreaming vision, Fox Dreamer."

Wild Hawk did have visions come to him in his dreams. As he walked in the golden afternoon, he thought of the second dream he'd had the night before.

A strange woman had come to him, a woman he had never known in real life. Very beautiful, she had hair the color of dark autumn leaves. It had been braided with a single rare white hawk feather woven in it. Another woman had appeared beside her; this one he did not know either. She was older than the first. Her hair was black, as were her eyes. She, too, wore the white feather. It had become clear in his dreaming mind that these two were Oglala Sioux. His mother, Rain Lily, had been this, just like these strange women. She had joined the Wahpekutes when she became Red Hawk's wife and had never gone back to her father's tribe.

Who were the strange women in his dream? Wild Hawk wondered as he returned to the temporary camp. His eyes sought and found Audrina, then rested on her for a moment before he mounted. He had left her to herself for a time, for she had been bound to his wrist with a length of rope for many days now.

"It is Wild Hawk's desire that she know who her master is, that in time she will never wish to escape me," he told Fox Dreamer.

"I understand this, that you do not wish to harm her. You only want her for your own." Fox Dreamer was looking at Sadie as he said this, knowing the time would come when he would be one with her.

Audrina saw Wild Hawk watching her, and then his look beckoned her to join him on the horse. "Come to me," his dark, dancing eyes conveyed while he held out his hand, palm up. She walked, her limbs like lead, then when she stood beside the horse, he bent down and swept her, weightless, onto the mount behind him.

Just then Left Hand and Tawena rode up for orders,

reining their mounts beside Wild Hawk. "Tawena may ride the gray mare, Left Hand the swifter horse," he announced.

"Where are we going?" Tawena asked, looking at her chief curiously. "Are you sending us out to scout the area before you enter it?" Her eyes rested on the rope Wild Hawk had refastened between his wrist and Audrina's. Eaten up with jealousy, she looked at Wild Hawk's face. "Do you suspect white men in the area up ahead?"

"So many questions," Wild Hawk said in Dakota. "You only need do as I say, Tawena, as always." His horse stood still and he looked over his shoulder past Audrina, saying, "I have seen many on horses come suddenly and go just as quickly on the horizon. You will scout the area *behind* us and hide wherever you must to discover who tracks us from afar."

Slyly, Tawena and Left Hand exchanged glances that said this was their chance to speak with the Rebel Indians, the *Hoha*. Tawena could not help but stare at Wild Hawk's lovely captive. Unbelievably, the white woman was even more striking with the stupid old hat on her head, her skin tanned deep gold, her hair streaming in a long, fat braid down her back. She even had some new brown spots across her straight, narrow nose, which made her look all the more interesting. Tawena's blinding jealousy returned, like powerful poison in her savage blood.

Sharply, angrily, Audrina stared back at Tawena. Why did she always have to stare so rudely? What was the matter with her?

Tawena's eye's were like burning coals, her curiosity as to what was going on between Wild Hawk and the

207

white woman nearly uncontrollable. She wanted to question Wild Hawk fiercely, to ask him what he was going to do about the *winu* once they reached his father's village.

"For pity's sake," Audrina grumbled at Tawena. "Will you quit your staring, you black-eyed witch!"

A low chuckle rumbling from Wild Hawk's chest, he said softly in English, "Watch out, little fire, Tawena is Warrior Woman. She had gone through all the tests of endurance that a young man goes through to become a tried and tested warrior. Tawena can kill you as easily as look at you."

For a moment Audrina sat stunned. Wild Hawk had not said this much to her in days. Feeling audaciously brazen, Audrina wrinkled her nose at Tawena and turned her head with a toss, her braid flying. Be brave, she kept reminding herself. Don't let them squash you into the ground like a bug.

Tawena glared, then slowly dragged her gaze back to Wild Hawk. She toyed with an idea, smiling cheerfully at Wild Hawk and beginning spontaneously, "My Chief." He acknowledged her address with a nod of his head. "Before my brother and I take care of this matter, I suggest that we rest for the remainder of the afternoon." She nodded to Audrina. "Precious Fire looks weary, as does the white hair . . . ah . . . Snow Maid. We will take them to the stream"—Tawena pointed—"there. Then you may council with your braves and give them instruction."

"But you know what to do, Tawena. You and Left Hand can lead and speak for me"—he smiled warmly —"in this matter."

For the first time ever Tawena pretended shyness. "I

208

would bathe, too, Wild Hawk. My time of *isnati* has come." Tawena hated to say she was menstruating when she really was not.

Wild Hawk stared into Tawena's dusky face. "You must stay away from the other braves then."

Tawena's head shot up. "Oh no, there is no need for that."

"You know the rules, Tawena. We will set up the tepee for your isolation."

"You need not go to the trouble, Wild Hawk." Tawena shot her brother a frantic look, while Wild Hawk took a moment to scan the soft green hills undulating across the graying horizon. Tawena set her mouth into a grim line. "What about when the palefaces' time comes? Will you set up the tepee for each of them?"

"That will be my decision, Tawena." He wheeled his horse about. "Now, go and take them to the stream." To Audrina he said in English, while placing a warm, vibrant hand on her arm, "You can get down now and go with Tawena to the stream. Take Snow Maid with you. You may share the tepee this night with Tawena, or not. It is up to you. She is—" Wild Hawk changed his mind about what he'd been about to say. He only nodded at Tawena.

The warrior woman knew she had stuck her foot in her mouth, as the white man says. She had only wanted to spend some time alone with the captives to warn Snow Maid to keep silent on certain matters. She did not believe she had warned Snow Maid enough. But now, with the lie she had told Wild Hawk, she had placed herself in isolation while the others rode out. She smiled cattily then. Much time would be spent with the captives in the tepee, all the time she would need to make them understand they must hold their silence on any and all subjects if they wished to remain among the living. They understood sign language well enough.

"What is going on?" Sadie asked Audrina on the way to the stream as they followed Tawena. "I thought we were going to keep going. All of a sudden we are striking camp?"

As Sadie walked, she stripped off her soiled pink blouse right down to her camisole, and Audrina caught a flash of bruised flesh in her side vision. She whirled to face Sadie, catching her by the hand to stop her. Sadie stared squarely into Audrina's face, unblinkingly.

"What is it?" Sadie was alarmed. "You seem to be staring at a ghost . . . or something."

"Those bruises on your arms," Audrina said. "Where did you get them? Who did this to you, Sadie? Those are finger marks. Who has been hurting you? And why haven't you told me?"

Sadie looked toward the stream. As the sun set with brilliant orange streamers flaring across the sky, tears brimmed in Sadie's eyes. "I can't tell you. Look," she cried, "Tawena is way ahead of us. Come on, Audrey, we've got to catch up with that Indian shrew or else she'll—" The words stuck in her throat.

"So," Audrina snapped, "Tawena has been tormenting you." Infuriated, her green eyes narrowed. "Why?" She squeezed Sadie's hand. "Tell me, Sadie. Maybe I can help."

"You can't do anything about it," Sadie said, lowering her eyes. "Besides, no one ever sees her do it. She's so quick and nasty about it. If you tell Wild

210

Hawk, he won't do anything about it, either."

"How about Fox Dreamer?" Audrina asked. "Have you told him of Tawena's cruelty? You can always use sign language, you know."

"I can't!" Sadie interjected. "If I tell, it'll only get worse. Tawena said I'm not supposed to talk about anything."

Suffused with curiosity, Audrina said, "Wait a minute! How can Tawena tell you anything? She does not speak English."

"Sign language. Indians are good at it. I was griping one day on the way to the water when she whirled around and pulled my hair. I could have sworn she told me to shut up in that strange Dakota tongue. She warned me with a knife to my throat to keep quiet. She can speak some English words, too."

"She did the same thing to me when . . . the night . . . they killed . . . Left Hand kill—"

"You don't have to talk about it, Audrey. I know it hurts you even to think about the dear woman. I loved her, too. She was good to want to take me in like that."

Audrina's face hardened. "If she hadn't picked you up that day, you would have been spared all this. You never would have been taken captive."

"I'm glad I was." Sadie looked down at the dirty blouse she held. Audrina was waiting to hear more. "I would never have met Fox Dreamer. I'm afraid I like him very much," she sighed with a hopelessness born of fear of the future and what it held, "too much."

Gently pushing back the long silvery wave from Sadie's dark brown eyes, Audrina murmured affectionately, "You are very special to me, Sadie, so I am going to talk to Wild Hawk and tell him what's—"

"Henala!" Tawena ground out, standing not far away and tapping her foot in irritation, arms folded over her beaded bodice. "You come . . . Tawena."

"See!" Sadie hissed low. "'You come . . . Tawena,'" she mocked, snorting through her pert nose. "I can't stand much more of her. She's always watching me; it makes me very nervous to think I have someone always peering over my shoulder, keeping tabs on every movement—even private ones."

"Sadie," Audrina warned softly, "do not give Tawena the satisfaction of seeing your frustration and anger. She loves it because she can only taunt you more. I believe she hates you because you are so pretty and have hair like the golden light of the rising sun, and added to that, two braves are always vying for one look from your big lovely brown eyes."

"You really think I'm that pretty? Do you think Fox Dreamer is aware of how pretty I am?"

Unconsciously, Sadie looked down at her rounded breasts while running a hand along her shapely hips on up to her slim waist, then raising it to rest on the hank of heavy blond hair.

Audrina chuckled. "Of course he does. Why, I remember that barn dance where all your beaux fought to whirl you around the floor. . . ."

"Henala!" Tawena shouted. Enough. "Come . . . Tawena."

Taking a deep breath, Sadie whispered, "Here we go again."

"Courage, Sadie."

Stepping behind them abruptly, Tawena took Sadie by the nape of her neck and shoved her forward. When she reached for Audrina's neck, the auburn-haired

212

woman ducked, thinking to herself, *Your day is coming, Tawena.*

Tossing back his head, Left Hand shrewdly laughed at the English words. "Tell me more, Wild Hawk," he said, wishing there were more time to learn them all in one sitting.

"Why do you want to learn the *wasicun* tongue now?" Prairie Wolf asked, looking from Left Hand to their leader. "You did not wish to know when Standing Hawk was teaching our village, nor when Red Hawk did the same."

With a shrug and a sly look, Left Hand explained, "I would like to speak to the white dogs that follow us. If I kill one or more of them, I would like to tell them of my hatred for their race."

Wild Hawk's face darkened. "If these are whites that track us, Left Hand, I want no senseless killing and scalping. If they are only settlers that seem to follow, leave them be. Only if they are the wicked *wasicun* soldiers will you attack. If they are of many numbers, do not attack but lead them away from this camp. Do you remember the *wasicun* who was with Precious Fire in her relative's house? Take that one alive if he is with these who track us, for it is my wish to deal with that one myself. Is this understood?"

It was Left Hand who spoke next as they passed the pipe around their circle. "I remember his face well. You told me in Mankato that he is the *wasicun* soldier who would not let you collect Red Hawk's possessions."

"*Sha,* yes," Wild Hawk said. "Now, if those who track us are the Hoha Indians, I would like you to slay

213

as many as you can. Take one or two captive if you must. We are close to Dakota Territory now, and we can move faster and easier away from danger of the white soldiers. Soon we will come to my father's village. My heart tells me that the Hawk People have gone to hide in the Pahasapa Hills and there is no one left in Red Hawk's village."

"It is your village now," Left Hand reminded. "Your people, Wild Hawk." He looked aside with glittering black eyes of envy and bitter resentment.

One of the other young braves asked, "Will we move on in the golden light of the rising sun?"

"Sha," Wild Hawk said, standing now, arms folded Dakota fashion over his strong, wide chest. "Bring me as many of the rebels as you can catch alive. I wish to question them, torture them if need be—" Left Hand shuddered as Wild Hawk added, "—for the murder and scalping of Audrina's beloved relative!"

The savage blood in Left Hand drained from his face, leaving him looking almost pale. He turned away from Wild Hawk, afraid to look him in the eyes, afraid the Indian leader would read the sudden fear in his own. There was hatred in his slaty eyes, too, hatred for all white people—especially for one with moss-green eyes and dark fire hair, who was bringing much trouble and danger to him. Wild Hawk would not ride with them, so great was his fear of losing Precious Fire.

As Left Hand strode from the circle that was breaking up, his mind worked furiously and with desperation to find a solution. It was becoming increasingly difficult to find a way to get rid of Audrina, but get rid of her he would. He must find the white soldier Powell, even if he had to ride all the way back to the Minnesota River Valley. Time was growing short. If Audrina spoke to Wild Hawk, if she told him that she had seen Left Hand do the killing and the scalping, Left Hand was dead, as sure as the tree stump blocking his path at that moment.

The moon was making an appearance in the twilight-blue sky by the time Left Hand neared the stream. He crept up and watched the women bathing in the smoky purple shadows lent by the scrub pines, tall brush, and rock outcroppings.

Lustfully, Left Hand grew hard, watching Snow Maid trickle water from her slim fingers onto her shapely white thighs and run her hand around to the curve of her bottom. She squatted, rinsed a torn piece of petticoat in the water, and then stood to wring it out. Snow Maid was relaxed and content with her world, for now. . . .

Just about to ask himself where Tawena could be, Left Hand felt a cold object slide beneath his throat. The deep feminine voice snarled, "Brother, what are you gawking at?" Then Tawena lowered the blade and laughed low in her throat.

Disgruntled for the moment, Left Hand felt his desire droop as he watched the knife being drawn away. Swiftly, he brought Tawena's attention back to the bathing women. "Look, they stand together now and speak softly."

"They only wonder at my disappearance!" Tawena made a disgusted sound. *"Hau!"* She glanced up at the sky. "It grows late. I must return to camp to put up the tepee." She looked aside. "I am much ashamed of deceiving my chief."

"Why did you do it?" Left Hand asked his sister

215

softly. "That was stupid of you; you have only confined yourself when you need not be."

"I want to warn the captives to hold their tongues. I must keep an eye on them. I was just pondering a way to warn the red hair that she must keep silent on the matter of her relative's killing."

"I have learned some of the *wasicun* tongue this night. I will tell you quickly, then you must take Audrina back to camp." He kept his eyes on the captives all the while he explained. "You must do this: You will warn the firecat woman that Snow Maid will get the same as the deceased one if she ever speaks of that night to Wild Hawk. There is no other way. I know it is dangerous, for she will be suspicious and Wild Hawk speaks the white man's tongue well.

"I think we must move quickly. It grows late," Left Hand continued. "I will have to join the other braves soon. Wild Hawk will stay with the camp. I knew he could not leave Precious Fire to track with us. If it is the rebels who follow us, I will warn them not to show during the day. They might even have to slay some of Wild Hawk's braves if they get suspicious."

"You will do what you must to keep the secret of our alliance with the *Hoha* safe, Left Hand. Now, I will leave you with Snow Maid." Tawena's eyes twinkled knowingly at her brother's excitement in watching the white hair. "You will make certain she never talks?" Her brother nodded, his eyes gleaming with lust. "Good. Work fast, my brother, and enjoy." Tawena returned to the captives.

"Where is Sadie?" Audrina asked when they reached

216

the clearing, which was a small valley hidden from view of any who might approach. It was as deep as the height of a tepee, and this was where Tawena would set up the temporary dwelling. She walked to the travois and Audrina followed, repeating her question.

Tawena only grunted. She knew what Audrina was asking and she wanted to ignore the white woman as long as possible. Then Tawena looked up and her face sagged in disappointment. Left Hand had forgotten to give her the *wasicun* words!

"I asked you a question." Audrina was frantic now. "Sadie was with us when we left the stream. Where is she now?"

Worry began to gnaw at Audrina's taut nerves as she glanced over her shoulder toward the path that led to the stream. "Sadie might be in trouble. I am going to look for her!"

Before Audrina could walk ten feet, Tawena was upon her, the knife threatening her throat, her other hand yanking the braid. "Say-Dee . . . *Sunihanble*. Say-Dee *Sunihanble*."

"Sunihanble?" Audrina shook her head perplexedly. "What does that mean? Is it a name?"

Audrina could not know that Tawena was saying Fox Dreamer in Dakota, trying to make her believe that Sadie was occupied with Fox Dreamer in the woods. But Audrina did not have to be convinced of anything. She knew Tawena was keeping her from going back for Sadie and this made her all the more determined to see for herself.

"Say-Dee—"

Tawena never finished. "You lie!" Audrina shouted, whirling and jabbing her elbow into Tawena's ribs.

217

"Sadie is *not* all right!"

The Indian woman's strength was far greater than Audrina's. But Audrina gave it all she could, whirling about to knock Tawena on the side of her head. Momentarily stunned, Tawena's grasp loosened on the knife and it fell. It skittered across the clearing and came to rest at the tips of Prairie Wolf's moccasins. He grinned as another brave joined him, and they stood watching as the slimmer woman launched her full weight against Tawena.

As the fight continued, with the dainty *wasicun* holding her own, Prairie Wolf asked Red Feather, "Where is Wild Hawk? I think he would not like to see his pretty captive in this battle. He would be worried that her lovely flesh would be marred. See how Tawena tries to scratch her? Perhaps we should stop them now. Warrior woman might kill the little *wasichu*."

"I do not think so."

"She is not as strong as Warrior Woman. She will soon tire."

"I still do not think so," Red Feather insisted.

"Tawena has been trained as a Sioux warrior." Even as he said this, Prairie Wolf was surprised at how Precious Fire kept out of harm's way. She resisted all the blows by sidestepping.

Astonished and full of admiration, Red Feather nodded his head laconically. "The white girl is strong for one so small, and she fights like a wildcat. *Hau!* Look how she tries to tear Tawena's hair out by the roots!"

"But look, Tawena goes for her fallen knife! I do not think we should allow her to cut the little firecat up into ribbons. Her pretty face will be scarred for life."

218

"We will wait and see," said Red Feather.

"Where is Wild Hawk?" Prairie Wolf wanted to know, in case the fight started to get out of hand.

"He is speaking to the warriors and examining Cold Knife's horse. The Paint might be lame and—Look! Tawena is close to her knife."

"*A-i-i-i*, but the little cat kicks it aside!"

Audrina tangled her legs with Tawena's, and down they crashed into the grass and dirt. Legs and thrashing arms poked every which way; long-nailed fingers tried to claw; black hair and red hair came loose; skirts climbed thigh-high, and first one was on top and then the other. They breathed hard, they panted, their faces red and labored. Their high-pitched shrieks rent the air.

For a moment, the two braves cheered as Precious Fire sat on top, pinning Tawena facedown in the dirt. Then she flew off as Tawena heaved with all her might, unseating her tiny tormentor. They whirled about, facing each other again. Wild Hawk had heard their cries and he was swiftly coming to investigate. . . .

Tawena led the way along the path, walking Indian file. Audrina was in the middle. Sadie took up the rear, humming a tune softly to herself. . . .

Left Hand's attack was swift as a striking snake. He came up from behind, clamping one arm across her breasts, the other across her mouth. Alarmed, Sadie tried yanking and clawing her attacker's hands away, but she only succeeded in having both her arms twisted up behind her back. Her eyes were wild and frightened, her heart thumping wildly in her breast.

219

Suddenly, she was being dragged into the clustering bushes. She looked up at last and saw her attacker through shocked and frightened brown eyes. Her mind raced toward some way she could possibly escape, but Left Hand had her locked in his evil clutches. There was no way out.

Tears stung Sadie's eyelids as Left Hand squeezed and pinched her soft flesh. His hand came up between her legs, and his cruel fingers pushed aside the raggedy bloomers and probed until Sadie cried out in pain.

"Damn you, you evil savage!" Sadie cried out, but to no avail.

Left Hand grunted in what sounded like satisfaction at finding Snow Maid still a virgin. If he had only looked down at his hand, he would have been very surprised as what he saw. As it was, he was just in too much of a hurry to notice the red smear of blood.

Sadie knew terror as Left Hand shoved her down into the new green sprigs and spongy moss and shucked his leggings. She gasped when she beheld the huge, throbbing organ as it sprang to life.

"Don't you dare!" she cried, horrified at what she saw.

Left Hand smiled now. Her fear only served to make him all the more excited and eager to mount her. She was so soft, so alive, so womanly, and his lust was fueled by hatred.

Oh God, she prayed, make the sky fall down on him. Don't let him do this dirty and nasty thing to me. I'm a maid untouched, Lord, and I want to remain one for the man I love. *Fox Dreamer,* her mind cried out because her voice would not function. Please, *please,* someone, stop this torment and let me go free!

Falling on top of Sadie, Left Hand at once spread her legs wide, so wide that Sadie thought her flesh would tear where her legs met. He gathered her soft buttocks in his hands to lift her body from the ground, then his hard body clenched as he readied himself for the powerful thrust.

"No . . . no . . . no . . ." Sadie gave the weak utterance. "No. Not you." Please, Lord, *not this man*.

Sadie's head was rolling from side to side, pathetic tears sliding from her cheeks to drip forlornly onto the ground. Dear Lord, she had never been so afraid in her life. If only there were some way to get out of this!

"Snow Maid, now you will know what it is like to have a real man. Your first . . ." He breathed deeply of her womanly scent, which was driving him wild. "Your very first."

Sadie stifled a tortured groan, begging, "Hurry, will you? Get it over with . . . or forget it!"

Left Hand tried out his newly acquired English on her. "Not want woman like this. You not fight." He shook her. "You fight. I like woman fight!"

Dumbstruck, Sadie blinked as she looked up at Left Hand. His pronunciation was slipshod at best, but she could understand him. "You—you can speak English! Get off me! Can't you see it's my time!"

Blushing from ear to ear, Sadie showed him the evidence. Left Hand shot off the white woman as if she had the plague. He brushed himself off vigorously, as if he'd caught a disease, and pinning her alternately down with his feet, he climbed into his leggings as swiftly as possible.

"You fool Left Hand!" he hissed down at her while she adjusted her clothing as best as she could under the

221

circumstances. "Fool Left Hand . . ."

"No!" she exclaimed softly. "You fooled yourself, idiot!"

Left Hand reached down and pulled Sadie to her feet, then stood away from the "dirty" woman. Sioux females at this time of the month were outcasts, isolated from the rest of the tribe. Tawena should not be in the *isnatipi,* but Snow Maid! He was angry, spitting mad at this turn of events

All of a sudden Left Hand's body came alert. One of the braves was giving the bird call; it meant he should come immediately. His fingers throttled Sadie's delicate throat, and he hissed into her face, "Keep mouth shut."

"About what?" She stared up at him curiously with her lovely brown eyes. "I don't understand. Speak clear, will you?"

"Kill Precious Fire," he began slowly. "Kill . . . Kill . . . Precious Fire." He shook her to make her understand.

"What?" Sadie looked horrified. "You are going to kill Audrina? My friend?"

"Sha, dead," he said with a vigorous nod. "Audrina be dead. You no talk of Left Hand killing old *wasichu."* He made a motion to describe a plumper woman.

Sha must mean "yes," she deduced.

"Wasichu? Woman?" Sadie inquired. She frowned. "Oh, I have it. You don't want me to . . . ah . . . talk about the night you killed," she gulped, "—the night you killed Audrina's aunty?"

"Kill aunty." He nodded again. His slaty eyes grew dark and ominous then. Sadie stepped back. Left Hand pointed to himself and snarled, *"Kill Audrina!"*

"Oh!" Sadie gasped. "You will kill Audrina if I tell." She shook her head. "I don't understand." For a moment, Sadie frowned at the ground and then her face lit up. "Wild Hawk doesn't know about this then?" Sadie heaved a sigh of relief. "Thank heaven! I thought he ordered you to do the killing because he wanted to be rid of her . . . b—because he thought she was a nuisance. But you are the one who thought that. You are the one who hates white people. You would kill Audrina or me at the drop of a hat"—her eyes narrowed—"if Wild Hawk was not here!"

"Kill Audrina!" Left Hand hissed again, eyeing the blonde darkly.

Sadie frowned and pursed her pink lips. "Someone is coming. You go." She shoved at his back and he flinched away. "Go on, go on, before you are caught with me." She shivered.

Finally understanding what Snow Maid was telling him, Left Hand moved. Then he frowned perplexedly, slipping quietly and stealthily away in the direction of the bird call.

So Left Hand thought. Actually, he went toward the last bird call, which had been a real bird. The first bird call had sounded near the path where Fox Dreamer now walked. He had been alerted to Snow Maid's disappearance when he and Wild Hawk had come upon the two women deep in battle. Fox Dreamer had searched the area while the chief had been breaking up the fight, and Wild Hawk himself had almost killed Tawena with his bare hands. He had choked her until she turned purple. The only thing that saved Tawena was the little firecat coming to her rescue, incredible though that seemed, too.

Fox Dreamer's main concern now was for Snow Maid. Tawena and Left Hand had been acting peculiarly, and Left Hand was nowhere to be found, either. Fox Dreamer hoped there had been no foul play.

"Snow Maid," Fox Dreamer called softly. His black eyes darted here and there, watching for any movement in the grass or brush. Wild Hawk had given them permission to use their Indian rifles now that they were close to Dakota Territory.

Fox Dreamer carried his rifle horizontally at his hip, the feathered thongs blowing softly in the night breezes. It was growing steadily darker, and soon all he would be able to make out would be blurred images. He moved fast and lightly on his feet.

"Snow Maid," he called in a near whisper. "Where can you be, my flower?" He was afraid she had come to harm; he could not stand it if she had been hurt.

Suddenly two soft hands slipped from behind and over his eyes. Fox Dreamer swallowed hard. It was a woman; he could feel shapely breasts pressed against his back. There was a playful whisper in his ear.

"Guess who?"

Dropping his rifle, Fox Dreamer whirled about and pulled a shivering Snow Maid into his fierce embrace. He was crazy with desire for her. He had never kissed her; he had only ridden close to her on his horse, and that had been enough for Fox Dreamer to realize Snow Maid was the woman of his dreams.

Sadie's heart beat crazily as Fox Dreamer lowered his boyishly handsome face, and like the gentlest whisper of wind, his firm and silken lips captured hers in a tender kiss.

224

Fox Dreamer's head lifted suddenly and his beautiful Indian words tore through her like fire: *"Tecihila,"* he said over and over, the Dakota words meaning "I love you."

Tenderly, Sadie touched his chin with a finger. "What are you saying to me? What does it mean?"

Fox Dreamer realized she had asked what the word meant. With a pained expression, he looked at her and his heart repeated it, hoping it was in his eyes. *"Tecihila, I love you."*

While Snow Maid gazed at him wonderingly, he touched her lips, pronouncing the word, teaching her, wanting her to repeat it.

Sadie understood what he wanted and listened carefully, then copied his lips. "Tay-CHEE-khee-lah." She stood on her toes and kissed his lips. "I love you," she said with all her heart and soul.

It was in her lovely brown eyes. Fox Dreamer slowly bent his knees and retrieved his rifle, never taking his eyes off Snow Maid. She wanted to tell him about Left Hand but knew she must learn the Sioux language in order to do this. She could use sign language, but something dark and terrible in Left Hand's eyes kept coming back to warn her to hold her silence—or else!

With arms about each other's waists, they walked slowly back to the camp. They understood each other very well. They were in love.

Chapter Nine

The shallow, flat-bottomed valley was shadowed in a dreamlike field of ghostlike fog as Wild Hawk stood on the highest hill overlooking the camp. Raising his jet head, he gazed at the obscure moon, then lowered it again to gaze at the fuzzy outline of the small tepee Tawena had erected.

Wild Hawk recalled what had taken place down there not long ago. The sight he had come upon would always be stamped upon his mind. He had never witnessed such an energetic and lusty scrap between two women. Precious Fire had been holding her own— no, she had done better than that. She had fought like a mountain cat defending her kittens!

This Dakota warrior was puzzled, for Precious Fire indeed seemed to be protecting something—or someone. He had watched as Snow Maid returned to camp with Fox Dreamer. Wild Hawk realized how much Fox Dreamer already loved and cherished the fair, ethereal girl.

He felt the slight tug on the rope at his wrist and

226

turned to look at Audrina. Her head moved and she met his gaze. His eyes studied her features, slowly taking in her loveliness until he came to rest on her dusky lips. He lifted a finger.

"Woman." He spoke to her in a firm, husky voice. "Beautiful woman . . . Precious Fire. It is good you are unharmed."

A spark of excitement raced through Audrina's nerve ends as Wild Hawk's fingers sensuously trailed along her arm. Was he her hero or her enemy? "I only have a few bruises, Wild Hawk."

Audrina shivered as she anticipated Wild Hawk's wondrous touch, which brought hunger and ecstasy. She did not even resist. He was like the sun she needed for warmth and growth to stay alive. She had waited so long for him to touch her tenderly again. His index finger traced the outline of her lips, then slipped to her throat, across her collarbone, and down the length of her arm. The finger was joined by several more sensitive, caressing members. He moved ever so slowly.

Freeing her braids, he then ran his coppery-hued fingers through her abundantly thick hair. She breathed of his scent deeply, and the dampness of his buckskins added to the heady, masculine essence that was Wild Hawk. His caresses grew bolder, pressing her into a delicious intimacy.

When Wild Hawk felt her breasts, Audrina experienced the shimmery tension that made her glow within. His hands became even bolder, going inside her bodice, arrogant in the power he wielded over her. He pulled her tightly against him and Audrina could feel his bold, swelling desire against her belly. With the rope between them as a reminder of her imprisonment, Wild Hawk

227

bent and slowly captured her lips. He cupped her chin as he taught her to meet and explore his thrusting tongue. He tasted the sweetness of her mouth. She tasted him.

In the pale light of the moon Audrina and Wild Hawk stood kissing, one bronze hand spread at the small of her back, hers wound at his nape, stretching as far as the rope would allow. The fingers of his other hands were caressing and rolling the sensitive points of her breasts, going from one to the other. They stood out in excited twin peaks beneath his knowing fingers.

Forgotten were the suspicions and mistrust they had harbored for each other. There was only the crimson flame that grew and continued to radiate between them, their bodies feeding each other heightening pleasure.

Pushing the bodice of the shift aside, Wild Hawk lowered his head to her breast. With the tip of his tongue he flicked the nipple. Audrina's hands flew to Wild Hawk's silken hair. Her fingers threaded through it as he swirled his tongue around the responsive bud, driving her to ever higher excitement.

Soon Audrina would share his bed, know his thrust, and grow even closer to the savage who owned her body and soul.

Wild Hawk was thrilled, triumphant, that she had learned to want him as he wanted her. Beneath her shift, his fingers moved back and forth across her silken mound. When she moaned in hot wanting, his thumb entered her slowly, then moved faster and harder until she sobbed in shameful wanting of release.

"Oh, Wild Hawk," she cried, "I want you."

"So you will have me, and Wild Hawk will have

228

Precious Fire. We will be one, as it should be."

"Yes . . . oh, yes."

Audrina could feel her thighs quivering as he lifted her off her feet and carried her in his arms. He moved swiftly then, setting her down near a tree trunk as he stripped off his leggings. He removed the rope still binding them together at the wrists and tossed it aside. Audrina pulled the deerskin shift over her head and let it fall at her feet.

A thousand joys shone upon Wild Hawk's face as he looked down at the shift, then at her naked splendor. The throbbing pulse of Indian drums could be no wilder in her veins or louder in her heart and mind as Wild Hawk came to her. He felt her swollen breasts, delighting in the creamy texture of the mounds and caressing her nipples, which were erect and eager with passion and desire. She moaned softly. The primal rhythm surrounded them while they stood with their flesh touching and then began to move in a slow, primitive dance of love and passion.

The sudden bite of his teeth in the shadows of her shoulder teased and tormented her. Audrina tipped her head back, arching her neck and exposing a throbbing vein that he stooped to nibble. She straightened and stared into the dark pools of his eyes. Audrina's hands slid to his waist and held him while she swayed toward the flat muscles of his bare stomach. She boldly pressed her body closer to his, her secret place seeking contact with his swollen shaft as he gracefully lowered her to the ground beneath the tree.

Brazenly, Audrina arched her hips, and in that single motion Wild Hawk took her shapely behind in his hands to help her in the pleasurable endeavor. He slid a

229

hand between her thighs to stroke her and she moved eagerly against his hand. Then he lifted her. With an animal grace, he fitted himself to her body. He wrenched back momentarily, gaining momentum. Then his engorged shaft plunged to enter her—hot, hard, and swift. The movement was so powerful and sudden that she jerked in a convulsive reflex and cried out, not in pain but in pleasure.

"Love me," she murmured against his ear. "Love me, Wild Hawk. Just keep loving me and never stop."

In the heat of passion, he answered her in Dakota, "I do love you, my Petala. My heart loves you completely. You are my reason for being . . . my heart . . . my soul . . . my flame!"

Her passion taking on greater fire, she lifted her hips to meet the next thrust and gasped at the savage sensation of their mating. Slowly, deeply, he moved inside her, taking her wonderfully, deliberately, with skill. He bunched and relaxed his muscled thighs. Now he moved faster and harder. Now slower again. Faster. Faster.

In a wild mating rhythm his body plunged and lifted, and she slid her fingers into the damp silk of his ebony hair. Piercing the dark recesses of her womanhood in a savage fashion, he sought deeper contact, pulling her hips gently down to sink her feminine core upon his shaft.

The mist-shrouded moon rose ever higher, casting a pale bluish light over the hill. It made the earth look unreal, the trees and the ghostly waters and life itself. Tentacles of jeweled mist wrapped around the naked flesh of the lovers, dreamily blurring the bronze warrior and his captive white beauty.

Audrina leaned her head against his shoulder and her eyes drifted shut in ecstasy. When the waves of incredible pleasure crept up on her again, she lolled her head back, still undulating her hips. Her auburn tresses flowed wildly over her naked shoulders, over his arms. Cresting ecstasy, she came with him in a passionate fluttering, soaring to the heights of passion.

Beautifully, the night scene changed. The unearthly fog lifted. Midnight mist lingered. The stars came out and glittered like diamonds and the moon glowed like a yellow topaz. Wild Hawk's eyes drank in her moonlit loveliness. Their bodies investigated and mated again and again. Wild Hawk discovered and charted every quivering, sensitive inch of Audrina's sensuously slim body. He skillfully brought her to peak after peak of soaring ecstasy.

Rapturously, she sat in his lap as he loved her. Then she pressed his powerful frame back to the place where they had warmed the earth with their mating. Wild Hawk felt hot passion build in his loins as she explored his lean waist, his taut thighs, his firm behind. As he lay back she stationed herself above him. He was suspended in awe, impressed by her newly found skill as a lover, a temptress. With her hands on his hips, she pulled him to her until he rested on his elbows. Suddenly, he found even greater pleasure when he moved to her rhythm, her hips swaying to the undulations of love.

The lovers spoke no words; there was no need for them. He carried her to the twinkling waters of the stream and washed her. Her face glowed and her eyes were like dark gray-green jewels. Then he allowed her to wash him. When they came out and lay upon the

231

mossy bank, he slid his tongue over her breasts, her waist, her belly. He parted her secret lips with his fingers and his tongue began to slide back and forth across her turgid flesh. A strand of his long ebony hair blew sensuously across her thighs and Audrina arched.

A mysterious excitement raced through her. He slipped between her auburn curls and she gripped his muscled shoulders. Then she pushed her fingertips into the damp silken strands of his thick ebony hair. She clutched handfuls when he became bolder, licking her supple body, possessing her and thrusting in a miniature play of love.

Never had she known lovemaking could be this way. She peaked over and over, and then his manhood revitalized and he took her again. They soared to a passionate fulfillment, her release even stronger and more abandoned than before. Fire seared them together for a moment in time, and then she saw her glorious savage above her. His white teeth flashed as he smiled like a triumphant warrior whooping his final victory.

Audrina was in the crook of Wild Hawk's arm, just about to sigh her delicious contentment, when a strange bird call sounded from the wood and the brush.

Coming instantly alert, Wild Hawk shot to his feet, dragging her and her shift with him. A finger was crossed over his lips as he motioned with his other hand for her to dress swiftly. He was into his leggings before she had the shift tugged down to her calves.

She stepped out into the moonlight. "What is it?" she asked, looking over her shoulder. "Oh!" she cried when he dragged her back into the shadows.

"Do not ever show yourself until I give you leave to

do so!" he warned darkly.

Audrina frowned her displeasure. "What do you mean? It was only a little bird. See, there is no one there."

"You do not know who could be out there. You must let Wild Hawk check it out first to see if it is safe."

"You mean it could be my people?" she asked.

"That is what Wild Hawk means—yes. Your people would not treat you kindly after you've been with Indians. They would believe the worst, that Audrina Harris has been sleeping with Indians."

"Willingly, of course," she said. "But you are right. I have been sleeping with an Indian. Willingly or not, they would frown upon me. I understand. I would be welcomed at first, then they would treat me as an outcast." *What if they were to learn of my Indian blood, as surely they would, once I was brought back to Mankato? Either way, I am a captive.*

"You will always be with Wild Hawk, Audrina. Now that I have tasted of your love, you will be my captive forever."

"I don't want to be a captive. I want to be free, Wild Hawk. I will grow to hate you if you keep me like a caged bird."

Pressing her back to his chest, he growled against her damp hair, "Love me or hate me as you will, but you will never be taken from me! And you shall never leave me, Audrina!"

She felt hate. She felt love. Fear. Joy. Anger. Lust for revenge. A desperate need to escape. To stay. Her eyes stared sightlessly at the moonlit swath upon the earth. How could she experience so many tangled emotions at the same time?

233

Audrina broke from his hold and whirled to face him. "I do hate you, *I do!* You have taken enough from me, Wild Hawk. I will not let you steal more of my heart." She noted that his eyes glittered strangely but she went on. "You have made me your captive . . . your harlot. I will not be that for any man ever again, especially not to a full-blooded Indian!"

Wild Hawk's body went rigid. His eyes like black stones, his brow looking thunderous, he took her arm in a viselike grip, snatching her close to his hostile face. "You were not so ashamed to give yourself to an Indian many times this night!"

Her chin jutted upward. "I did it because you wanted me and you would have forced me if I resisted," she answered shakily.

Force. He almost laughed outright at the word. He listened for the bird call again, and when he was satisfied it was not one of his braves returning, he gripped her shoulders again. "You allowed Wild Hawk to come into you because you wanted me as I want you. I can feel you shiver. You would lie with me again if you could. But you cannot. You are angry now and there is no love in Precious Fire now. You have hidden it beneath a dark blanket."

Embarrassed and ashamed, Audrina looked aside. How could she tell him that she was afraid all of a sudden, more afraid than she had ever been? She was falling in love with Wild Hawk more each day. More each minute she stayed with him. Before long, she would be completely his. Heart and soul. Body and mind. Oh Lord, she had succumbed much too easily to his touch and the thrilling persuasion of his lips and husky voice. What if she became pregnant with his

234

child? Where would she be then? A sinning heathen. A stupid squaw forever pregnant and slaving over a primitive cook fire.

"You are angry too, Wild Hawk. We are always in conflict with each other. It will always be like this. You are an Indian and I am a white woman. We come from entirely different worlds." She hung her head dejectedly. "I am your captive. You are my . . . fear."

"Fear?" He held her face between his hands so she couldn't turn away from his penetrating eyes. "What do you mean by this? Audrina, I do not understand your mood or your words."

"I will never be anything but your captive," she answered brokenly. "You could never make me your wife."

"Why could I not, Audrina?" He looked at her incredulously.

Her lashes flew upward. "Why?" she asked, a sad, faint smile crossing her features. "Because you are an Indian and—" *I am part Sioux Indian, too, but he would never believe me.* "As I said, our worlds are as different as night and day. There is nothing romantic about huddling beneath a blanket or a hide to keep warm. I could never live in a tepee or a lodge with dirt for a floor. I want curtains, windows, a stove, a real bed." She shrugged. "Things you could never give me, Wild Hawk. Things you would not want for yourself because you are not civilized and you shun progress. I've had all these things and could never live long without them. I want to work as a seamstress, as my Aunt Kate did; that is a challenge all women of the 1860's face. I want to be free—free to be my own person, my own woman."

235

Pushing his face close to hers, he gritted out, "And you would not have a white man to share your bed if you were forced to stay with me. That is what Audrina really wants. A white man. White babies. You would be ashamed to have a child who would turn out half Indian." He shook her. "But most of all, you would want a white man to make love to you—Powell!"

Audrina leaned away to look into his dark, furious face. She immediately said, "Joe? You mention him again. . . . The first time you were jealous, then you mentioned that together we had taken your father's medicine pouch. Why do you always bring Joe into our conversations? Joe is not my lover, Wild Hawk, and—"

Holding her by one arm, Wild Hawk gazed into her willful face, then gave her a little shake. "Powell is the man you would wed." Raising an eyebrow inquisitively, he went on more harshly than intended, "You would escape and go back to the *wasicun* warrior. This is why you are angry. I keep you from returning to your lover."

"Joe was never my lover. I tried to tell you." Audrina's shoulders jerked in frustration. "Why can't you listen to me, Wild Hawk?" She turned aside. "It does not matter, anyway. You and I can never be one."

"You are like a whore when you speak this way. You let me love you through the night and now you swear we cannot be one," he ground out, his face shadowed by a frown.

Audrina flinched sharply at the harsh spoken words. "I said we can never be one, and I mean it, Wild Hawk."

"Why do you keep your fear? You fear everything. The future can be ours, Precious Fire. It takes both rain and sunshine to make a rainbow."

236

Wild Hawk stared at this white woman who had gotten into his blood, his mind, who had wormed her way into his heart. He had made his own vow before taking her captive. He had told Audrina she would be his, in every way. Now she was. This night his lovemaking had been passionate, more than the first time, and had bound them together even tighter.

Taking up her wrist, Wild Hawk bound her to him with the rope once again. "You will ask me no more questions. You will not tell me you cannot live the Indian way. You will not dream of Powell any longer and wish to return to your home."

Audrina frowned. "Asking me to do all those things is like asking me to stop breathing. But for one: I do not dream nor moon over Joe Powell. He is as far as the most distant star to me."

"I am not asking," he hissed. "I am demanding! Now, follow me."

"What about the medicine pouch?" Her voice was low, and when he turned, she found herself gazing into sable-dark eyes surrounded by the hard planes of a face that was beautifully wild and primitive. "What are you going to do with it?"

Freezing in his tracks, Wild Hawk faced her squarely. "You were at the execution in Mankato, were you not?" he demanded harshly.

"Y—yes," she answered, utterly confused. "But what has that got to do with it? Everyone in town was there." She shrugged. "Well . . . almost. You were there, too. I saw you." She could not help but smile. "It was the first time I saw you, in fact."

"One of those braves was my father, Red Hawk," he proudly told her.

"Oh." Audrina felt a rush of compassion for Wild Hawk. "You watched him hang."

"I did not wish to humiliate my father by watching him suffer. I turned away before he—" Wild Hawk did not go on.

"What does that day have to do with the medicine pouch?"

Audrina suddenly answered herself: It had everything in the world to do with it. That was the day the hawk had dropped the pouch at her feet. She could not tell him this, for he would never believe such an incredible tale and it might only make matters worse between them.

"I will say this one thing. There is a spiritual aura that emanates from the pouch. You are lucky you did not destroy its value. It is forbidden for a woman to touch these personal pouches, so much more a white woman. You should be punished for touching it, and the usual method is to remove the hand of the guilty one." He heard her gasp and he went on stonily, "We will speak no more of it this day." Through the lightening twilight, he could see the weary braves returning. "Perhaps one day you will tell me what you and Powell were doing with it."

Audrina's mouth fell open. "Powell did not have a thing to do with it, and furthermore—"

"Henala!" He told her that was enough.

Audrina was pulled along by the persistent tug of the rope. "I don't even care if you kill me," she grumbled wearily, "and scalp me. Go ahead, take my hair. You already possess everything else I own—or *used* to own. You took my beloved Aunt Kate. You took my medicine pouch. My maidenhead. One of your fair

238

maidens even took my boots. What did I get?" She glared at the bronze shoulders that rippled with every catlike step he took. "A pair of moccasins. And an Indian lover."

"Where is Precious Fire?" Left Hand hissed outside the tepee as Tawena poked her head from the entrance, finishing the plaiting of her black shiny braid.

"Is she not sleeping outside in her blankets?" Tawena inquired.

"She is not out here," he told her. "I have searched the area and Wild Hawk is not anywhere to be found. He is gone, too."

"They must be here somewhere. You have not looked hard enough."

"I have told you, woman," he persisted. "They are nowhere in the camp."

"They they are outside the camp," she returned haughtily.

"Do not mock me, Tawena. I am your blood brother and we are in this together."

The Indian woman shrugged. "What did you find out? I am impatient to hear what happened."

"Keep your voice low," he demanded. He watched her nod. She clenched her hands tightly together and waited. "First tell me if you threatened the girl enough so that she will not speak of matters better left unspoken."

"*Sha, sha,* yes! Now tell me what you have learned. I am weary. I have not slept a wink this night. Look"— she raised her bleary eyes—"twilight comes. Tell me quickly before Wild Hawk and his woman come from

239

their love nest."

"Love nest?" Left Hand snarled in gnawing anger. "I am disgusted that Wild Hawk is seduced by that white beauty. She might come down with child. I wish to see no more half bloods in our tribe." He spat upon the ground near the tepee. "We must keep the Indian breed pure and noble."

"You say these things with venom in your blood, and yet you would mate with Snow Maid yourself. Are you two-faced like the white man?"

"No!" he immediately exclaimed. "I may lust after the white *winu,* but only with the thought in mind to degrade her and punish her for the white man's deception to our race. It is one way to get revenge."

"You are right. But if she comes down with child, you must seek the special herbs to destroy the babe before it comes.

Left Hand said nothing. He would not tell his indomitable sister that he had failed with the white woman. It was not his fault it had been Snow Maid's time.

Glaring at her brother, Tawena read the truth of the matter. Snow Maid had returned to the tepee all aglow and full of confidence. She had been with Fox Dreamer, but Tawena had been occupied otherwise and did not pay the couple much mind. It had been right after the fight between her and the firecat woman. No one had won. Wild Hawk had put a halt to the battle. Tawena was confident enough to realize she could have slain the white tigress if he had not come along just then.

"I would hear what you have learned," Tawena said sharply. "Was it the Rebels?"

240

ACCEPT YOUR **FREE GIFT** AND EXPERIENCE MORE OF THE PASSION AND ADVENTURE YOU LIKE IN A HISTORICAL ROMANCE

Zebra Romances are the finest novels of their kind and are written with the adult woman in mind. All of our books are written by authors who really know how to weave tales of romantic adventure in the historical settings you love.

Because our readers tell us these books sell out very fast in the stores, Zebra has made arrangements for you to receive at home the four newest titles published each month. You'll never miss a title and home delivery is so convenient. With your first shipment we'll even send you a FREE Zebra Historical Romance as our gift just for trying our home subscription service. No obligation.

BIG SAVINGS AND **FREE** HOME DELIVERY

Each month, the Zebra Home Subscription Service will send you the four newest titles as soon as they are published. (We ship these books to our subscribers even before we send them to the stores.) You may preview them *Free* for 10 days. If you like them as much as we think you will, you'll pay just $3.50 each and *save $1.80 each month* off the cover price. *AND you'll also get FREE HOME DELIVERY.* There is never a charge for shipping, handling or postage and there is no minimum you must buy. If you decide not to keep any shipment, simply return it within 10 days, no questions asked, and owe nothing.

GET FREE GIFT

MAIL IN THE COUPON BELOW TODAY

To get your Free ZEBRA HISTORICAL ROMANCE fill out the coupon below and send it in today. As soon as we receive the coupon, we'll send your first month's books to preview Free for 10 days along with your FREE NOVEL.

FREE

BOOK CERTIFICATE

ZEBRA HOME SUBSCRIPTION SERVICE, INC.

YES! Please start my subscription to Zebra Historical Romances and send me my free Zebra Novel along with my first month's Romances. I understand that I may preview these four new **Zebra Historical Romances** Free for 10 days. If I'm not satisfied with them I may return the four books within 10 days and owe nothing. Otherwise I will pay just $3.00 each; a total of $14.00 (a $15.80 value — I save $1.80). Then each month I will receive the 4 newest titles as soon as they come off the press for the same 10 day Free preview and low price. I may return any shipment and I may cancel this arrangement at any time. There is no minimum number of books to buy and there are no shipping, handling or postage charges. Regardless of what I do, the FREE book is mine to keep.

7-89

Name _____

(Please Print)

Address _____ Apt. # _____

City _____ State _____ Zip _____

Telephone ( ) _____

Signature _____

(if under 18, parent or guardian must sign)

Terms and offer subject to change without notice.

Get a **Free**
Zebra
Historical
Romance
*a $3.95
value*

Affix
stamp
here

"Only a few of them. I had to be very careful that the other braves did not see as I met with them."

Tawena's black eyes flashed. "How did you manage that without them seeing or growing suspicious?"

Left Hand's brow darkened. "One did see. Prairie Wolf came sneaking up on us."

With a gasp, Tawena said, "He saw you speak with Yellow Bear, leader of the *Hoha?*"

"One day I shall be leader of them, too." Left Hand hoisted his chin into the air. "I am almost that now."

"You covet the position of every young leader, Left Hand. Can you not be satisfied that one day you may be sub-chief to Wild Hawk?"

"You still presume you will become his bride?" He scoffed at her trampled vanity. "I witnessed the fight when I returned from the stream and saw for myself who Wild Hawk favored. He almost killed you with his hands and would have if the little firecat had not stepped in to beg him to cease."

"*Henala!* You know that it is not for us to meddle in our leader's affairs. Precious Fire is Wild Hawk's property, his captive. It was not for me to punish her. These were his own harsh words. I stepped out of line and he punished me instead of her. I hate Precious Fire! Now we must be careful in all we do. We cannot go against our Itancan and Chief, Wild Hawk."

Left Hand snorted. He would rather treat the captives like the white dogs they were, and it bothered him that Chief Wild Hawk insisted no one touch a hair on Precious Fire's head.

"Yellow Bear has killed Prairie Wolf," Left Hand said to change the subject. "He crept up on us and there was no other way. Prairie Wolf had already seen too

241

much. He saw how friendly I was with the Rebels. He was suspicious. When he began to move away quickly, Yellow Bear let his tomahawk fly."

Horrified by this news, Tawena shook her head sadly. "It is a bad thing to kill one of our own, Left Hand. The Rebels might do this, but I do not like senseless killing."

"Now Tawena sounds like Wild Hawk."

"I only say what I feel, my brother."

"We will not see the Rebels for a while. It is too dangerous." He laughed softly. "The Rebels have company, Tawena. Soon we can rejoice . . . when we are rid of the white beauty."

Excitedly, she asked, "Why is that? What has happened?"

"The *wasicun* soldier has joined the Rebels. He is the same one the firecat woman was frolicking with in her dwelling. He is Pow-ell. He has left his Army. He said he has come for Audrina Har-ris and he will do anything to get her back."

"He told you this? *How?*"

Slaty eyes glittered triumphantly. "He knows our tongue."

Angrily, Tawena demanded, "Why did you not tell me this before?"

He replied. "You did not ask. You were too busy flapping your own tongue!"

"Look!" Tawena alerted him. "Wild Hawk comes now." The playful sparkle left her black eyes, and she became serious and angry. "And look who walks behind him. *Ptah!*" Tawena spat and ducked back inside. "I wish to see no more."

Left Hand squared his shoulders before he went to

meet his chief. It was time to tell some lies . . . perhaps not too many.

Avoiding looking at Precious Fire, Left Hand walked right up to Wild Hawk and said," One of us is no longer." He glanced aside as the sun rose and the warriors stepped into view. "I will not say his name so his spirit does not return to earth."

Wild Hawk looked his men over. He, too, did not say the missing one's name. "How?" he asked simply, staring away from Left Hand.

"You were right, my chief. It was the Hoha Indians." He looked sideways to see if the warriors were watching. They all stared down at the gray morning earth, mourning the loss of a Sioux brother. "I got away, but the missing one was not so fortunate."

With a wooden stance, Wild Hawk said, "Did you bury our brother?"

Left Hand stammered for a few seconds, then when Wild Hawk looked at him sharply, he burst out with renewed vigor, "They took his body with them!"

"What do you mean?" Wild Hawk questioned harshly. He felt rather than saw Audrina come up beside him, staring from one to the other in curiosity at their rapid emotional bursts of Dakota. Unconsciously, he stroked her arm, unaware that Left Hand was glaring at her skin, thinking she was the shade of warm apricots.

Left Hand knew what his leader and his captive had been doing all night long. Hidden in the folds of his leggings, he clenched his hands with anger and jealousy.

Red Feather came to Left Hand's rescue just then. "It is true, Wild Hawk, great leader. They took the

243

body and rode away. We did not go after them."

"Why not?" Wild Hawk asked.

Red Feather, the youngest brave present, answered again meekly, "Left Hand said that more of them waited just over the hill. He said he had scouted that area and saw that their numbers were many. We could not have taken them, my chief."

The penetrating hawk-brown gaze turned on Left Hand again. "Is this so? There were so many that you could not fight them?" Wild Hawk's questioning was fierce, and Audrina looked up at him with a shiver.

As always, Left Hand felt the bite of Wild Hawk's prestige. "It is so. I have said this," he returned, his voice on the edge of irritation. "I do not lie."

"I believe you," Wild Hawk quickly stated. "You may go now and ready your mounts for travel. Give them water and let them graze until the sun lifts over the earth, then we will go from this place."

Catching the inflection in Wild Hawk's tone as he took her and their surroundings in at a glance, Audrina read into it: He wants to be gone from this place where they had shared such exquisite passion. He must have a great desire to forget what happened here.

Giving the muscular length of Wild Hawk's back a hostile glare as she set out to follow him, she thought, *Well, I feel the same way, too.*

Audrina winced angrily when he grasped the rope and tugged her along. She jerked back defiantly but soon saw the folly of her gesture when he snatched her up against his hard leanness. "Audrina," he began in a deep-timbered voice, "we can always go back into the woods if you wish to continue your defiance?"

Speaking in a suffocated whisper, she said, "No."

244

When he turned from her again, she walked with stiff dignity.

Cautiously, Audrina slowed upon eyeing Tawena at the opening of the tepee. Wild Hawk felt the pullback on the rope and stopped, turning to face her. Her flush deepened to crimson as his eyes raked her boldly, enigmatically, reminding her that they were now the most intimate of lovers.

"If you defy me and fight me, I will take you again and again. Remember this, Audrina."

Perusing her with dark, dancing eyes for several more moments, Wild Hawk then walked away, giving Audrina her freedom as he took the length of rope with him. With sign language, Tawena gave Audrina orders to help prepare for their leaving.

Sadie emerged from the tepee, her small face lighting up when she spotted Audrina. She had hated being confined with Tawena the night long. Before they had gone to sleep, Tawena had pinched and slapped her several times. Sadie wondered what she had done to anger the Indian woman, but she couldn't think of a single thing that might have aroused such burning irritation in Tawena.

"Audrey!" Sadie said almost in a whisper. "Listen close, I have something to say."

"There's no need to whisper, Sadie. Tawena cannot understand. Besides, even if she could understand *some,* she could not hear everything at the moment. She is too far away."

Grabbing Audrina's arm, Sadie stared around before speaking. "This is serious! I understand that Left Hand hates white people with a passion. . . ."

"That is nothing new."

"Let me finish, Audrey. Listen. You have to be wary of Left Hand. He killed Katherine, and Wild Hawk had nothing to do with ordering her murder!"

"I know Left Hand killed my aunt, Sadie, but I don't know if I believe Wild Hawk had absolutely nothing to do with it."

"I have reason to believe Wild Hawk is innocent." Sadie clenched her jaw and went on. "He doesn't even *know* that Left Hand was the one to kill Katherine."

Staring into Sadie's eyes, Audrina's brow furrowed with utter astonishment. "Are you saying it was all Left Hand's doing and none of Wild Hawk's at all?"

"Right. Left Hand threatened to kill *you* if I spoke about that night to anyone—especially Wild Hawk."

Audrina's green eyes conveyed the fury within her. "How did this conversation come about? Left Hand can't speak English, can he?"

"Oh, he speaks enough, all right." Sadie's voice rose an octave, then dropped quickly in volume. "But it's a little hard to understand; you have to piece it together. And don't I know from being around Tawena. . . . We can communicate with each other in a sign language of sorts. That's how different tribes speak with each other when they don't have the same dialect."

"Shh," Audrina hushed Sadie. "Act normal, as if we haven't even talked to each other yet, if Tawena looks our way."

Unconsciously, Audrina's mouth pursed tightly as she wondered how much of Sadie's account held truth. If Wild Hawk did not know about Left Hand being the one to slay her aunt, what would he do if he *did* know? It probably would make no difference. What did one more white person's life matter in this time of war

246

between the white man and the Indian? But the idea that Wild Hawk possibly had not ordered Left Hand to slay her aunt was something pleasant to think about. She would say nothing of this to Wild Hawk, however. Audrina was afraid she would put Sadie's life in danger . . . and very possibly her own, too.

A quarter of an hour had passed since Audrina joined Sadie. The morning sun had yet to find its way over the hill, but already it promised to be a warm day. Audrina found herself wondering what month it was. End of April? Beginning of May? And when would they reach their destination?

Audrina forced her eyes to meet Tawena's. "What do you want me to do now? I have packed the remaining pokeberries and the pemmican." She signed with her hands as she spoke. "I have rolled the blankets into bundles. I have helped you put the lodge poles on the travois. Is there anything else?"

Cold dignity created a stony mask of Tawena's face as she lifted her handsome nose in the air and walked away. Audrina knew when someone disliked her. In fact, Tawena *hated* her. When someone hated that much, she had to be awfully bitter. Too bad, Audrina thought. Tawena must not find much in life to be happy about, for she never had a kind word for anyone, and she hardly ever smiled at anything or anyone.

"I've never seen anyone so nasty and hateful," Sadie said, eyeing the woman who turned in a huff. "She really is a bitch."

"Sadie." Audrina shook her head in mock severity. "Where did you learn such language? Tsk, tsk."

"Pa used to swear a lot." The long lashes of her liquid brown eyes fluttered. "And whenever his friends came

247

over, they swore a lot, too. They used to get into the sauce and have some silly arguments over the Indians, and I never could tell who could outswear the other." She chuckled with happy memory. "Ma used to cover her ears and hightail it to the kitchen. Ma warned me to step outside the house. She always said, 'What goes in your eyes and ears has to eventually come out. And profanity is the worse thing to let in your body.' Like Ma said, if you take it in, you've got to let it out. The best thing to do is cover your ears like she did, I guess. But I thought it was kind of fun to hear Pa and his wild river buddies get all riled up and cuss. There wasn't much else to do at times."

"I know what you mean." Audrina combed the tangles out of her long hair as best she could, then she quickly made the thick braid that hung like a dark red arrow down her back. "Aunt Kate's gentlemen callers were always cussing out the Indians." Atop her head she placed the beloved slouchy hat, her face sober as she mused on the images that focused in her memory, subconsciously aware of the dull ache inside her breast. "I loved Katherine so much, Sadie."

"Please, Audrey, don't start crying or you'll get me going."

"I won't, I promise."

Sadie looked away and then back at her friend again. "Where did you sleep last night, Audrey? I didn't see your blanket out here anywhere when her Indian highness allowed me some privacy outside before bedtime. I thought I saw you up on the hill with Wild Hawk."

"You did."

"Oh. I see." Sadie dipped her blond head. "You don't

248

want to talk about it."

"I do not." Rubbing at her weary eyes, Audrina added, "Maybe another time, Sadie. But not now."

Catching sight of Wild Hawk standing at the crest of the hill, the emerald lights shifted in her eyes and her soft lips tingled in remembrance of his kiss—and other unbidden memories. His strong, muscular arms were upraised in prayer and praise, thanking *Wakantanka* for another day. Audrina offered up her own prayer to God for a new day, thanking Him that she and Sadie were still alive to enjoy yet another one. She also prayed fervently to discover a safe way to escape her bronze captor, the proud, powerful man she was falling more in love with each day.

"Did you get any sleep?" As she asked Audrina this, Sadie watched Fox Dreamer readying his horse on the fringe of the camp. "I mean," she went on when Audrina did not answer, "you look tired, Audrey."

"I am," Audrina said, then plunged on carelessly, "But you'll see . . . I will make it through the day."

Halfway through that same day, Audrina ate her careless words. Riding the extra horse that had belonged to Prairie Wolf, she began to slump over more and more with the rhythmic plodding of the horse's hooves. She was rudely brought alert when her horse strayed and she felt the tug on the rope strung between her and Wild Hawk's wrist.

Blessedly, Wild Hawk called a halt later that afternoon when she started to doze again. She awoke with a start, coming instantly alert as she noticed her surroundings. What looked to be a deserted Indian village also appeared to be an encampment that had been vacated *quite suddenly,* for possessions were

249

haphazardly strewn about everywhere.

As the rope was loosened, Audrina rubbed the chafed area that circled a band of redness about her wrist. Mildly surprised, she stared at Wild Hawk's long, lean back as he strode away without a single word, walking through the hastily abandoned encampment, leaving her in Tawena's harassing care.

Exasperated by her vulnerability to Wild Hawk, Audrina wished she could stoop down, pick up a stone, and throw it at his arrogant head. Her nostrils flared with fury. He was heartless, cruel to keep her bound to him all this time. But then her features softened as she reminded herself for the hundredth time that day: I am his captive. He is my captor, my enemy. How could she expect him to treat her any differently? She guessed she should be grateful he did not resort to torturing her physically.

Tawena nodded imperiously toward the sun-dappled creek beyond the wooded path that branched in different directions from the deserted encampment. With her bow and arrows slung over one shoulder, her back stiffly erect, she followed the captives to the creek to allow them to refresh themselves with a splash of cooling water and a moment of semi-privacy.

When that was done, they returned to the ghostlike encampment. Taking time to study her surroundings as she and Sadie walked behind Tawena, who was poking in and out of deserted tepees, Audrina experienced a sad, haunting feeling about the place. She saw Wild Hawk walking slowly among the tepees, the look on his noble face reflecting her own impressions.

Then the truth struck Audrina: This must have been his father's village. This was where Wild Hawk lived as

250

a boy during the summer months. Their habit must have been to move on before winter set in in earnest, but if that were so, why had they not taken the tepees? And why would they not be returning now that spring had warmed the land? As she asked herself this, Audrina noticed that the ground showed evidence of tepees that had been dismantled and taken away.

Turning around, Audrina caught sight of Wild Hawk emerging from one tepee that was more colorful than the rest, decorated with scenes of a great warrior in fierce battle and the daring buffalo hunt. She gazed at the arrangement of triangles, diamonds, and hourglasses in shades of turquoise, rusty red, ocher, and brown. The colorful border was much like the pretty design embroidered on her moccasins. Only a very skilled hand could have painted the scenes on the tepee, and she wondered where the Indians found their materials for dyes and paints. They must make their own, she guessed, out of natural, colorful substances from the earth and from plants.

Wild Hawk came to stand before Audrina, carrying several articles of clothing and something that looked like a crude bar of herbal soap. "There is a change of clothing here for you and Snow Maid," he said, handing the items over to her as his sensuous mouth curved into a smile.

"Snow Maid?" Audrina inquired, forgetting in her weary state that she had heard him pronounce the charming name once before. "Who is she?" Audrina cocked her head sideways.

"Your friend, Sadie." He watched for a sign of objection, but none was forthcoming. "Fox Dreamer has given her this name."

An indescribable thrill passed throughout Audrina as she stood looking at Wild Hawk in the shining brightness of the day. With a defiant toss of her head, she asked, "What is my name now, Wild Hawk? Why haven't you called me Precious Fire? Am I not to receive another of your precious Indian names to go by?"

"You are being willful again, Audrina." Wild Hawk's eyes sent her a private message. He went on, "If you are not careful, I will have to punish you."

Audrina tossed her gleaming red braid defiantly. "That will be nothing new, Wild Hawk. Knowing you has made me no stranger to correction. Every time I turn around you are breathing in my ear"—as she said this, he offered her a sudden arresting smile—"or taking something from me. . . ." She whipped the long, fiery braid over her shoulder. "This braid will bring many blankets or a—"

"You have said enough, Audrina." His uncompromising expression lost all humor as he turned his back on her to hand the items to Sadie.

"Come with me," Wild Hawk ordered Audrina in a crisp tone. "There is something I would show you." He led her toward the overgrown path branching away from the creek.

Tawena watched them go. Now, she thought, now the captive white beauty will learn what it is like to be treated as a slave.

Feeling a painful tug on her arm, Sadie reluctantly turned to face Tawena's hateful countenance. Tawena tried to take the armful of clothing from Sadie, but the white girl held on for dear life. When Tawena began to slap the young blonde and pull her hair, Sadie gave loud yelps and cries of fright. She would not have cried out, but her scalp was tender from Tawena's abuse the night before.

"What is this?"

Fox Dreamer had heard Snow Maid's cry and, leaving his horse with Red Feather, went to investigate. His dark eyes blazed angrily. "Why are you striking Snow Maid?" Fox Dreamer questioned Tawena harshly. "What has she done to deserve your correction?"

Tawena stood her ground to the boyishly handsome brave who was Wild Hawk's cousin and best friend. She answered, her eyes wide with false innocence, "She will not give me these things Wild Hawk told me to put into this tepee. See how greedily she hangs on to them. Wild Hawk said we must share these things."

"They are for you, too?" Fox Dreamer asked as his black eyes sharpened discerningly, knowing she was lying, for Wild Hawk had especially gathered these things for the white women's use.

"He did not say that," Tawena slyly answered. "He told me to take charge of these things. They are choice items left behind by Rainbow when they fled Red Hawk's camp in haste. He went into the tepee that Rainbow occupied after her father died. See"— Tawena reached out to finger the lovely doeskin material with decorations and beadwork created by Wild Hawk's sister's own hands—"Rainbow's own dress. She must have been in a hurry to have left such a pretty possession behind."

Fox Dreamer's jaw clenched, and his eyes narrowed slightly as he remarked, "Wild Hawk says that Strong Heart led our people to the Pahasapa Hills shortly after

253

Red Hawk's formal burial ceremony and when Wild Hawk left for Mankato. He thinks, too, they feared being forced onto the reservation. That is the reason they did not wait for Wild Hawk's return."

"I think it is so," Tawena said, grateful for the change in subject. "We have been gone a long time from the Hawk People." Tawena's eyes glittered like midnight ice. *All because Wild Hawk wished to return to Mankato to gaze upon the dwelling of his Precious Fire.* She knew this was true. There was something else Wild Hawk had returned to Mankato for, but she had no knowledge of what that could possibly have been. Perhaps to try to obtain his father's possessions? It did not matter to Tawena. All that mattered was finding a way to be rid of Precious Fire.

"I will put these things away now," Sadie said. She hesitated while they stared at her, then she employed sign language to convey her message.

After allowing the young woman to enter the tepee behind her, Tawena exhibited politeness toward Fox Dreamer, wishing to question the young brave before he vanished like morning mist. He was as quick and efficient in his movements as the Hoha Rebels, and he would have made an excellent warrior to ride with them. The problem was, there were too many *good* Indians lately. Wild Hawk did not wish to fight against the whites, but Tawena knew his mind could be changed. Perhaps a little poison in the pot and Wild Hawk's hatred could flare up again and burn as brightly and maliciously as before. Perhaps the captive beauty could be gently persuaded to poison his heart with loving deception. That is, if their forthcoming plans of action failed. But now for more important matters.

"I see how your eyes follow and caress Snow Maid," Tawena said in a kind voice to Fox Dreamer. She did not realize that he was studying not Snow Maid at the time but Tawena herself. "You should hurry to claim her before my brother does, my friend. Why do you not take her into the woods? I think Snow Maid would enjoy your advances."

"I will be the judge of that, Tawena." Fox Dreamer's eyes smiled gently into Tawena's shrewd face. "I will make love to Snow Maid when the time is right. Perhaps I will take her to wife first."

Tawena rasped out, "Take her to wife! Are you crazy, Fox Dreamer? You may take her as your captive mistress, but wife is out of the question." She could tell by the stiffening of Fox Dreamer's shoulders that he was becoming upset. So Tawena eased up. "Tell me, Fox, why did our great warrior Wild Hawk really make this overly long trip to Mankato? Surely," she laughed deeply, "not to take captives?" She peered up at the tall, boyishly handsome man. "There must be something else."

"I cannot speak, Tawena. It is not for me to say. All I know and can tell you is Wild Hawk felt compelled to return to Mankato after his father's hanging there."

Tawena's eyes narrowed a canny half inch. "Did he get something else there besides the silly and dull captive women? He has never shown interest in any woman before, neither white nor Indian. Why does this woman with fire in her hair seem so special to him?"

"She does not *seem* special," he informed. "It is

because *she is,* Tawena. Why do you think he named her Precious Fire?"

As Fox Dreamer left her, Tawena remained rooted to the same place, a deep frown set between her thin black eyebrows. Her nostrils flared angrily. It was too bad that no Dakota swearwords existed. If she had known any, she would have spoken them all!

Part Three

Savage Angel

A time to get, and a time to
lose; a time to keep, and a time
to cast away . . .
—Ecclesiastes 3:6

Chapter Ten

The sight of Red Hawk's Spirit Lodge aroused sad memories for Wild Hawk. The formal burial ceremony had already taken place without the body of his father. In Mankato, Red Hawk's body had been cut down along with the other thirty-seven warriors, placed in four waiting wagons, and driven to a shallow grave on a sand bar at the edge of the Minnesota River. The bodies had been covered in blankets and placed in two layers in the thirty-foot-long, twelve-foot-wide grave.

Wild Hawk's jaw clenched as he recalled what else had happened that night of December 26. *Wasicun* doctors from Mankato and nearby towns had descended on the grave and had stolen the bodies of the dead warriors, spiriting them away to use for anatomical studies and for dissection in their laboratories.

Now Wild Hawk set Audrina down, facing her toward the Spirit Lodge. Speaking low, with mystical reverence, he explained, "This is the Spirit Lodge of one of those Dakota who were hanged at Mankato. Red Hawk. This is sacred ground," he murmured.

"Ancestral ground."

"So," Audrina swallowed hard, "this is Red Hawk's Spirit Lodge."

He went on in a low voice to tell her that Red Hawk had wanted to be buried here, placed against a willow backrest inside the lodge set up on a hill, a low stone wall built indoors around the corpse. When she would have stepped inside, he told her, "There is no body there. As you must know, Red Hawk was buried with the others in the shallow grave at the edge of the Minnesota River. But his body did not remain there long. . . ." Wild Hawk could not go on with the sad account. It made him very angry to know he could not collect his father's corpse and bring it here—what was left of it after the *wasicun* doctors finished with it.

Instead, as Audrina stood transfixed, Wild Hawk went on to describe to her the procedure Red Hawk's body would have gone through. "As in the formal burial ceremony, which takes place with or without the body of the dead man, the Dakota Sioux pay their highest tribute to one of our leaders while building the Spirit Lodge. Before burial," he told her, "the corpse is painted and dressed in his best garments. The legs are bound together for a while, with knees somewhat flexed and hands folded over the chest.

"In the grave we place a filled pipe and a container of grease, along with all his personal possessions. The corpse is then dragged out of the tepee by a famous brave"—in this case it would have been Wild Hawk—"and carried to the Spirit Lodge amidst cries and much wailing."

"What would happen then?" Audrina whispered almost reverently, unhappy to see him look so forlorn,

260

his handsome face creased with his inner pain. She knew his age was nearing thirty, but at the time he appeared ten years older than that robust age.

"A warrior would cut off a braid from the hair of the deceased. Relatives closest to the dead man would gash their forearms and legs and wear their hair loose."

Remembering the fresh scars her fingers had touched when they'd first made love, wondering about them then and now, she asked, "Did you do this, Wild Hawk?"

"Of course," he answered. "We would remain in mourning until a man of eminence declared the period terminated. Four nights after the death there is a feast with ceremonial pipe and food offerings to the spirits. The braid is placed into a sacred bundle." He held up the familiar object and Audrina softly gasped. "Such bundles are highly regarded and carried by trusted women when the camp moves on."

"And," Audrina said with a loud gulp, "you say this is Red Hawk's medicine pouch?"

"That is correct."

Feeling suddenly happier than she'd been in a long time, Audrina smiled widely at the tiny white puffs of clouds in a beautiful Dakota-blue sky. With tear-stained cheeks, she stared at the hawklike face before her, hearing the song of the wind in the lofty pines.

"Then this has been my mission! I was chosen to bring it here!" She did not mention the name Minowa, but she would recall much later that she would have been spared much trouble if she had.

"Yes," he hissed, grabbing her wrist. "You might have been chosen to bring it here, but who stole it from my father? You and the *wasicun?*"

261

She stared at him before she could find her voice. "Why did you come to my aunt's house that night? What were you really doing there, Wild Hawk?"

"The sacred medicine bundle drew me there." For the moment, he would not add that he had desired to look upon her pretty face once again before he joined his people in the Dakota Territory. "I heard . . . things."

"You heard the drums and the Dakota singing?" she asked excitedly.

Instantly, he dropped his head, watching her with a keenly observant eye. "How would you know about that? You are a *wasicun*. Such things are not experienced by your kind."

"My kind!" Audrina tilted her dainty chin. "And just what does that mean?"

"You are of the white race," he replied levelly. Bitter anger deepened his voice further. "Your lover Powell kept me from going to my father in the Mankato jail to collect his belongings. He stole Red Hawk's pouch. I don't know his reason; you tell me, Audrina. He was the man you would have wed if I had not taken you. You were found naked as winter with him."

Fury almost choked her. "No! I would never have married that scum." She gave a low, desperate laugh. "He was always after me. . . . You have to believe me, Wild Hawk, there was nothing between Joe and me."

Suddenly, Audrina asked herself why it was so important that she convince Wild Hawk that Joe Powell had not been her lover. She did not have to prove anything to Wild Hawk!

Hauling Audrina near, Wild Hawk breathed close to her ear with the insistent pressure of his fingers at her nape. "If you choose to forget the *wasicun* warrior, I

262

will be more lenient with you, Audrina, when we arrive at my village."

Drawing in a sudden breath, Audrina stared up at his compelling face. "I thought this was your village. Why aren't your people here? What do you mean, you will be more *lenient* with me?"

Audrina studied the lean, coppery-skinned face.

"You are a defiant captive, Audrina. I would break you of this. You must forget Joe Powell and seek forgiveness for hiding the medicine pouch he stole from my father."

Exasperated, Audrina shook her bright head, saying, "I knew nothing about that! Joe did *not* give me that medicine bundle." Taking a deep breath, she forged on, "A—a hawk did."

The almost-black eyes narrowed suspiciously and there was a cold edge of irony in his masculine voice, "A hawk gave you my father's pouch? Do you expect me to believe that one of our Spirit Fathers flew down from the sky and dropped this pouch into your hands? You lie to save yourself from punishment, Audrina. And punish you I will."

Choking back hot tears, forgetting all about the hawk, she pushed the loose strands of brilliant hair back from her throbbing temples. *"How* will you punish me, Wild Hawk? Will you make me your love slave? Or are you finished with me now that you've sullied my virtue?"

"Because I made love to you a few times does not mean you will escape me the next time. I still want you. I am not full of Audrina yet. Yes, you will continue to be my woman and I will take you when I feel the desire or the need for release. If Audrina is defiant, I shall

263

make love to her until she cries out for Wild Hawk to cease." He gazed deeply into her huge green eyes then. "It will be an ungentle mating, Audrina."

"No!" She tried to yank out of his grasp but he held her fast. "No man will make a whore out of me," she ended on a soft whisper of words.

"Do not call yourself whore, Audrina!" he ground out with slow fierceness.

"That is what you made me, Wild Hawk." Her voice hardened. "Your savage tigress!"

Flinching at her hard words, Wild Hawk strove to check himself from striking her. "You will explain to me now, Audrina. Your friend Powell kept this pouch of my father's." He spoke slow and easy, to calm her. "When did he bring it to your house? Why did you keep it so long and not try to return it to its rightful heir?"

Quickly, she replied, "I did not know who the heir was. Powell did not tell me. . . ." Audrina went stark white. *My God,* he had twisted her tongue. How would she ever get out of this one!

His voice was uncompromising yet oddly gentle in tone. "We will speak of this no longer. There is no more to discuss now, Audrina."

"But . . . there is," Audrina cried, then silently watched as he bent low to place the medicine bundle inside the Spirit Lodge. Then, as she watched with a sickening lurch in her belly, he removed his long Dakota blade from its sheath and, pushing up his sleeves, gashed his forearms. Then he cut his ankles. Then he cried aloud in mourning.

Why was he doing this to himself again?

Clearly, his voice rang out, deep and resonant, carrying a unique force all its own: "This is Red Hawk's

264

Spirit Lodge. It will stand untouched until the skins of this tipi age and crumble, and the winds pull down the dried branches of the scaffold and it withers away. Then the last remnants of the great warrior's belongings will be scattered across the plain."

"My mission . . . my secret mission . . . This?" she asked in a voice that seemed to come from a long way off. With all the traumatic events she had experienced, this was definitely the most disturbing of all. Mission yes, but believed by no one.

Audrina had no idea how long she watched Wild Hawk stand rooted in his bereavement, praying. Dully, she watched the slowly gathering night spread purple shadows over the land. She stood like one in a trance, not realizing that the Moon-When-the-Ponies-Shed would come to an end at midnight. Tomorrow her calendar at home would read May 1.

The small party of Hawk-People-Who-Shoot-in-the-Leaves left the deserted village several days later. Before departing, Wild Hawk had ordered his braves to take what essentials would be needed and pack them on the two extra horses. Like a mad woman, Tawena rummaged in her father's old tepee and finally, after much searching, found some extra clothes—for herself.

Audrina wore a somewhat cleaner doeskin shift, and so did Sadie. They now had crude combs to remove the tangles from their hair and coarse bars of oddly shaped green-colored soap. They were grateful for any small luxury that came their way, and Wild Hawk looked upon the appreciative young captives with a secret smile of his own.

They were on their way again. There would be many rivers to cross, many valleys and hills to traverse before they reached their final destination. But Wild Hawk steered clear of whites who were plundering deserted settlements. Also on the plains were thousands of Yankton and Yanktonai who were thought to have joined the Minnesota Sioux. There were the Canoni, wanderers-in-the-woods, certain Dakota families who eventually came onto the plain. Wild Hawk did not want to have to fight for and lose his beautiful and tempting captive.

All the Sioux nation was on the move, the peaceful and the hostile. Dakota prisoners were being transported by soldiers into western exile in South Dakota and Nebraska. There were relatively few Dakota still living along the Mississippi, and those lived mostly in scattered villages and family groupings on land not thought to be all that valuable by the whites. These Indians were largely left alone, even in the heat of the war and now in the bitter aftermath of exile.

For the people who moved west, there were all kinds of problems. The *wasicun* missionaries were trying to break down the culture, and the government was trying to break it down, too. The traders with their firewater and all manner of Indian people from everywhere were all moving westward together like wild, vagrant winds.

Wild Hawk headed for the Pahasapa Hills, where he knew the Hawk-People-Who-Shoot-in-the-Leaves had gone. He was determined they not be confined, like the Dakota Indians at the Upper and Lower Agencies, on a narrow reservation along the Minnesota River. It had been there that land-hungry white settlers and the fierce Dakota had confronted each other when war broke out. There had been other smaller Dakota settlements in the Shakopee, Prior Lake, and Mendota areas, occupied by relatively well-assimilated Dakota. And when the war came, most of these people fled for their lives, for they feared retribution from the whites.

Wild Hawk did not wish to fear nor fight the *wasicuns* any longer. The only fight would come if someone sought to steal Audrina Harris from him. She was his. But would he endanger the lives of the Hawk People by bringing her to his village? Would he keep her then, if he had to choose between the safety of his people and Audrina? These were the questions that troubled him daily. That, and his growing affection for the charming white beauty who was his precious captive, precious heart.

Wild Hawk alternated between anger and tenderness toward Audrina. It continued to plague him why *she* had been chosen to carry the sacred medicine pouch to Red Hawk's Spirit Lodge—if chosen she had been at all. He, Wild Hawk, should have been the one to collect it from his father. But Powell had kept him from carrying out this noble deed. Perhaps, he continued to worry, she and Powell had stolen it from his father. But why would she do it? She did not hate the Sioux as Powell did. He had read the compassion in her green eyes the day of the execution. He had yet to learn what Powell meant to her. Could he believe Audrina when she said Powell meant nothing to her? That he is "scum"? He had heard the word before. . . . It meant that the person was low and worthless.

It became a daily battle for Audrina to remain indifferent and unmoved by Wild Hawk's virile presence, especially when he looked her way suddenly with an engaging grin. Then she would experience an unquenchable heat of desire, right in the middle of the blazing light of day. It was growing harder to battle this growing desire and to vanquish her nagging sense of fear concerning her future.

They were traversing strange wild land garbed with beautiful earth tones and verdant spring greens, with many rivers and empty distances and not one house or farm in sight for miles and miles. The pasqueflower was in bloom, with its hairy leaves and purplish blossoms that were shaped like cups.

This day, Audrina could make out jagged peaks against the skyline in the smoky distance. She gained Wild Hawk's attention, asking him, "Can you tell me where we are going? And will we be there soon?"

"It is safe to tell you we are going to Lonewoman Creek below the Pahasapa Hills. But these are not the hills you see up ahead. My father's former village has been moved beyond there."

"How do you know this?" Audrina wondered out loud.

"It is where Strong Heart said he would take the Hawk People if we were late in arriving." His wild-brown eyes scanned the green hills and blue rivers stretched out before them. "We will have to pass through the Badlands," he declared. "Surely Audrina has heard of this barren land?"

"Most certainly."

Indeed Audrina had heard of the Badlands, also known as the White River Badlands and the Big Badlands. The early French-Canadian trappers had called this part of southwestern Dakota *Les Mauvaises terres à traverser,* the bad lands to cross.

"Who is Strong Heart?" Audrina asked.

Resonant and impressive, Wild Hawk's voice captivated Audrina. "He is the bravest and strongest warrior among our people."

Audrina smiled. "While you are gone, that is."

"Your compliment makes this warrior proud," he returned with a smile of his own that lit up the earth as radiantly as the sun.

"It is so," she went on in a silky voice. "You are the leader of the Hawk People. How do you say leader in your language? I would like to learn some words if I am to live in your village." Only for a while, she thought, and then she would someday discover a way to escape.

"The word is simple," he said. "It is *Itancan.*"

"Wild Hawk." She pounded her chest, sitting straight on her horse. "*Itankan.* You will be chief when you join your people in the hills?"

"*Sha,* yes. I am chief; there are others in my village who will perform the duties of *Itancan.*" Then he laughed, displaying a row of perfect white teeth. "You are *Winu.*"

He looked her over, his dark, dancing eyes seeming to undress her right there in the bright sunshine.

Flushing beneath his intense scrutiny, Audrina was almost afraid to ask, but she was growing braver. "Well," she laughed, "tell me what that means. I have heard you and the others say this many times. I have an idea, but I'm not sure."

"Captive Woman."

"I see." Disappointedly, Audrina turned her head aside. She would not allow him to read her distress, but oh, she hated it when he referred to her as his captive. . . *Winu.*

She did not wish to spoil the day. The sun was shining with a lemon yellow brilliance across the earth. She felt a sense of well-being she did not wish to destroy by being defiant. All she wanted, for now, was peace between them. When he flashed her his white smile and treated her with kindliness, she felt wonderful.

Daring much, Audrina begged, "Teach me some more, Wild Hawk. I want to know the simple words like food, water, yes, no. Things like that."

While his braves rode on ahead to scout the area, Wild Hawk taught her. Audrina learned fast, but she had a hard time with some of the explosive and guttural sounds. She felt silly when she was forced to make her voice sound gruff. At these times, Wild Hawk tossed back his head and laughed, pleasing her tremendously.

Breathless and happy, Audrina allowed her animation to surface. "You are very pleasant to be with when you laugh, Wild Hawk. I love to be with you then."

The sun's rays had deepened Audrina's complexion to a dusky peach where her skin was exposed. She did not realize how beautiful she appeared to Wild Hawk, wearing her manly hat that somehow made her look ultra-feminine, with her fat braid hanging down her back and the innocent contours of her face alive with the gentle mystery of womanhood. The hazards and the discomforts of the savage journey to his village had not detracted from her haunting loveliness. In fact, she was more alive and beautiful and strong than when he had first taken her captive, with her defiant spirit yet intact.

Every evening Audrina dutifully followed Tawena to

a stream near their temporary camp. As she walked to the water one night, she noticed Sadie studying Fox Dreamer. And Fox Dreamer had done his share of watching Sadie. It was as if they could not get enough of looking at each other. Audrina realized that Fox Dreamer and Sadie were truly falling in love. Audrina noticed that Left Hand seemed to notice, too.

Audrina had learned enough of the Dakota language so that she could lightly converse with Tawena. When the Indian woman began abusing Sadie that night, Audrina used the word for "enough." *"Henala!"* Audrina snapped angrily at Tawena. The Indian woman stared at Audrina as if she had sprouted horns, then turned her back. But she did not bother Sadie any more that night.

Satisfied for the time being, Audrina smiled smugly, meaning to learn more Sioux every chance she could find. Wild Hawk was an efficient teacher, and he seemed to enjoy these comfortable sessions with her while they rode over the endless prairie.

One captivating night, in the pale light of the rising moon, Sadie knew a restless desire to meet with Fox Dreamer. The urgency was almost unbearable. While everyone slept, with Tawena snoring loudly in her blankets and Audrina a distance off slumbering peacefully beside Wild Hawk with the rope between them, Sadie made up her mind swiftly and moved to sit up. Tawena stirred and smacked her lips.

Suddenly Sadie became ecstatic. Tawena had forgotten to tie her. Still, every move she made caused Tawena to stir restlessly.

Holding her breath, Sadie slowly eased to her feet, but when Tawena rolled over, facing her, the young blonde panicked and stood galvanized. Damn! If only she could rise and go for a walk in the moonlight, maybe Fox Dreamer would be stirring, too.

Sadie's dream came true, for out of the misty dark emerged a handsome figure. She knew at once it was Fox Dreamer. Her young body flushed with the pleasure she always found when he was near. He had experienced the same aching restlessness as she had . . . and he had come for her!

He came to her like a soft whisper on the water, reaching for her hand and taking her quickly away from the night-shrouded camp. Sadie never saw Wild Hawk look up from his bedroll, smile, roll over, and then close his eyes again. She gasped when a fleet-footed deer crossed their path, going to the moonlit stream to drink.

Sadie was only vaguely aware of her surroundings as they came to stand beneath the small clump of cedar trees. It was the presence of Fox Dreamer and her heart leaping about in her chest that preoccupied her the most. A beautifully primitive love chanting began when he tipped her chin upwards and her eyes met his in the semi-dark. And there was no need for words as Fox Dreamer drew her into his thrilling embrace. In fact, there was no way they could readily communicate, for they did not fully know each other's language. Theirs was the language of love.

Kissing her at once, Fox Dreamer's slim male lips brushed Sadie's rhythmically, and she experienced an eager affection coming from him. She gave him wild encouragement and he groaned his desire, murmuring thick in his deep male voice. He was instantly aroused, and Sadie was delighted if not a little frightened of the feelings he built in her. But she instantly calmed her fears, for the answer to this burning need that grew by leaps and bounds lay with him.

Fox Dreamer knew a warmth deep within as he kissed Snow Maid fully for the first time ever. Desires that had been sleeping in him for so long were fanned. This tender and fiery warmth was something brand new to him, and he knew that when they came together, as surely as the rising Dakota sun set the earth ablaze with its warming rays every evening, there would be some pain, for it would be an ungentle mating at first.

"Fox Dreamer, love me," Sadie softly urged when he pulled away for just a moment. Gazing up at his moonlit profile, she tried to learn every inch of his face by heart.

In Dakota, Fox Dreamer spoke to her softly, tenderly, trying to convey to her his fear of hurting her for the first time. Holding her at forearm's length, he gazed deeply into her eyes that were as dark as his in the night's shadows.

"I am not afraid, Fox Dreamer," she whispered, pulling him close to her heart. She knew what was bothering him; it was as if they could wonderfully communicate with their minds. "I have never known a man intimately before. There have been many young men who wanted me. I never wanted to be made love to by any of them." She shook her silver-blond head, hoping he understood her. "I knew from the very first time I locked eyes on you that it was you I wanted—forever." Hers was a wistful smile; his was thoroughly attentive. "Even though I hated you at first, I could not resist the heartfelt tenderness of your look, your gaze. Oh, Fox Dreamer, I want to be with you always! You

are the gallant knight I have always dreamed about—
even if you *are* Indian."

In Dakota Fox Dreamer answered, cupping her
lovely face beneath the full-orbed moon. "I promise
you my heart forever, Snow Maid. Nothing will stand
between us. My world has become brighter and
happier since you came into my life circle. You will
always be my only woman, I promise you this. This
night we will make love for the first time and you will
forever be at my side. No longer will you have to suffer
Tawena's guard. You will be under my protection and
keeping from now on. Do you believe this?"

"I do not know what you are saying or asking me, my
love," Sadie said, as amber lights danced in her eyes
when he turned her in his loving embrace. "But I know
it is beautiful and good. Now," she moaned in her
feverish desire, "hold me, Fox Dreamer. . . . Hold me
close . . . I am yours."

With a swift bending of his knees, Fox scooped
Sadie up into his arms and bore her to a grassy love-
nest beneath a tree where, together, they melted into
the warm earth. Like a man dancing gracefully in a
sensuous dream, Fox began to make love to her. He
knew this was what she wanted. It was what he wanted.
Feverishly, he had waited for this moment. Never had
he forced a woman, and his knowledge of making love
was very slight.

"I have saved myself, as I think you have, Snow
Maid," he murmured huskily, drawing her close. "For
you are as pure as the winter snow; this is why I have
named you Snow Maid."

He kissed her tenderly, and Sadie's heart drummed
rapture's melody in her breast. Intense desire coursed

through him and he held her closer and closer until their bodies met in a wildfire union. Each was aching for the fulfillment of the other's lovemaking.

She tensed, fearful for only a moment as Fox Dreamer pressed his sinewy body into her softness. Something in his manner soothed her then, and he murmured Indian words into her ear. Her chest rose and fell, and she fully relaxed the tense nerves in her body. He undressed her slowly; his own buckskins were off in a flash. He remembered something, disappeared for a moment, then returned to set his long Indian rifle within reach.

Dreamy and filled with quivering excitement, Sadie's eyes closed as he moved over her body slowly, carefully, so as not to alarm her with his intense craving. Black lashes lowered as he kissed her reverently, moving from her shoulders to the lush mounds of her breasts. When he took her nipple into his mouth, she moaned softly and arched upwards, giving him full access to suck the rosy tip. At the same time, Fox tugged her slender hips closer, his bronze hand sliding across her silken belly, eliciting sounds of pleasure from her pink mouth.

Fox Dreamer moaned as his desire for this white woman grew into flaming primitive passion. In between suckling her breasts, he breathed love words to capture her heart as well as her soul, praying that she would be his forevermore.

Sweetly, erotically, his Dakota words set Sadie afire. She knew he loved her as much as she loved him. It was in every word, every gesture, every caress, every sweet thrust of his desiring soul and body.

The heat expanded and grew between them, and

Sadie leaned toward his manhood, the glimpse of his strong bronze body making her heart beat more rapidly. Fox slid down the ivory length of Snow Maid's body, then bent to kiss her thoroughly. She cried out from the half-savage, half-gentle assault, clutching handfuls of his ebony hair. His searching kisses found what they were looking for and his moist tongue thrust into her, searing the innermost center of her pulsing flame, opening her to him like a flower seeking the sun. He kissed her inflamed secret core, his bronze fingers cupping her closer and closer.

One hand slid around and down her taut, quivering stomach to the swell of her hips, setting off tiny tremors that swept through her loins. He lifted his head and his body rose above hers.

Fox knew he must hurt her for a few moments.

"Oh . . . *yes,*" Sadie softly pleaded, knowing the moment was at hand, feeling her heartbeat throbbing in her ears as Fox knelt between her opened hips and rocked forward in one smooth, swift thrust.

Curling into the curve of Fox's body, Sadie experienced no pain, only unending pleasure as his silken flesh became one with hers.

Bemusedly, Fox gazed down upon his fair beloved, knowing her pain had been almost nonexistent. After the initial thrust into her maidenhead, he moved slowly, careful so as not to tear her tender flesh and cause her unneeded pain, for he was very heavy and full.

Fox's ardor was surprisingly, touchingly restrained, and she discovered happily and thankfully that he was a gentle lover. They moved to the savage love song of their rapturous hearts. Sadie felt her pleasure mounting as he clutched her tiny waist and thrust in and out of her. Her body arched naturally, in a glorious expression of love.

Poking and threading pale fingers through his ebony hair, Sadie tugged him closer and closer, and Fox melded into his beloved. His thrusts becoming stronger and more sharp, Sadie lifting higher and higher until together they discovered a tempo that bound their bodies as inseparable, in loving ecstasy. His expert touch sent her to even higher levels of ecstasy, so wonderful she thought she might die from it.

Fox Dreamer sunk himself shaft-deep, and Sadie raked her fingernails into his flesh as they came simultaneously, their naked bodies passionately straining, their mutual release striking them so fiercely that they both shouted softly, and then finally relaxing, moist and aglow in the shimmering moonlight.

Love flowed in Fox Dreamer like warm, wild honey. Sadie, too, was filled with an amazing sense of completeness.

Making love once more, they soared even higher this time, until the peak of delight was reached. After walking back to the edge of the camp, Sadie felt a wave of sheer loneliness as he kissed her, then pressed her lips tenderly with his fingertips. When he murmured words of love to her, Sadie felt a deep peace enter her being. Then he vanished into the shadows and Sadie lay wide awake. She stared into the starry heavens for hours before she slept at last, replete for now, dreaming all the sensuously heightened colors of fire, passion, and love.

*   *   *

They were pressing deeper into Dakota Territory. The scenery became even more rugged and wild after they had deviated south to cross the wide brown Missouri where the river was somewhat narrower and calmer. Even at that, Audrina thought for sure she would drown if she fell from the horse, for she could not swim; she had never learned how and had never been in water above her waist.

Mounted on the big Appaloosa, Audrina secretly watched the play of rippling muscles in Wild Hawk's bare coppery torso as he lead the Bear. She was so engrossed in her delightful task that when she felt her small bundle of possessions slipping from her fingers, she slowly dragged her gaze to her empty hand.

No! she thought frantically, *not the armband Wild Hawk gave to me!* She didn't know what she'd do if she ever lost the beautiful possession that was so precious to her. Reaching for the bundle, she groped a little too far and found herself slipping into the neck-high water. Sadie saw her disappear into the swirling gray water for a moment and screamed.

"Audrey!"

Coming down off Fox Dreamer's horse, Sadie fought to reach her friend in the dragging current, but she had a hard time trying to keep her own head above water. Fox Dreamer came to Sadie's rescue and lifted her back onto his horse. The others were also fighting the strong current, trying to hold onto the frightened horses.

Tawena moved like a sleek fish in the wild current. Even so, one of the horses was carried away and there had been no saving him, although Wild Hawk had fought furiously to reach him. Holding onto the Bear's

278

tail for dear life, Audrina watched the poor head bob away from them, the big liquid eyes of the horse looking resigned to its fate. And then she imagined herself floating after it, never to be seen alive again!

"Audrina . . ." Sadie cried. "Help her!" Fox tried to get to her but Wild Hawk had already heard Sadie's distressed cry.

Thrashing around in the water, Audrina thought this was surely the end as she coughed, choked, and gasped, until strong arms clamped about her waist and lifted her up.

Wild Hawk finally manged to get Audrina back onto the Bear. On the riverbank, she flopped over onto her back like a drowned mouse. Staring up at Wild Hawk, her eyes turned deeply green. She had no idea how ridiculous she looked, clutching her little bundle of rescued possessions to her breast with one hand and a handful of horsehair with the other.

"Wild Hawk," she panted, her fingers circling his wrist. "Thank you. I was scared out of my wits. I've never been swimming in such deep water."

"You did not swim, Audrina," Wild Hawk said while a muscle quivered at his jaw in restraining laughter. "You rolled about like a fat buffalo heavy with child." He said this to the braves over his shoulder, repeating it in Dakota.

Audrina saw that they all got a good chuckle at the expense of her intense embarrassment. "Thank you again, Wild Hawk, you humiliate me so well," Audrina quipped, rising to her feet dripping wet. "Well!" She stared around. "What are you all staring at? Not one of you look much better than I do!"

"We know that," Sadie said with a giggle. Then she

pointed. "But what are you going to do with that bunch of the Bear's tail you're hanging onto for dear life?"

Peering down at her balled hand, Audrina blinked wide with surprise. Tossing her sopping auburn braid across her shoulder in a defiant gesture, she said testily, "What do you think? I am going to make a *Bear-tail* necklace!"

With a mock-serious face, Wild Hawk said, "A necklace?" He looked at the hair dubiously, giving her a mocking grin.

"Well, maybe an armband." When she saw his doubtful face, she shrugged. "Don't believe me then." She stuck her chin in the air, walking away to seat herself upon a rock, taking her possessions out one by one to dry them.

The grinning braves pressed Wild Hawk for Sadie's question and Audrina's answer; they laughed heartily when their willing chief translated. There were only two among them who stood still and did not even smile. Tawena and Left Hand turned their backs on the others, going to remove blankets and other damp items from the horses, laying them out in the sun to dry.

Selecting several of the longest strands, Audrina set to work on her task. Painstakingly, she wove the horsehairs for hours as the Indian party waited for their possessions to dry out. She sat there on her rock, while Sadie fell asleep peacefully under a blanket after she'd stripped down to nothing, her damp clothes hanging on a nearby branch.

Only once did Audrina look up to enjoy the beauty of nature, for a little songbird had come to perch on a branch of a big old box elder tree. The soughing in the pine trees continued. Another hour passed. Wild

Hawk, trying to suppress a grin, stopped near Audrina's perch. He was munching a prairie turnip and held it out for her to take a bite.

"It is good nourishment, little one."

Audrina shook her head no. She did not look up but kept her head studiously bent low over the thing she was making.

Dragging his eyes reluctantly from Audrina's river-soaked bodice, Wild Hawk walked away with a curious smile. Tawena and Left Hand strolled by, shifting their eyes over Audrina with surreptitious glances, and then straight ahead again with displeased smirks. They could not help but be curious over the thing she was working so hard over.

Sadie sat up, blinked, and looked at Audrina on her rock. "Lord, aren't you done with that thing yet? How much longer is it going to take?" Sadie reached over to feel her clothes to see if they were dry.

"Don't know."

"We'll be leaving soon. Most of the clothes are dry." Sadie looked at Audrina sitting in her still-damp shift. "Aren't you going to change your clothes and dry the ones you're wearing? Just a little? You must be uncomfortable sitting there like that." Under the blanket, Sadie tugged her clothes on. Just then Left Hand strolled by, his eagle eyes shifting over her and Audrina. Daringly, Sadie wrinkled her nose at the vulgar-eyed warrior and he in turn warned her, with a look, that her time was coming. "Not with Fox around," Sadie dared in a singsong voice, knowing Left Hand could not understand a word she said.

Peering over at Audrina, Sadie shrugged. "I might as well be talking to a tree. You don't even know if it's

281

night or day, if you're afoot or on horseback." She heaved a deep sigh, asking, "What are you going to do with that, anyway?"

"Going to give it to Wild Hawk." She stood then, brushing the extra hairs off her skirt. "It's an armband," she proudly revealed.

"How nice," Sadie crooned, studying the perfect little squares of weaving that closely, intricately held the thing together. The narrow band had been fashioned for a large arm. "But how does he get it on and off?"

Unaware that she was being closely observed, Audrina showed Sadie the loops at one end of the armband and the braided tie at the other. "You pass it through the loops, draw it tight over and under, then let the little bit left over hang loose—like this, see?"

Sadie's lips parted in delight as she asked, "Who showed you how to weave like that?"

"Aunt Katherine," Audrina answered, going poignantly back in her memory to the day they had sat outside on the hard bench in front of the Dakota Hotel, fashioning bracelets.

"Your Aunt Katherine showed you," Sadie echoed, excited when she thought of making something for Fox Dreamer. "Can you show me how to do it? Not now, some other day when we have time."

"Of course," Audrina said, looking around for Wild Hawk. "There are many natural things you can make the bracelets and armbands out of. But long pieces of animal hair and dried flexible plants work the best."

"What is it, Audrey?"

A second ago, Audrina had looked down sheepishly. Now she said, "I have to admit I did not know what to

282

do with that handful of horsehair, Sadie." Her cheeks burning with remembrance, she added, "Not at first. I felt really stupid." She was feeling much better now. Audrina even saw the humor of the earlier incident and began to laugh happily with Sadie. "I must have looked mad as a hatter and wet as a drowned hen," she said between gales of giggles and laughter.

"Yes . . . you did." Sadie hooted, clutching Audrina's arm. "Oh stop laughing, Audrey, I'm getting a stitch in my side like you do when you run too fast!"

Across the clearing, Tawena exchanged dark frowns with her brother, who worked on the other side of the horses. "They are like crazy women. There has been too much happiness and joyful matings of the eyes when those four are in one another's presence. This makes me sick."

"You do not like it any more than I," Left Hand growled. "Perhaps when we go through the Badlands we can make a few accidents happen. One for the white hair, the other for the fire hair."

Tawena's voice hardened ruthlessly. "We will give them to the white warrior who has joined the Rebels. I have a feeling we will meet him soon. We have to be careful, my brother, that *we* do not cause these accidents you speak of. The white man is our answer. You will see."

The sunset hovered just above the rolling horizon when they made camp some distance from the Missouri on a tributary of the White River. When Audrina presented her gift to Wild Hawk, he turned it over in his hand. That done, he smiled benignly and handed it back to her. "It is nice. You have done as good a job as the craftswomen of our tribe, Audrina."

"It is for you, Wild Hawk," Audrina said, handing it back. "I made you a gift."

His expression stilled and grew serious as he looked down at her bare arm. "You do not wear the gift of the armband that I gave you."

"I am saving the armband. It is so pretty and special that I don't wish to wear it every day."

Wild Hawk's eyes bore deeply into hers. "Do you mean this, Audrina?"

"Of course. Why do you think I pulled such a foolish stunt as to get off that horse in the middle of the river?" She gestured in a sweeping motion with one slender arm. "I was not fishing for trout, Wild Hawk."

Holding up a string of fish, he said, "I have already taken care of that, Audrina."

"They are good-sized ones, too!" Audrina's mouth watered. "I love trout."

"Do you, Precious Fire?"

"Yes," her answer was whisper-soft.

His grin flashed brightly, dazzling against his deeply bronzed flesh. "Thank you for the gift. Wild Hawk will cherish it always. Now, let us walk to the stream before you clean the fish. Audrina knows how to clean fish?" His eyebrow rose inquiringly.

"Oh, yes . . . of course." *But I'm not going to tell you how much I despise doing it!*

The sun sank low, the salmon sky paling above the cobalt blue of the hazy horizon. As they stood there in the breathless Dakota twilight, the glow of the sky was reflected momentarily on the fluttering, multi-veined wings of slow-flying insects. They circled and landed

284

awkwardly among sparse grass clumps.

Basking yet in Wild Hawk's appreciation of her gift, Audrina stared at the odd-looking insects, wondering what they could be. Seeing her interest, Wild Hawk instructed her, "They are called water scorpions." He stood next to her by the scarlet dappled stream.

Frowning with concentration, Audrina continued to watch the strange bugs. She had never beheld such odd creatures. Reddish-brown, about an inch long, they clung to the pale green grass, forelegs outthrust, long breathing tubes projecting to the rear of their bodies.

"It's like a small brown twig caught among the plants. Oh . . . they almost look helpless."

"Do not let their position fool you, Audrina." Wild Hawk gazed at her with a gentle smile. "They hang downward in the leaves, awaiting the approach of their prey. At dusk, the adult insects take flight."

The fading light of sunset bathed Audrina's face in a winsome portrait of shifting watercolors. "Where do they come from?" she softly asked.

"Right here, from the White River. They travel far, Audrina, to the rangeland waterholes beyond the wall where the Badlands end to the north, and along the White River, far into the south."

Between a thumb and forefinger, Wild Hawk plucked one of the bugs from the grass's stem. Audrina jumped back, watching the creature's forelegs move rapidly as it rubbed roughened patches against its frail body.

Catching the faint high squeak of its strident sound in her ears, Audrina shuddered. "It's a little ugly, isn't it?" she said, at the same time feeling a certain oneness with the little creature.

As Wild Hawk continued to hold it captive between his strong bronze fingers, the insect suddenly ceased all movement. Audrina blinked as it stiffened, and she couldn't know that it feigned death.

"Oh," she breathed sadly. "It died. Did you crush it, Wild Hawk?" Audrina stared up into his watchful eyes. She held her breath and after a moment it stirred again.

"The creature has fooled us," he murmured, peering into her eyes intently.

"Oh, Wild Hawk, release it . . . please."

Tossing it into the air, he watched as its gauzy wings unfurled and it fluttered away to safety. Time stood still as Audrina looked up at her bronze captor. He had allowed the tiny creature its freedom. What about her?

Together, spellbound, they watched as the creature was silhouetted against the dim, scattered light, then swallowed up in the gray world of sundown.

The captive and the captor let their eyes meet, misty green and compelling black, locked in mutual understanding. She was his captive, yes. . . . Would he ever let *her* receive her gift of freedom as he had the silken-winged creature? Only time would tell, Audrina knew.

When Wild Hawk saw Left Hand approaching them, he released Audrina from his dark gaze. "You must go now to clean the fish," he ordered sternly. "And cook them well. Wild Hawk does not like raw fish."

The Indian leader narrowed his eyes as Audrina made an abrupt about-face. He and Left Hand watched her go, both noticing that her slim hips sashayed more than usual. Left Hand reluctantly dragged his heated gaze from the slender beauty, hating her for growing more lovely and charming and willful each day.

"What are you going to do with that one?" he asked. He went on when an answer was not forthcoming. "Our young chief pays more attention to the fire hair than he does to his braves. Is she so very special to our great leader that she takes up every moment of his life?"

Is this what his braves had begun to believe? That Precious Fire was more special than they were? Indians believed that it was wrong to treat a woman as if she were more important than anything else. Precious Fire should be serving him, not the other way around. Had he become weak in his men's eyes? This was bad. He must show more force. Yes, he must be the leader Red Hawk would be proud to have left behind to serve the Hawk People.

Wild Hawk briskly answered, "I will think on this, Left Hand."

Left Hand held out a finger. "Did she give you a gift?"

"It is so," Wild Hawk said. "She is talented."

The black slaty eyes glittered. "In many ways . . . It does not go unnoticed."

"The braves are jealous of the woman of their chief?" Wild Hawk asked gruffly. He did not await an answer. "She is my captive. They have taken captives before. They should not be jealous. This is the first white woman I have taken and intend to hold."

"But you do not torture her as you should, Wild Hawk. Even now she is left to roam free. . . ." Left Hand shut up quickly. He told himself he should not force this to Wild Hawk's attention. It was good that Precious Fire was allowed to roam as she pleased.

When everything was ready, it would be that much easier to be rid of her once and for all.

All that seemed to have gone into Wild Hawk's ear was the word *torture*. The image of Precious Fire being stretched between four stakes rose painfully in his mind. Her stunningly beautiful body scorched by the heat of the Dakota sun. That creamy olive-gold face marred by sun blisters. Her moist lips cracked. The water in her body depleted and shriveling her up like a prune . . . her beauty dried up.

The dark, enraged look on Wild Hawk's face drove Left Hand back several steps.

"I have spoken too freely. I am sorry, my chief; I will speak of this no more."

"It is good that you do not," Wild Hawk warned. He watched Left Hand go to join his sister, who stood guard over Sadie and Audrina as they cleaned the fish. Fox Dreamer was there, too, keeping his eye on Tawena lest she lay a hand on Snow Maid in needless cruelty.

After they had finished the meal of fish dipped in ground meal and cooked to golden perfection, the brave who had been acting as guard rushed into camp, waving his hands in the air while speaking rapid-fire Dakota. Wild Hawk snatched up his feather-thonged rifle and walked a little distance from the camp. When he returned, he was not alone. With him were three Indian women and one very young brave. Audrina and Sadie watched as they trudged wearily into their camp.

"Oh," Sadie moaned, "they are so pretty." Her worried eyes scanned the camp in search of Fox Dreamer, and finding him beside Wild Hawk, she kept her eyes trained on Fox's appraisal of the young Indian

288

women. Sadie grimaced, adding, "Especially the one with the longest black hair."

Audrina looked the Indian women over. "Yes . . . she is lovely."

Audrina, too, was watching, watching Wild Hawk as he bent his head while conversing softly in Dakota to the women. "They must be from the same tribe or neighboring tribes. Wild Hawk told me that the Dakotas are divided into three grand sections: the *Isamjati* who are the Santees; the *Ihanktonwan* who are the Yanktons, the prairie tribes; and the *Titonwan* who are the Tetons. The Assiniboins separated from the Dakota a century ago and are known as the *Hoha* or rebels. The present-day hostile Indians go by that name, which is like a curse on them, even now."

"What does Dakota mean?" Sadie asked, keeping her eyes glued on the prettiest Indian girl and Fox Dreamer.

"Dakota means *allied*. The confederated Dakota tribes were called the Nadowsioux by the French and the Algonkins. Sioux means the snake, or the enemy."

"You have learned a lot," Sadie said. "Wild Hawk has been teaching you. I see when you ride next to him that you and he talk deeply. I see him smile often. When you turn away, Audrina, his beautiful eyes watch you very closely. He studies every inch of your body when his braves aren't looking."

Audrina felt her face turn sunset-red. "Fox Dreamer does a good share of his own staring. I watched you and him leave camp the other night." Audrina eyes were full of fun and mischief. "You and your handsome brave did not return for over two hours."

"We were gazing at the stars." Sadie blushed and

looked away from Audrina. Then she grew serious. "I would really feel like a slut, Audrey, if the man were anyone but Fox Dreamer. I gave myself to him because he's the only man I will ever be with or love. Love makes it all right. If Fox Dreamer dies, I'll become another kind of Snow Maid—an *old* one with white hair, remembering the memories I had with my beloved savage."

Audrina felt confused and frightened by Sadie's words, though her own feelings were much the same. All of a sudden, she faced Sadie and took hold of her wrists.

"Sadie, I have to ask you something. I—I don't think I want to stay with Wild Hawk. Escape is something I have been thinking and planning for some time now. I do not want to be a captive, a *Winu,* the rest of my life. I want to live in a real house . . . with a civilized man. I love Wild Hawk, but it just won't work out—it never will."

Sadie placed her pale hand over Audrina's darker, more coppery one. "Well, then," she began softly, "you better stop giving him your body and your love. The way he looks at you, Audrey, I don't see how he could ever let you get away. He would kill anyone who tried to help you escape. He might force you to slave for him if you try to escape too many times. It's as if he can read your mind. Does he know that you have Indian blood yourself? Oh, my God," Sadie gasped, "Wild Hawk's looking over at us right now! I told you he can sense things. He knows about me and Fox Dreamer, too, and his looks seem to say it's all right, it's good."

"It is good," Audrina murmured, "—for you." Sadie went back to brushing her long hair, but Audrina surreptitiously watched as Wild Hawk continued to converse with the new arrivals. Coyly, shyly, they were admiring him, that much was clear. Audrina felt an unfamiliar stab of jealousy. She also felt desire for Wild Hawk to come to her, to let her know she was the one he wanted above all others. But did she really? What *did* she want?

A short time passed and Audrina was just closing her eyes, trying to force her ears not to hear the sound of women's laughter, when she felt a presence on the edge of her blanket. Peering upwards, her heart picked up a crazy rhythm when she made out the tall form standing there.

"Come, Precious Fire," Wild Hawk murmured, pulling her up with him.

Taking her arm, he fastened the rope between her wrist and his, his eyes never leaving hers. Audrina glanced down at the rope that stretched tautly between them as he began to walk. She followed her bronze captor, and already the wild drums of desire were pounding out a crazy rhythm in her blood.

Chapter Eleven

"Wild Hawk, who are the Indian women? Are they from your tribe?" Audrina fired the questions as soon as they stepped from the fringe of campfire into purple shadow. "Will they be traveling with us now to your village?"

Wild Hawk answered truthfully. "They are Minnesota-Sioux from Lake Traverse. They had been in exile from Minnesota and escaped from soldiers who had been bringing them to live on a reservation." He made a sound of irrepressible disgust.

Audrina fought to control her swirling emotions. "Are there more?" she inquired, walking slowly, her hips gently asway.

A secret smile ruffled Wild Hawk's sensitive mouth. "More women? No," he said, his stride long and fluid beside her smaller, tighter steps. "I do not think more are coming, Audrina. Why do the Indian women catch your interest?"

Wild Hawk turned to her and touched her cool hand while gazing deeply into her warm, expressive eyes.

292

Audrina shivered with sweet exquisite feeling, warmed by his demonstrative affection.

"Audrina, let us sit here, on these rocks near the stream." When they were seated, he asked, "Why should this be of special interest to you? Is there something that worries you about them?"

Yes! They are pretty and perhaps they might interest you. That is what worries me most. "I just wondered what they were doing here." She hugged her knees to her chest, then stared into the dark copse of pines.

"Ahhh, Precious Fire, that is not all." Taking her hand, Wild Hawk experienced a tingle of excitement that raced through him like uncontrollable wildfire. "I think perhaps there is more Audrina is not telling me."

A delicate frown creased Audrina's brow. "Why do you use my name as if we are discussing someone who is not present? Do all Indians do that? *Sha?*" She tried out one of the Sioux words he had taught her. "Yes?"

"Sha," he said. "Yes, they do at times. You say some very strange and funny things at times yourself, Audrina."

Reflected moonlight glimmered over his savagely handsome face like beams of muted radiance. As usual, his head was held high with pride, his profile strong and rigid in bearing, the ends of his midnight hair lifting to dance with the soft night winds.

"But now Audrina must tell *Wild Hawk* what really bothers her about the pretty Indian women."

Aha! So he had noticed they were pretty, just as she had thought!

"You do not speak," Wild Hawk said. "Why do you pull yourself into your own thought-world when I put questions to you?"

"I think you are reading more into it than what is really there."

"I do not think so, Precious Fire," he purred deep in his throat.

Oh! She loved it when he whispered his Indian name for her in that special way.

Suddenly, he was very close.

"Wild Hawk, can we go back now. I am very tired," she lied, ending with a tremulous sigh.

"You are jealous, I believe," he said close to her ear. "I want to make love to Precious Fire. She has made me desire her very much."

Audrina did not realize it when her cheeks blushed responsively, desire sweeping through her like a strong north wind. "Are all women considered expendable to you?"

"What do you mean by this word, Audrina. I have never heard it before—*ex-pendable?*"

"*Sha.*" Audrina watched him closely as she explained. "Able to be sacrificed to the lusts of—of you savages."

Frowning darkly, Wild Hawk slowly shook his dark head. "You call me savage again. I will not allow this kind of talk any more, Audrina. I am not a savage," he said sharply.

"You are not very civilized, either," she dared respond.

"Audrina!"

She was barely able to control a loud gasp of surprise as he yanked her to her feet, speaking bitterly. "White men are the savages, Audrina. Did you know it was the French traders who began to murder and scalp the Indian first? Did you know that the Indian followed

294

the white man in torturing captives? And rape?"

She hung her head in shame, shouting, "Yes, yes! I know all that!" Audrina clamped her hands over her ears. "And I do not want to hear more about how the white man introduced all those evils to the *gentle* savages!"

"*Do not* call me savage!" he snarled. "Not even a *gentle* one."

"I did not!" she retorted tartly. "I meant . . . oh, I don't know what I meant." She moaned, awash with turbulent emotions. "Why do you confuse me so?"

"If Precious Fire prefers to be Wild Hawk's defiant captive then he prefers to punish her as he sees fit. I will not be so gentle with Audrina this time."

"No!" she cried out, wrenching away. "Don't punish me, Wild Hawk—not like this."

While Audrina protested with hands that were like the frail beat of a butterfly's wings, Wild Hawk grasped her upper arms and brought her about. He shoved her down into the new carpet of spring grass and unceremoniously pushed up her shift.

Dark rough hands grasped her tender thighs. "No . . . you cannot mean to—"

Swiftly, he unfastened his breeches, but did not remove them. He said something in Dakota, but all Audrina could fathom was the flat, guardedly emotionless tone of his deep male voice.

Suddenly, she was being pinned to the ground, and above her, she could see his black eyes narrowing dangerously. His movements no longer slow, his compelling gaze riveted on her startled face, he moved over her body sweetly, maddeningly, possessively.

Releasing the hardened length of himself from his

fringed buckskins, Wild Hawk dropped between her legs. There was a tingling in the pit of her stomach and she could see the dark fires raging in his eyes. He did not remove her shift.

A quiver surged through her veins as she realized that he was going to make love to her with all their clothes on!

Suddenly, Audrina felt ashamed, humiliated. This was not love, but rape.

"Now you *are* going to show me just how much a savage you really are," she boldly admonished him. "Go ahead, Wild Hawk, make—make me hate you. I—I want to hate you completely."

He said nothing, but his body stiffened.

"But please," she begged, the pulse at her throat beating with feverish rapidity, "be quick."

Audrina lay quietly as he cupped one of her taut-nippled breasts. She prayed he would not hurt her too much.

There was a heavy sensation in her stomach as Audrina tensed her thighs for the painful entry. She was utterly surprised when the hard thrust did not arrive and she felt indescribable pleasure instead of pain. Magic . . . savage magic all over again.

Amazingly sweet, Wild Hawk was kissing and nibbling the throbbing vein in her throat. Against her murmured protests, he sucked at her skin, moving ever downward as he brushed one shoulder of the shift low on her arm. He paused, pulled away, and lifted his sable head to stare at her for a long, thrilling moment. Audrina stared boldly back. She was inflamed by him but still tried resisting his manly charms and persistent touches, his flaming kisses.

Then, before Audrina could think twice, their lips met in a kiss and she was buffeted by the strains of a hauntingly savage melody. Wild Hawk's kiss was not punishing and angry, but tender, sending the pit of her stomach into a wild swirl of exquisite torment.

As he left her lips, he buried his face at her silken throat, breathing a tender kiss into her singing flesh. Lower . . . lower . . . a jolt of pure sensuous fire went through her as he captured a nipple and forced it to attention with his flicking tongue. Pushing her shift way down, he kissed her breasts devouringly and Audrina arched her hips in natural abandon.

Meeting her graceful thrust with his hand, Wild Hawk's supple fingers explored her thighs, and then moving upward, he searched for pleasure points.

In a blur of motion he removed her shift, then gazed almost reverently at the shapely, graceful beauty of her naked body. Then his own clothes vanished. Naked steel met feminine velvet.

Rapturously, wildly, Audrina moaned her pleasure. . . . It was all so perfect. So shining. So right. She did not even want to pull away. Not now. Not ever, she thought as a hot, exultant tear trickled down her cheek to spill into the velvet-soft grass beneath. Audrina gasped with pleasant surprise as Wild Hawk lifted one of her slender feet to kiss its instep, its heel, and then each toe, one by one. Such sweet, exquisite feeling . . . *Ah, Lord.*

The excitement between them intensified a hundredfold. Sensuous silken black hair brushed her face, creating wild tremors along her already-tingling spine and buttocks.

She should be afraid . . . *but she wasn't.*

She should hate him . . . *but she could not.*

She should fight him, deny him . . . *but she wanted him.*

"Wild Hawk, Wild Hawk," she softly exclaimed, her body aching for his savage possession. She felt wanton.

He groaned, his voice full of deep tremors. "My Petala!" She curled into the curve of his hand and his finger entered the special throbbing place.

His touch ignited the core of her womanhood. She wanted to belong to this man, wanted to be Indian, as he was!

Dear God, she was; she was *Indian, too!*

Instinctively, her body arched toward him. "Wild Hawk, make the world go away!"

"You mean the white world, do you not, Precious Fire." It was a statement, not a question.

Nudging her thighs apart, he entered her hotly, urgently, the fire growing like a wild sunflower nurtured by sun and shower . . . and wind . . . like a wind aflame!

She cried out, clawing his back like a tigress in heat, her breath stretching out in long, surrendering moans. The pleasure intensified with each thrust and Audrina grew afraid she would die from so much exquisite torture. Wildly, she caressed the length of his lean, muscle-rippled back.

It was like a tumultuous storm raging within, one struggling for release, the other wanting to hold onto passion's raging torment as her body strained beneath her Indian lover's.

Gracefully, she arched her back, welcoming each hard driving plunge into the willing receptacle of her woman's body. Taking her slim hand, Wild Hawk guided it to himself so she could feel what he was doing to her, and Wild Hawk couldn't control her cry of delight.

Sensually, he brushed the rigid staff of his manhood against her fingers as he pulled himself almost all the way out, then plunged within once more so she could fully realize how deeply and sweetly he fitted into her. As he performed this delightful magic, he murmured into her ear, stimulating her with the expressive language of love.

Exultantly, he heard her muffled cat-sigh of pleasure at his shoulder. Shocking her even further, he reached a hand between the apex of her thighs, pushing a finger into the auburn tangle of wonder-soft curls, his gentle touch stroking and fondling as he continued to plunge in and out. Her flaming hair was spread out beautifully in the grass as her head tossed wildly.

Then Audrina heard herself sobbing out loud, begging for final fulfillment. Embracing her thighs with his own, Wild Hawk cupped her buttocks as turbulent bursts of pleasurable energy ripped through his body, shaking him with thundering rapture, flooding Audrina's entire feminine frame with pulsations of liquid jetting fire. Audrina abandoned herself to the pinwheel of bliss and moved on to tumultuous rapture, catching every nerve end in her body on fire until she sensed her soul shimmering inside and out with thrillingly vibrant ecstasy.

Gloriously, she floated back to earth. Her moonlit surroundings refocused at last and she lay still, panting hard. "How very . . . very beautiful. I know what it's like to be a shooting star," she gasped, rolling over to face her lover. "I love you, Wild Hawk."

299

If Wild Hawk had heard, he did not reply. His eyes were closed. . . . She ran her fingers over them to see for herself. He hadn't heard her, she thought, and snuggled down, satiated, full of a sense of well-being.

But Wild Hawk had heard. Every word. He wondered how much she would love him when he introduced her to his Indian village, his world that was so unlike her own.

Upon reaching the Badlands several days later, the party halted to rest where an awesome spectacle of fluted, seemingly inaccessible hills rose jaggedly against the skyline. There was little vegetation, except in the flat low areas and on the tablelands.

Even in this forbidding, withering country, songbirds, predatory birds, jackrabbits, coyotes, and prairie dogs abounded. Audrina had even caught a fleeting glimpse of bison, antelope, and mountain sheep.

She beheld the rolling grassland, cut by a number of streams. On either side of the White River were the Badlands, their eroded sections banded in soft colors and carved into unusual shapes, interspersed with numerous well-grassed flat-topped tablelands. She had never seen such a strange landscape. Wild Hawk belonged to this. He was part of every strange formation of rock, with their abrupt beginning and termination, their barren appearance and unproductive crisped soil, their precipitous sinkholes and monotonous, weird appearance, inspiring wonder and awe in every beholder. Looking up, Audrina spied the wild hawk making circles, and she felt a kindred spirit with the beautiful bird.

Audrina was spellbound, mystified if not frightened a little by it all. The semi-barren landscape, though threatening, had its own beauty and wildness. Columns of hard rock and other irregularities resulted in the many box canyons and gullies, pinnacles and ridges. There were clay beds, weathered into rounded hump-backed surfaces.

"We will skirt the wildest and roughest areas," Wild Hawk told her.

Indeed, the party avoided the areas cut into thousands of deep, tortuous gullies, with intervening saw-tooth divides that extended from the main rivers back to the tablelands.

After several days of riding, they entered the Black Hills, where ponderosa pine, spruce, aspen, white birch, and cedar prevailed. There were extensive pine forests and hardwood groves among the hills where they rested, along the banks of the various streams that flowed through the Territory. Here were small belts of timber consisting of cottonwood, elm, willow, box elder, and some live oak. "Soon, Audrina, very soon we shall be at my village."

"I am glad, Wild Hawk." But was she really?

At long last, the weary party came to a small Indian encampment hidden in the beautiful enchanted woods. "There is a certain peace here," Sadie said. "Or at least, I am *hoping* there will be. It's like a Dakota paradise."

This was the end of their journey, Audrina thought. Here she would find either freedom or captivity; love or hate; happiness or despair.

The Hawk People greeted their new leader with cries of joy and exultation. Small children danced up and down, doe-eyed maidens watched every move Wild

Hawk made, their youthful faces shining with pride and happiness. One girl, especially pretty and dainty, stood out from all the other young women. Her dark eyes were glued on Wild Hawk and shone joyfully. Part of her waist-length hair was pulled up in one fat braid and left to hang with the rest of her thick, shiny tresses that floated exotically down her back. She had slim hips and a tiny waist, pointed breasts, and dusky rose lips no man could resist wanting to kiss.

Audrina noticed that the three Indian women and the young lad who had ridden with them were treated kindly and taken in with welcoming arms, but when the eyes of the village rested on Sadie and herself, she felt the hostility strike her like a cold, hateful wind. She had an impulse to turn away, or they would destroy her confidence and make her feel deadened with hopelessness. It was important that these people like her, but she couldn't say why. Especially not if she was planning escape. Who cared what they thought of her *then*, she told herself, as she would be far gone. The only problem would be convincing Sadie to go along with her.

Without even looking at her, Left Hand took the reins of Audrina's horse and motioned for her to dismount. Tawena looked smugly over the shoulder of a tall, handsome warrior who hugged her lightly, as if he wanted to be quick about the greeting and get it over with. Then he turned, his black shiny eyes contacting Audrina's.

Next to Wild Hawk, this tall, robust Indian was almost as good-looking, but not quite. His nose was much larger, his lips more full. She had been shocked to find that when their eyes met, he seemed to be peering

302

into her very soul. Instinct told her he was a man to be trusted.

Audrina's first impression had been accurate, for when Wild Hawk brought the tall Indian over to her, she saw only kindness and welcome in his large black eyes. Audrina could not help but smile when his sensuous mouth turned up at the corners and he nodded to something Wild Hawk was imparting to him in Dakota, all the while watching the dainty Indian maiden with the silken hair and lovely doe eyes.

"Let it be known that this is my woman and no one is to touch her or tell her what to do. If Precious Fire is to be punished, I will do the punishing. No one lays a hand on her; if they do, they will surely die, *Cante Tinza.*"

Strong Heart, the man Wild Hawk had just called by his Indian name, grinned and clamped a big hand over his leader's shoulder. "It will be as you say, Wild Hawk. But surely, one of the young women like Rainbow will be allowed to teach her things and show her our ways? And surely she will be allowed to come and go freely to the stream to bathe?"

"Sha," Wild Hawk said. "Only with Rainbow and myself." He looked around for his sister just then, and when he saw her waiting patiently and respectfully just off to his right, he held out an arm to her.

"Wild Hawk!"

Ecstatic, Rainbow flew into his arms, hugged him fiercely, then stood back while he cupped her lovely face between his large hands.

"You are more beautiful than ever," Wild Hawk murmured, his eyes adoring every inch of her. "Though it has not been all that long since we have looked upon

303

each other."

"Too many moons," she replied.

With sinking heart, Audrina watched the most beautiful girl in the camp sharing a loving embrace with Wild Hawk. My God, Audrina thought sickly, angry with herself. *What a fool I have been.* Of course, why didn't she realize it before. Or had she? Wild Hawk had had a woman—a beautiful doe-eyed squaw— waiting for him all the time. All those nights . . . all those tender, loving nights she had lain in his arms in passion. She groaned inwardly, mercilessly gripped by pain.

Audrina walked meekly behind Wild Hawk when he motioned for her to follow him, but she did not feel meek! Inside she was boiling and angry! Oh, how Wild Hawk must be laughing at her now! She wished she could see his face, but he just kept walking straight ahead, lord and master of his kingdom. And Audrina kept walking with her head down—but not too far down, just enough to give the impression that she was subservient to her lord and master, The Savage Wild Hawk!

What am I doing? Audrina asked herself. *I will hold my head up and walk straight as an arrow!* Her relationship with Wild Hawk had taught her that Indians frowned on fear and trembling and smiled on lionhearted valor.

Puzzled, Rainbow frowned as the captive woman was led away. She had tried to meet the pretty woman's eyes but Audrina had kept them downcast, as if afraid Rainbow would read something in them. *Perhaps she does not like me,* Rainbow told herself as she turned away, not seeing the flame-haired beauty walk coura-

304

geous and tall of a sudden. "I cannot blame her. She does not even know me. She is white. I am Indian. But she is so pretty . . . I was hoping we could be friends. Does she know Wild Hawk is my brother?"

"You can be friends. . . ." came a soft, sweet voice in front of Rainbow. "You speak English very well," Sadie added with a friendly smile.

"Thank you. I think the one with the sunset hair is pretty. You are very pretty, too," Rainbow said, reaching out to touch the beautiful blond hair. "What is your name?"

"Sadie. But Fox Dreamer calls me Snow Maid."

"How lovely. I am Rainbow, Wild Hawk's sister." She looked his way for a moment, watching him enter their tepee. "My brother has never become so possessive over a woman before. This is what is different about him. Now I see." Rainbow smiled and waved as Strong Heart entered his own tepee, then she blushed, wondering why the Indian had affected her this way. This had never happened before, for they had always been best of friends, nothing more.

"My friend Audrey is sad about something," Sadie said. "I wonder what is bothering her."

"I do not even have to know her to see that something is wrong. I, too, wonder why she is so sad," Rainbow said. Then she held up her hand, saying, "How, Fox Dreamer."

"How, Rainbow. Come . . . Snow . . . Maid," Fox Dreamer said in his halting English. "To my tepee."

Sadie's eyes lit up and she shook the dust from her feet when she saw Fox Dreamer holding the flap open to a comfortable-sized tepee. She was ecstatic. Their own home! Dear Lord, they were going to be all alone . . . together . . . just the two of them? "The only thing that is missing now is marriage," she said aloud, knowing Fox could not understand. She would have to teach him some more English so that he could understand she wanted to be his wife, not just his mistress.

"Come, Snow Maid."

"I am coming."

Sadie's mouth dropped open when she saw the old woman seated upon a pile of mats and robes. Certainly the old woman was not . . . she didn't . . . Sadie turned to Fox Dreamer with a question in her eyes.

In halting, half English and sign language, he informed Sadie that the older woman was a relative.

"How close a relative?" Sadie wondered out loud. "And is she going to stay with us?"

With a puzzled frown, Fox Dreamer shrugged and said nothing, just seated himself upon the mats circling the cookfire. The old woman rose to serve him, going to spoon some mysterious savory stew into a bowl. Along with this, she added some corn pones, and then she shuffled back to her mats.

Fox Dreamer patted the mat next to him and Sadie walked over, looking down at the food. Her stomach rumbled noisily, even though the stew did not look all that palatable.

"Do I have to wait to eat?" Sadie asked. A few times on the trail, Tawena had made Sadie and Audrina wait until the men had finished, as was the old custom. Here, in this tepee, it appeared she was going to have to wait again.

The older woman, Autumn Beads, viewed the young woman from beneath wrinkled eyes. So, she thought, her dead daughter's son looks upon the white hair with love and gentleness in his eyes. This is good. The girl is comely and looks strong. She will bear my grandson many fine warriors.

Autumn Beads sighed, her bones creaking as she stood. The white hair will have a hard time of it at first, Autumn Beads determined. The other maidens who have looked upon Fox Dreamer with longing eyes will not treat her kindly . . . not at first. What did it matter? Her grandson would take care that no harm came to his lovely young bride . . . if bride she would someday become.

Sadie looked up as the old woman handed her a bowl of stew, then nodded when the young maiden just sat staring, wondering if she should really take it. They exchanged smiles then as Autumn Beads pressed a pone into Sadie's hand and gave it a friendly squeeze. Beaming from ear to ear, the old Indian nodded sagely, then shuffled away.

"She likes me," Sadie said out loud happily. She ate hungrily, looking forward to the moment when the old lady would leave her and Fox Dreamer alone.

"What kind of stew is this?" Sadie asked Fox Dreamer.

Seeing her pointing at her food and inquiring about its contents, Fox Dreamer picked up a stick and drew a prairie turnip, and then he proceeded to draw a snake.

"Snake!" Sadie exclaimed. "What kind of snake?" She nodded at the picture in the dirt and he picked up the stick again.

Fox Dreamer added something to the snake's tail, and Sadie swallowed hard. "Rattlesnake!" She recovered quickly as hunger asserted itself. "Oh, well," she sighed. She dug in again, telling herself it was actually very good. "Very, very good," she said aloud, licking her lips to express her satisfaction.

Fox Dreamer smiled happily across the tipi at his grandmother. He looked down at Snow Maid's corn-silk head then, wondering how happy she was going to be when she discovered that Autumn Beads did all his cooking and sewing, and hardly left the tepee at all—even slept there.

Wild Hawk's eyes were hooded as he watched his lovely captive. He could see that Audrina was jealous, jealous of the young woman who bustled about serving him, smiling happily and musically speaking to him in Dakota.

When the pretty doe-eyed squaw paused before the white woman to offer her a bowl and two pones on a straw mat, Audrina looked up in disbelief. She was going to allow her to eat? Now? Audrina shook her head to clear it.

"I don't want any," she said stiffly, shaking her head no.

Suddenly, Wild Hawk paused with the pone halfway to his mouth.

"Why not?" Rainbow asked. "You are not hungry? You have traveled so far, my brother tells me, and you must be very empty in the stomach. Eat. It is all right. I will eat, too."

The word *brother* did not register in Audrina's head—not as it should have registered.

She watched as the friendly girl served herself and then sat down. Audrina sat in stunned silence for a

308

second longer, then blurted, "You spoke English."

"Yes." Rainbow's voice was soft, her manner gentle. Her doe eyes turned to Wild Hawk, and in her peripheral vision she caught the worried look flash across the white woman's face. "May I speak?" she respectfully asked Wild Hawk.

Wild Hawk rose fluidly to his moccasined feet. "You have already done a good share of talking." With that, Wild Hawk kissed the top of her shiny dark head, while Audrina looked on dejectedly. "I must go. There is much work to be done and many older braves must be visited before this night sees Wild Hawk on his mats."

Audrina looked up at him. "Where are you going?"

"I have to meet with Strong Heart and the Elders, I have said. Do not worry. Rainbow will not bite you."

Wild Hawk made his way to the huge lodge in the center of the summer encampment. This was Wild Hawk's new village; he was the Hawk-People-Who-Shoot-in-the-Leaves' new chief and he had many matters to tend to.

Nodding to the guard who would keep an eye on his tepee when he was gone, the stalwart young chief entered the lodge, meeting with Strong Heart and the few elders who were left in the tribe. They sat and smoked, passing the pipe, then they talked, speaking of matters foremost in importance and then following up with trivial matters.

The People had not really had to go into hiding from Colonel Sibley and his men, for there were so many scattered villages like this one in the Dakota Territory. It would be virtually impossible for Colonel Sibley to round them all up. The war between the North and South had just ended and there were not many white soldiers who wanted to participate in another battle. Wild Hawk tried convincing the others and himself that they were safe. But white hatred for the Indians ran very high right now. He felt that somewhere in him there was another battle left, another battle with the white soldiers, but he did not cherish the feeling that he was going to have to kill again some day.

Some eight hundred Lower Sioux and four thousand Upper Sioux roamed the Dakota Territory. The Upper Sioux had left their villages near Lakes Traverse and Big Stone because they had little faith in Colonel Sibley's promise of safety if they surrendered.

This was the way things stood now. They would stay here until it was time to move on. But Wild Hawk knew they could never return to Minnesota, not as long as Audrina was his captive. There was no need to go there now, for his people were scattered like the four winds, in a wilderness of frustration.

"Oh Great Spirit," Wild Hawk prayed outside the lodge, "teach the white man to appreciate the beauty and wonders of nature and the wildlife. Let them learn the uselessness of wars and conflicts. The Indian people you have put here, Great Spirit, weep for what has happened. Keep us free in this holy land of the Sioux, the Paha-Sapa. We will drink the healing waters that flow from the holes in the rock walls, the tears of Wakantanka, and drink to cure our souls. We have not climbed the peaks in the Black Hills because they are visited by the Thunderbird. I know my father chose to give his great spiritual gift to me. I will use the gift of the Great Spirit to be a mighty leader of the Sioux. Send a voice to me soon, Wakantanka. Show me what I must do. Must I send the defiant *winu* back? Make her my wife? She is a part of me. *Give me a sign.*" Wild Hawk

310

continued to raise his arms to the empurpling sky and pray.

In the big tepee, Audrina felt ill at ease now that Wild Hawk had walked out, leaving her alone with his pretty squaw. She gazed into her soup, wondering about the bits of gray meat floating around, looking but not really caring about the contents of the food.

Rainbow saw, out of the corner of her eye, that Wild Hawk's enchanting captive had set her bowl down. She sat quietly, as if meditating. Rainbow turned around to face the white woman.

"I will not bother you if you are praying," Rainbow said, moving toward the flap.

"I am not . . . praying," Audrina said, wondering why she should have to explain herself to Wild Hawk's squaw. "I suppose I do have to tell you everything now, though."

"Were you speaking to me?" Rainbow asked, facing Audrina again.

"I said," Audrina began, "you will be giving me orders from now on, I suppose. It's only natural. You are his wife. . . ."

"Wife?" Rainbow moved closer. *"Me?"* She pointed to her chest. "I am not a wife . . . not yet."

"You aren't?" Audrina could not believe that Wild Hawk would merely keep her as his mistress. All of a sudden, Audrina frowned. "I am telling you this . . . I will not share him with you. You . . . you can have all of him. Even though you are only his mistress."

"I am mistress to no man, Aud-rina."

Audrina blinked her confusion. "Well, then," she shrugged, "who are you?"

311

The pretty Indian girl giggled. "I am Rainbow," she smiled coyly. "Wild Hawk's sister."

"Oh . . ." Audrina gave a long, drawn-out moan. The heavy lashes that shadowed her cheeks delightfully flew up. Then, a serious look crossing her face, she asked, "You are . . . really?"

"Sha, yes." Rainbow giggled, showing Audrina even white teeth as she leaned backward. She pointed at Audrina. *"Oh . . .* you thought I was Wild Hawk's *squaw.* No wonder you looked so sad when you saw us embrace." She sobered then. "Do we not look *anything* alike?"

Audrina studied the girl closer, now that she was not afraid to do so. "Yes, you do. But—" Audrina began slyly "but I am a captive. A *winu,* he calls me—or Precious Fire. But now—"

"Now?" Rainbow wondered what she had been about to say.

"Now that I have made him angry, he will probably call me Slave. You see, it all had to do with a medicine bundle that belonged to Red Hawk."

Rainbow looked sad all of a sudden. "My father," she said dropping her head. "Red Hawk was our father. I should not say his name. It is not respectful to mention the name of a departed loved one."

Audrina pressed her lips together. "I was there—in Mankato."

"You were *there?"* Rainbow looked confused. "How can this be?"

"I live in Mankato." Audrina's shoulders moved in a light shrug. "I *used* to live there. Now I live . . . here."

Tears glistened in Audrina's eyes, and Rainbow felt sudden compassion for the pretty white woman her

312

brother had taken captive. "Audrina, my brother has never taken a white woman into captivity before. You are the first."

The green eyes gazed at the lovely and kind Indian girl for a moment longer, and then the dam broke. "Ohhh," Audrina moaned between sobs. "Y—you would not u—understand, Rainbow," Audrina groaned. "I do not want to be a captive. I want to be free! I—I have always been free."

Her arm going around Audrina's shoulders, Rainbow said, "Wild Hawk is a good man. He will not beat you. He has never done this to anyone before and I believe he will not start now."

"H—has he ever spoken h—harshly to a woman before?"

"No. I do not recall that he has." Tawena came to mind, but Rainbow preferred not to mention the Warrior Woman.

"Ohhh," Audrina wailed. "Well, he growled at me . . . many times. H—he even shook me and—and pushed me away."

"Maybe it is because he loves you and is jealous because Precious Fire wishes her freedom."

Audrina grew still. "Loves me? He thinks of me only as a possession he can drag around and order about. He even had me tied to his wrist for a while."

"Why?"

"Why?" Audrina blinked damp eyes. "Because I tried to escape. Why shouldn't I?"

"You are right." Rainbow sighed. "But you would not have gotten far."

"How would you know?" Audrina dried her eyes to look at Rainbow. "You said he never had a captive before."

"I know my brother well." Rainbow got up and started to clean around the cook area. "He would not let you get away. There is love in his eyes, Audrina. I saw this at once and now realize what is different about my brother. You have made Wild Hawk different. He seems to be more gentle and caring. He acts gruff, true, but I read the new gentleness in his eyes. You are very fortunate. There are many young women, from here and neighboring tribes far and near, who pine just to belong to Wild Hawk."

"But they are *Indian.*" Audrina had forgotten for the moment that she, too, possessed some Indian blood. But she'd been white in her heart for so long that it was going to be difficult changing to an Indian's way of thinking.

"Yes, you are right," Rainbow said. Then she stared at Audrina and she felt an odd sense of something. "Who were your parents, Audrina?"

"My father's name was Frank Harris."

"And what was your mother's name?"

That question made Audrina want to cry, but there were no more tears in her to be spent.

"Her name was Melissa. She died giving birth to me."

Audrina decided she would not, could not, tell Rainbow her secret—that she was one-quarter Oglala Sioux.

"Was there not the love of someone else who cared for you when you were a babe?"

"Oh, yes. My Aunt Katherine." Choking back a small sob, she said, "Katherine loved me very much but she is dead now."

Gently, Rainbow asked, "How did she die?"

"Wild Hawk had her killed!" Audrina said bitterly.

314

"No! Rainbow cannot believe this. Why would he do such a thing?"

"I don't know," Audrina answered, her face troubled and unhappy. "Why don't you ask him; he's your brother."

Unable to believe her brother capable of such a cruel act, Rainbow pressed on to extricate the truth. "Was it Wild Hawk who did the actual killing?"

Audrina shook her head. "No. It was—"

The bells tinkled at the doorway of the tepee.

Having kept her ears peeled, Tawena entered the tepee just then. "I hope you do not mind, Rainbow," Tawena said. "I saw that your flap was open, so I accepted the welcome." Her black eyes swept Audrina with a hostile glare. "I see you have been talking to Wild Hawk's defiant *winu*. I do not care for all the English that is being spoken around here. . . ."

"Please . . . I heard what you said. Do not call me that," Audrina snapped. "I do not like the word *winu.*"

"What did she say?" Tawena questioned the dainty young woman, enviously eyeing a new doeskin shift Rainbow was wearing.

Slowly, the elfin face swung to Audrina. "Tawena would like to know what you said." Her eyes twinkled in camaraderie. "Should I tell her?"

"No. Let her stew." Audrina picked up her cold food and began to eat as if suddenly assailed by great hunger.

The bowl was almost full, and Tawena eyed it for only a moment before she advanced stealthily, then suddenly kicked her foot upwards, sending the stew flying into Audrina's face and down the front of the only clothes she owned besides the Indian shift she sometimes wore.

315

"Oh!" Audrina shot to her feet. "Look what you have done, you—you she-devil!"

"Watch out, Audrina," Rainbow warned. "Tawena has a bad temper."

"And so do I!" Audrina stepped closer to Tawena. "I've already had a go at it with her!"

Rainbow gasped. "You have fought with the Warrior Woman? How did you manage to come out alive and with your face unmarred?"

"Wild Hawk saved her."

The owner of the husky deep voice stepped casually into the tepee, ordering Tawena to leave at once. "Do not ever come into this dwelling place without being invited." When she began to defend herself, he told her to be still. "Hear me and obey. Otherwise I will have you punished, Warrior Woman."

"Me?" Tawena's nostrils flared in outrage. "You would never do that to *me,* Warrior Woman."

Stepping closer to Tawena, Wild Hawk peered down from his ominous height. "Do you try me, woman?"

"Oh, Wild Hawk!" Tawena threw herself at him. "Do you not know how I care for you? I only sought to make the white captive behave. She always wants to fight with me. She hates you. She would kill you if she found the chance. Can you not see this?"

"Stand back from me!" Wild Hawk hissed, unwinding Tawena's arms from his neck. "You sicken me with your lies. Take care," he said as she backed away, her eyes angry and bold. "I will banish you from this tribe if you dare to interfere in what is mine again, Tawena!" he snarled just as she was ducking out the opening. Then, demandingly, he said, "Bring Audrina fresh clothes to wear in the morning. I do not care where you

316

obtain them. Bring them here, even if they are your own clothes."

"Sha!" Tawena hissed; then she was gone.

Rainbow was busily fussing over Audrina, trying to clean the stew off her bodice. Then she stopped and hunkered back on her heels. "I have a nice clean shift you can wear for the night. It is soft," she told Audrina, and shyly she added, as she brought it out of her possessions, "If you like it, you can have it for your own." Rainbow handed it to her new friend.

"Oh, it *is* soft." Audrina caressed the tender hide that was almost a golden shade. "How did you get it like this? It is almost like a cotton nightgown."

"I do not know *cotton,"* Rainbow said. "But I labored on the hide for a very long time. I scraped it and rubbed it with animal brains to soften the hide. Then it hung many days in the tanning. I sewed the beads and quills into it, and this took much time, too."

"You worked so hard on it . . . I don't know how I could accept this fine garment."

Pressing a flushed cheek to the soft hide, Audrina looked up at Wild Hawk, praying that he was not disappointed in his sister's generosity.

"Just accept." With a light shrug, Rainbow added, "We share, Aud-rina. Indians do not have to be reminded to feed those who are hungry, to give shelter to those in need, to clothe the poor. We do it instinctively and with pleasure and . . . sincerely. We visit the sick and afflicted, and are sympathetic to those who suffer misfortune or disaster. We place importance on being *wastecaka,* generous."

"Wastecaka." Audrina nodded. "I like this word."

Audrina would learn just how important this was as

317

she came to know the Sioux Indians better. In fact, she would come to know that generosity was a cardinal virtue of the *Dakota oyate,* the Dakota people.

Do I belong here? Am I really to be one of them? Time would tell, she answered her own question.

Over the next several weeks, Audrina learned more from her new friend. Wild Hawk had years ago taught his sister to speak English, and lately Rainbow had even mastered connecting the name Aud-rina and now said it quickly. They were each learning the other's language and customs.

Wild Hawk often left Audrina in his sister's care. Audrina was puzzled that Wild Hawk did not seek her out at night. A week passed, then two, and still he left her alone. There were times when he did not even share the tepee with her and Rainbow. She learned from Rainbow that Wild Hawk would sleep in the Big Lodge with other high-ranking warriors, for they would discuss issues far into the star-studded night and doze off until the morning star was the last twinkle in the sky. Then they would rise and go about their day-business.

Audrina saw Wild Hawk one chilly rain-swept day just returning from a hunt. Daringly, she stared his way, feeling thrills race along her spine when he looked at her. His feet were clad in high-ankled moccasins. His leggings were richly ornamented with quills, and each bore distinctive crosses, the black marks earned only by saving a fellow warrior's life in battle. His deerskin shirt—the one he wore only in the coolness of early morning—bore two bands of quillwork across the shoulders and bands on each arm. Audrina had asked Rainbow about the hair fringe along both arms, for she had not seen any of the other warriors with this style.

"The hair fringe is worn only by important chiefs."

"I see." Audrina found herself idly wondering what it would be like to be married to such an important man. She watched as he walked through the village. He made no sign to her.

Audrina learned more and more about the Hawk People and the Great Spirit *Wakantanka,* who was much like her own God. The Sioux were shocked to hear the paleface use the name of the Great Spirit in jest or carry on licentious conversations. In fact, Rainbow said, no tribe of Indians that she knew of had a word with which to take the name of the Great Spirit in vain, nor did they have curse words such as the *wasicun* had.

Audrina learned about name-giving and how it is one of the most important events in a Dakota person's life.

"How is a child given his name?" Audrina asked.

"When the child is born, the grandmother and the Medicine Man give the child his first tribal name. They are the only ones who know this name. If the grandmother passes on, the oldest woman relation takes her place."

"When does the child receive his real name?"

Rainbow answered, "When the child is about fifty moons. That would be about four years old. Then they name the child after what Wakantanka had created or something linked to the clan of his grandfather. If a young man goes on a vision quest, he can choose his name that way, from what he sees in his special vision,

319

like an eagle, a hawk, a bear, a fox, and whatever that animal is doing in his vision, like running, stalking. During my brother's vision quest, where he dreamed and entered a world where the spirits of all living things dwell, he rode on the back of a powerful hawk. He felt very wild, very free. He saw the hills look up as he flew over, the valleys, rivers, and creeks passing under. He saw more, but this he does not tell anyone, not even me, his sister."

During these talks, Audrina and Rainbow would sit or walk outside on the clear, bright Dakota days with puffy white clouds sailing in an azure sky, and always two pairs of hostile eyes followed. The brother and sister fought to keep their hatred under control, especially when their leader was near, but it was becoming harder and harder for Tawena and Left Hand to restrain themselves from murdering the whites as they slept.

Often Tawena and Left Hand would leave the encampment during the night. No one stopped them, for the guards thought they went out to hunt. The brother and sister were very quiet and did not return sometimes for days at a time. And they did not always go to hunt. . . .

What no one knew, not even Wild Hawk, was that they had gone out to meet the Hoha Indians in the hills where they encamped, in the sacred grounds that were forbidden to be entered. But they did not care. They did not stay there in order to see the Thunderbird; they were there to hide out. This was Indian Territory and they were still Indians, even if they were called Rebels. They were considered outcasts of the Sioux Nation.

Another individual had joined the Hohas. His name

320

was Joe Powell. His enlistment time in the Army was up, so he could do anything he wanted, and what he wanted most in the world was to find Audrina Harris. After he found her and made her his possession, he could reenlist with Captain Bellum's New Ulm militia. Only now *he* wanted to be captain and he would make this come about in any way he could.

Tawena and Left Hand passed the site of an abandoned Sioux village and came to the mouth of a canyon. Within its high protecting walls grew a tall pine whose large bottom branches were more than six feet above the canyon floor.

"We will meet them beyond this point. Not far now," Left Hand informed Tawena.

"Good. Will they have the *wasicun* soldier with them this time?" Tawena was eager to meet the man who would become the instigator in their plot—without his knowledge.

"*Sha,* he will be with them."

They spent another fifteen minutes or so riding carefully over rocks, skirting thorny bushes and brambles that created a painful barrier to any swifter passage.

Suddenly, Yellow Bear sat before them on his war horse, a picture of wickedness in the harsh light of day. His hair was more iron-gray than black. The hank of it was gathered into two long braids, both of which bore wolf-trimmed braid wraps. The strong face was typically Sioux: eyes set wide apart over high, broad cheekbones; nose long and wide and heavily bridged; chin like a vise. His whole face was seamed and stitched like old leather. His body, tall and large-framed, was still sinewy with muscle, but the skin that was gathered

321

in places betrayed his age. He was only fifty, but he had aged swiftly because of enmity for his own people. He was also fat around the middle—a sign of overeating and lack of exercise.

Tawena received her first look at Joe Powell as he rode out from behind Yellow Bear. "Surely he is a paleface," she whispered with a sneer to Left Hand. "Even though the sun has tanned him above the blue collar of his shirt, I can still see what a paleface he is." Below the waist, Powell wore stained buckskins and old Army boots. Tawena took in the blond wavy hair, a nose that was only a little crooked, and noticed that he was built solidly, with a substantial amount of muscle. All in all, Powell was good-looking—for a *wasicun*. White man or not, Tawena was happy to see him, for it meant that Precious Fire would be leaving the village soon to return to Minnesota with Powell.

Joe took one look at Tawena and noticed the menace in her slaty eyes and the curled lip of pride and haughtiness. Long blue-black hair had been braided and slung over one reddish-brown shoulder, bared by the sag of the loose shift she wore. His gaze dropped to the long Indian rifle that rode at her hip, aware without being shown that she knew how to use it—expertly.

There were several more moments of taut silence, and then he spoke. "This is the Warrior Woman you told me about?" Powell inquired, and Yellow Bear nodded. "Why has she come with Left Hand?" he asked in Dakota.

Coldly, Tawena whipped out an answer, causing Powell to swing his gaze around to her. "Because, paleface, he is my brother. I go where he goes, especially when it is a matter of importance."

322

Piqued at her insolence, Powell wanted to ignore her, but she had said one word he had not understood. He asked Yellow Bear to translate and the older man grunted, "Paleface. Tawena has called you paleface," he said in English and chuckled. It was not a happy sound, but more like the sound of a man who is sick and tired of everything in general.

"Speak no English!" Tawena ordered sternly.

"Hiya! You are too outspoken, Warrior Woman," Yellow Bear spat viciously. "Be still, bitch. You are only a female. I do not care if you are Warrior Woman. You listen and be still. If you do not obey, I will rape you as I did once before for your brazenness."

For all her deep bronze color, Tawena paled visibly. She remembered the day. She had called him *p'tay,* fat buffalo cow. She remembered the tearing punishment of his organ, his hot, eager thrusts and his hard, hostile hands pawing her all over. Never, never would Tawena allow Yellow Bear to force her through that agony again. She would kill herself first.

As the Indians and Joe Powell conversed quietly, Tawena could tell that the *wasicun* Powell was very eager to get his hands on Precious Fire. Why did all the strong, virile warriors, white and Indian, want that red-haired vixen? Even Strong Heart had been looking sweetly at Audrina Harris and it vexed Tawena to no end. But Tawena knew a secret no one else knew: Strong Heart loved Rainbow but was too shy to do anything about it. Tawena wrinkled her nose in disgust, wondering why love made strong warriors into men weak in the knees.

The low campfire cast a reddish-bronze glow over Left Hand's wily face as he spoke to the other men. "We will make our move when Wild Hawk goes to council with the Sissetons."

"When will that be?" Powell asked.

"In fourteen moons," Left Hand answered. "If all goes well in the Sisseton Camp and they do not call off the meeting again."

Powell glanced at Yellow Bear, who was swigging at the whiskey jug. Yellow Bear wanted Precious Fire for himself, but Powell had promised to get him supplies, blankets and food enough to feed them for many months. Yellow Bear looked surreptitiously in Powell's direction. He had brought Powell this far, but once he had all those things he would take Precious Fire for his own.

That night Tawena and Left Hand stayed in the jagged green hills with Yellow Bear and his men. She was the only woman there that night—and she was in trouble.

Tawena had been abused by many in a drunken party before. The savages were passing tall green whiskey bottles around, and before long they were reaching for her skirt and moving it up to feel her leg.

Tipping a bottle now and then, Joe Powell sat back against a thick-trunked pine, chuckling to himself. Inebriated Indians were as crazy as loons, he thought, watching as one of the eager braves mounted Tawena and shoved her skirt to her thighs. He was about to thrust into her when she unseated him, and when she managed to pin him to the ground beneath her, she withdrew a wicked-looking blade that she at once pressed to his skinny throat. Drawing blood, Tawena watched it trickle into his greasy black hair.

"You will leave Tawena alone," she bit out slowly,

harshly. Then, letting him rise to his rubbery legs, she waved the knife around, warning all the savage drunkards in a hissing tone that they had better watch themselves and make no sudden moves toward her. "Tawena chooses who she will bed with."

"And who will you choose, Warrior Woman?" asked Yellow Bear, almost in a stupor where he lounged against a tree, wrapped in a buffalo robe.

"Powell."

"What?!" Joe shot up straight, his back scratched by the tree. "Wait a minute . . . I'm not looking for any fun tonight." He patted the bottle against his chest. "This is all I want to cuddle up with. Besides, I'm dreaming about what I'm going to do when I get Audrina back."

Tawena snorted, having heard the name Audrina. Finally, she arose to walk away.

"Be still, *sunka ska,*" Tawena hissed, calling Powell white dog.

Disgusted and bitter, Tawena glared at the *wasicun* soldier who had begun to snore, the half-empty whiskey bottle cradled at his chest. He wanted Precious Fire. Wild Hawk wanted Precious Fire. . . . Audrina . . . Audrina . . . She was getting sick of that woman. *"Ptah!* Precious Fire. I spit on all her relatives' graves—*Ptah! Ptah!* Maybe I will even spit on Precious Fire's grave soon."

Soon . . . Tawena's eyes glittered maliciously. In fourteen moons Precious Fire would be gone and she could sink her claws into Wild Hawk. He would be sad. He would need to be consoled. She would be there, not the *wasichu* woman with the grass eyes and dark fire hair. Not Audrina, Precious Fire. Tawena, Warrior

Woman, would stand beside the great Chief Wild Hawk. She, Tawena, would bear him many fine sons ... many ... many. ...

At that moment, miles down into the moonlit valley, Wild Hawk and Audrina were making love in a wooden copse near Lonewoman Creek. "My beloved captive," he murmured. "Let me always be with you. Let me feel the earth beneath my feet, the sun against my face, and you by my side. We are as one, man and woman, like husband and wife. Without you I will become as nothing. I would hear your voice in the wind. Your eyes would look at me from everywhere. The sky. The sun ... the grass. My heart would be lost without your precious embrace."

"Wild Hawk," Audrina said, smoothing back his long black hair. "I am not going anywhere." At least, not yet, she told herself silently, feeling tears burn her eyelids.

"Do not ever leave me, Audrina."

Audrina gazed into his moonlit eyes. "What if someone takes me away?" she asked softly.

"Do not speak such words." Fires burned in his eyes as he jerked away from her. "I will kill anyone who would try that! I would bring you back, and he would be staked to the ground and I would peel his skin from his body. I would slowly remove his eyes and his ears, his nose—"

"Oh ... please. Stop!" Audrina begged. Pressing into his warm, vibrant body, she peered into his moon-glazed eyes. "That is terrible. Then you really are a savage."

Ducking beneath his arms, she sat up at once, looking deep into the shadows with a look of worry and bewilderment. She felt the turmoil deep inside again. Why had she made love with him again? Was she crazy? One minute she was walking to the stream with him, the next she was lying flat on her back watching the fiery streaks of sunset above her while he thrust in and out vigorously and ravenously. Breathlessly, rapturously, she had met every thrust, feeling the unleashed strength of his powerful body . . . his lust . . . his love . . . his seed.

Audrina made a motion to stand, but he grabbed her back down beneath him. "*Hiya,* Precious Fire. You have defied me again by calling me savage." She was still so moist that he entered her with ease. With urgent desire coursing madly between them, they made love fiercely again, finding that quivering rapture together for the fourth time that moonlit night.

As she dressed Audrina almost wept, for every time they joined it was like a sweet expression of love. When they stayed away from each other and did not make love, it was as if a part of her were sorely missing.

With a smile in his voice, Wild Hawk said out of the blue, "I believe Audrina defies her captor so that he will make love to her. Is this true?"

"You are learning English better and better, Wild Hawk."

"This I know. I have a talented teacher."

"I have two," she said happily. "Wild Hawk and his lovely sister, Rainbow."

By the time Audrina and Wild Hawk returned to the tepee, she was asking herself for the hundredth time since arriving in his village, How could she leave him?

Her heart had been filled to overflowing this night. She was certain Wild Hawk had experienced it, too. But he was a proud warrior; he would not readily admit it. But their loving, embracing bodies had triumphed and attested to the burning truth: They loved deeply, totally, irreversibly.

It is love, Audrina told herself before she fell asleep between Rainbow and Wild Hawk. It is a precious passion, not just physical. No. Their love was growing . . . by leaps and bounds. It was terrifying.

Chapter Twelve

Audrina was becoming fluent in the Dakota/Sioux language. Every day Rainbow tutored her, telling her what different words meant and helping her to pronounce the voiceless guttural "throat-clearing," "gargling," and "explosive" sounds. She would always end up on her back, giggling or laughing hard.

There was a bluff close by, and Audrina went up there often just to be alone. Peaceful, happy for the time being, she would sit there, facing the setting sun. There was always someone watching her, she knew. But she did not care, for she blotted the invisible presence of the "guard" out and let her thoughts flow.

Gazing downward, Audrina could see the tips of the tepees and some patches of canvas through the trees. It was beautiful here, wonderfully peaceful, with the sun shining in a vast blue sky on clear days, sometimes bits of clouds drifting lazily overhead. When the men were lucky in the hunt, there was plenty of meat to eat. Otherwise, there was an abundance of juniper and cedar berries and the fast-maturing vegetables the

Indians had planted early in the season. Audrina had lost several pounds, but still she could not be called skinny. She was slender, and her breasts were not too small but like "two perfect doves," Wild Hawk had informed her while capturing the soft fullness of one breast, then the other.

Audrina sat in awe and cried softly in delight when a mighty hawk with a wingspan of five feet soared high above the ponderosa pine. She watched the hawk until he was well out of sight. She stared down into the deep green shady woods below the grassy bluff then and wondered who had been ordered to watch her this day, hoping earnestly it was not Left Hand, for she could not stand his slaty eyes that always seemed to be undressing her.

Breathing deeply of the pine-scented air, Audrina leaned back then forward again in a rocking motion, feeling serenely peaceful. The sun was setting behind the woods, its glimmering rays pushing between the tree trunks and foliage. It set the village aglow with a heavy stroke of wild rose and touched the water of Lonewoman Creek with spindrifts of fire. This western section of the Dakotas was like an enchanted savage paradise. She loved the pine-smelling woods, the wildly winding trails where Indian moccasins had softly trod for years and years.

Audrina was almost at perfect peace. If only she would be able to live happily with Wild Hawk and the *Odakota,* "the real people," "the friends." To learn their ways fully and be satisfied to want for nothing more but Wild Hawk's splendorous love.

But did *he* really love *her?* Would *he* be willing to live like the white man? Or, would *she* be willing to abandon the white man's luxuries to live in the wild with her wild beloved, her tender warrior? Which one of them would give in first? What if neither of them did? Though it was like paradise here, she missed Minnesota. She missed having a comfortable chair to sit in. She missed sleeping in a bed that was soft and off the ground. What if she became pregnant and had children by Wild Hawk? It was entirely possible. How could they be educated in the proper white man's way? They would be brought up in the red man's world. Would they want to discover the other world she had come from? There were so many questions.

Audrina sighed. The preacher in the church in Mankato once said, "You can usually tell how bad a person wants something by realizing how much he's willing to give up for it." The message had dealt with loving and obeying God, how much you were willing to give up in order to follow Him. But the same concession could similarly be meant for lovers also.

"Your treasure is where your heart is." Where had she read that line? Had the same Preacher Williams quoted it? Was it from the Bible? She couldn't rightly recall, but it had been engraved upon her memory and the single line stood out profoundly in her mind just now.

The last rays of melting sun had vanished and a low moon was hanging romantically in an evening-blue sky. Audrina stood slowly and brushed off her skirt. The low voice came to her on a gentle breeze, sighing over the treetops.

"My *Petala* . . . Audrina . . ."

Precious Fire.

Her beloved warrior was calling from below. With a

quaint wistfulness on her face, Audrina turned calmly and went to meet him. The world seemed to stand still in the blurred lavender of dusk.

Silent as shadows, they walked hand in hand. As the red sun blended into the earth moments ago, they too became one with the earth and melted and joined and shared a fierce and fiery Indian passion. She had cried the name Wild Hawk again . . . and again. . . .

It was a long time later when they went to seek their night's rest, unaware that each was as troubled as the other. Their uncertain future plagued them deep into the night, until at last, exhausted, they fell asleep, fingertips contacting lightly, as if afraid to lose the other's beloved caress.

Audrina slept like the dead until she felt the sun hitting the side of the tepee and warming her flesh like a heavy, suffocating blanket. She sat up with a guilty start. Noticing she was all alone in the tepee, she wondered why no one had tried to awaken her.

Looking around as she rose from the buffalo robes, Audrina noticed that Wild Hawk's Indian rifle was gone, as were his other weapons. That could only mean one thing—he had gone hunting.

Just then Rainbow entered the tepee, cheerfully greeting Audrina in Dakota. Audrina said "Good morning" in the same language. Then, in almost the same breath, in the same language again, she asked if Wild Hawk had gone hunting.

"He has gone to meet with warriors from other tribes. He is the leader of the Cante Tinza."

"What does that mean?" Audrina asked, removing

the sleeping shift and pulling on a fresh one for day wear.

"It means Brave Heart Warrior Society." For some reason, as she said this, Rainbow remembered the bitter look on Left Hand's face as her brother became leader of the Cante Tinza. Left Hand had always coveted that position. She had watched Left Hand when her brother was readying his horse just that morning. Left Hand's eyes were still full of daggered envy. She was grateful to the Great Spirit for one thing—that Left Hand did not lead them in any of the honorable societies. Left Hand was desperately competitive and greedy for power. Rainbow had always kept it to herself that she did not trust Left Hand and his sister Tawena.

"My brother is Chief of the Hawk-People-Who-Shoot-in-the-Leaves," Rainbow told Audrina. "The only other warrior here who could take his place is Strong Heart. He will be sub-chief someday." For a moment, her eyes took on a dreamy expression.

Audrina softly chewed her lower lip before she spoke. "Why didn't Wild Hawk tell me he was going to this meeting?"

"Do not be unhappy, Audrina. You were sleeping and he did not wish to awaken you." Rainbow saw her friend's inner turmoil. "What is it, Precious Fire? Has something made you sad?"

"It is nothing. I—I just felt a little sick, that's all." Now, why did you have to go and lie! Audrina chided herself. Then again, come to think of it, she did feel a little nauseated.

Reaching out, Audrina touched Rainbow lightly on the shoulder. "Uhmm, let's go to the creek. I would like to wash myself and—and some of my clothes."

Upon reaching the creek, however, Audrina was dismayed to discover that there were other squaws and maidens there, and she did not have a chance to speak with Rainbow about what was troubling her. The desire to pour out her soul was leaving her fast. She shrugged as some of the squaws began to chatter, a few of them giving her dirty looks, still not liking her very much. By the time they were ready to return to camp, Audrina felt surly and did not wish to discuss anything, especially not Wild Hawk!

The time for confidential conversation arrived several days later while Audrina sat mending Wild Hawk's and her clothes.

"Sit with me for a while, Rainbow. I—I need someone to talk to." It was difficult to get Rainbow to stop moving, even for a minute, but finally the young woman saw that this was somewhat serious and she listened—with half an ear.

"Rainbow, stop, can you please listen?" Audrina groaned. "You aren't really paying any attention to what I'm saying."

With a sheepish turn of her head, Rainbow said, "I know what Audrina wants to say. It is not good."

"No," Audrina insisted, lifting her cool green gaze to the Indian girl. "You do not know what Audrina wants to say. I have started this conversation several times, but you always steer it to something else."

"You wish to talk about how much you hate being Wild Hawk's 'winu, captive woman?' Say what you want to say. But if you want me to help you escape my brother, the answer is no."

"I would never ask you to do that, Rainbow."

Rainbow's liquid black eyes narrowed curiously as she asked, "Then what is it that Audrina wants?"

Audrina pursed her lips. "It all began when your brother took me captive." She thought for a moment, then changed her mind. "No, that's not when it all began. Listen closely to what I have to say, Rainbow. The day your father was executed in Mankato"—Audrina cleared her throat—"a big hawk dropped a medicine bundle at my feet. Don't look at me like that, Rainbow, I am telling you the truth." Rainbow's black eyes widened. "A beautiful hawk just swooped over me and—and dropped it. I took it in my aunt's house and kept it in her closet. The first time she saw it, she shrieked."

Rainbow started to rise. "I have to make supper. Perhaps Wild Hawk will re—"

"*Oh!*"

Audrina wanted to scream. Sighing heavily, she begged, "Sit back down, Rainbow, please. I am not finished talking."

"But Rainbow is finished *hearing.*"

"Please, Rainbow, don't be afraid of what I have to say. There's no one else for me to talk to because Wild Hawk surely doesn't want to hear."

Rainbow nodded and returned to the mat. She almost whispered when she leaned to Audrina. "A hawk dropped the medicine bundle at your feet? This is really true?"

Audrina nodded, praying that Rainbow could enlighten her where her brother hadn't.

"This does not happen to white people, Audrina.

That was a sacred bundle. In it were Red Hawk's smallest possessions, very valuable ones."

"They didn't make much sense to me. The clay pipe was broken, no doubt from the fall after the hawk dropped it to the ground. There were feathers, swatches of hair—"

"From scalp locks."

"Oh." Audrina looked as if she might become ill. "Well anyway, I did keep the bundle, despite what Aunt Katherine kept telling me. She said if I didn't find the rightful heir or give it to a Sioux from the same tribe, I would be under a curse. Finally, a woman by the name of Moving Voice, or Minowa, visited me and—"

Rainbow went very still for several moments. As Audrina paused, the Indian girl softly inquired, "Minowa?"

"Yes. My aunt asked her to come see me." She began to tell her friend about that meeting with Minowa, unaware that Rainbow's thoughts had begun to stray elsewhere.

The Indian girl did not say, but she was puzzled that Rain Lily's sister Minowa had been the one to visit Audrina. Her mother, Rain Lily, had been dead many years now. Minowa had gone to live with her husband on the Lower Sioux Indian Reservation in Minnesota, not all that far from Mankato, where Audrina said she had lived.

"Tell me again," Rainbow began. "How did you happen to have this pouch in your possession? I wish to know if it was before or after my father's execution. I would like you to tell me everything you can about that day. If you were at the execution, how long you stayed, if you saw my brother there . . ."

336

Audrina took a deep breath and then began to describe that day, and the day three months later when Wild Hawk burst into her house—when she was naked with another man. . . . Did she have to explain *that?*

When Audrina finished telling Rainbow about the hawk dropping the medicine bundle in the yard, she failed to see the shadow lingering right outside the tepee. She was totally unaware that Wild Hawk had returned until Rainbow jumped up from the mat and rushed to throw open the door flap.

Audrina was just getting to her feet when Wild Hawk entered, bloody rabbits dripping from his hands. Those large, bronze hands, she saw, were clenched tightly over the floppy ears. It came to her in a sudden rush of faintness: *He has heard much of what I just told Rainbow.* And when she looked up into his eyes, she knew it was so.

Forcing a smile, she all but whispered, "Wild Hawk."

"Why has my devoted captive not come to greet me?" he growled like a bear. 'Why does my sister have to hurry to do my bidding when there is a strong and healthy *winu* here?"

He looked so angry that Audrina thought he would prefer to lunge across the tepee to throttle her instead of speak to her. "So," he began, while Rainbow instantly busied herself in preparing the rabbits, "you still hold to those same lies."

A surge of anger bolstered Audrina's courage. "If you are so sure that they are lies, then tell me, How *did* I come to have the pouch in my possession? Tell me that?"

"We have been through this before briefly, Audrina,

337

and you continue to lie for your lover."

"That is not true, Wild Hawk. You know yourself I have not had any other lover but yourself." She felt her flesh color hotly, knowing that Rainbow must have overheard.

"I only know that Audrina was with Powell—and she had my father's pouch with her a long time before I discovered it on her person."

"Oh," Audrina groaned. "I suppose you heard the part about Minowa, too?"

"Minowa?" His eyes darkened suspiciously. "Why do you mention my mother's sister, Minowa? We have not seen that woman for a long time." He moved closer to her, every step menacing and bold. "Tell me, how did you come to know that name, sister of Rain Lily, my deceased mother?"

"She—she came to see me."

"*Hiya,* why would Minowa come to visit a paleface?"

"My Aunt Katherine sent for her. Minowa told me that the medicine bundle was occupied by the spirit of a man—a very powerful one."

Like the lightning strike of a snake, Wild Hawk caught Audrina by the arm. "Again, you lie. How can this be? Such things of mystery are known to happen— but not in the white man's world."

"Well . . . then I must be an Indian, too," Audrina said.

"You are a *wasichu* woman." He shook her, and all of a sudden her vulnerability surfaced. He saw it, but he continued to torment her. "And whites cannot be trusted."

"That's just not true! And you know it."

"I know nothing but the lies I have heard here today.

338

You have kept the pouch from me so you could return it to your lover, Powell."

"This is ridiculous!" She gasped and Rainbow turned back to her chore once again after having watched their heated exchange. Too late, Audrina realized her drastic, far-reaching mistake.

Unceremoniously, he pulled her over to where his possessions lay and bound her wrists with the rope behind her back. Her eyes looked up into his like a wounded creature's. "Why are you doing this to me?" When he began to walk away, she called to him, "Wild Hawk . . . please . . . don't tie me up again."

When he put his back to her, she decided she had already boldly ventured this far and she might as well go all the way. "You know I have heard the drums and Dakota songs coming from the pouch. All of what I've said is God's truth. If you cannot accept the truth, so be it."

Audrina looked to Rainbow to bestow support upon her, but the Indian girl kept her back to her. She did not understand that the Great Spirit meant for Audrina to come here, that there was a purpose for her living among the Cetan/Wahpekutes. At the moment she only knew that her brother must not show weakness before his people. He must be the master here and his captive must be subdued.

But Audrina had begun to see much for herself. She came to the conclusion that no matter what she said or did, Wild Hawk would always trust his own cynical beliefs first. She would always be *wasicun* . . . and he the Sioux Indian. She was nothing more than a female captive. He had said it himself; she was not to be trusted.

And he, she thought spitefully, watching him exit the tepee like a savage master, he might be responsible for the death of my aunt, but he will never, never cause the death of *my* spirit!

Night was slowly enveloping the village as Wild Hawk returned to the tepee to check on Audrina. She had remained rooted to the spot where he had left her fastened to a lodge pole. But she had grown weary and fallen asleep on the mat, having refused to eat anything Rainbow had offered her. Wild Hawk had left Rainbow at the tepee of Strong Heart's younger female cousin, telling her he was going back to check on Audrina.

"Please, do not be too harsh on Precious Fire," Rainbow had begged. Her brother was surprised, for she had never begged him for anything before, not even the white man's pretty trinkets he could have gotten for her by trading Indian blankets and pelts at the Dakota and Minnesota forts.

"I will deal with her as I must, my sister."

"Yes," she said, knowing her Indian friend was watching her curiously. Rainbow sat down again, cross-legged, and they resumed the storytelling, which was a favorite pastime with the Dakota Indians. But Rainbow listened with half an ear; she was concerned for Precious Fire and what her brother would do to her new friend. . . .

Audrina stirred, feeling a silken sensation along her thigh as she opened her eyes to the dark. Someone was kissing her and running warm, vibrant lips up her leg.

"Wild Hawk!" Furiously, she began to struggle.

"How dare you come in here and seduce me while I'm asleep . . . especially after treating me like dirt."

"My *Petala* . . . Precious Fire is not dirt." His lips moved over her throat, while his long, dark fingers pushed aside the bodice of her shift. "And Wild Hawk dares anything."

"Do not call me your 'little fire,' either!"

"Be still, or surely I will take Audrina by force."

"You wouldn't!" Audrina gasped, wondering if he really would or not.

For answer, Wild Hawk ran his fingers through her auburn-dark hair, unbound and falling free about her softly rounded hips. Reverently, he kissed her hair, her nape, her breasts. He began to remove the shift, slowly, realizing agonizingly that underneath she wore no other garments. Her body was olive-gold and naked; he could see her from the moonlight that filtered in from the fire-hole.

He finished removing the shift and Audrina drew her arms in front of her with an instinctive, meaningful gesture, and then, seeing the naked demand in his moonlit eyes, she suddenly felt wanton and brave. Flinging her head up, she laughed with throaty delight as she threw her arms around his neck, nuzzling his throat and deliciously nibbling here and there.

Wild Hawk had prepared an erotic torture for her, had meant to leave her hanging in the lurch after he had brought her to a feverish pitch of aching desire. But he was the one pleasantly surprised. He had never seen Audrina like this, clinging to him in absolute surrender. His strength was hard against the naked splendor of her soft, feminine flesh.

Wild Hawk only purred deeply in his throat, running

his fingers through her fiery dark hair. They stroked at her temples, and up and down her moist throat. They dropped lower, and Audrina tingled with bold responsiveness as Wild Hawk fondled her taut-nippled breasts. Sighing, she pushed up to meet him, heated by his magical caresses that expertly discovered all the special hills and valleys and flat planes of her body to make her passionately come alive.

Taken slightly aback by her bold surrender and delightful abandonment to his advances, Wild Hawk kissed her all over. He bent on his knees, burying his face in the cleft between her creamy mounds, pressing her dovelike breasts to his cheeks, then shifting slightly to taste fully of the ripe auburn fruit and cream with his encircling tongue.

"Oh, love me, love me, my bold, handsome warrior!" she cried, clinging now. For the moment her worries had vanished, his kisses melting her resistance like spring snow, his male sensuality sending a flickering heat throughout her body until she felt like a trembling flame.

"Ahhh, sweet tigress," he groaned, for that was what she was to him that night, bold and wild and beautiful.

You are my enemy, Audrina thought with passion's fervor, *and I love you!*

Boldly, he staked his claim on her body, nuzzling and kissing her hips and sides and abdomen, and the two soft, sloping angles where her feminine form slanted deliciously inside her thighs . . . then the velvet-soft lips.

"Oh . . . beloved!" Audrina panted. "My beloved warrior!"

White-hot images spun through Wild Hawk's mind,

342

whetting him to an intolerable tension, making him realize he had never experienced such blazing heat in his groin before, in fact, all throughout his male body. His heart. His soul. His whole body was afire for one special woman.

Lifting her up into his arms, he carried her outside to a natural grass bed behind the tepee. Beneath the spindrift of moonshadow, he laid her down. At once Audrina's arms fell wide across the earth, her slim, bare calves and buttocks experiencing erotic delight against the dew-kissed grass.

Gazing into the great heavens, Audrina felt a oneness with everything. A falling star drew its fine, bright line deep into the Aurora, the Great Dipper towering above the shafts of mystic light. In the whole expanse of the star-studded sky there was not a single cloud, only the celestial lights moving in the northern sky.

Under the stars, they resumed making love. Audrina soared to the hawk's domain with her beloved savage. Wild Hawk kept one hand cupped to her shapely breast with a gliding, kneading motion while he gazed down at her in the moonlight. With his other hand he unfastened his breeches. With energetic passion, they fused together at once, and everything in the heavens became even brighter.

Ecstasy washed over the moonlit lovers. Wild Hawk and Audrina were so eager for each other by now that the shattering climax was over before they were hardly aware of it. The sudden release came as a pleasant shock and then there was only a slow drawing of sighs.

When Wild Hawk felt the final pulsations beneath his body, he raised himself on his elbows and shifted his weight so that his still rigid staff slid all the way out.

Standing to his feet brusquely, he pulled Audrina up so fast that she was startled, and then he almost dragged her forcibly back into the tepee. "Put this on," he ordered after bending to retrieve the discarded shift.

"You are punishing me—why?" Audrina stood holding the shift.

"Surely you must know!"

"You believe I told a lie." Audrina stood, shaking her bright disheveled head.

"For telling *many* lies," Wild Hawk said.

He tied her up again, then he went out. Cold. Impersonal. Audrina felt the loss like a knife in her chest. She felt abandoned. So very alone. Crawling into the buffalo robes, she covered herself as if she'd come down with a cold and a chill. Her whole body shivered and would not cease its violent tremblings.

"I have to get away from him," she told herself. "He loves me one day; the next he despises me because my skin is not red."

She thought they had shared an ecstasy so wild and glorious, but she was now sorely disillusioned by anything to do with love.

"He will not humiliate me again. . . . Oh, and to think I wanted him to make love to me again after he had finished this night!"

Audrina comforted herself with the words, "I will escape, I will. One day my chance will arrive and I will snatch it, dear God, even if it means my death!"

344

Chapter Thirteen

Wild Hawk's suspicions had flared anew. The image of Audrina in the arms of that *wasicun* Powell kept haunting him. The picture of her running naked in the moonlight with the young soldier . . . over and over he envisioned erotic mind pictures of her and Joe Powell locked in intimate embraces, even though he knew she had been a maid untouched when he had taken her; the painful memory of her even touching and kissing Powell would not allow him a moment of temporary peace.

Lifting himself in an agile leap, Wild Hawk mounted the Bear and went for a cooling ride through the moonlit woods along the foot of the hills. Could he believe Precious Fire's incredible story of the hawk dropping his father's pouch in her aunt's yard? Such things of mystery were known to happen, but not in the white man's world, not that he knew of.

Audrina was a paleface, and they could not be trusted. He would do well to remember that. . . .

Returning to the moonlit encampment, Wild Hawk

345

brought his horse to the corral, and meeting Rainbow halfway, he walked with his sister back to the silent tepee. Rainbow said nothing, realizing Wild Hawk's thoughts were elsewhere.

Fox Dreamer had made a mistake in leaving Sadie alone with the older woman, Autumn Beads. Left Hand was quick to take note of it. He asked around and discovered that Fox Dreamer had gone with several other braves to go look at some horses in a distant Sisseton village.

Left Hand had also gleaned some useful information just by hanging around a few old squaws whose favorite pastime was indulging in good-natured gossip. Left Hand was patient; he took his time and listened well. He not only learned that Fox Dreamer was planning to make Snow Maid his squaw, but he also discovered some very interesting facts about Wild Hawk and his precious captive.

For now, Left Hand decided to use the bits of savory gossip about Snow Maid. Later, he would recall what he had learned of his Itancan's woman.

Anger and corrosive bitterness gnawed at Left Hand. Wild Hawk's unusual treatment of his captive was not being frowned upon by any of the other leaders and elders. Their attitudes seemed to say, "Wild Hawk will handle his captive as he deems best."

Contemptuously, Left Hand sneered in the direction of Wild Hawk's tepee. Prisoners might be adopted into a tribe, but they were usually jeered at, abused, and even tortured. They should be groveling slaves! he thought with unrelenting rancor. It was not uncommon, however, to marry a captured woman. There were several of these in neighboring tribes, but never had there been any such practices here. Not that he knew of in their past history, anyway. The Oglala Sioux had taken white captives for wives and so had some of his Sisseton relatives.

As he walked and made his plans for later that evening, Left Hand thought to himself how the People should keep the Indian breed pure and noble. In the past they had adhered strictly to their own customs. Now, as in many civilized societies, there was a double standard. Elders carefully watched over the behavior of young women, while a young man was expected to make love without serious intentions. Feminine chastity was highly prized. It was only a virtuous girl for whom a suitor was likely to offer many horses, and certain tasks at sacred ceremonies could be performed only by a woman of irreproachable purity. He, himself, had found no such woman of purity he would like to make his wife. He was a fighter, a warrior. Marriage was not to his liking, not in these perilous times when his people were struggling to survive—especially himself and Tawena.

Now there were two white females in their tribe, and Left Hand was afraid that Wild Hawk might be as foolish as Fox Dreamer. If they had children and those children mated with others in the tribe, what would be the final outcome? There was already "captive blood" here, kidnapped half-breed children.

Left Hand spat on the ground. What was so good about taking a white woman? He had never had one . . . then again, he could not be certain. He had been very drunk when they had overtaken a white settlement one night several summers ago. All he could recall was that the white man's firewater had made him very ill in the morning, with a head as big as his horse.

This night he was going to discover for himself what Fox Dreamer liked so much about Snow Maid that he would lower himself to take her for wife. Left Hand decided that if Snow Maid were to prove herself special on the mats, then he would capture her and take her away for himself. He would hide her up in the hills, to use her whenever there was a need to taste white flesh. If she proved to be fertile, he would slay the child. If there were more, he would slay them, too.

Left Hand rubbed his hands together as he joined Tawena and Grandmother in their tepee. He only dared hope that Snow Maid was yet untouched. He would be angry to find that Fox Dreamer had gotten to her first. Snow Maid, he told himself, would have kept herself pure for her husband. . . .

And it was almost true. Sadie bustled about in the tepee, humming to herself, happy that Fox Dreamer had asked her to become his woman . . . *his bride*. They had only made love once.

Sadie stopped what she was doing to stare off into space. Actually, it had happened more than once that first time, but only on one night. She was thrilled that Fox Dreamer treated her kindly and held her in high respect. She was breathlessly and radiantly happy. Suddenly, she erupted into girlish giggles. Even on the rainy and wintry days, she knew Fox Dreamer would keep her warm . . . oh, so very, very warm.

She had the tepee all to herself. There was no need for a guard; Fox Dreamer trusted her, and Autumn Beads had been asked to stay with Tawena's grandmother this night, for she was feeling poorly.

The request had come all of a sudden this afternoon when Left Hand had come for the older woman. Autumn Beads had turned and asked Sadie if she would be all right alone. Sadie had been ecstatic but tried not to show it. An afternoon and an evening all to herself . . . it would be heavenly, she had thought, whirling around the tepee after Autumn Beads had taken a few things and gone out with Left Hand.

Guiltily, Sadie thought about walking to the other end of the village to visit Audrina. Then she thought, I didn't before, so why should I when Fox Dreamer is gone? I want to relish this time alone, anyway. Maybe when Fox Dreamer returns, I will ask him to come with me to visit Audrina and Wild Hawk. . . .

It was a moonless night; only the stars glittered in the heavens. Stealthily cautious, Left Hand prowled about to make sure the village was asleep. He crept by Wild Hawk's tepee, and judging from the silence and the unlit walls, he determined that they, too, were asleep. It was very late, and Wild Hawk's "activities" had undoubtedly tired him out, Left Hand thought craftily.

If only Wild Hawk were not here, he could go into the hills and summon Powell and the Rebels, Left Hand told himself. But the time was not ripe. When it was, there would be two less troublesome captives in the camp. Powell was eager to come and fetch Precious Fire now, but he had been forced to restrain his wily tactics. Yellow Bear was no fool; he did not want Wild Hawk to find him out and have the chief's wrath fall on his head. And they had to be very cautious when the right time arrived.

Like darkness and shadow itself, Left Hand lurked like a hunting cat outside Fox Dreamer's tepee. He had learned, while gleaning his information that day, that Snow Maid knew the Sioux language well enough to understand the threats he was going to lay heavily upon her this night.

The embers were burning low inside the tepee as Sadie snuggled into the fur robe and sighed happily. She had spent a delightful afternoon all by herself. She was gazing up at the shining white stars through the smoke-hole when she became aware of a great sense of evil surrounding her. All of a sudden she was not so happy to be alone.

There was a stirring at the tepee flap, and she sat up with a start. Then she relaxed a little, thinking that maybe Fox Dreamer had returned. Her pulse raced when the person who had entered her tepee spoke no greeting.

"Who is there?" she asked. When no answer came, she repeated the question in Dakota.

Like a flash of deadly lightning, the shadowy figure lunged for her and quickly moved to lie on top of her. As soon as he spoke, Sadie knew who had attacked her. His full weight was pressing her down, and she felt as if she would suffocate.

"*Hiya,* Left Hand," she begged in Dakota. "Please go, or I will scream!" she protested, struggling in his lusty embrace.

"Scream all you want," he said, dizzy with triumph. They could communicate. This was better than he had hoped. "You have learned our language well, Snow Maid." His words grated on her raw nerves. "I have wondered what you have been doing all this time cooped up with Fox Dreamer and that witch Autumn Beads."

Sadie had trouble piecing together his whole sentence, for he had spoken swiftly and raspingly. He was totally aroused, that much she could tell from lying beneath his full weight.

Exceedingly alarmed now, she could feel the hard shaft grinding against her. His hands moved over her cringing flesh, trying to intoxicate her with his greedy lust. He did not kiss her mouth, but his hands touched her everywhere, and she knew she would only prolong the misery by fighting him.

Sadie was horrified to find her body responding to his burning lust. He teased her unmercifully, undressing her swiftly and pressing the rounded tip of himself into her softness.

Sadie gasped when Left Hand's finger gained entry and moved slowly, tantalizingly. Her mind whirled, and to her horror she found herself swelling, her breasts tautening. He must stop, she thought agonizingly, he *must stop*. She tried to think of Fox Dreamer, her mind recalling what it was like to have his muscled body joined with hers.

Automatically, Sadie's arm crept around Left Hand's neck. She pressed her creamy breasts against the smooth chest. This was her love, she imagined plaintively in her tortured mind. She was lying with her beloved, with Fox Dreamer. He had stolen her heart. She wanted him . . . deliriously . . . madly.

Left Hand triumphed when he felt her resistance fading. Snow Maid was ready for him; he knew it when her body arched, begging him to enter her, dragging

351

her sharp nails across his back.

Sadie cried out when he plunged into her moist warmth. He rode her swiftly and hotly, thrusting in and out until she began to feel it beginning to happen. Her climax increased until she exploded into shameful ecstasy, and when it was all over, when Left Hand had met his gigantic peak, she lay beneath him, crying softly in humiliation and shame. "Oh, Fox Dreamer," she cried in English, "please . . . please forgive me."

Left Hand took her again and this time she did not willingly respond. He slapped her hard, until her mouth and nose began to bleed. Shaking her, he demanded her submission this time. "If you do not, Fox Dreamer will die."

"No," Sadie sobbed, "you cannot be so cruel."

He hissed into her anguished face, "If you do not yield to me again, Snow Maid, first Fox Dreamer will die and then you. You were not a virgin after all. You gave yourself to that young pup?" He shook her again until her teeth rattled. "Who was it?"

"Fox Dreamer!" she cried. "And he will be mine again and again. I hate you. You are an evil monster!"

Spreading her thighs wide, he penetrated and forced her to respond once again. When he felt her reluctance leaving, he made love to her almost tenderly. He forced her to reach the peaks with him again and again. When that was done, he moved down over her and kissed her warm, wet stomach.

The woman Fox Dreamer had named Snow Maid flinched again and yet again while his tongue throbbed and beat against her flesh. Sadie tried to transport her mind elsewhere, picturing serene lakes and blue skies, imagining herself walking through lush ferns in a quiet

352

forest, walking to a moss-and-woods-bordered stream to meet her beloved Fox. . . .

Left Hand understood that she had fled elsewhere and he hissed, *"Henala!* Enough of your daydreaming. Return to me, for now you will taste my fierce and deep hatred for your kind. Do not try to blot out the reality of this night. Now . . . feel my hate and contempt for your race!"

Sadie tasted bitter revulsion and humiliating pain when he had his way with her twice more. Before he left her alone to her abject misery, he forced her to secrecy—otherwise he would kill Fox Dreamer when next he saw him. He also forced her to agree to meet him secretly, whenever she could get away.

When he was gone, Sadie turned over and wept. As the Dakota Indian said, *It was a good day to die.* But Sadie told herself that that would be giving in to the cruel gods of fate.

Sadie's heart beat dolefully. She did not want to die; she wanted to live. She wanted to love, she wanted to spend her days with Fox Dreamer, to have his children, and if there was a way out of this, she would find it. Someday, if there truly was a God, she would discover the narrow path. . . . She didn't want Fox Dreamer to die. She would live, if not for herself, then for her beloved brave.

Tears coursed down her cheeks. She forced herself to get up and wash the putrid sex smell of Left Hand from her body. Then she tried to get some sleep but could not. She rose and washed again, then combed the tangles out of her hair. The blinding tears came, falling upon the buffalo robe.

Sadie hardly slept, but by morning she was dozing

restlessly, tossing and turning with sweat dotting her forehead and body. She sat up suddenly, wiping her bleary eyes. Her heart leaped to her throat. She heard undeviating steps approaching the tepee. They paused; they stopped. . . . Sadie's heart stood still and her face wore a waiting expression.

The door flap opened, and she made out a tall, lean form silhouetted against the glimmering dawn. "Fox Dreamer!" she cried, dragging the buffalo robe over her shoulders. "Fox Dreamer!" She ran to him and threw herself in his arms.

Chuckling, Fox Dreamer said in Dakota, "This is a pleasant surprise. I will have to go away more often. You make my heart sing in gladness, Snow Maid."

Shakily, Snow Maid's lips touched Fox Dreamer's and he became instantly alerted. He held her away from him, then drew her closer again, touching her bruised lips with his fingertips. His boyishly handsome face darkened with rage.

"What have you been doing, Snow Maid? Your lips are bruised by lusty kisses."

Sadie's heart began to hammer in fear of discovery. "I—I ate the prairie turnip again," she answered haltingly in Dakota, grateful to Autumn Beads for teaching her some words. She had understood enough of Fox Dreamer's words to realize he'd spoken about kisses. "*Sha,* the prairie turnip."

"I thought you did not like it."

She turned and chewed her lip as he continued to stare at her with suspicion. "I wanted to try it again."

"You broke out in a rash last time."

"What did you say?" Sadie stammered. "I did not understand that. Repeat it, please, Fox Dreamer."

"You broke out in a rash from the prairie turnip. You should not be eating it, Snow Maid." He communicated additionally by signing.

"I—I know. It tasted so good that—" Sadie fought against her voice cracking, then she rushed on, "that I ate the whole thing, Fox Dreamer." She pictured the vegetable with her hands, patted her stomach, then threw her hands wide.

Lies, lies, lies! Sadie's heart was breaking, for the last thing she wanted to do was to lie to her beloved brave. But she had to, she thought with sickened dread, otherwise Left Hand would kill him.

"Your lips puffed up like that?" Fox Dreamer waved a hand, beginning to show signs of feeling sorry for Snow Maid.

"Yes. It happens when I eat strawberries, too." Her stomach was churning and she was afraid she might be sick.

"You must come and sit with me and tell me what you have been doing while I have been away. Snow Maid must teach Fox Dreamer more of her English words."

"You were not gone very long," Sadie pointed out, trying not to show him how sick she was in her heart and soul. Her body was hurting everywhere, but it was the mental torment that hurt the most. . . . Oh, how it hurt to think she had deceived Fox Dreamer!

"We had to turn back. Three strangers were sighted several hours outside the village." He used his hands to sign for the words she had not learned yet. "We chased them up into the sacred hills, and then we could not go further, for it is bad to go up there where the Thunderbird lives if we do not mean to pray and seek a vision. We had doubled-back, so our leader decided to return to the village before we set out again."

"I am sleepy . . . Snow Maid." He reached for her hand. "Will you sleep . . . beside me? . . . "

"*Istima,* sleep, Fox Dreamer," Sadie murmured, reaching out to brush the long black strands out of his handsome young face. "*Istima.*" The tears poured down her soft cheeks.

The sun climbed slowly on the distant horizon and began to bathe the village in its rosy glow. Fox Dreamer had fallen asleep in the buffalo robe next to her. Sadie's eyelids drooped. It was going to be a beautiful day, already she could see patches of brilliant blue through the door flap.

It was early June, Fox Dreamer had told her, the Moon of Making Fat.

Audrina awoke to the first bright twinklings of light. She was alone in the tepee, guessing Rainbow had gone to the creek with the *mni* skins to fetch water and Wild Hawk must have been summoned to the council lodge when the earth hung suspended between the wee hours and dawn.

After turning from the cooking area, Audrina gasped, for a motionless figure stood at the door flap. She found herself looking into the frightening countenance of a very troubled young woman. "Sadie!" Audrina cried, rushing to take her friend by the shoulders. "What has happened? You are as pale as a ghost. Are you sick? Here, come and sit down. I have some hot broth."

"I haven't slept, Audrey." Sadie waved aside the

herbed broth, and Audrina set it aside with a look of concern.

"Where is Fox Dreamer? Why isn't he with you?" Audrina could not help firing questions at Sadie. "Your face is colorless and your eyes are glazed. *Sadie,* talk to me, please!"

Drawing the back of her hand across her reddened nose, Sadie almost whispered, "Fox Dreamer is gone again. He left hours ago, and I finally managed to drag myself here."

"Where is Autumn Beads? Isn't that the name of the grandmother who is staying in Fox Dreamer's lodge?"

Sadie waved her arm as if it were of no concern or importance. "She left yesterday afternoon to go and stay with Tawena's and Left Hand's grandmother."

"They left you *alone?*" Audrina shook her head, the long hank of hair she had braided early that morning brushing her shoulder. "No guard? Nothing?"

"Fox Dreamer cherishes me and trusts me completely, Audrey." She moaned as if racked with pain. "He has . . . faith . . . in . . . me."

When Sadie burst forth in a torrent of uncontrollable tears, Audrina moved closer and put her arm about her friend. "God, Sadie, what is wrong?" This is serious, Audrina thought, a cold feeling freezing her blood. "Did Fox Dreamer do something to hurt you? Does he know how miserable you are?"

"Fox Dreamer is gone. . . ." She shook her head dazedly, staring but really not seeing anything.

After a good shake to Sadie's shoulder, Audrina pulled her around. "Look at me, Sadie. Tell me. What is wrong? *Please.*"

Sadie's head moved back and forth slowly as she

murmured, "I wish I were dead, Audrina. I—I would be better off."

"Sadie, you may wish you were dead, but you are not! You are alive! And if I have anything to do about it, you are going to stay that way. Now tell me . . . tell me all!"

"L—Left Hand r—raped me, A—Audrey." Her lower lip trembled and her chin shook. She stared at Audrina glumly.

Audrina's stomach turned over with a sickening lurch and she felt her own tears begin to collect along her lids. She steeled her shoulders and cleared her throat. "Now," she patted Sadie's hand, "the first thing we have to do is let Fox Dreamer know as soon as he returns. . . ." Audrina frowned. "Sadie, when did this happen? If it happened while Fox Dreamer was away, why didn't you tell him when he returned this morning? Rainbow told me that the braves had returned after we heard the hoofbeats arriving at the crack of dawn. So I know they were here briefly before leaving again."

Sadie shook her blond head and moaned. "I can't tell Fox Dreamer, Audrey. I just can't."

"Why *not?* Left Hand should get what's coming to him."

"Audrey, you wouldn't tell Wild Hawk if *you* were raped!"

After Sadie had reacted with such violent emotion, Audrina rocked back on her heels. She was just coming to her feet when Wild Hawk entered the tepee, his dark, penetrating gaze moving between them. His eyes came to rest on Sadie.

"Something is amiss?" He did not receive an answer, for just then Autumn Beads entered the open flap and stood beside Wild Hawk.

She greeted him and smiled her toothy grin, pressing her bundle to her sagging bosom. "I have come for Snow Maid."

"She is here," Wild Hawk said, his all-knowing eyes taking in the tearful Sadie, and then reading the sorrow and vexation stamped on Audrina's features.

"Come, Snow Maid," Autumn Beads said. "It is time to return to our tepee."

"Wait!" Audrina cried when Sadie slowly, wearily, came to her feet.

Three sets of eyes turned to her. Audrina could tell that Sadie was begging her not to speak. With an almost imperceptible nod, Audrina turned back to making the morning repast. Then Autumn Beads and Sadie were gone.

"I would like to talk to you," Wild Hawk said, his strong voice filling the space, his dark brows drawn together.

As she had her back turned, Audrina spoke the simple Dakota words over her shoulders, "I am here. Speak."

Delighted and refreshed by Precious Fire's presence this morning, Wild Hawk suddenly smiled. His woman was beginning to sound more like an Indian squaw each day. Then his face grew serious as he said, "If Snow Maid is having trouble with Fox Dreamer, it is none of your affair, Audrina. You may speak to her of it, but do not advise her what to do. Fox Dreamer is taking Snow Maid for his wife in the Moon When the Cherries Are Ripe."

"When is that?" Audrina turned with their savory breakfast in two bowls. She was still sick over what

Sadie had told her and didn't feel like eating much, but she would force herself. Wild Hawk was displeased when her eating habits were poor.

"Your people say the month of July."

"What is it now? Is it June?" Audrina watched as he nodded. "I know this one, it is the Moon of Making Fat."

That is right, my love, Wild Hawk was thinking. He smiled to himself as he sat with crossed legs upon the mat. He gazed into her eyes, not saying the words: I will make you fat, Audrina, fat with my child so that you will never leave me. You are my captive rose, my savage maiden, willing or unwilling, but mine you will always be! Never, never will you belong to the paleface man who haunts your thoughts night and day!

Audrina was not thinking about Joe Powell; he was the farthest person from her mind. Her thoughts and her heart were in turmoil. One day Wild Hawk treated her kindly, that next he treated her as if nothing out of the ordinary had happened. She couldn't forget what had taken place a few nights before when Wild Hawk had left her so coldly, as if he had found her touch repugnant to him. What did he want from her? How did he wish her to act? She had no secrets any longer, for he had taken the pouch. . . . Yes, she did have one secret: her plan to escape him and the hurt he inflicted upon her aching heart, day in and day out.

Now, look at him, she peevishly thought. He is silent again sitting there as if nothing is amiss. Couldn't he see that she had to get away from him? She needed time to think, to be alone, but when Wild Hawk went away for a long time, she was lonesome for him. It just did not make much sense. Perhaps love never did make sense . . . not when two lovers were as different as night and day, as black and white.

Sewing materials gathered, Audrina sat down to mend a torn buckskin shirt, one of Wild Hawk's. It was a new chore for her, mending his clothes, but he had asked her, and it was only one of many chores that she was slowly growing accustomed to. But could she ever get used to the thought of living out the rest of her natural days as a Sioux mistress? She hardly thought so, especially the way things were going now. . . . And then there was Sadie's new problem. How could they ever hope to live harmoniously with Indian lovers, let alone a whole village of Sioux?

Without another word, Wild Hawk stood, taking up his practice bow and arrows, and went out of the tepee as silently as he had entered it.

Audrina wondered why he had become silent all of a sudden. Something was troubling him, deeply. Was he afraid they would get into an argument over the pouch again? Wild Hawk, afraid? Audrina scoffed at her own wayward thoughts. "It is I who should be afraid . . . but I am not." Suddenly, her face turned unpleasantly downward as she stabbed the bone-needle into the taut fabric with a vengeance.

"But I love him," she murmured, rubbing the material against her face. "It's crazy, but I love that black-haired savage." Sighing deeply, she went on, "I must learn to be patient and wait for him to understand and believe in me about the medicine pouch, and other things. I think he is still jealous about Joe Powell. But Joe never meant a thing to me . . . he never could." Audrina wondered if Powell would ever try to rescue her. If Joe came for her, would she go with him? What was worse, to stay with Wild Hawk and wonder what her shaky future would be or to leave with Joe and return to Mankato? She could live at the little house. . . .

Frowning with concentration, Audrina stuck the needle into the hide to finish the repair on the shirt. It was not a very large separation and it should not take much longer, she told herself, hoping she could get to visit Sadie later. Something had to be done about her friend's horrible situation. Sadie was afraid of something, perhaps of Left Hand's threat. She was sure that was it. Left Hand was evil, he was covetous, and he wanted to keep the Indian breed pure and noble. But where was Left Hand's noble blood? Who was the real savage here? How in God's name could Sadie be helped? Wild Hawk would not wish to unman Fox Dreamer by interfering, not in a million years.

Audrina set the finished shirt aside. She stood and went to peep outside the flap. Many of the braves were disappearing into the meeting lodge, and then she spied Wild Hawk on his way there, too. The braves would smoke together and plan for a secure future. Children were playing games at the far side of the encampment, away from Sadie's and Fox Dreamer's tepee.

Looking this way and that, Audrina could see no guards about. . . .

A light breeze played through the door flap. This was her chance to go and visit Sadie and see if she could talk some sense into her head. No one saw her as she slipped from the tepee and made her way to the one that was Fox Dreamer's.

She was in further luck, for there went Autumn

Beads, walking with a *mni* skin down to the sun-dappled creek for water. Autumn Beads waved to Audrina and kept walking. It would be a while before Autumn Beads returned, as the old woman was in the habit of stopping to gossip with every squaw and child she met on the way there and back. For a moment, only a moment, Audrina thought of escaping with Sadie, but her friend was in no condition to leave now . . . and it was all Left Hand's fault.

Throwing back her head, Audrina breathed deeply of the warmed earth and savored the heady scents of summer, smiling at the pasqueflower nodding in the slight breeze. She had brushed out and left the wavy mane of her hair unbraided. The sun's rays kissed the top of her head, and the wind of her passage stirred the hem of her doeskin skirt and the tendrils of hair at her cheeks. It was great to be alive, to be strong, healthy, and full of vigor. She had seen her reflection in the waters of Lonewoman Creek, and she liked this new tanned and rosy-skinned Audrina she had seen. Now, if only she could get her friend to look and feel just as strong, perhaps one day soon they could steal away from the encampment. But it would take much doing. They would need food. Horses. Blankets for the cool nights. Wild animals roamed the dark in search of prey, too! Oh . . . it would be such a risk. . . .

Audrina visited with Sadie briefly, but the young blonde was more silent and subdued than before, and she looked very tired. After telling Sadie she loved her, Audrina finally rose and departed when her friend fell asleep on the buffalo robe for the fourth time. Audrina glanced over her shoulder as she went out. Sadie wouldn't miss her. She was fast asleep, hopefully an untroubled sleep, for Sadie sorely needed her rest to recuperate from the shock her system had earlier received.

Summer was fast growing sultrier and the days were longer, hotter, and stickier. Some days were dry, and then there would be a cloudburst that would drench everything. Then the sun would pop out in a sudden blue sky, and it would be warmer and moister and sometimes unbearable.

Audrina made frequent trips to the creek to bathe, to swim—which she was getting better at—and to wash out her clothes. Sometimes she would linger there, with her toes in the water, leaning back on the bank in the lush green grass with the sun beating down on her face. Wild Hawk would come for her if she stayed away too long. He seemed to trust her, she thought, or were there secret eyes watching from the bushes? That would be awful, for a person needed some private time to herself. But the Indians did not seem to have time for the simple luxury of being alone. Especially not the women; they never seemed to get away by themselves.

One day Audrina followed Tawena to the creek. The woman had been acting strangely, peering about as if trying to be sure no one saw her making her way there. That is odd, Audrina told herself, putting aside the wild berries she'd been rinsing outside the tepee . . . very odd.

She walked, thinking how good it was to be alive with the sun on her face and the blue sky above, and then she hurried to the creek, telling herself she was foolish for worrying about what Tawena could be up to. . . . But Wild Hawk had been gone for hours. Where could *he* have gone?

For some curious reason, she slowed her pace and crept up to the trees that flanked the creek. She should really go back and not be spying on Tawena, but something drew her onward. . . .

Audrina gasped aloud when she saw Tawena kissing Wild Hawk! He was naked as a jaybird, and she could see his clothes hanging on a branch near the creek bank. She could see the sinewy muscles of his buttocks and flanks as he flexed. Tawena was pressing her voluptuous body closer and closer. Wild Hawk was doing something with his hands, no doubt fondling her large, pendulous breasts!

With a small cry, Audrina whirled from the disturbing sight. Her heart hammering wildly, she thought at once of planning escape. She and Sadie would make plans as soon as possible; she had to get away from here! One day it was like a sunny paradise; the next it was a lonely, frightening place. . . . Now, at this moment, it was hell!

Instantly alerted, Wild Hawk's keen eyes caught sight of Audrina's bright head shining like a beacon in the afternoon sun.

Their eyes met and clashed like blades in combat. Then he saw her mouth fall wide. Angrily, she whirled, her arms outstretched as if she fought to regain her balance. Her shiny braids flew behind her and Wild Hawk could see the soles of her moccasins as he fastened his breechclout. He gave one last sneering glimpse at Tawena, where he had knocked her to the ground. Her jaw was already swelling. Hatred was alive in her black eyes, but Wild Hawk had no time to wonder or especially care who this intensely vile emotion was aimed at.

She runs like a deer, Wild Hawk thought as he saw Audrina heading toward a grassy knoll. He was not worried about what Audrina had seen, for it had been nothing. Sneakily, Tawena had caught him bathing and he had been angry that she had intruded on his private time. He did not have much privacy of late, for he had begun to take on the responsibilities of chief, and this made him very busy. He was also Itancan of many groups and warrior societies.

He had almost caught up to her. Not much farther. He told himself Audrina could be made to understand. He was confident of this. He was not interested in Tawena. His manhood had remained limp during Tawena's hasty embrace. It had stayed that way . . . until now, when it had begun to rear like a wild stallion sniffing out its mate in her time of heat.

Audrina heard Wild Hawk gaining on her. She was already out of breath, and her aching legs felt like collapsing. Still, she would not give up. She stumbled halfway up the grassy incline then, when, she began to claw her way to her feet, she felt herself being tackled from behind. He held her loosely, and she began to struggle and roll with him, only a short ways down, where they nestled in a bed of sweet-smelling pine needles.

It was a beautiful hidden spot, like a natural grassy cove, halfway up the green knoll. She looked up and saw him staring down at her with a mischievous grin. In a deep voice, he said, "Precious Fire is jealous."

"Oh . . . I am not!" Audrina shoved and tried to heave him off her. "You weigh like a ton of bricks, Wild Hawk." His hard chest grazed hers, making her nipples tighten. "Now get off! Go back to your lusty warrior woman. Make wild love to her. . . . I'm sure you already had a good start before I came along to spoil it!"

"There was nothing to spoil, Audrina. Tawena does nothing to excite me." Wild Hawk's eyes roamed her delightfully flushed face.

"What were you doing a few minutes ago? Having lunch by the creek?"

"What is *lunch?*"

"What?" Audrina blinked, her long lashes moving slowly, sensuously. "You really don't know what *lunch* is?" When he shook his head, she explained. "Lunch means the afternoon meal."

"I would rather share lunch with my beautiful captive princess," he said huskily.

In unconscious shyness, Audrina had crossed an arm over her breasts. She realized, daylight or not, she wanted Wild Hawk badly, so much so, in fact, that she was trembling from head to foot, trembling with desire.

Leaning over her, he brushed his lips across hers, then the kiss deepened and he removed the offending arm that shielded his chest from meeting hers. Audrina's blood began to sing in her veins, and her senses swam dizzily.

When he pressed into her body, Audrina brought herself closer to him. She could feel the damp breechclout against her legs and realized her skirt was well above her knees.

"Get off me, Wild Hawk." Spreading her arms, she

rolled her head aside and tried to rise on an elbow. Her blushing gaze traveled along his bronze, muscled length, sweeping down to linger for a moment on the hard evidence of his desire. He pressed her deeper, more intimately into the spoon of earth and soft, spongy grass. "Go make love to your dusky Indian love," she hissed jealously.

Grasping her shoulders hard, he gave her a shake. "She is not my love. Why do you speak this way?"

"Oh, she is not?" Audrina's lips puckered angrily. "Then what was she doing in your lusty embrace?"

"*Tawena* was embracing Wild Hawk. If you would have stayed to watch, you would have seen her being knocked to the ground. I did not even harden with desire."

Her face turned three shades of red and her eyes skittered off to stare at a little red bug in the grass. He was that way now, though, she could tell.

"Oh, and I am supposed to believe Tawena pounced on you as soon as you came out of the water."

"She attacked me, yes. It is well known she wants to become my bride."

Audrina hid her sudden jealousy and fear. "I—I did not know that. I—I mean, I knew she wanted you, b—but I did not know she wanted to be your wife, Wild Hawk."

"You are as tense as a snared rabbit." His voice was a husky caress.

He silenced her with a kiss. It was a kiss that started out gentle and warm, and then, as it grew fiery and eager, Audrina's nipples came to hard little peaks as his hand moved over the outside of her shift. His other hand reached under her hem and cupped her throbbing

368

womanhood, while the kiss grew deeper and sweeter and wilder.

Wild Hawk groaned as if in pain when Audrina reached downward to stroke his fiery shaft. She moved her fingers over the turgid length, back and forth until Wild Hawk wrenched away, whispering her name. He moved atop her swiftly now, the palm of his hand slipping beneath her shift to the softness of her stomach, then tenderly moving lower to massage the auburn darkness between her creamy thighs, deliberately prolonging her sweet torment.

Audrina's soft breasts melted under his hard, muscled chest and her quickened breath attested to her readiness. With a tiny groan of impatience, she removed her shift swiftly and opened her arms to her Indian lover. Her eyes were heavy-lidded as she felt the rigid organ standing up between them, and a cloud of passion quickly enveloped her.

Sensually, Audrina's fingers dove into the thick ebony hair and clutched handfuls of the silken strands in both hands as his flaming shaft entered her auburn forest. Eagerly offering herself to him, she cupped the sides of his head as the thrilling, savage thrust went on and on, plunging into the warm, satiny sheath of her body. He was her bronze captor; she was his stolen heart.

Wild Hawk plunged deeply within his love, so tight and hot around him, the rounded tip exciting the tiny bud when he wrenched back and then forward again with the powerful driving force of his lean, muscled buttocks. Savagely, he savored the surging upthrust of her body, which moved like a dainty dancer on the wind, her long, slender legs tightening around him. His bronze hands lifted her buttocks higher as he strove to go deeper into a sensual world of pleasure.

They continued to make love, first savagely, then tenderly, then sweetly, now harder again, and Audrina was in her first mind-spinning tumblings of release when her slitted eyes gazed up into the sky. She spotted a hawk, sweeping the towering updraft in a breathtaking ascent, each swift circle carrying it hundreds of feet aloft. Rapturously, Audrina climbed with the bird, panting under the bittersweet pleasure only Wild Hawk could give her.

Wild Hawk noticed the change in his beloved, and he traveled with her to the savage sky of love and bliss. They were kindred spirits: He was making her wild with his ever-increasing rhythm, triumphant and thrilled with her delicious acceptance. She continued to watch and pant and arch her slender hips. The hawk lifted above a green mountaintop, going up and up into the blue until, still turning, it was only a small speck in the vast blue of sky and the blinding whiteness of sun. The shattering climax went on and on, and they strained until the white-hot blaze of ecstasy began to descend.

"I love you, Wild Hawk . . . I love you."

"And I love you . . . Precious Fire!"

Wild Hawk clutched his beloved, drawing her damp face against his chest. They stayed like that for a long while, each listening to the other's thundering and then slowing heartbeat.

Thin, airy music rose and fell around the lovers, the haunting strains of wind in the needles of the sweet-smelling ponderosa pine and the shiny green leaves of the cottonwoods.

370

Wild Hawk shook with an eerie feeling of the supernatural. There had been a profound difference in their joining this time. Their hearts and souls had married. She had walked with him in the Dakota land of enchanted visions, in the eye of the sun. He gazed down into her glassy eyes and saw with a jolt that she was staring up at him as if mystified by what they had mutually experienced. She had come so close to being an Indian a few moments ago when time had ceased to be. He had felt it. So had she. For a space of time, she had actually become a Sioux.

"Precious Fire, my heart is filled with joy. . . ." Tenderly pushing back a dark auburn strand of hair, he murmured thickly, "Who are you, Audrina Harris? . . . Who are you really?"

Audrina wet her lips. She had no answer for him. All she could do was drop her bewildered gaze to his chest and close her eyes.

Chapter Fourteen

The heavy blanket of gray clouds had been steadily pushed aside by a dazzling blue sky. Now, the early morning was beautiful, with velvet-winged butterflies flitting amongst the wildflowers in the lush grasses flanking the forested village. Children were laughing and playing, in imitation of their elders. Little girls, pretending to be squaws, had put up miniature tepees, and young boys had brought them rabbits and other food as though they were adult men returning from the hunt. Boys were also imitating the performances of the military clubs and indulging in all sorts of pranks, including snatching the meat from the racks set up in camp and then dashing off to a safe distance for a leisurely feast. Laughter and play abounded in Wild Hawk's village.

Standing together outside Fox Dreamer's tepee, Audrina and Sadie watched as, below the tranquil blue sky, Wild Hawk and a party of five other warriors returned after a night's absence.

Sadie smiled adoringly as Fox Dreamer approached,

and together they laughed joyfully while he hugged his beloved around the waist and they disappeared within his tepee, the blonde's soft giggles floating in their wake.

Discreetly, Autumn Beads had slipped out only moments before to afford the young couple some privacy to greet each other. The old woman chuckled to herself, staring up at tiny white puffs of clouds in the summer-blue sky.

Wild Hawk spoke with Strong Heart for a moment longer, and then a boy who was standing by took the reins of the Bear to lead him away.

Separating from the other young braves who had wished a word with him, Wild Hawk neared Audrina, his sable eyes locked upon her dewy, flushed face. Attired in only a breechclout and high-topped moccasins, Wild Hawk walked steadily toward her, his bronze, strongly muscled chest rippling and glistening moistly. Her heart took up an even stronger rhythm as she lowered her gaze to his long, sinewy limbs.

Leading a beautiful, prancing Paint, Wild Hawk wore a brilliant, attentive smile, his white teeth contrasting with his coppery countenance.

How handsome he is, she thought, adrift on a savage dream of her own making. Her whole being seemed to be filled with waiting. She tried not to stare with longing at him, but she felt the wildfire racing through her.

Halting before her, he reached out lovingly to push aside a lock of red hair that had strayed loose from her braid during her morning tasks. Smiling softly, Audrina delighted in the feel of his tender touch against her cheek. She had missed him . . . and he had only been gone one afternoon and one night.

Almost in a whisper, she said, "It is good to have you home, Wild Hawk." *Home?* Had she really said that? Did she really mean it? she swiftly asked herself.

"My heart sings at the sight of you, Precious Fire." His dark eyes savored the lovely sight of her, dressed as she was in the soft doeskin shift Rainbow had given her. Bending forward, he murmured into her ear, "I have a gift for you. . . ." Tautening the reins around his wrist, he brought the mare closer. "She is yours. You may name her whatever you choose."

Audrina's heart leapt with happiness and gratitude as she lifted a hand to the soft, velvety nose and laughed delightedly when the beautiful mare nuzzled her hand in greeting. "Mine?" Audrina inquired. "Are you sure, Wild Hawk?"

"I am very sure. You may keep her always as your very own." His eyes feasted ravenously on her delighted face, wishing he could take her in his arms right here in the middle of the village and kiss her thoroughly. As he stood there with this passionate thought, his breechclout stirred, for his manhood was growing large with steamy desire.

"Thank you for the mare, Wild Hawk. You are far too generous, for this is a wonderful gift."

Wild Hawk smiled broadly. "You may have anything your heart desires, Precious Fire."

"Anything?" she asked, as her heart stood still.

"All but one."

"My freedom?"

"Sha, yes."

*   *   *

Jealousy alive in her narrowed eyes, Tawena covertly watched from a short distance away. Alive also were the feelings of hate, animosity, and hostility. She would have her revenge, and it would be sweet. Wild Hawk cared not a whit for Tawena, for he had eyes only for Precious Fire. This was too bad. He could have had Warrior Woman. . . . Now the virile warrior would have nothing but a paleface woman who had enticed him to lead her to his mats.

Tawena caught Strong Heart also looking with a steady gaze toward the enamored couple. Strong Heart seemed to watch them exactly as she did, envious of the couple's affection for each other. A tempting strategy crystallized in Tawena's brain. "I could always get Strong Heart to seduce Precious Fire," she said under her breath. Then Tawena felt a sourness in the pit of her stomach, for she knew, even before she set forth to devise such a stimulating plan, that Strong Heart would never go along with it. The handsome warrior was too faithful to his leader—and honor ran strong between the two men. Besides, Tawena concluded, Strong Heart practiced a code of high moral conduct. She knew of a few young braves who could be persuaded to fall, but not Strong Heart.

Walking back to her tepee, Tawena's mind ticked with further plans for revenge. Soon, she thought mentally, rubbing her hands together, soon Wild Hawk would travel to the Sisseton Camp, and he would be forced to leave his beloved captive behind.

Audrina cherished the Paint she had named Bo-ton-ton, the Sioux word for confusion. "Exactly the way the Paint's coat looks," she said, laughing into Wild Hawk's shining eyes.

"Bo-ton-ton is a little bit wild, I am afraid," he said, watching for her reaction, his sable gaze boring into her soft green one.

"I am sure we can remedy that."

Looking up and down her graceful form, he said, "We can *remedy* anything, Precious Fire."

The implication sent waves of excitement through Audrina. Could he fix the differences between them? she wondered, half in anticipation, half in dread. Could everything ever be all right between them? God help her, how could she truthfully deny there was no attraction between them, that her brazen heart did not love him in full measure? What was she going to do? she wondered as she watched Wild Hawk return to the corral with Bo-ton-ton.

For the next several days, Wild Hawk instructed Audrina in the training of Bo-ton-ton, always careful lest his braves see him lavishing too much attention upon his beloved captive. In private times, however, in the tepee while Rainbow was away visiting her friends, Wild Hawk wooed Precious Fire like a gallant swain courting his bride-to-be.

Indeed, Wild Hawk began to make plans to take Precious Fire as his wife, but he wanted her completely willing, with no desire remaining in her heart and soul to return to the white man's world. He wanted her desire to be solely for him, to want to be in his Life Circle until *Wakantanka* called for them to come to

Eternal Paradise.

Keenly aware of something different about Wild Hawk, Audrina began to wonder indeed why he had not kissed and caressed her lately. Why was he holding back? Did he not want her anymore? She quivered and burned with desire whenever Wild Hawk came near, or when he "accidentally" brushed against her in the corral while training Bo-ton-ton. There was much exciting pleasure in merely looking at Wild Hawk, merely being with him, but her healthy young body hungered for more, a hunger only Wild Hawk could satisfy.

Wild Hawk was taut as a bow string. He wanted to make love to Precious Fire, but he would not break his own promise to himself to leave her be until he made her his and said *mitawicu* to her, "I take this woman for wife."

One beautiful summer evening a lovely doeskin dress, bleached white, was brought to Audrina. Pleasantly surprised, she watched Rainbow approach, carrying it across her forearms, saying, "This is for you, Precious Fire."

"For me?" Audrina softly breathed, taking the Indian dress from a widely smiling Rainbow. "You shouldn't do this."

Onyx eyes twinkling merrily, Rainbow said, "This one is a gift from my brother."

"Why?" Audrina looked astonished. "First the Paint, and now this."

"I think maybe my brother likes you a little?" Rainbow's voice lifted, as did her pert little face.

Profoundly touched, Audrina caressed the wonderful material. "So precious . . . so soft." Her eyes searching Rainbow's face, she asked, "What is the occasion? Is there going to be a special party for someone?"

"*Sha,* yes." Rainbow giggled softly. "Wild Hawk would like for you to try the dress on. He will come to see you after you have finished dressing. Loosen your hair and put this on your head." She handed Audrina a white beaded headband. "He would like to see you wearing this with the dress."

"You still did not tell me what the occasion is to be, Rainbow. I hear no ceremonial drums." She canted her head, hearing only the little bells upon the tepee tinkling in a soft summer breeze.

"Do not stand there staring at the dress, Precious Fire. Put it on!"

"All right—if you say so."

Swiftly taking her tresses out of the shiny braid, Audrina brushed them until crackles of electricity were heard in the tepee. Next she secured the narrow strip of white leather around her forehead and tied the ends in back, the four little feathers hanging tip-down among her gleaming red tresses.

After slipping off the shift and donning the soft white one, Audrina turned about, asking, "Well, how does it look?"

Wild Hawk stood there in place of Rainbow; there was no sign of the Indian girl anywhere in the tepee. Wild Hawk's warmly assessing gaze roved her feminine form, and though she had no mirror in which to see herself, his look of admiration was louder than words.

"You take this warrior's breath away, Precious Fire." When she lowered her lashes shyly, he reached out to lift her chin, bringing her green gaze back into

378

contact with his thoroughly admirng perusal. "I would bring you to the creek so that you could see your lovely image in the water if the Night Spirit had not already blanketed the earth with darkness."

Embarrassedly, Audrina cast her gaze aside, asking again the question foremost in her inquisitive mind. "What will be the occasion to which I'll wear this dress, Wild Hawk?"

Bluntly, he answered, "Our wedding ceremony."

"T—tonight? O—our wedding ceremony?"

He chuckled, "Do not worry so quickly, for it will not take place this night."

"Why?" she asked, waving her hand in the air. "I mean, why have you decided to take me for your wife?"

"It has long been my wish to take Precious Fire for my wife. I have thought on this long and hard for many moons now. I wish for you to be the mother of my children. I desire for you to join me on my mats, to pleasure me, to give pleasure to you, to wake up with you beside me in the morning. Sometimes you have been defiant and have caused me to become angry. Most times you make my heart sing with gladness and I believe the Great Spirit has chosen you to walk beside me the rest of my life. I have been angered many times, and one of those times was when I discovered the pouch—my father's pouch—on your person. Now I believe you were indeed chosen to carry the pouch to my father's Spirit Lodge."

"What made you come to believe this, Wild Hawk?" Audrina asked.

"I do not have full knowledge yet, Precious Fire. I have had dreams and I believe these dreams are linked with your past. The women in my dreams perhaps could be relatives of yours."

"Why do you say this? Do these women resemble me then?"

"Yes. There is something about the two of them that make me wake up with your image on my mind. It burns there and it is as if the women in the dream had much desired for me to learn something."

Should I tell him? Audrina asked herself. *Should I tell him that I have the Oglala Sioux blood flowing in my veins?*

"What about *my* wishes?" Audrina asked Wild Hawk. "Don't they count, too? What if I did not wish to have you as my husband?"

"You are my captive, Audrina. Defiant and willful as you are, you are still that. You must do my will and never question my wishes. I wish for us to join in seven moons before I go to council at the Sisseton Camp."

"I—I am flattered that you want me for your wife, Wild Hawk. But our customs are worlds apart. Your path is not my path. My life has been so very different"—she waved an arm to indicate her surroundings—"from all this. Those people out there are full-blooded Indian and I don't know if they will ever come to accept me. I still see angry looks coming my way, from young maidens mostly."

"That is because they are jealous of your position in my life. I know everything you say carries some truth. What is it that troubles you most of all, Precious Fire?"

"Well, for one thing, who will perform the ceremony? Will it be the ceremonial chief? I am Christian. . . ."
You are heathen, she'd been about to say, but she did not actually believe that, for Rainbow had told her about *Wakantanka*, the Great Spirit, who was so much

380

like her own Christian God.

"*Mazakutemani,* Little Paul, as the whites call him—he will marry us. He has become a Christian. He used to be head speaker for the Wahpeton Sioux. Now he carries your Christian Bible everywhere he goes. Little Paul is elected Spokeman of the Farmer Indians and Deacon in Rigg's church."

Slowly, she asked, "He will marry us . . . in this Rigg's church?"

"No. Little Paul will make the special trip here to join us as man and wife.'

"Why a Christian?" she asked Wild Hawk. "Why not your usual ceremonial chief?"

"My wish is to please you, Precious Fire. You can have a little of both worlds—for a while longer yet."

"I am not an Indian. . . . I cannot live among your people, Wild Hawk!"

After Audrina had spoken these words, she realized she had not entirely spoken the truth. *She was part Indian.* But she did not wish to *live as an Indian,* to bear many children, to be a squaw, a slave to hard labor.

Recalling to mind the near-visionlike trance of their lovemaking and how close Precious Fire had come to being one of his own kind, Wild Hawk shook his raven-dark head in bewilderment. "You once told me that the whites of Mankato called you half-breed. What Indian nation did they mean? Cheyenne? Cherokee? Blackfoot? Sioux?"

"*Sha,* Sioux," Audrina blurted almost unthinkingly.

Moving closer, he questioned softly, his eyes dark and compellng. "*Are* you part Indian, Precious Fire?" Rubbing his strong fingers up and down her peach-skinned arm, he inquired, "Do you have Sioux blood as

I do? How much of you is Indian and how much is white?"

Sighing deeply, Audrina confessed, "I have told a lie, Wild Hawk. I wish to change my words to ones of truth. Aunt Katherine—" her voice cracked, "before she d-died, she told me of my Indian parent."

"*One* Indian parent?"

"Of course," Audrina said, holding out her arm. "Look at my skin, Wild Hawk. It is not as darkly copper as yours." Taking hold of her fiery braid, she said, "Look, my hair does not have a single black strand—" Abruptly, she halted her words, for he was ready to speak again.

"I mean"—Wild Hawk's eyes narrowed—"do you not know of the ancestral line of your father's and mother's people?"

"No. I have no knowledge of their parentage."

"Your skin is not as dark as mine, nor as red. Yet your hair has dark fires in it, as does Rainbow's possess a tint of this fire." He nodded, his sable eyes shining wishfully, curiously. "Which of your parents possessed Indian blood and how much of it?"

"My mother was . . . half Indian."

She heard his quick intake of breath before he spoke again.

"What was your mother's Indian name?"

"Gray Dove." The long sweep of Audrina's lashes lifted and lowered.

'What branch of Sioux?" he fired at her rapidly.

"Oglala—"

"Good," he whispered, squeezing her hand hard. "That is very good, Precious Fire!"

With that, Wild Hawk turned and went out of the

382

tepee while Audrina simply stood there, blank, amazed, shaken.

She finally blinked from out of her trance, the one she'd been enveloped in several moments after he had exited the tepee. "But," Audrina began, "all I have known is in the white man's world." She waved an arm slowly about the tepee, continuing talking to herself. "I can never become used to—to all this. It—it is plain drudgery, slavery almost. My path cannot be the same as Wild Hawk's or his people's. Yet, I am not convinced that my father's white race—his parents, and their parents—were more happy and content in their wood dwellings than the Indians were through the centuries on the mountains, deserts, and prairies, as I am not certain that I could finally, one day, become happy and content to live as an Indian, traveling from camp to camp."

Audrina could just imagine Wild Hawk's attitude a couple of weeks after their marriage: "Wife, do this; Wife, do that." Then, after a year or so, or more: "Squaw, keep baby (or babies) quiet. Wild Hawk wishes to sleep."

Grimacing with distaste, her frantic thoughts raced onward. "And think about the winters. He said we would stay right here, for this is the winter camp they were at already. . . . I'll freeze to death under a thin blanket." Her conscience argued, *But there are many blankets—thick, heavy ones.* She argued right back, "Too, my back is already killing me after sleeping on buffalo robes and mats on the ground." *Perhaps that was only from cleaning the tepee the other day.*

"The food is okay. . . ." Audrina shrugged. "Love or luxury?" she asked herself. "Buckskin or calico? Braids or bows?" She sighed up at the stars sparkling enchantingly beyond the smoke hole.

Love . . . Love . . . Who was there to love her back in Mankato? No one cherished her friendship there, not a single solitary soul.

Unconsciously puckering her forehead, Audrina said to herself, "There is Aunt Kate's house . . . the memories . . . the sewing I could take in. I know enough to become a seamstress, just as Katherine was." The people of Mankato could not snub her then, for there was only one other woman who took in sewing and she was elderly. There were hems to be lifted or lowered, bodices to be ripped out and made larger as the girls in town grew to womanhood, men's suits to be altered, party dresses to be made, pressing to be done. . . . Lord, she could go on and on. She would never want for anything. . . . She would have everything—every comfort, enough food, and maybe in time, there would come along a kindly man to love her. . . . He might be an *older* man. . . .

Suddenly, Audrina's thought switched with a passionate burn to Wild Hawk's kisses, his wild caresses, his mere bold touch. His lips . . . his tongue . . . his embraces that made her melt like butter in the sun.

Settling down for the night, Audrina sighed, with a tender, hungry yearning. Sleepily, she murmured, "He is forcing me. . . . Wild Hawk is . . . forcing . . . me."

Gentle . . . force.

384

Chapter Fifteen

In the midst of a stand of mountain pine, Joe Powell stood motionless, only hearing for the moment the wind breathing restlessly in and out of the trees and bushes. Then he hunkered down suddenly when he detected another sound—just some Indian children playing close by. Joe made himself stand stock-still and waited until they ran squealing happily back into the camp, then he resumed his watching of the tepees for Audrina to step out from one of them.

So far, he'd had no luck.

Rubbing the coarse blond bristles of a new beard, Joe thought how furtive and clever he was to have tracked Tawena and Left Hand back to Wild Hawk's village. Not for one moment had either of the two detected his inconspicuous presence behind them. Powell had moved from bush to tree like an Indian.

When Yellow Bear and the Rebels were out raiding, Joe always stayed behind up in Thunder Butte. Not this time, however, for he had returned to the place where he had tracked Tawena and Left Hand—to the edge of

Wild Hawk's Winter Camp. He knew this was where they usually stayed during the cold season, beginning with the Moon of the Popping Trees, December, to late in the Moon of the Dark Red Calves, late February. Wild Hawk had not moved his people on to a summer camp, and this was wise because soldiers from Minnesota were roving the Dakotas in search of those escaping from exile onto reservations.

"This is better for me this way, too," Joe told himself in a low voice. "Better they stay in one place where I can keep my eye on their activities so I can plan to make my move." He spat in the eye of a nodding wildflower beside his booted heel. "I don't need any help from that brazen Warrior Woman or that slaty-eyed brother of hers."

Joe prided himself in having become quite the adept hunter and expert tracker; he was getting better at it each and every day. When the time was ripe to snatch Audrina from Wild Hawk's camp, he was going to accomplish the perilous task all on his own—without Yellow Bear's aid.

Yellow Bear had something treacherous on his mind, Joe told himself. The fat old Indian had devised a scheme, and Joe knew it had to do with Audrina. When referring to her, he always said "the Fire-hair Woman," with a greedy look of lust in his rheumy eyes.

And Yellow Bear wanted Joe to be the one to appear guilty, caught red-headed so to speak, not himself, in the event that they should be seen trying to spirit Audrina away. Yellow Bear, Joe read into it, wanted the Fire-hair Woman for himself. "Otherwise, why would Yellow Bear have remained in the Hills of Thunder Butte with me?"

Powell didn't want any stupid Indians messing up his plans. "I'm going to do this thing on my own," he snarled under his breath. "And when I get that pretty piece in my clutches, I'll have me not only a squaw to warm my bed when we reach Mankato, but I'll also have the bed and the house—Katherine's house!" His pale eyes darkened to stormy blue. "First I'll have to make sure Katherine doesn't make it on the long journey back home."

Emboldened in body and mind, anticipating his next surreptitious move to visit this spot, Joe crept away from the concealment of bushes and trees that flanked the village and made his way stealthily up to where his horse was waiting on the grassy incline beneath some camouflaging willows.

Over the next several days, Audrina found herself in low spirits. She was slicing wild vegetables for a stew and for the thousandth time she asked herself, as she paused with her blade on the edge of a rock, "How can I really be in love with an Indian? Well," she went on, slicing through the wild turnip, "you're part Indian yourself."

Was Wild Hawk using gentle force? Or did he have *wakanda,* the inner magical fire, as the Sioux called it. "With this force one can affect and control others," Rainbow had informed her, "and to possess something with great strength can only increase one's inner potential and power. I believe Wild Hawk has this, in a way, but I believe he only uses it during conflicts with other hostile tribes, not with those people he loves. Many times I believe he has used this fighting hawk

387

spirit to count coup on the enemy. . . . He can ride up to a soldier in the middle of battle and *touch* his enemy and never get hurt himself. He is known for doing this. . . . Wild Hawk is there but no one can see him. What is the word for this?" she had asked Audrina, who had answered, "Invisible."

She returned to the present, from her reflections. "Am I not only the captive of his body?" Audrina asked herself, "but of his mind as well? How can I survive in his world with true contentment? Oh . . . I do not believe I can live the Indian way." And Wild Hawk could not become an "apple," red on the outside and white on the inside. Never. She and Rainbow had laughed over this. "There are not any apples here, Audrina." Rainbow had fallen into a fit of giggles, ending with a spell of coughing, as she did of late.

"There might not be apples here," Audrina had replied, waiting for Rainbow to finish coughing, thinking she merely had a cold, "but there certainly are some slimy worms. One male, one female."

"I know of which two you speak, Audrina," Rainbow said, catching her breath, having no liking for Tawena and Left Hand herself.

It was a beautiful and stirring sight to watch Wild Hawk and his warriors ride out on the hunt. Many deer had been spotted flitting through the forest just five minutes before, and now they were mounted and ready with weapons to seek their delicious prey. Audrina had put aside her preparations for the stew momentarily, hoping they would return with fresh venison for the pots.

"Hiye!" the cry rang out as the thunderous sound of many hooves pounded out of the village. With a thrill

388

dancing in her soul, Audrina stared over at Wild Hawk—his primitively handsome face, his long raven hair tied and drawn over one shoulder, streaming down his broad chest in front almost to his waist. Shooting a glance over his shoulder, Wild Hawk lifted his bow in a salute, encompassing Audrina and others waiting outside their tepees, and then he was away like the wind. With a groan, Audrina turned aside, biting her lip, her brow creased. She was of two minds: to go or to stay. Which . . . oh, which? If only she did not have so much fear of staying!

Sadie was suddenly standing beside Audrina, Autumn Beads lingering in the background near several of her neighbors.

Quickly, Audrina turned to her friend.

"Sadie, what do you think about leaving?" Her eyes searched the contented little face with the charming brown eyes and rosy cheeks. "Do you still want to?" Audrina inquired, her hands nervously pressing into her shift.

"Oh no, Audrey. Everything is wonderful, and right after your wedding, Fox and I are going to finish making plans for our wedding. I am content."

"I don't want to stay, Sadie." Sadness caused her piquant features to droop. "We do not belong here, don't you see that? In a few years we will be large fat squaws, with babies riding in cradleboards upon our stooped backs. Our hands will be rough and dry. . . ."

"Rainbow's are not," Sadie said defensively.

"Rainbow is not a squaw, Sadie."

"But she has been doing the work of an Indian squaw for many years," Sadie argued. "Her hands are soft as the doeskin she sews upon."

"I am afraid, Sadie, afraid I will die here of—of something. Like starvation, Sadie, have you not heard that this will be the fate of the Indians a few years down the road?"

"Folks have been saying that for years, Audrey, and look, they have plenty to eat. Are you worried for yourself? I thought you were afraid of becoming too fat?"

"I—I—"

"You are afraid of loving Wild Hawk, that is what is troubling you, Audrey. You are afraid to love an Indian. Look at me. I do not have a drop of Indian blood, but you do. I should be the one to fear, not you. How can you say all these things, Audrey? Wild Hawk has been good to you. These Indians are not savages."

"What about Left Hand? Did you forget about him? Aren't you afraid that he will rape you again while Fox Dreamer is away? I, too, am afraid of that. Left Hand might have me in mind as his next target."

Sadie laughed scoffingly. "Left Hand would not dare do anything to cross his chief, especially not with Wild Hawk's woman," she ended emphatically. "He is crazy, but I don't believe he is *that* crazy."

"Oh . . . I do, Sadie. And are you going to wait around to see if he does rape you again? What will happen to you next time? Will you lose your sanity and become just like Left Hand? Then they will give you to him, and the two of you can be crazy together. Fox Dreamer will not want you when you walk the land of the lost spirits."

"You are beginning to sound just like an Indian, Audrey."

"So are you, Sadie." Urgently, she went on, "That is

why we must try to escape, to leave here before we become . . . *squaws!*"

"I am not going, Audrey. I am more afraid of leaving than staying. Do you not realize what could become of us out there in the Dakota wilds? We could find ourselves captured by some really hostile Indians who would torture and enslave us for the rest of our lives!"

Audrina shook her head, her long fat braid brushing her shoulder. "I don't think so, Sadie, not if we are careful and take enough food with us to reach one of the Dakota forts."

"Fort Pierre, the nearest one, is hundreds of miles from here."

Lifting her shoulders impatiently, Audrina asked, "You cannot know that for sure, Sadie?"

"Really, Audrey, do you believe Wild Hawk would live so close to a fort of the white man?"

"Sadie, think of this, seriously. What would you do if you were to discover you carried Left Hand's child?"

With a gasp, Sadie looked around to see if Fox Dreamer was anywhere nearby, then she remembered that he had ridden out with the others on the hunt. There was no one else who could understand Audrina's words.

"Audrey, I—I do not wish to talk about this any longer. I have to return to my tepee and prepare a stew pot." She wiped her suddenly damp hands upon her skirt and, turning to go, smiled one last time at her friend. "You better do the same, Audrey, Precious Fire. Wild Hawk will be home soon. Maybe even before tomorrow's sun rises."

With a stunned expression riding her fine features, Audrina watched her friend return to Fox Dreamer's

391

tepee, Autumn Beads trailing meekly behind, as if she were the blonde's slave instead of the other way around.

Audrina made her way back to Wild Hawk's tepee alone, trying to stave off the feeling that she was being suffocated. For over an hour, she prayed for a sign. Then, when she was done, she prayed some more. What to do? When would this conflict ever end?

"Give me a sign; give me a sign," she mouthed repeatedly, along with her incessant pacing.

Standing still, staring up through the smoke hole at the first evening star, Audrina whispered urgently to herself, "I want to be free. To come and go as I please. But I love him," she went on contrarily. "I love Wild Hawk. . . ." Pressing her fingertips to her aching head, then to her mouth, she found herself shivering uncontrollably, as if she'd caught a severe, bone-penetrating chill. "But I do . . . not . . . want . . . to . . . *live with him.* He is a savage, no matter what he says. On the other hand, I do not believe he is a cold-blooded murderer. Sadie was right. . . . Left Hand had taken it upon himself to murder Katherine and possibly, yes, just possibly Wild Hawk had nothing to do with it. . . ."

Suddenly, there was the muffled sound of steps outside the tepee wall. Could it be a wild animal of some sort? she wondered as her body stiffened reflexively. Or, she relaxed as she thought, just some children playing outside her tepee? Yes, that must be—*Wait a minute!*

Shrinking back, Audrina watched as a long-bladed knife poked through the tepee wall. The hand that held the weapon sliced downward with a neat stroke, making a slit large enough for a person to bend down and step through. . . .

Joe Powell shot forward to clamp a heavy hand over her mouth.

"Don't be afraid, princess. I'm here to rescue you!" Joe began the lies. "You've got to come back to Mankato with me, and posthaste, Audrey. Your father has returned and is searching for you this very minute. We've got to get out of here before Wild Hawk and his warriors return."

"How do you know Wild Hawk is away?"

"Never mind that now."

Audrina's head snapped up. *My father!!*

"I was wondering when that bit of news would hit you. Come on, we've got to hightail it back to Mankato before Hank leaves town, thinking you're not there."

"I'm *not* there," Audrina said simply.

"That's right . . . you're here. I told Hank to wait here because I knew where to find you and I'd be bringing you back as soon as possible."

"Hank?" Audrina blinked her confusion. "Who is Hank?"

"Your father." Joe gave a quick grin. "Hank Harris?"

"I thought my father's name was Frank, not Hank. At least, that is what Katherine used to tell me."

"Used to?"

"K-Katherine has passed away. . . ."

With a sly eagerness to his pale eyes, Powell said huskily, "Let's go, princess. We can talk better outside, among the trees where no one can see us."

"But there are eyes all over out there, watching every move everyone makes."

393

"Well," Joe chuckled low, "they must all have the same name tonight—Sleeping Eyes. I have been feeding the dogs on the sly; they know me now. Come on, let's get out of here, princess!"

Audrina paused, struggling with her troubled heart. Joe made the decision for her, grasping her arm and pulling her along behind him, through the slit. He muttered huskily, "Now, stay right with me, hear?"

Audrina whispered, "I'm right beside you, Joe."

"Good girl."

Despite Joe Powell's bad treatment of her, Audrina couldn't believe how good it was to see someone from the past, from the civilized world. A white man.

A Dakota moon had appeared in the sky, and suddenly being outside, in the cooler evening wind, Audrina felt a certain euphoria rise up in her. *This is my sign*, she told herself. It was time to depart from her Indian love. She was going home . . . home to her father who was waiting. *Her father*.

"Wait!" Audrina halted suddenly, tugging at Joe's sleeve. "I cannot leave Sadie behind."

"Who?" Joe blinked, and then groaned. "Oh, *that* Sadie. Was it Peterson?" He received an immediate nod from Audrina. "Do you think I want to risk getting caught now that we've come this far?"

"What was that?" Audrina asked, suddenly alarmed at the muffled step she'd heard.

"Look," Joe whispered, directing a finger toward a dark, huge silhouette, "there is my horse. *One* horse."

Fixing Joe with a look that spoke volumes, Audrina pulled his hand back down. "Really? Is that the only horse you have? We cannot—"

"Yes, we *can* ride him. Look, he's a big, strong

394

tallion and he's black as night—good for keeping idden," Joe went on emphatically. "But he won't carry ree."

Black . . . big. Like Wild Hawk's Bear . . . Audrina uddenly realized she was leaving her heart and her appiness behind.

"I can't go," Audrina said slowly, firmly. "Sadie will e lonely without me. I'm the only other white erson . . . here."

Scoffingly, Joe said, "I seen your sweet Sadie in the oods this afternoon, with a young, handsome savage. he didn't appear to even know what the word lonely as all about. Come on, princess, Sadie'll never miss ou."

"Joe, how do I know you will not try something gain, like you did back in Mankato, at the house? I ouldn't like to be put through that again."

"I won't try that again, Audrey. I was drunk that ight. I'm not drinking now, honest. I haven't touched drop since that night, you can believe me."

"I . . . don't know," Audrina said. Sadness was ready in her heart as she stared around at the moonlit ncampment, the dark silhouettes of hills. The land round them was wild and raw, and the Sioux lived pon it and cherished its wildness. But it was hard for udrina to accept. There was no road filled with the ust of moving carriages, wagons, and folks attending aurch services on Sunday. Life was so different here.

"You look just like an Indian princess," Joe suddenly .id.

Audrina touched her fat braid, saying, "I do?"

"Yup. But we can change all that once we're back in vilization. You know how to sew; you can make yourself some pretty dresses just like you used to."

"If we get caught, they will kill you, Joe. You know that, don't you?"

"Hell, I've chanced it this far. Audrey, come on. Look, there's no guard near the corral. Is there any special horse you want to take?"

"We couldn't!" she gasped.

"Sure we can. Half the village lads are gambling in the big lodge way over there in the center of camp, and the rest, like your Wild Hawk, are out hunting. They'll get themselves lots of deer, but they have to bring them down first, and then gut them and butcher and clear them."

"That's not what I was referring to, Joe. I don't like to steal from anyone, not even from Indians." Especially not Indians, she thought.

"But these Indians stole plenty. . . . They even stole my girl."

"I am not your girl—or anyone else's, Joe. I want that clearly understood right from the start."

"Okay. Then let's just ride Blackie; he can take us both."

"You also have saddlebags? Blankets? Food?" She received a nod for each one of her questions.

"Yup, all that, and *mni* skins filled with water."

"You speak Sioux?"

"That, too."

Sighing resignedly, Audrina said, "We will take Boston-ton."

"Who?" Joe followed Audrina's steps now, trying to catch up with her briskly moving, moccasined feet. "Who the hell is he? A scout?

"My horse," she announced, sneaking stealthily up

to the corral, "Bo-ton-ton—a 'she.'"

"Oh . . ." Joe shrugged. "Well, let's get *her*."

On the new sun, Wild Hawk and his exultant warriors returned from a successful hunting-of-the-deer. They proudly carried the meat from the three creatures on a travois, meat that would be used carefully and sparingly in the stew pots; not a single portion of the animals would go to waste.

Feeling a chill of foreboding race along his spine, Wild Hawk slowly turned to stride toward his tepee. Something was amiss. All the anticipation that had ridden with him over the long miles to home had suddenly vanished.

Rainbow greeted Wild Hawk at the entrance to his tepee. Slowly, regretfully, she opened her mouth to speak of Precious Fire's disappearance, but Wild Hawk beat her to it. "She is gone," he said slowly, trying to still the hard pounding of his lacerated heart.

Gasping, Rainbow said, "My brother, how did you know?" She covered her mouth then, trying to hide her persistent cough.

"You are ill again," Wild Hawk noted.

"No, my brother, it is only a chill I have caught," she replied, breathless from coughing. It had kept her in the sweat lodge most of the night, as she endeavored to release the phlegm that choked her breathing.

Wild Hawk frowned worriedly. "It should have left your body by now," he growled, clenching his hands at his sides. "How long has Precious Fire been gone?"

"I could not say. I believe she has been gone for several hours, for the cookfires in the tepee have burned down to dying embers." Rainbow beheld the sun descending the highest hill. "I believe she left us in the darkest hour, my brother, when the moon had met the middlemost arc in its path across the Heavens."

"Several hours after I rode out of camp," Wild Hawk said, thoughtfully staring at the ground.

"There is something else, my brother."

"What is that?" Wild Hawk asked, going around to the back of the tepee as Rainbow followed close behind.

"Look," Rainbow said, and Wild Hawk's gaze lifted to the severed wall of the tepee.

"I must ride!" he said urgently. "She has been taken!"

"Wait, my brother. Look more closely and you will see that there is no sign of a struggle."

"She was carried. . . ." Wild Hawk began to follow the tracks, and what he saw changed his mind. "You are right, my sister; Precious Fire went willingly."

"I will leave you alone with your thoughts now." Rainbow turned and moved slowly away from the tepee, taking down a *mni* skin from a pole nearby and making her way to the stream to fill it.

Pain stabbed Wild Hawk so deeply that beads of perspiration stood out on his forehead. A fire in his heart began to flicker and burn. He was enraged, yet the sweat on his brow, the twist of his heart increased painfully with visions of what danger Precious Fire could be in. Would he ever see her again? Would he ever hold her in his arms again? His bright white teeth clenched in his mouth. . . . She was to have been his bride come the end of this week.

"What is it that troubles you, my chief?" Left Hand

walked up to stand beside Wild Hawk, frowning at the hole in the canvas of the tepee. "What has happened?" he inquired swiftly.

"She is gone," Wild Hawk replied simply.

"Precious Fire?" Left Hand's slaty eyes narrowed. Elation filled his chest then. . . . *She is gone.* "You will ride out in search of her?"

"Sha."

"I will ride with you then."

"Good." Wild Hawk turned brusquely, heading for the corral for a fresh horse. "We will go at once; the day stretches long before us and there is much tracking to be done. You will ride with me for part of the day, and then I will go on alone." Wild Hawk held up his hand in a halting motion as Left Hand was about to question the purpose of this move. "It will be as I say; I wish to ride on alone if she is not found in the first half of our search."

Left Hand followed close behind, and he could not help but wonder what was on the warrior chief's mind. Maybe Wild Hawk wanted to count *coup.* The acquisition of scalps or tokens of the bravery and skill of the warriors was very important to the Sioux. There was plain evidence that Precious Fire had gone without a struggle. He could tell by the tracks as they mounted up and began to follow them that there were only two horses—Precious Fire's Bo-ton-ton . . . and Powell's big black.

Yes, Left Hand corrected his thinking, it was good that his chief went on alone, for he did not wish to be present when Powell cried out that Left Hand, too, was in on this deception.

Part Four

Lost Embrace

Weeping may endure for a night,
but joy cometh in the morning.
—Psalms 30:5

Chapter Sixteen

Night fully shrouded the forest below as a lone Indian reined his horse to rest atop a softly moonlit hill. His mount was weary, but Wild Hawk's heart was even wearier. Heavy. Aching.

Precious Fire was lost to him. "She has gone from me, of her own accord. I do not know where to search next." He was saddened deep in his warrior's heart. "She has vanished from my Life Circle, like thin smoke rising to meet the wind."

A sudden night breeze lifted ebony strands from his wide shoulders. "O, Great Spirit, I cannot track her any further than I have already, for I must return to stay with my sister. She is ill. Rainbow needs me at this time of her strange coughing sickness." A tear sparkled in his beautiful dark eyes. He loved Precious Fire, but if she chose to go from him, there was nothing he could do. He was letting her go. . . . He was letting her take his wounded heart with her. He was still for long moments.

After Left Hand had returned to the Pahasapa

camp, Wild Hawk had gone on alone. He had tracked and backtracked, but somewhere along the banks of Kills-Himself Creek the soft prints of two mounted horses disappeared. It was as if they went up into the air at that spot. . . . Or perhaps the Great Spirit did not allow him to find her at this time. But why? he wondered. Why was he having such difficulty with his tracking? Why would the Great Spirit put this strange affliction on him?

The moon, now more than half full, ascended slowly toward the zenith of the cloudless sky. The hills rose with the moonlight full above them, and they seemed to glow and glimmer, to be illusory and insubstantial. The whole surrounding midnight scene extended away in the silvered light, vague and dreamlike and spectral. It was a still world, magic with bleached moonlight and the howling of coyotes and wolves.

The lonely sound of a coyote shivered the silence of the night. This did not send chills down Wild Hawk's spine; he was used to the sounds of night predators, feeling a oneness with all wild creatures. The only thing that chilled him was the terrifying thought that Precious Fire could be in danger—or worse. But his feeling was that she was not dead, that she was safe—for the time being.

"Or she is being warmed within the arms of her lover?" His stoical face darkened to an almost black-bronze in the moonlight, casting him in an all-powerful image of the pure and noble Indian. "Powell," he hissed. "The *wasicun* soldier has come for her at last and she has gone willingly back to the white world of comforts with him. With the paleface," he spat. Then he said, *"Hanke-wa wasichu,"* calling Audrina half-breed in his frustration and anger.

He snarled hotly as he whirled his mount to descend the hill, "She is not Petala to me any longer. She is merely Audrina Harris, Powell's woman!"

In the anguished days that followed Audrina's flight, Wild Hawk was not able to track her any further than he had already, to Kills-Himself Creek. Beyond there lay danger for him and his people at this time, for news had been brought to him from the Sisseton Camp that the soldiers from Minnesota were out looking for Little Crow and his men. Early in the year, accompanied by about sixty braves, Little Crow had gone to Fort Garry, where he received some provisions. He had pleaded, but in vain, for Canadian intercession to obtain the release of the Sioux people held prisoner in Minnesota. Little Crow had returned to the state in early summer, on a horse-stealing foray. With him went sixteen men, a squaw, and his son sixteen-year-old *Wowinapa,* The Appearing One. Several murders were reported in the Big Woods area, where warriors of Little Crow's party were operating.

"Do you think, my great cousin, that Little Crow's braves are guilty of all these murders?" Fox Dreamer asked, seated upon the mats in his tepee.

"We cannot know this for truth, Fox," Wild Hawk answered truthfully. "Soon the soldiers from Minnesota might come this way," he explained to Fox and a teary-eyed Sadie as he sat with them in his cousin's tepee. "I cannot place our people in any more danger

405

than I have already by bringing the captives to this village." He did not mention the name of Precious Fire, for it brought pain and frustration to his heart at this time. "Also, there is danger from another military group led by a man named Captain Jones. He is searching for Red Iron and Standing Bear, who have escaped from the reservations also. I never want to be placed on a reservation with our people. We will remain free as long as there is breath left in my body." He whipped his long black hair back over his shoulder as he tossed his head with a fluid motion.

"There are so few Sioux left with our hard-won freedom," Fox Dreamer said. "You are correct in saying so, Wild Hawk. To go after her at this time might mean putting our people in further danger. I know your heart is saddened. I pray that she will be returned unharmed, somehow, some way."

Wild Hawk sighed deeply and drew the back of his hand across his moist eyes.

Rainbow appeared just then in the open flap to the tepee. Her lovely face was drawn with weariness, as if she had spent another sleepless night staying up with her coughing spells. "I am sorry to disturb you, my brother. But Spotted Elk and Flies-with-the-Owl wish you to meet with them in the council lodge. Some of our Blackfeet brothers have come to speak with you and Strong Heart, and those Elders I have mentioned. They are worried that the white soldiers who search for Little Crow will come this way," Rainbow ended on a spurt of muffled coughs beneath her hand. "I am sorry; this chill has not yet left my bones.

Smiling tenderly, Fox Dreamer arose from the

sitting mats. "You have pink health in your lovely cheeks, Rainbow. Now we must hear you end that cough. I believe it will be soon that you will have regained full strength from your spring chill."

"But it is summer," Sadie reminded him in halting Dakota. She could have bitten her tongue then as she thought how hastily she had spoken, without thinking.

"Yes . . . so it is." Sheepishly Fox Dreamer looked around for a moment longer before following Wild Hawk out of the tepee.

"Sha, come along with me," Wild Hawk invited Fox Dreamer. "You are welcome to attend these meetings with me any time you wish, for you have sound wisdom in your opinions and you hold principles that guide our everyday life."

Fox Dreamer beamed. "Thank you, Wild Hawk, my great cousin!"

Wild Hawk's powerful voice, at the time a little weary in tone, drifted away as the tall figures walked to the council lodge, leaving Sadie and Rainbow together to visit.

"Please sit, Rainbow," Sadie invited. "I have some herb tea for us to share." She turned away to prepare two cups, hiding her worry from the ailing Indian maiden.

All of a sudden a loud snort and buzz sounded from back of the tepee. Sadie giggled softly. "Autumn Beads is noisy about her sleeping and frequent napping, but I'm happy the beloved woman does indeed sleep so soundly. Otherwise, Fox and I would never have any time alone during the romantic summer evenings."

Despite feeling a little ill, Rainbow smiled her

407

cheeriest. "Autumn Beads retires early, I hope?"

"Oh yes, very early in fact." All of a sudden Sadie cast her gaze aside, her expression forlorn, her dark brows gathered in worry.

There was the softest of touches as a gentle hand rested upon Sadie's arm, and the blonde looked up into a pair of beautiful, compassionate eyes, dark as obsidian. "You are sad that your friend—and my friend—has gone away, I know this is so."

"*Sha,* yes, Rainbow. Precious Fire and I were good friends, but it was not always so. We lived several miles apart, but when I visited her in town, the rumors were that she was half-breed." She looked into the understanding face of the Indian maiden. "Can—can we talk about something else? I am curious, Rainbow. May I ask you something?"

"Now you have Rainbow curious, so you must ask your question."

"I hope you will not be offended." Sadie licked her lips before she went on. "Why are you not spoken for, Rainbow?"

Sighing, Rainbow looked first at her hands and then at her feet, saying, "They are too big, that is why."

Having followed Rainbow's line of vision, Sadie couldn't believe the words she had just heard. "Your hands and feet, Rainbow? They are small, dainty . . . perfect." Then she happened to look up in the dark eyes that moment and caught the mischievousness in them. "Oh . . . you—you were just funning me."

Rainbow nodded, indeed fond of mischief, even in her illness. "Yes . . . just joking, having fun with Snow Maid. You are my friend, too," she stated firmly.

408

"My answer to Snow Maid's question is this: There has never been a brave, young or old, fat, skinny, or perfect like your Fox Dreamer, who has caught this maiden's eye. Perhaps . . . Strong Heart." Rainbow coughed once, then heaved on a sigh, happy there were no persistent coughs to follow at this moment. "I am yet young, Snow Maid," she said ever so softly, "and I have many years ahead in which to catch the man of my dreams. Now," she gracefuly rose to her feet, "I must return to my brother's tepee to prepare his evening meal. Fox Dreamer will return to you soon, too. Good night, Snow Maid, let us pray we hear some good news of Precious Fire soon."

"Good night, Rainbow." Sadie waved from the tepee entrance. "Sleep well," her voice dwindled so that only she could hear herself, "and I pray that tomorrow will find you in perfect health, without that nagging cough. Oh, dear . . . " Biting her lower lip anxiously, Sadie turned and went back inside the tepee. "Rainbow and Audrey are in your hands now, Lord."

Exhausted and hungry, Audrina clung to Bo-ton-ton's reins; several times now she had almost fallen off in her weariness. They had been riding for what seemed an eternity. She wondered if Joe was ever going to come to a halt and rest for the night. She had been pushed to her limits of endurance before by Wild Hawk as they had traveled across Dakota Territory, but this time was different somehow. This time Wild Hawk was not here to protect her. This time she experienced a lonely, cold feeling, as she had when Katherine had died and tears burned her eyelids until she dashed them away with the back of her hand.

Audrina wanted desperately to turn back to the green hills and fly into her Indian love's arms. Her mind and heart were worn out from trying to convince herself she did not need her Indian lover, that she could suppress her love and shameful desire for Wild Hawk. But was it indeed shameful? Was it forbidden desire? She answered no to both these troubling questions. She would never yield and give herself to a man she did not truly love. She made a heart's vow never again to lie down with another man.

Stroking Bo-ton-ton's silken mane, Audrina reflected back to the wonderful day Wild Hawk had gifted her with the mare. She had witnessed love and trust shining in Wild Hawk's sable eyes, eyes that darkened to ebony whenever lust and desire for her shone in their liquid depths.

Love.

Trust.

"He has finally come to trust me, and I throw it all away by running from him," Audrina muttered under her breath. "Lord, what is to become of me? Of Wild Hawk?"

"What did you say?" Joe asked as he kneed his big black closer. "Were you talking to me," he chuckled, "or were you talking to yourself?"

"Myself," Audrina conceded.

"Ah, I thought as much. You must be plumb tuckered out to do that. Up there, we'll stop by that stream. It's already pretty dark out, anyway; soon the moon will appear alongside those hills."

Why does he go on and on sometimes? Audrina wondered feeling not only bone-weary but thoroughly bored with Joe Powell's presence and his constant stating of the obvious.

After they had watered and bedded down the horses, they sat without a campfire, sharing the meager sustenance of Army hardtack and jerked venison. Joe looked hot and sweaty, darkly tanned where his clothes exposed parts of his body. When he removed his low-brimmed hat, there became visible a band of skin across his forehead that was shiny and white.

Under the Dakota moon, Audrina appeared more lovely and dusky than ever to Joe Powell. She was like an Indian princess, and it had long been his plan to make her his humble slave, one he could tyrannize over. Just the way she was dressed right now, in soft doeskin shift, beaded moccasins and headband, soft white armband, braided fiery hair, this was how he would parade her around town, walking a few paces behind him. His own Indian slave; this made him harden just thinking about it. He would be the envy of the town.

Joe continued musingly. He could hear the delicious gossip. *Powell has got himself a beautiful squaw to do his bidding. She goes with him everywhere. Her real name is Precious Fire and she was once the great, famed warrior Wild Hawk's woman. She cleans Joe's house and his mother's, and does everything he says at the snap of his fingers. He has brought her to heel. Yeah, he sure does have that girl trained. Wish I had me a pretty squaw, instead of a nagging bitch of a wife. But do you think Joe'll marry her?*

"Hell no!" Joe answered the imaginary gossipers. Ruminatively, he dumped the settled coffee grounds from his cup onto the ground.

"You must be plumb tuckered out, Joe," Audrina taunted. "You are talking to yourself, just as I was a short time ago." She snuggled beneath a blanket and gazed up at the silver Dakota stars, feeling lonelier than ever.

"It wasn't anything." Joe coughed embarrassedly. "Really. Nothing."

"The way you sounded it must have been *some*thing. There was a strength in your voice that was very determined and defiant." Huge green eyes looked over at his moonlit face and then she returned to stargazing. She was silent for a moment longer, then asked, "What does Frank Harris look like? Is he handsome? Big? Tall? Broad-shouldered? What?"

"Who?" Dumbfounded, Joe stared down at her unblinkingly. "Frank? Oh . . . yeah. Frank Harris— your father. He's kind of . . . ah . . . just average-looking. Medium build . . . ah . . . green eyes."

Rolling over onto her stomach, unaware of Joe's lecherous gaze following the hump of tender buttock, Audrina's curiosity broke from the lethargy of her weariness. "Green eyes?" She sounded excited suddenly. "I can't wait to see him. . . . My father." Softly, she said to herself, "Green eyes; I don't recall ever meeting a man with eyes the color of my own."

"Is he kind?" Audrina wondered out loud, slapping at a pesky mosquito that had finally chanced the fatal landing upon a tender vein in her arm.

"Kind?"

412

Joe didn't seem to acknowledge that such a word existed in the English vocabulary.

"You know." Audrina shrugged against the grassy earth. "What is his personality like? Is he soft-spoken? Or is he gruff, with frowning brows?"

"He's"—Joe cleared his throat—"normal."

Audrina pouted impatiently, saying, "That's nice to hear, Mr. Powell." She rolled over onto her side, putting her curvaceous backsides to him. "You're such a help when it comes to describing a person accurately. It is almost as if such a person does not even exist, and you're just telling me all this to get me to return to Mankato. I don't know if I really believe your tale of my father being alive and in Mankato waiting for me."

"You're mocking me, Princess."

"Mocking? Why would I wish to do that? All I want to know is if Frank Harris is truely searching for me, that he will be there when we arrive in Mankato."

"How do I know?" Joe asked with a shrug. "For all I know, he might be out searching the countryside for you when we get there."

"Good night, Joe."

Lustily, he continued to stare at the luscious hills and valleys of her womanly form, aching to reach out and touch her. Not yet, you arrant fool, he warned himself. You'll have plenty of time for that once you've got her where she can't escape, locked up in a house where she'll learn to become a willing slave and satisfy your every whim and lustful craving. And if she continues to defy you, you can always tie her to the bedposts and let her go hungry. She'll be begging your mercy and kindness before the week's out . . . once you get her

413

home. There'll be no one to come to her aid, either, because no one wants to befriend a *hanke-wa washichu*, a half-breed female!

"Sleep tight," Joe murmured, while delicious plans ticked in his mind as he closed his eyes.

Sleep! Audrina thought angrily. How can one possibly sleep with all these huge mosquitoes buzzing about one's head? Besides that, my world is coming to an end. . . . She fnally fell asleep, her fingertips resting upon the white buckskin armband Wild Hawk had given her, so soft . . . and yet so strong. It could endure forever. . . .

Audrina was running—running fast—but her feet took her nowhere. She seemed to be running in place, and someone chased her with a tomahawk. Just when the sharp, wicked blade was about to descend to split her skull in two, she leaped with renewed vigor and left her motionless stance. Her bare limbs were moving swiftly again, but this time she was gaining some headway. Her attacker still pursued, with the tomahawk held high, glinting threateningly at the corner of her vision. Slicing downward viciously, the stranger who wielded the tomahawk sliced off one of her hands. In horrible fascination, Audrina stared down at her severed member, the dripping blood.

Audrina mumbled and squirmed in her disturbing nightmare. *Now her attacker was on the other side of her, and she tried shifting her weight to keep from losing another hand as the blade chopped downward again. A miss this time . . . Audrina chanced to look upward into the eyes of the one who harmed her. His eyes were slaty . . . wicked . . . full of soul-destroying hatred and jealousy. On the other side of her suddenly appeared the female counterpart of the first evil one. The she-devil wielded a weapon also, this one a long-bladed knife. Up ahead loomed a tall, princelike Indian, and she heard what the people of the village— the Hawk People—were chanting: Wild Hawk, free her . . . free Precious Fire! She has brought the sacred medicine bundle . . . this signifies her importance in our village. . . . She is one of us now; this is in the Prophecy.*

The terrible sister and brother continued to pursue, their shining weapons chopping and hacking bits and parts of her away. Breathing deeply, her eyes terrified, she saw sections of her anatomy falling to the left, falling to the right.

Wild Hawk, help me.

Up ahead, Katherine appeared like a ghostly apparition calling to her sweet niece, holding out her arms. Audrey . . . Audrey . . . Audrey Tina . . . White Feather . . . Don't let them get you, too, darling. . . . Live, live, for your love. . . .

The ominous Indian pair were after Katherine, but she only laughed merrily, saying they could get her no longer. Katherine turned back to Audrina once again. Wild Hawk is not responsible for my death. . . . Audery, listen to me well. . . . I know, you in your own heart do not believe that Wild Hawk ordered to have me slain. He could not have done this. Left Hand and Tawena are the evil force in Wild Hawk's village. Watch out, Audrey, watch out. . . . They are not finished. . . .

As Katherine drifted away like a wispy, vaporous wraith, Wild Hawk appeared. When he came to her, shining like a magnificent bronze statue, he took her into the circle of his strong embrace and she became whole again. . . .

Her heart pounding hard, Audrina surfaced from her savage dream, feeling more alone and frightened than she had ever been in her entire twenty years. Then a wild wind arose and caressed her until she felt safe and secure once again . . . but alone . . . still so very alone in the starlit world that encompassed her.

Miles to the west and in a slumbering Indian village, Wild Hawk walked in his dream. *Somebody wished to speak with him. Again the savage angel came to him, so clearly that he knew there was no mistaking her. Precious Fire drifted away, and he strove to reach her, to help her, but she was pursued out of his dreaming vision. She was not the one who had wished to speak with him, for she was in trouble and he could not reach her just now. Into his dream walked another woman, this one much older. She is going to reveal something of great importance. She is Tashina, White Feather's grandmother. Who is White Feather? Wild Hawk's dreaming mind asks. You shall see. Behold, a sacred voice is calling you.*

Into the vision steps Wild Hawk's father; he has a noose about his neck and his eyes are sad. Wild Hawk's father summons the sacred hawk to deliver the medicine pouch into the hands of his son's beloved. In

416

*the powerful talons of the hawk is the medicine
bundle, and in his powerful beak is the sacred white
feather. They sail to the ground and his love picks them
up. . . . Precious Fire is transformed into a shining
image in white Indian dress. In her hair is the white
feather. She is joined with the leader of the Hawk
People. She gives birth to a strong, handsome son who
is to be named White Hawk . . . White Hawk . . .*

"This . . . is . . . our . . . destiny," Wild Hawk gasped
as he came fully awake. "I must go and find my
beloved." He rushed to his feet and took up his
weapons. Fool! he called himself as it dawned on him
that no white woman but a very special one—with
Indian blood at that—would have heard the pouch sing
and drum for her. "She was wearing the rare white
feather in my dreaming vision. The women in my
dream are her relatives. This time only one of them
came to me—the older one. *Tashina!*"

On swift-moving feet, Wild Hawk went to the corral
and readied the Bear. He was mounted in five seconds
flat, furiously riding like the wind out of the sleeping
village. Into the night he rode, the Bear's hooves and
his heart pounding out the message, *My love, my wild
love, be safe, be strong. I am coming for you. You and I
will be one. Wild Hawk and White Feather!!*

Love's wild wind carried him far into the night, over
the hills and stretches of flat land, under moonbeams
sifting down through heavily foliaged branches. All the
while he rode, not knowing exactly where the Bear's
fleet hooves would take him but heading east all the
time, Wild Hawk reflected back to several days
before. . . .

Tawena had tried to get close to him again, and he had shoved her away. "There is only one woman for Wild Hawk, Tawena. Keep your distance from me, Warrior Woman."

She had laughed in his face, saying, "Precious Fire? Hah, she is only your whore! Your defiant captive has run away from you, into another man's arms. Do you hear laughter, Wild Hawk?" she taunted him further, calling Precious Fire whore for the last time.

For the first time ever, he had been forced to have a woman beaten and Fox Dreamer had been the one to carry out the punishment; he seemed to have some punishing of his own to mete out on the fiercely jealous woman. Following the fierce but deserved beating of Tawena—who was unable to sit or walk for two days afterwards—Wild Hawk had planned to move farther onto the Plains, but he had been preoccupied with Rainbow's delicate health, for it had taken a turn for the worse on the tail of Precious Fire's absence. She was now confined to her mats and Snow Maid waited on her, bathing her hot brow and spooning thin soup into her mouth. Suddenly, Rainbow's coughing had ceased and everything had gotten better, for she was up and about that morning—the morning before Wild Hawk had the revealing dream.

Before Rainbow's health had taken a better turn, Wild Hawk had been sullen and moody, promising himself that they would keep on the move once Rainbow was well. He would raid and be proud of his exploits. He would take women, many captives, have many wives to warm his mats. Then he had glanced around the village. This was where he had loved

Precious Fire. She would forever be impressed within his mind and in his heart. Never would he forget her beauty, charm, and defiance. Yes, even that he missed. Her flashing green eyes, her pouting pink mouth.

"In my heart," he had told himself, "she is truly my wife. I have given her the white armband that joins our hearts and souls as if we were already one in wedlock."

The Great Father saw them as one. If Wild Hawk had not believed this before, he now did so with every ounce of his being.

Before the revealing dream, he had told himself he would take another woman to his mats. In fact, as he had gazed up at the split-tailed swallows flying all around his tepee, he had decided to do it right away. He had come to a halt outside Pretty Swallow's tepee, knowing she would welcome him to her mats again and forgive him for showering so much attention on his captive *winu*. But his heart had not been in it. Not this soon after losing Precious Fire, he had told himself achingly and had walked away from Pretty Swallow's tepee.

Now, with a renewed burst of energetic determination, guiding the Bear with the thrust of his bare knees, Wild Hawk came to rest atop a windswept hill. There was nothing but dark shadows below, where the moon did not cast its pale white illumination. In all this vast, wild country surrounding him, finding Precious Fire would be like—what did the whites say? Finding a needle in a stack of hay? Nevertheless, he was going after her.

"I will allow no man to take her and keep her from me, not while I live and breathe!"

With those words ringing over the earth, Wild Hawk kneed and whirled the Bear back down the slope, going east, ever eastward, searching for his lost ecstasy.

For Audrina, the ride had become long and grueling. The bugs were the worst. She had red, swollen bites all over her body, and she had to hide beneath her saddle blanket at night or be eaten alive.

As Bo-ton-ton plodded behind Joe's big black, Audrina pressed her mind for remembrance of the dream she had had the night before. Hard as she might try, the elusive dream would not fully come to her, but she knew there had been evil and good in it. She had been trying to escape someone or something. She had seen Wild Hawk in her dream, too, and she had heard Katherine's voice, but beyond these things she could not remember. Bits and pieces were coming back to her, and she had to snatch at them furiously in the morning. She dreamed again that night when they camped out under the stars.

But this dream differed markedly from the others. *"One more week,"* Joe was telling her, *"and we'll be in Minnesota, White Feather."*

"It can't be that soon!" she had cried back, tears burning her eyes.

"Oh yes, we will be out of Dakota Territory and heading toward the Minnesota River Valley."

She turned once to look back. "I love you, Wild Hawk." Then she rode on past Joe Powell and did not look back in the direction of the Black Hills again.

Audrina's heart was aching as she listened to the

calling of the coyotes under the mysteriously veiled moon. Dark wisps of clouds floated by the face of the moon, a moon that had started out as a deep orange and now, higher in the sky, was as gold as a Spanish doubloon. Trees swayed to and fro in the restlessly tossing wind, and the air was humid and hot. Audrina was grateful for the wind that blew away some of the pesky bugs, but the mosquitoes clung to the flesh now and then as if they had landed on glue.

All of a sudden Audrina knew that she did not wish to return to Minnesota. His savage heart was calling to her in the peaceful beauty of the evening and she knew she must go to him.

"Joe! Wake up!" Audrina shook his shoulder, angry that he did not awaken and only smacked his lips loudly. This should get him awake, she thought. *The Indians are coming!"*

"Wha—what?" Joe was instantly alert and sitting up in his blanket. "Indians? Where?" He shot to his feet, holding his head as if he were feeling unsteady.

Audrina, her head pressed to the ground, pretended she heard something, and then she gasped, for she actually heard the pounding of many hooves. "Oh dear Lord . . . they are coming!" She came to her feet, her head moving swiftly back and forth. "Oh, think fast, Powell, where can we hide?"

"Yellow Bear and the Rebels!" Joe ground out.

"Maybe Wild Hawk!" Audrina cried, hope growing in her vivid green eyes. "Dear Lord . . . let it be he." Suddenly, his words struck her and she turned to face him. *"Yellow Bear? The Rebels?* Who are they?" Peering into the sheepish face of Powell, Audrina felt that

421

something was drastically amiss. "These Indians . . . you know them . . . these rebels?"

"They're friends of Left Hand's and Tawena's. Come on," he rasped, grabbing her hand. "It's only about an hour before dawn and we have got to get out of here!"

"Joe!" Audrina shouted at his back as he yanked her along to the tethered horses. "What is this all about? Something is wrong and you must tell me, please. I wish to know what is going to happen!"

"I can't tell you now, Audrey. First we have to get going before they find us. They're coming fast. Get mounted . . . and, damnit, forget the clothes drying on the branches!!"

Chapter Seventeen

Yellow Bear and his band of Rebels, accompanied by Left Hand and Tawena, rode furiously after their cleverly elusive prey. After a half hour, when they came to a skidding halt, having lost the swift pair in the thickly wooded area, Tawena decided to speak what had been bothering her mind all the while. Watching each face closely for a reaction to her words, she spoke quickly and coaxingly.

"Wild Hawk has gone himself to search for Precious Fire. He started out alone and then a band of his braves joined him. Their numbers are larger than ours. When I was gathering my possessions to leave, I saw them ride out to join Wild Hawk. I believe twenty of his braves are with him even now."

Yellow Bear grunted angrily. "Why did you not say this before? I do not wish to have Wild Hawk's wrath upon my head. I do not wish to be tracked and plagued the rest of my days by Wild Hawk and his braves. I wish to drop out of this hunt. I do not care to pursue the flame-haired *wasichu*. She is too much trouble. I am growing too old for such chases." With his feathered lance in his right hand, he whirled his barrel-chested pony about, ordering his men to follow. "Come, let us go from this place. There is even more trouble in the wind. The white soldiers with their leader, Cap-tain Jones, come this way, we have been told by one of our scouts. We will go far from here to raid the small camp of the Yanktonai we spotted yesterday."

Watching the band of Rebels ride off, Left Hand hissed the perplexing question that had been plaguing his mind, one he'd been unable to ask while Yellow Bear was speaking. "Why have you spoken so hastily, my sister? We could have persuaded Yellow Bear to help slay Wild Hawk and be done with this troublesome matter once and for all."

"Why do you worry about Precious Fire? The *wasicun* soldier has taken her."

"Do you not see, Tawena? If Powell is caught by Wild Hawk, our leader will question him and discover our hand in this."

"It is too late!" Holding out her arm, Tawena showed her brother the brand that had been burned into her flesh. "Wild Hawk is my leader no longer."

Gasping, Left Hand snatched up her arm, careful not to touch the still-tender flesh. "When did this happen? When did Wild Hawk banish you from the tribe?"

"I called Precious Fire a whore."

"You did that?" Slaty eyes narrowed. "What else have you done while I have been away with the Rebels? Have you spoken of our plans?"

"I have learned more," Tawena said, halting his interrogation for the moment. "There are rumors in camp that Precious Fire has the blood of the Oglalas

424

and that Wild Hawk is eager to find Precious Fire and take her for his wife at once. I overheard him speaking to Fox Dreamer about a dream that he had. Precious Fire had had the honor of carrying the medicine pouch of Red Hawk to his Spirit Lodge. This is what Wild Hawk and Precious Fire were doing at the lodge; he brought the sacred medicine pouch there."

There shone a new, wicked light in Left Hand's eyes and now he was very much in haste to be away from his sister. "I ask you again: What else have you told them?" he demanded.

Tawena confessed what she had admitted to Fox Dreamer. "I have never seen Fox Dreamer the way he was just this last sun. First Wild Hawk had me beaten for calling Audrina a harlot. Fox Dreamer became curious about other things. He said he did not believe Snow Maid's story that she had not been intimately touched by another. He read great fear in her eyes. He knew that something was wrong with the girl. He questioned me fiercely, wanting to know if you had touched . . . Snow Maid."

"Did you tell him?" Left Hand hissed angrily.

"He broke me down, Left Hand. The pain was awful; I could not bear it a moment longer."

"You told him that I ravished his woman?" Left Hand's eyes were wild and frightful.

"I am sorry, my brother."

With a strangled sound, Left Hand sat down heavily upon a nearby boulder. "You are a fool! He will kill me."

"I know his love for Snow Maid is great," Tawena whined. "Just as Wild Hawk's love for Precious Fire is great."

"And what little love I have carried for you is finished!" Left Hand yelled as he whirled on his sister, ready with a long-bladed knife. He plunged it into her stomach, lifting upward to end her life swiftly.

After he had accomplished the brutal killing, he stepped away, bent down, and unceremoniously wiped his blade in the grass. Gritting his teeth, he vowed, "I will find Powell! We will make plans with the white soldiers. They will make a surprise attack on Wild Hawk and the braves. I do not feel sorrow that Wild Hawk will perhaps perish before the day is out. He will never wed his Precious Fire." He stuck out his naked chest, gruffly vowing, "Now that I know she has the blood of the Oglalas *I* will take her to wife after Wild Hawk is dead!"

That afternoon, after followng the twisting creek for hours, Left Hand came upon the camp of Joe Powell and Precious Fire. The sun filtered through the feathery pine branches of tall, spindly trees and set Precious Fire's long braided hair afire. Her peach-colored flesh drew his lusty gaze, and the soft rise and fall of her innocently wanton breasts as she lay down in the long grass to rest, with her arms stretched upward, caused his savage blood to pound and drum in his veins, his manhood to grow tight and swollen.

"I will have you yet, Precious Fire. You do not make me fear you any longer. You do not hold power over this warrior now that I know you have the blood of the Oglalas. You may hold power over Wild Hawk's heart and soul. You are still a *hanke-wa wasichu*, a half-breed in my eyes. My desire for you does not involve the heart or the soul, for I want only to degrade your kind and punish you for the white man's stealing of our

426

lands. Your kind will steal no more when I am finished." He chucked evilly. "Snow Maid and Precious Fire will both be mine. Slaves to my every need and lustful craving. I will make you my first woman, and then I will bring you down to degrade you and make certain you never hold your head high in Left Hand's village."

Just then Left Hand saw Joe Powell coming his way, carrying a water skin to be filled at the stream. *"Pssst,"* Left Hand hissed, drawing Powell's attention off the path and into the bushes where he had concealed himself.

"What the hell—? Left Hand?" Powell went for his gun, then he realized he had left it resting against his saddlebag. "What do you want? What are you doing here?"

"I came to tell you much important news, Powell." Left Hand's eyes glittered greedily as he imagined himself having his way with Precious Fire once he got rid of a few encumbering nuisances.

"What is it? Be quick about it," Powell ordered in perfect Dakota. "I have to fill this skin and get back before she gets scared because—"

Left Hand cut Powell off. "Look, between the trees. She sleeps."

"Ah, well, that's good. Now, what the hell do you want? I've got what I came for and took what you wanted me to get rid of."

"I see you have Precious Fire. But I have news. . . . Wild Hawk is not far behind."

"What?" Powell again reached for his invisible gun, then cursed again for not remembering to strap it on.

"He will ride through this area by sunfall." When

427

Powell would have moved on, Left Hand grasped the man's wrist. "I have other news. Yellow Bear has warned me that the white man's cavalry is near. There are many of them."

"What has this to do with me? Hurry up, speak your piece and then I have to—"

"You may be rid of Wild Hawk and his braves."

"You mean he is not alone?" Powell ground out. "Damnit to hell, what's the story?"

"Wild Hawk started out with Left Hand, tracking with him. Then I let him go on alone. I would have tried to cover your tracks, but you were very clever to ride in the shallow creek beds. But now Wild Hawk is coming with many braves; Tawena has told me this when she came out to meet with me and Yellow Bear."

Peering behind Left Hand, Powell asked, "Well, where is Tawena? And where are the Rebels?" He shivered, hoping they were not too near.

"Never mind them, paleface. I have a plan that will rid you of Wild Hawk and the small band he rides with. This man whose name is Cap-tain Jones and his Minnesota soldiers are not far away. It is my idea that you could lead them to Wild Hawk and his men."

"Is that right?" Powell thoughtfully chewed his lower lip and his drab eyes brightened to chilly blue. "Now, that sounds like a good plan, Left Hand. What about Precious Fire? Who will watch over her while I go and talk to Captain Jones? You sure he's coming this way? It's my old friend John Jones and the cavalry?"

"You can trust Left Hand," the wily Indian said. "I will watch Precious Fire. You need only give me some of your tobacco. This is a fair trade?"

"You'll return her to me once I've alerted Captain

428

Jones of Wild Hawk's whereabouts?"

"You have my word," Left Hand said slowly, cunningly. He held a hand out for the tobacco and Powell went to fetch it, keeping an eye out lest Audrina awake.

"Now . . ." Left Hand pointed in the direction Powell should go to encounter Captain Jones and his cavalry. He had not lied about this one thing, for they were indeed passing below the bluff this very moment, only a quarter of a mile away.

Left Hand would wait, for he must know the outcome of this sudden battle between the white soldier Jones and Wild Hawk and his small band. Only then would he return to his village to relate the sad tale of the loss of many braves—and Wild Hawk.

Rubbing his hands together, Left Hand waited in the bush, watching over Precious Fire . . . waiting . . . like a venomous snake for the poison to take effect.

Earlier in the day, a detachment of cavalry, under the command of Captain Jones of the First Minnesota Mounted Rangers and the Third Battery of Light Artillery, had chanced across the tracks of a small band of Sioux, their trail moving northeast along a ridge that overlooked a small stream of the White River. Jones had halted his men, calling for one of his mixed-blood scouts—Michael Drum.

It was mid-June. Some four weeks earlier two Sioux chiefs, Red Earth and Standing Bear, had escaped from the Indian reservation far to the north. Once in familiar terrain, the two chiefs had parted company. The younger, Standing Bear, and his followers had disappeared to the north. Red Earth's group, made up mostly of elderly men and women, had soon been discovered by searching cavalry; the old chief had surrendered.

Standing Bear had still not been found. Another who constantly eluded capture by the cavalry was Wild Hawk, rumored to be the new chief of the Hawk People. For over a year, troops of cavalry had fanned out to the north and west, searching for the trail of the elusive and dangerous Wild Hawk. Jones's detachment was one of these search parties. His troops and their horses were fresh, the mid-summer weather remained uncommonly dry and lukewarm, and Jones wondered as he waited for Michael Drum, his chief scout, if he were about to be uncommonly lucky.

The wily Drum was more skeptical. "There are not enough tracks to be Wild Hawk's war party; he always rides with many more braves," he said.

Rubbing his chin with one hand, Captain Jones looked down at the ground, his mind in deep thought. After a moment, he lifted his head. "How many are there, would you estimate?"

"Two dozen at most. Could be fewer if they have extra horses packing meat."

"A hunting party, Sergeant?" Jones asked Drum.

"I think so, sir. There would be more if it was a war party."

"Could it be a *hunting* party from Wild Hawk's band?"

"It could be, sir."

"Why do you think it's Wild Hawk and not Standing Bear?" Jones asked Sergeant Drum, squinting at the hills to the west.

430

"From what we was told at the Dakota Agency, Captain, this Standing Bear broke out some time around the first of June. The way he lit across Dakota Territory, seems like he was making seventy or eighty miles a day; the cavalry couldn't keep up with him."

"That sounds reasonable, Sergeant," Jones said approvingly. "Wild Hawk and a few other young chiefs are still on the loose, too. Heard it at Fort Pierre that Wild Hawk took himself a couple of white captives a few months back. They can't find hide nor hair of any of them. Wild Hawk moves with the purest animal instinct. He claims the Great Spirit of the Sioux leads and protects him every inch of the way."

"That sounds like Wild Hawk," the scout said.

Wild Hawk! Captain John Jones could not suppress the sharp thrill that made him sit ramrod straight in the saddle. At West Point, Jones had listened to lectures about the older Red Hawk, hanged at Mankato, and other great Indian war leaders of the plains, like Wild Hawk's grandfather, Standing Hawk. Red Hawk had fought at Acton, at the two battles of New Ulm. He had been among that confederacy of Sioux and Cheyennes who had been a scourge to the United States Cavalry for a dozen years. Stubborn, recalcitrant, and proud— Wild Hawk was all of these, as his father and grandfather before him had been. But Wild Hawk had even more cunning. He had attended a few peace conferences and had simply acted as if the *whites* were intruders. "All the white people have to do to end hostilities," he had said in perfect English, "is to withdraw from Sioux hunting lands and sacred burial grounds."

Captain John Jones snickered to himself now. Wild

Hawk's terms had been outrageously simple, and he was not amenable to any sort of bargaining over them. Why had so many Sioux chiefs acted this way? Many of the Sioux had come wearily into the reservations, all fight gone out of them, yet a few maverick bands held out, harassing forts and trails, carrying on the hopeless battle. Wild Hawk was one of these, and perhaps the most honored of the young Sioux war leaders still in the field. He was being blamed for leading the Rebel Indians, for some of his men—and one warrior woman—had been seen riding with the Rebels.

"That's all I needed to hear, Drum," Captain Jones said with a grin. "We'll see where these tracks lead us. Oh, and send me that rebel Sioux scout of yours; I'd like a word with him. Maybe it takes a Sioux to catch a Sioux."

"He is gone, sir," Drum said.

Taken by surprise at this announcement, John Jones shrugged lightly, realizing no Indian was to be trusted—not even Michael Drum.

"Their tracks lead north," Joe Powell said as Jones approached. "There's good reason to believe they'll move out in the same direction. Once they're clear of that heavy cover—"

"We'll give them reason to keep going," interrupted Captain Jones. "You're excused, Roberts," he ordered the young corporal who had been conversing with Powell. "Where the hell did you come from, Powell?" He looked from Powell to the scout, who remained rooted to the spot where he'd been listening to Powell's conversation with Roberts. Drum began to step away,

432

and Jones snapped, "Stay, Sergeant."

"Right, sir."

Turning back to Powell, Jones inquired, "Well? What are you doing here, Powell? I thought your time in the cavalry was up. And how do you know so much about Wild Hawk's movements?"

Not wishing to mention anything about his precious captive, Powell said, "I hear you need a few good men, Captain."

"You saying you're joining us, Powell?"

"That's right, sir."

"We're not going to get us any Indians, charging up the tails of the Sioux," Jones growled. He grinned deviously then. "That will be our new recruit's assignment. You'll do it right, *right,* Lieutenant?"

"Right!" Powell readily agreed. He turned away, paling considerably, for he had not counted on getting into the action. Audrina Harris was a more tempting diversion than battling Sioux. All he was really bent upon was returning to her as swiftly as possible, so he could settle down in Mankato with Precious Fire as his willing slave. This was all he could think of as he reluctantly readied himself for battle.

Chapter Eighteen

The first rifle shot cracked from a point south of Wild Hawk's Indian party. Its report was as brittle as the snap of a dry branch in the frigid air of a wintry Dakota morning. Everything happened swiftly after that.

Directly in front of Wild Hawk a young brave of no more than twenty summers looked up at the blue sky in surprise, made a tight gurgling sound in his throat, and as his spotted pony jumped nervously ahead, the young brave slid sideways from his mount to pitch onto his face in the bed of fragrant pine neddles.

On the dying echo of that first shot a noisy and furious charge surprised the Indians from the rear.

In the pandemonium of that surprise attack, Wild Hawk perceived many things. He understood that he had not listened attentively enough to the whispering of his hunter's instinct; all he had been thinking of was finding Precious Fire.

Wild Hawk now realized that the blue-coated

434

oldiers, many of them wearing civilian garb, out-numbered his band many times over. He noted that they were attacking along the bed of the stream as well as along the higher ground on both banks, but the main attack was along the bottom.

Galloping hard, Fox Dreamer sidled his mount close to Wild Hawk's horse. "Something is wrong. This attack is too late, as it is too early!"

"You are correct in saying so, my cousin! Too late, for they failed to catch us resting and watering our mounts at the approach of dawn! Too early, because the whooping of the soldiers and the careless rifle fire and the sound of their bugle warned us and allowed us to take flight before many had been struck down."

"The bullet that killed one of our warriors was fired from some distance. . . ."

"No!" Wild Hawk cried. "It is not so!"

Alarm struck Wild Hawk like the stabbing of an enemy blade.

"What are you saying?" Fox Dreamer tried not to show his fear, for all Indian hunters and warriors were trained from the time they were small boys to face danger and hardship bravely and never to show fear or to complain.

"That one shot was fired from horseback or from the riverbank. It came from above us . . . from a lone sniper in a tree," Wild Hawk explained.

And the cavalry attack that followed his words was more like an Indian raid than a typical maneuver of the pony soldiers.

Wild Hawk's band was already racing along the bottomland in panicky flight—exactly as the white chief had planned. *"Sha!"* The noise, the bugle, the premature shooting . . . all deliberate, all part of the strategy. Wild Hawk had a strong feeling that Powell's devious hand was at the bottom of that plan.

"Wait!" Wild Hawk shouted. "Do not flee, my braves; it is a trick!"

But Wild Hawk's cry was scattered like dry leaves to the wind. His braves were already racing tumultuously ahead, out of his control. Wild Hawk exchanged a knowing look with Fox Dreamer, tears burning in both their eyes. The best cover of the trees was already behind them!

They were still contained by the shallow flanks of the meandering stream, but up ahead, as Wild Hawk and many of the others remembered, there was the open plain. No Indian believed that he could be caught in the open astride his favorite horse or pony. The white chief had counted on that, too, Wild Hawk thought bitterly.

Wild Hawk hung low over the Bear's neck, trying to drive the horse on by the force of his will to overtake his fleeing band. "Halt!" his deep voice rang out commandingly. "Turn back, my braves, this is not a good way to die!" As a shot zinged past him, and then another, he hung precariously over the side of his galloping mount to avoid the speeding bullets. There was not time in the white man's attack to slip his arm through a loop so that both hands would be free to shoot arrows. . . . Everything was happening too fast. He had to try and stop his braves from running, to turn back and take to the trees. But it seemed futile.

Wild Hawk's urging arrived too late, carried away on the streaming wind. The first fleeing warriors swept

oward the opening that appeared on the left bank
f the stream where the broad plain beckoned. Just
s the fleeing warriors reached that opening, a wall of
lame crackled from the high ground above the east
ank. Two horses buckled simultaneously, horses and
iders plunging into a tumult of dust and flying limbs.
Another warrior tossed his arms high and screamed,
onvulsed in agony.

Wild Hawk whirled his mount. The white chief had
lanned well. His riflemen were shooting the ponies
nd swift horses.

Warrior's rage seized and filled Wild Hawk. He
ould no longer hope to stop the others. He had been
utwitted, his braves routed. But if this were the end of
is hunt for his woman, he would not succumb like the
oft-eyed deer in frightened flight but like the keening
awk whose nest has been violated by a stranger's
rasping hands. *He had to find Powell and kill him!*

Wheeling his horse in a skilled and astonishingly
uick maneuver—almost in the instant of decision—
'ild Hawk turned about and was racing back along
s own tracks, straight into the fury of the cavalry's
ursuit. *Wakantanka,* protect me, he prayed, I must
ve to see another day. On the other hand, if I die, let
e walk into the afterlife with honor. But tears filled
s eyes, thinking of leaving this world for another
ithout his heart's love . . . his savage angel.

Their charge had closed the gap on the fleeing
dians, and in seconds Wild Hawk was amidst them.
orses and men reared and plunged around him.
hough he held his Indian rifle in one hand, he made
 effort to fire. Instead, seeing a slender figure with a

437

sword brandished high in his right hand, Wild Hawk swung the Bear toward him. Captain Jones finally saw him at the last moment, and his eyes widened in astonishment that the compelling Indian dared come at him so bravely.

Whirling past the man who raised a long knife instead of a rifle—indicating that he was an officer— Wild Hawk reached out and touched him. Then, as suddenly as he had swung his mount about, he was through the lines of the bluecoats, a thinner and more ragged bunch than he had first guessed.

Swiftly, Wild Hawk plunged on past the astonished faces, men who had never seen him before this very moment. They could not move, nor could they lift their weapons. The Indian broke clear, racing along the river bottom while the noise of battle faded away. For the first time since the opening rifle shot of the brief battle, Wild Hawk saw that he might live to hunt and love again. Only if he found Precious Fire would he know the continuance of love's joys and bittersweet pains. Perhaps he would live even to see his own son . . . maybe daughter . . . then more sons. . . .

He had lost the battle, but he had counted *coup* on the white chief who had defeated him, even though there was no Indian witness to give that *coup* the merit it deserved. . . .

No one, that is, but Joe Powell, who had just taken an arrow in his chest, forever stilling the beat of his greedy heart. And one other had seen. . . .

Just then Fox Dreamer hunkered down in the grass and ran along at a lope, reaching his pony before any of the bluecoats could notice his stealthy presence in he grass. The avenging Indian returned his bow and rrows to their places—minus one arrow—and leaping nto his pony's back, he lit out after Wild Hawk.

Astonished by the Indian warrior's bold maneuver, Captain John Jones, like all his men, had been too slow o cut the hostile Indian down when he whirled about nd plunged directly into their lines. Jones had seen the ark, glittering eyes fix suddenly upon his as the auntless warrior changed his racing mount's course. n that moment, the young officer had experienced the rst bowel-deep fear he had known in his life. A chilling onsciousness of death descended upon him with a wiftness and certainty he could not alter or evade.

Instead of the crushing blow, there had been only ard fingers clutching briefly at his arm. Nothing more. here was a nightmarish vision of long, shiny braided lue-black hair and deeply bronze skin and several agle feathers bobbing in the wind. A young, hand-ome, noble face. Muscled, ramrod straight back. Then le Indian had vanished like thin smoke in a stormy ind.

Plunging on, the chill of panic still gripping his neck nd his insides, Jones had reached the open plain efore he was able to rein in his speeding horse. By then le battle, such as it was, was over.

A half-dozen Indians and at least as many horses lay prawled in grotesque positions along the river bottom nd the widening valley. Puffs of dust and dark specks a the valley showed a few surviving Indians in flight cross the plain, the cavalry in hot pursuit.

439

Eagerly, Jones looked up, searching for sight of Powell. Not long ago he had been standing on the bluff overlooking the stream, waving his rifle over his head and shouting in exultation, his face red with triumph. It was as if his face had caught the glory of the setting sun—and then Powell disappeared from view.

Triumph? Captain Jones wondered briefly. And where was Powell at the moment? Coming down from the bluff?

Captain Jones felt relief and nothing more for carrying out his part in that small victory with the Sioux. He had been through many a battle, but looking around at the crumpled postures of death, he felt no pleasure this day.

Sergeant Drum rushed up to him just then, reining his piebald horse to a skidding stop, his black eyes shining with excitement. "It was him, Captain! It was *him!*"

"Him?" Jones repeated stupidly. "Who are you talking about, man?"

"The Indian who counted coup on you, sir."

"I didn't see him until he was right on top of me. It—it was like he was invisible. Just like a huge hawk swooping down to touch but not kill. Well, who was that Indian?"

"He has *wakanda*. Wasn't he fearful and awesome?"

"Who, damnit, who the hell *was* he?"

"You have been touched by Wild Hawk himself!"

The hills loomed close, a humpbacked southerly range of the Black Hills, notched by deep canyons. Wild Hawk knew these rugged hills well, as he knew al

440

he windswept rocks and canyons, all the valleys, and rivers of these ancient hunting grounds of his People. He rode as if one with nature, pausing like a deer suddenly gone still, then alert again like a mountain cat.

Wild Hawk was heading southwest toward the nearest hills. Far behind him came the pitifully small, dark figures of the pony soldiers in dogged pursuit. He could not estimate how many followed. A dozen bluecoats, perhaps less.

The thin report of a rifle shot reached him belatedly, the sound carrying where no bullet could fly. Wild Hawk nodded, then dipped out of sight.

The canyon he had chosen lay straight ahead. At the last moment he veered south over rocky ground. A figure on horseback appeared suddenly, and Wild Hawk relaxed his tense body as he saw the grinning face of Fox Dreamer. Smiling, yes, but there was also sadness in the liquid depths of the young brave's black eyes.

"So," Wild Hawk said, "how many of my warriors are gone?"

Fox Dreamer's face sobered. "Half, my cousin. The rest are fleeing across the plains." He smiled again, lightly this time. "I have seen you count coup, Wild Hawk, on their white leader."

"And were you lucky, my young cousin?"

"I have slain the white soldier who has grieved your heart by taking your woman. He took an arrow in his wicked heart."

"So," Wild Hawk began, "you have ended the foolish *wasicun's* life; this is good." Then his brow

441

furrowed as another thought plagued him. "If this is so, if Powell took Precious Fire, where is she? How do we know that it was not someone else who took her from our village?"

"She went with Powell," Fox Dreamer said. "Come with me, Wild Hawk, I have something you might like to see."

Wild Hawk followed close behind, reining the Bear in when they came around a huge boulder. There, before him, was the big black, almost a twin to his own magnificent horse. "How did you get him?" Wild Hawk questioned Fox Dreamer.

"This is Powell's horse. See the marking on his flank?"

"Aiyee, Powell has stolen this beautiful horse from our Cheyenne brothers."

"Look again. . . .the hooves. This is the same horse that led Precious Fire from our village, as she was mounted on Bo-ton-ton." He nodded at the fiery black horse. "Powell could not have bought this from the Cheyenne. There is not one Indian who would give up a horse such as this one."

"He is as great as the Bear. You will take him to our village and you will keep him, Fox. Or you will take him to the Cheyenne village to the north. This is up to you."

"He is mine now; I earned him and I will keep him."

"Good. You might have to fight a Cheyenne brother for him, but that is your fight." Wild Hawk nodded, looking toward the hills. "I am going in search of Precious Fire. You may come, or you may return to the Pahasapa Camp."

"I will join you for a time; then I will go to tell the

442